Morph: Demise of Knacc
© 2025 Tim Ferguson

Published by Red Leg Press

ISBN (Paperback): 978-1-9192860-0-6
ISBN (eBook): 978-1-9192860-1-3

TIM FERGUSON

Book One of the MorphEn Files

CHAPTER 1
THE APFEL

Washington DC, USA
Saturday 17th September 2016

Henkl and Zebra didn't stand out. They looked like any other Washington residents. Sporting Redskins caps and stonewashed jeans, they fitted comfortably into their environment, years of training paying dividends. Only fellow special forces agents might notice a difference in their demeanour. Maybe the steely glint in their eyes or the heightened observation skills they were currently deploying; just a few small 'tells' that might give them away should a fellow expert be watching them.

But there wasn't. It was a busy Saturday, people were thronging about, enjoying their weekend blissfully unaware of the two killers in their midst.

Zebra had already carried out a dry run of the route their 'mark' would take. Careful and meticulous planning had ensured that there should be no surprises today. The cameras covering the front and rear of Georgetown's gymnastic hall had all been sabotaged. The week earlier he had tested the university staff, examining their reaction time by exiting via the rear fire escape. It was as he had expected, a low-level maintenance manager had mooched slowly down from his office to see what the problem was. He did nothing, he pulled the escape shut without even bothering to investigate the rear alley, not that he would have found anything. He didn't even radio it in; he just went on his way, probably assuming students were just clowning about. But today would be different – very different.

Henkl caught his eye and nodded. Not a great movement, more a twitch of an eyebrow and a flash of his eyes, but Zebra knew; he always knew. Across the street, Connor Evans and his coach were approaching the main doors. Connor walked with the lithe spring in his step of an athlete on the up, a promising young gymnast carrying the hope and suggestion that he might make the next Olympic team. Only time would tell. Although Henkl knew that no amount of time would tell for this particular athlete. Zebra tracked his path and noted the time. It was 2 p.m.; he was 20 minutes early, but nothing to be concerned about. Today was competition time, heavy traffic would be expected and any serious athlete would want to remove any such stressors. Two hours till the competition would finish and a further 40 minutes till Connor would have completed his warm-down and stretch. Then he would shower, on his own for the first time that afternoon. That would be when Zebra would strike.

Henkl would be running the OP, the observation post. It was always the same. Work in pairs, one to strike and one to act as lookout – safe, secure and conservative. If anything looked out of place or different, then just walk away. Carrying out a kill wasn't like the movies. Ad-libbing didn't happen and if it did then things weren't just bad, they were dire.

Connor certainly lived up to his file notes: the all-American boy next door, blond hair, blue eyes with a strong jawline framing a confident, smiling face. Life had been easy for Connor, straight A's throughout school life and a promising sports career also beckoned. Not that he hadn't worked for it, but it was always easier putting the work in when the results came your way. And they had. A sports scholarship to Georgetown almost seemed a waste. Connor could have got on to any course based solely on his academic ability, but that wasn't his style. Connor was an athlete and, the way he saw it, he had to gain his place on sporting prowess alone.

Today was a relatively low-level comp for Connor. It wasn't about winning the event, that was a sure thing. Today was about his routine, all in front of a judging team containing one of the US Olympic selection panel. A good performance would ensure further discussions. A great performance, according to his coach, should lead to a squad training invitation. Nothing less than great was acceptable today.

Henkl broke the silence for the first time in 40 minutes, which wasn't unusual. He and Zebra had worked together for over 10 years. They got on and they trusted each other. And trust was by far the most important part of their relationship. Henkl was the boss and Zebra was his lieutenant; an important lieutenant, nonetheless. They had two teams deployed to make four hits and today was Team 1's play.

"Check comms," Henkl said.

"Roger that," Zebra replied.

Zebra adjusted his earpiece and checked his mike. Then, with just a telling look, he vacated the van and started walking up the street. No look back, no stutter, just a normal pace, melting instantly in with the other passers-by.

"Two parked cars, one van and a bike 100 metres north," came Zebra's first on-air report.

"Roger that."

A minute passed then he broke the silence again.

"One family of four, three couples and seven others in the coffee house."

"Roger that," said Henkl. "Any sign of campus security?" he asked.

"None so far," replied Zebra.

"Complete your perimeter, check in every two minutes."

"Roger that," came Zebra's reply, still with a slight South African undertone in his accent.

Zebra hadn't been back to South Africa in his 10 years since working for Henkl, but his accent was always there, just a hint nowadays though, but it was there and it probably always would be. Some things are just impossible to hide and, for him, his years in Cape Town and then the South African special forces had seemingly had a permanent effect on his accent.

He completed his perimeter walk-through and comms check and was back in the van 30 minutes later.

"All good, chief," he grunted.

Henkl tried to stifle a wry smile, he was on a job and it was serious time, but he couldn't. Zebra used the term 'chief' infrequently, it was the closest he came to using a term of endearment and Henkl knew it. Usually it would be 'Boss', but just sometimes he would switch to chief.

Henkl's mobile broke their conversation; it was the burner phone ringing which meant it was either Harry or Bush from Team 2.

"Ja," he answered, reverting to his mother tongue, which he usually did when saying yes to anyone, no matter the language he was conversing in.

Zebra could hear the faintest tinny voice through the phone and was unsure who was speaking, but the moment he heard Henkl's more abrupt and colder response he knew it must be Bush. There was little love lost between Henkl and Bush. He had often wondered why Henkl put up with Bush, but then no one liked Bush and Bush pretty much didn't like anyone, so maybe it all made some sort of sense.

Bush had failed selection and ever since had gone to great lengths to both hate all other special forces operatives whilst proving to them that he was better. Harry called Bush 'Fish' as a nod to the massive chip he had on his shoulder. Bush hated Harry more because of it, but it didn't stop Harry.

Zebra had spent years working with the two Brits and always wondered at the efforts they made to piss each other off! He liked their sense of humour and the way they never moaned when things turned to ratshit – which was often – but he found it strange how they seemed to thrive off hating each other.

"Walk-through completed, Boss. Everything is OK for tonight," said Bush.

"Roger that."

"We go at 10," said Bush.

"Roger that. Check in on completion," replied Henkl and then put the phone down. "I fucking hate that Scheiße," he grunted, reverting to his favourite German description of Bush.

Zebra wondered if his boss could go a day without calling Bush a Scheiße! Probably not. He didn't reply. In the early days he had asked why Henkl used him and had instantly regretted it. It wasn't that his boss had defended Bush and it wasn't that he had been annoyed at being questioned. It was something far more subtle, Zebra reckoned it was just the fact he had reminded Henkl of a wart on his body that he had been putting up with and just forgotten about. Just a little annoying thing that most of the time Henkl forgot could be cured.

In the arena, Connor was preparing to start his floor routine. It was one of his better elements and he had been doing the same routine for over a year now. He knew it well; he'd refined it, tweaked it and was as comfortable as he could be. It was now or never. Only a great routine was acceptable.

A nod to the panel and to his coach and then he started. Connor sprinted along the diagonal; the greatest length of floor available. At full sprint, he went in to a series of front handsprings, over and over and over, finishing with a double tuck and an inch-perfect landing, feet together. Connor felt great. His confidence was up, his blood was pumping and he had his inner warmth inside him. He called it his 'inner warmth', his coach called it 'Zen time'; the time when his moves just worked. Connor turned 90 degrees and shot down the side, another sprint ending in yet more handsprings and a double front pike. Floor work followed.

All routines had mandatory parts, but in truth most gymnasts appreciated the break in the tumbles. Most spectators saw the bits in between tumbles as boring, but for gymnasts it allowed them to clear their minds and focus on the next section. Connor was no different. Years of training had involved a great deal of mental rehearsal and focus. Now his training was paying off. Connor's floor routine was just over three minutes. Three minutes of pure power, speed and strength, all carried out under technical precision and inch-perfect footwork. Connor nailed it; he knew he had the second his first tumble landed. He gave his biggest, beaming smile the full works, grinning at both the judges and his coach before finally turning to where his parents were sitting watching. A single raised fist in the air and then both arms aloft.

"Yes, yes, yes," he shouted.

And with that, Connor left the floor, returning to his coach, who bear hugged him like never before.

"You nailed it, Blimp, utterly nailed it. Brilliant, Blimp, just brilliant," said his coach.

Blimp was the nickname that only his coach called him. A cross between blond and chimp, his nickname had started when he was 14.

"Is it enough?" said Connor.

"Yes buddy, it's enough," said his coach.

Connor's coach wasn't one for being overconfident. If he said it was enough, then it probably was. Even so, the wait for the scores would still feel long. Connor knew he had won, but that wasn't what the nerves were about. He didn't need a perfect 10.00, just anything higher than a 9.70. His coach had told him as much for the previous three weeks. His floor routine carried the same technical difficulty as Corey Brown's, the golden boy of the US gymnastic team. At the recent US trials Corey had scored a 9.70.

The arena went quiet as the judges finished their work and announced the scores – 9.74!

"Yes, get in!" screamed Connor. Another bear hug from his coach squeezed him close to fainting.

"Well done, Blimpy, well done. That's it, Blimp, that's it, buddy. You are there, you are there, you are there," said his coach.

Connor freed himself and ran to his parents. More hugs and congratulations followed. Tears were in his mum's eyes and the biggest grin was on his dad's face.

"I'll see you after cool down, Dad," said Connor, before disappearing in the direction of the warm-down mats. Connor's coach left him to it and went over to chat to the judges.

"Time check, Zebra," said Henkl.

"Twenty minutes, Boss."

"OK, good to go," Henkl replied and with that the pair exited the van, crossed the road and entered the building through the same doors as their mark had done a few hours earlier. Not quick, not slow, just an unremarkable journey by two Washington-ites at one with their surroundings. Once through the main doors, the bright sunshine was replaced with easier lighting, no squinting needed. Zebra walked directly to the male changing rooms – not quick, not slow.

Henkl followed Zebra but pulled up at the comfortable seating conveniently situated in the open recess between the changing rooms and the main atrium. He took a seat, dropping his rucksack to the floor whilst removing a copy of the *Washington Times*. He relaxed, took in his surroundings and opened the paper. Now everything was serious. Now everything mattered. His years of training kicked in; heightened observation skills honed in the classroom, refined in the field and practised over and over and over. Training mattered and Henkl trained. Henkl was the oracle when it came to training. He took account of all incomings and outgoings, the leather-clad motorbiker waiting by the main doors, the couple with a teenage daughter probably waiting for an older child to exit the main arena. Every person in or out was noted. He wouldn't go on air to Zebra unless there was anything to report. If the job went as they planned then there would be one on-air report telling Zebra the 'mark' was on his way alone, and a reply to confirm received, finally followed by a single 'on air' confirming completion – simple. But nothing was ever simple, planning made things easy, but simple didn't really exist. Trained operatives like Henkl and Zebra made things appear simple, but they weren't.

Zebra entered the changing rooms and walked towards the far end, past the open access area, past the urinals and toilets, and straight to the private team rooms. There were four in total. Rooms A and B were both locked, he knew they were, but he checked them anyway. Check and double-check. Always the same, every job, check and double-check. Room C was unlocked and empty and this would be the room Connor would use, Zebra walked on and went to room D. He locked the door before going immediately to the interconnecting door to C. It was locked, but not for long. Zebra made short work of the lock – it wasn't designed to keep intruders out, just a simple lock to give privacy from one changing area to another – and then he waited.

Ten minutes passed and finally the 'mark' exited the arena. Henkl didn't flinch, he just sat and continued reading the paper. Connor turned right and started towards the changing rooms – alone.

"The job is on, 10 seconds to you," came Henkl's curt 'on-air' report to Zebra.

"Roger that."

And then Henkl just sat there, motionless. Motionless but seeing and hearing everything; now it was all about Zebra.

Connor entered the changing rooms and made his way down to room C. The same route he had taken hundreds of times since arriving at Georgetown. He entered the room, dumped his bag on the bench, turned around and locked the door. He was still feeling his inner warmth. It had become a glow, life at that moment couldn't be much better.

Connor undressed, grabbed his shampoo and went to the nearest shower cubicle. The showers were great on campus, warm, powerful and revitalizing. As the jet of water partially massaged his back, Connor smiled to himself as he reflected how well his day had gone.

Slowly, quietly and carefully, Zebra opened the connecting door. He had heard the shower turn on, he had heard the shower cubicle close and he had heard the change in noise as the shower stopped jetting the cubicle wall and started pummelling Connor's body. The time to move was now. He closed the door behind him; he was in stealth mode, making not the slightest of sounds. Zebra stopped behind the wall recess between showers and benches. And then he waited, Glock in hand, suppressor fitted. He just waited.

Connor finally finished, turned the shower off and exited the cubicle, grabbing his towel from the hook en route. Part walking, part towelling, Connor made his way to the bench. A journey he never completed.

As he passed the recess, Connor part heard the dull *psst* of the first of two shots both to the back of his head. He was dead instantly, hitting the floor in a crumpled mess. Blood sprayed the wall and started pooling on the floor around Connor's head. Zebra spent some time calmly checking the job. It was good. It was always good. Then he moved, not quickly, not slowly, to the connecting door, relocking it behind him before exiting room D and making his way towards the main entrance.

"Job completed, moving out," came Zebra's 'on-air' report, breaking the silence.

"Roger that," came Henkl's reply, whilst casually folding his newspaper, returning it to his rucksack. Not quickly, not slowly, he stood up and started towards the exit. Zebra was 20 metres back. They both headed to the van, no comms, no breaking stride, a picture of serenity as they made their exit.

Once in, Henkl started up, checked for traffic, indicated and moved out. No comms, no fuss, efficiency personified – job one done.

Twenty minutes later and they were five miles from the campus. Henkl broke the silence first, but not to speak to Zebra. There was nothing to be discussed. He had to file his report and that meant only one thing, call Xav.

The phone rang, three, four call tones and then on the fifth it picked up.

"Is it done?" came the unmistakable voice of Xav, a Swiss national with a neutral British accent.

"Connor Evans boxed," Henkl replied.

"Any problems?" he returned, never one for long sentences.

"No, Boss," came Henkl's just as short response. "Team 2 moves tonight and we go on Monday," he interjected before Xav could respond.

"Good, call me once the Woods job is done," he replied.

"Yes, Boss, will do," and with that he put the phone down.

"Always Xav, never her," muttered Henkl to Zebra.

He didn't really want a reply and Zebra was never going to respond. Henkl liked her, the 'her' being Louise, and consequently he didn't like Xav. But Xav was everything Henkl wasn't; smooth, sophisticated, exceptionally bright and very well connected. But most importantly, Xav wasn't a thug. Henkl wasn't either, but Louise didn't see it that way. She knew too, she knew that Henkl liked her. And she used it, she used it against Xav and she used it against Henkl.

Zebra didn't quite get it. The charms of a woman, good-looking or not, had always been lost on him – and not because he was gay, no, not at all. Being gay had never clouded his judgement concerning women with charm. He just couldn't understand why smart, talented people got sidetracked and controlled by others just because of a superficial little trait. And Henkl was smart – very, very smart. Zebra hadn't worked with anyone as good as Henkl in the 20 years he had been working special ops. But it didn't matter, Xav was with Louise, as much as anyone could be with Louise, and it was never going to change.

"Food, Boss?" came Zebra's eventual reply, albeit a change of subject.

"Ja. Steakhouse near the hotel good?" he suggested.

It was Zebra's turn to suppress a smile. Henkl offering a steakhouse for food was his way of saying 'good job'. Yes, their relationship was good, very good. He was ever grateful that his boss always paired Harry with Bush, leaving Henkl and Zebra as Gruppe Eins. He felt a little sorry for Harry, that was for sure, but not sorry enough to offer a swap. Harry understood. He knew that being second in command meant he was never paired with Henkl on two-man jobs. None of the Apfel liked Bush, and as the head of Apfel, why would Henkl put himself on jobs, sometimes lasting weeks, with a man he despised? The simple answer, he didn't.

Zebra didn't feel guilty, Harry was paid more as second in command and the consequences left Harry holding the shittier end of the stick.

"Good for me, Boss, good for me," answered Zebra.

Harry was sitting in a matching white van to the one Henkl and Zebra had. They had rented them as a pair when they landed stateside. Bush was in the passenger seat, silent, motionless but watchful. Across the road was a lively-looking bar full of local Georgetown students enjoying their Saturday night out. Their 'mark' had been in the bar since eight. Sarah Woods was a Georgetown starlet. Her file described her as a talented musician and an even more talented athlete. But her real strength was her academic abilities. Sarah had not just got straight A's through school, she had scored the highest SAT score in over 10 years in gaining admission to Georgetown. Her university had practically begged her to accept Georgetown. She had. Her parents were both successful, mid-level public servants having started government life as analysts before moving into administration positions. At least that's what their files said, but Xav knew better. And if Xav knew better then so did Henkl and that meant the Apfel knew.

The Apfel was BioDS's covert security team. Not to be confused with BioDS's private security team, who were just a bunch of rent-a-cops in brown uniforms. No, the Apfel were something much more special and much more deadly. The name had come from the word 'core' and then mutated to 'apple core' and shortened to 'apple'. Only Henkl was German, and Xav was a native German speaker and so Apfel had come about. Still Harry liked it. It was an innocent term with deadly connotations.

The Sarah Woods file contained a great deal of information concerning her parents too. Her bio described an innocent but highly talented young lady. It even suggested that she might have little or no idea about her parents' professional lives. Analysts was indeed the correct description for her parents' occupation, only they weren't political analysts like the cover suggested; they worked for the CIA and had done so for over 20 years. They were lifers, a term used within the CIA for career CIA staffers.

"Comms check," said Harry, breaking their silent vigil.

"Roger that," replied Bush.

The Apfel always followed a strict protocol. Henkl's training programme was very clear, no room for misinterpretation and no allowances for deviation. Two-man jobs always meant the same system. The lead ran the job, the second actioned it, with the lead running the OP. Harry knew why it was this way round and so did Bush. They all knew. If the job turned to ratshit, then the likelihood was that the OP was the one that would get away, and so hierarchy dictated the junior team member got the riskier role.

Bush inserted his earpiece, attached his mike and departed the van. It was dark outside now. The street was lit by intermittent lamps and the occasional nocturnal establishment. There were a few bars and restaurants open, their windows helping light the street. He started his walk around, reporting in every couple of minutes. There wasn't a great deal to report, but that wasn't the only point of a comms check. Kit needed to work, and therefore kit needed to be checked. 'On-air' comms was at risk of interference from certain electrical signals, localized electricity surges, large buildings and a variety of other factors that could all impinge on the comms. He would carry out a perimeter walk-by. Years of training had drilled the basics into them – always the basics. Check, double-check and then check again. They had recced the area twice already; once in daylight and once at night. There had been no comms issues on either occasion, but triplicate checking mattered!

"At the junction, all clear," came Bush's first report.

"Check the alley to the left as you pass," instructed Harry.

He replied in a flash, "Roger that."

Harry had the van to himself for 30 minutes and he appreciated every second. Bush was a twat! Just sitting next to him irked, but life wasn't perfect and so he accepted that, at times, he had no choice but to work alongside Bush. That was the job.

"Fish, you there?" came Harry's follow-up to his instruction. It was deliberate, a chance to call him 'Fish' by pretending he had missed Bush's reply. It was totally unprofessional and if Henkl knew he had done it a serious bollocking would ensue. That was the difference between Henkl and Harry. Henkl was 100% on the job at all times, no matter what. He would never go off-piste for the chance of a cheap joke. But Harry just couldn't resist.

"Roger that, you hear? **ROGER THAT**," came Bush's reply.

Harry grinned to himself; the response from Bush was full of anger, more a growl than actual words.

"Continue on your perimeter," he said in a calming voice, still grinning as he visualized a seething Bush, probably picturing a grinning Harry in his mind's eye.

"Roger that," came Bush's reply.

Thirty minutes passed before Bush returned to the van. Being five minutes longer than on the previous occasions, Harry guessed he had slowed a little to quell his anger. Bush had failed selection and was 'returned to his unit' and this had left a permanent scar on his psyche. He'd only lasted another 12 months in the Parachute Regiment before signing off. On a joint operation with the Navy SEALs, Bush had got into a fight. The fracas alone wouldn't have been a problem, there was a constant flow of incidents between special forces operatives and almost all were dealt with in-house – a quick rap of the knuckles plus a 'non-mention' in your file. But Bush had done the one thing you never do. He had taken down a Navy SEAL officer and then told his own regiment officer where to stick it! There was no way back. He had effectively kissed his future in the Paras goodbye. So he jumped before he was pushed; a better result all round.

He went down the tried-and-tested personal security route after mustering out. Iraq, Afghanistan and a whole host of other seriously unstable areas of the world cried out for people with his skill set. Work was plentiful and well paid. He thrived making the most of his opportunity to prove he really was the best of the best. And he was! The problem was, Bush always carried his chip and no matter how well he did, the world of mercenaries didn't hand out accolades or medals. They paid you well, very well, but they never gave what he craved; a commendation announcing to the world that he was the best, which was never going to happen. Life for him would continue to be an unhappy and frustrating path to an even crappier place. And Harry was determined to help Bush get there as quickly as possible.

"All good, Harry, the alleys are quiet," said Bush as soon as he was back in the van. "The second alley is still the one we go with," he said without interruption.

"Roger that." Harry wasn't going to get into a discussion with Bush about the choice of alley to use. Bush was a top operator, quite probably better than Harry. He was running the OP and he was more than happy to give Bush some leeway on the precise spot for the hit.

"Have we got the green light on collateral?" said Bush.

"Yes, that's a green light... ONLY IF NEEDED!" he urged.

Bush wasn't trigger-happy, that wasn't what Harry was concerned about. He knew that Bush would only do exactly what was required. His reticence was purely based upon the numbers game. Kill one person and you get a few headlines in the US; multiple killings and it gets front page. And front page meant more police resources and a multi-agency response. No, 'collateral' was easy for Xav to approve, but he wouldn't be the one rotting in a US penitentiary if they got caught. He was cautious because he liked his life exactly as it was.

"OK, let's do it," said Harry as he climbed out of the van and made his way into the bar.

Bush started picking up the distinctive sounds of a party – laughter, loud music and lots of chatter – nothing clear, just the indistinct but very recognizable sound of fun and happiness. The bar was rocking, mainly full of twenty-somethings with their lives ahead of them and not a care in the world. Harry didn't stand out though; the bar wasn't off limits to a man of the world. Harry was 41, trim, weathered and sinewy. He fitted in seamlessly – nondescript, unnoticed, he was Mr. Bland. The training helped and so did the preparation. Arriving in DC two weeks ago had helped the entire team soak up the surroundings. New clothing bought instantly and worn each and every day since helped make their appearance look a little tired and worn. The odd local item helped too, nothing OTT, a Redskins cap or a T-shirt sporting Georgetown. Look like a local not a tourist, that was Henkl's mantra.

Harry scanned the room; he had already seen the 'mark', but that wasn't what the scan was for. Before he had made his way to the bar he had clocked the female toilets, the bar staff door leading out back, presumably to the kitchen and stores, and his line of sight to the street.

He got to the bar and waited his turn. It was busy, not too busy that you couldn't get a place to lean up, but busy enough that the barman tending the right-hand end could only catch your eye to say he was getting to you in due course. Harry used the time well, two minutes waiting to order a Bud was time well spent. The bar was typical of bars across the States. A large mirror giving a full view of the general bar room was his perfect instrument. He saw Sarah Woods and her three friends stood by the jukebox. He watched the group of lads standing next to the four girls, in part enjoying the music but in reality looking like they were calculating the odds of striking up conversation with the girls. It was a decent match up; they looked like a good fit. Harry considered the lads 'to be in', but looks alone were never enough! He knew this more than most. He never put himself above average on the looks scale, but personality counted greatly. And he excelled in this department. He always reckoned his personality took him from a five to an eight on his one to 10 spectrums. Did the lads have it in them? He knew Sarah did, he had seen her file, and by association he reckoned she would only have fun, interesting friends.

"What can I get you?" The barman broke Harry's thoughts.

"A Bud please," came his reply. He tried to reply in his best US accent. It wasn't great, but it certainly sounded US rather than European. The bar was noisy and he figured the barman hadn't noticed. He didn't mention anything, so all was good in his mind.

The barman returned with a Bud, he passed him a 10-dollar bill before the barman could state the price. It was busy, the barman was happy to crack on, Harry was happier to keep conversation to a minimum.

He took a bar seat, taking a slow slurp, eyes on the girls whilst all the time scanning the rest of the room.

"Have eyes on, subject with three girls." Harry spoke whilst withdrawing the Bud from his mouth. Unnoticed to all, but at the other end Bush heard everything loud and clear.

"Roger that," Bush replied.

Harry settled in at the bar, supping his Bud slowly, keeping eyes on the target but at the same time keeping his head down and avoiding eye contact. The last thing he wanted was an unwelcome approach from any of the merrymakers.

Forty minutes passed. Harry got another Bud; it would be his last of the night. It was approaching 11, the lads had tried and failed to make an impression and the girls were clearly on their last drink. Ten minutes later and the girls had finished their drinks. Sarah and her blond friend walked towards the exit.

Harry came on air, "Subject exiting, you are on."

"Roger that," came Bush's instant response.

And then Sarah turned to the toilets, with Blondie following suit. Her other two friends had started to move too, both ignoring the toilets as they moved through the bar doors and on to the street.

"Cancel that, cancel that, subject in the toilet," replied Harry.

"Roger that."

"Two brunettes street-side now, expect subject plus Blond in two," came Harry's quick response.

"Roger that," Bush replied. Although he didn't say, he expected two to be more like five minutes. It didn't matter, he was ready. He was always ready.

Sarah and her friend exited the toilets, joining her friends on the street. A few minutes passed as the four girls said their goodbyes and then they split. The two brunettes started east down the avenue and the subject plus Blondie headed west.

"OK, it's on you, the subject and Blondie are coming to you now," came Harry's final report.

"Roger that. Have eyes on," Bush replied.

Harry didn't move at first, he let a few minutes pass, checked the bar one last time and then calmly and casually swivelled in his seat and exited the bar. If all went as planned then his work for the night was finished. He crossed the street and walked the 300 metres west to where the van was parked. He slid in the driver's side, started the engine, checked for traffic, indicated and pulled out, heading west. Two minutes later, he passed Bush on the right-hand side of the street and a further 50 metres on the left was Sarah and Blondie. Harry kept on going, past the next crossroads, past the two alleys and past the diner before turning into the retail park half a mile further on.

Sarah was walking arm in arm with Blondie in a world of their own, chatting and giggling to each other, totally oblivious to the man in the shadows. It wasn't that Bush was ducking and dodging; that would stand out. The art of surveillance was to be grey, and he was every shade of grey there was.

The two girls got to the crossroads and paused a second, a final chat, a little hug and then Sarah crossed over and kept going west,

CHAPTER 1 THE APFEL

Blondie turned left. Ten metres later, Blondie took one final look over her shoulder, called out and waved bye. Bush thought he heard her say 'See ya later', but she wouldn't. She didn't know it yet, but there would be no later for these two friends.

Sarah was alone now and her destiny rested in Bush's hands – not a great destiny. He sped up, not noticeably, but quicker nonetheless. It took him 60 seconds to come level with the 'mark', but he still had to cross the street. Timing was now key; he looked east, then west. It was deathly quiet, perfectly quiet. Bush started to cross and ended up 10 metres behind Sarah who had finally taken notice of him. She looked over, not scared just observantly. Bush didn't look threatening, clad in an unzipped, grey Georgetown bomber jacket, blue jeans and trainers. He was intentionally capless; following a subject in a hoodie or cap puts people on guard. It's human instinct, comfort is gained from seeing faces, fear for most comes from the unknown or the unseen.

He smiled back and then continued walking, not quick, not slow.

Sarah kept walking, relaxed, happy and oblivious.

The second alley drew closer. He slipped his hand into his jacket and retrieved his Glock – timing was everything.

Sarah drew level with the alley and appeared to make a start at looking behind her. She never got that far. The sounds of two *'pssts'* from a suppressed Glock from eight metres were heard. Both shots were deadly accurate, to the head causing instantaneous death. Sarah hit the ground – job done.

Bush hurried over, gun reholstered. He dragged her down the alley and left her body behind the second bin.

"Sarah Woods boxed off, Harry," came Bush's 'on-air' report and then, before Harry had a chance to reply, a second 'on air'. "Heading west, good to go, Harry."

"Roger that, en route," Harry replied.

Bush walked west, Harry drove east and 45 seconds later Bush was back in the van.

"Problems, Bush?" asked Harry as he continued driving away.

"Sweet matey," Bush replied. "Just the girl, no collateral."

"Good job, Bush," Harry replied grudgingly. Even with perfectly executed jobs, he always struggled to be complimentary. He just couldn't bring himself to do it. Bush didn't care though; he didn't want Harry's compliments. Bush wanted what he couldn't have. He knew it and Harry knew it.

They drove in silence for a further 10 minutes and then Harry called in.

Henkl picked up on the third ring.

"Ja, is it done?" came his slightly inflected German tones.

"Sarah Woods boxed off, Boss," Harry replied. He always called Henkl 'Boss', as did Zebra, and Henkl appreciated it. He never said, but he did and they both knew he did.

"Good job, Harry. See you back at base." And with that he put the burner phone down.

Whilst Harry and Bush headed back to their base, Henkl picked his second phone up and reported in.

The time in DC was 11 p.m. meaning Geneva was not quite awake, but at 5 a.m. Xav would answer. He always answered. *On the second ring too, impressive*, thought Henkl.

"Is it done?" Short, sweet and to the point came Xav's clipped opening.

"Sarah Woods boxed," Henkl replied.

"Any problems?" he asked.

"None, Boss. All to plan. We move on Monday with Skinner and Tuesday with Sanchez," replied Henkl.

"Good, call me after the Skinner job," said Xav.

"Roger that," he replied and with that he ended the call.

CHAPTER 2
THE PICK

CIA HQ, Langley, Virginia
Wednesday 21st September 2016

Deep in the bowels of the large building, located at 1000 Colonial Farm Rd, Langley, Virginia, was a room bathed in dim, industrial lighting overhead and sharper VDU screens. Human eyes took a few seconds to adjust to the strange green and white glow upon entering the Arena. Originally called Stem Centre, the room had been renamed.

No natural light and, with a silent hum, soft voices added to the surreal surroundings. This was Ram's environment. This was his Arena. Roman Schubert was the archetypal computer geek; scruffy appearance, soft hands and weak chin.

Ram had been his nickname since high school. Others often assumed it was an abridged form of Roman, but this wasn't the case. The name had come from his time spent abusing and bastardising PCs with extra memory and upgrades. His schoolmates had enjoyed the double use of the word, Roman 'ramming' his PCs with extra RAM.

Ram had been recruited directly from Harvard into the CIA's specialist 'anti-hacking' programme, which he had always thought to be the definition of irony, given he had never spent a minute of his time preventing CIA hacks and just about all his time and energy had been spent hacking his way around the globe. But Ram didn't care. In fact, far from feeling guilty, he loved it! He was paid to legally, well almost legally, hack into anything and everything he could. When he wasn't given a direct assignment, Ram would spend his time inserting 'stonefish' into all and sundry that might be useful at a later date. This was how he trained, and practice made perfect. A 'stonefish' was his name for a concealed, dormant code, camouflaged but ready to act when needed.

Today was different though, very different. Ram was two weeks into a genuinely exciting 'pick'; he hated the word hack, it was crude and common. He saw himself as an artist, likening himself to a virtual 'cat burglar'. Ever since university, Ram had adopted the word 'pick', such as to pick a lock, when describing his work.

Martin Pawlowski, Pav for short, had assigned a very interesting 'pick', which had initially involved hacking into the Russian politburo. Gaining access via a back door, from there Ram entered a covert programme called 'Knacc'. Knacc, the Russian for 'class', was a secret programme based near Omsk. Ram liked the fact that his boss let him use his moniker. He knew it was a real feather in his cap, for only a select few were allowed to use 'Pav'; the plebs in the department all had to say 'sir' – and they had to mean it. Ram though was in Pav's circle, his very, very small circle.

He was close now. The last two days, he had managed to insert his 'foundation code' undetected. He could have inserted his 'pick' within a few days, but this would have been detected – detection was not an option.

So, for the last week, he had been working on getting his 'foundation coding' inserted undetected. Once inserted, it would allow him to insert his 'masking programme' and then he could proceed with his 'pick'.

Pav hovered over his shoulder, staring at the dual screens and the overhead master and slave screens. Ram knew most of what Pav was looking at didn't really mean much, but equally, he knew never to misjudge him. Pav wasn't assistant director of the CIA for nothing.

To get to that lofty position required a high level of conniving intelligence, cunning, political astuteness and, most of all, an ability to claw your way up a very tricky and dangerously slippy 'greasy pole'. At just 43, Pav had managed this with aplomb.

"How close are you?"

"Getting there, Pav, getting there," Ram replied.

"How long?"

"The masking programme is loading now, an hour max. Then I can upload the pick," returned Ram.

"Good job, Ram, good job. Call me as soon as the pick's inserted," and with that Pav turned for the door.

"Will do," replied Ram, grinning as he said it. He felt the warmth in Pav's voice and that in turn would lead to better things to come, that Ram was sure of. But most of all, he loved it when Pav called it a 'pick'. It was his word, his and his alone.

Pav closed the door behind him and started up the long, featureless corridor. Bland didn't do it justice. The corridor went on and on, with just doors breaking up the plain walls. As he made his way his mobile rang. Three shrill tones managed to break the silence before he could get to the call button.

"Yes Wendy?" came his abrupt answer.

"We have eyes on in Omsk, Pav. Drake and Kaspov have just made comms," she replied.

"Good, meet in my office for briefing. Ram isn't far off, maybe an hour."

"There in 10," Wendy replied and ended the call.

Pav continued his way; it was a 10-minute walk to his office from Ram's gloom. CIA HQ wasn't just big, it was enormous. Hundreds of acres of sprawling office space meant for long walks between certain areas of the site. He set a brisk pace; as always time was precious. The clock was most certainly ticking.

Back in the gloom, Ram tapped away on the keyboard to his left with an alarming speed. The screen to his right was filled with an almost undecipherable code. A multitude of characters scrolled continuously down the left-hand side of the screen, occasionally interrupted by flashing warning boxes.

Above his head were two larger monitors, centre right was the slave screen, currently mirroring his desk monitor, yet this was a split screen, only half was a mirror, the other half displayed a strange-looking vector diagram. Arrows moved from box to box, occasionally disappearing, then reappearing with more speed and boldness. Ram glanced from desktop screen to slave and back, but he never stopped typing. Twelve hours a day, six days a week was his life in the Arena. He left the Arena for food and toilet breaks and nothing else. He was never summoned to Pav's office or Wendy's. People came to him, not the other way round. He was no gym bunny, no scary physical specimen. But in his 'Arena', Ram was a gladiator and right now he was winning big.

Pav arrived at his office to find Wendy standing over his secretary. Clutching a plain brown file, Wendy was on the phone. Upon seeing him enter the outer office, she finished her call and hung up.

"No calls," instructed Pav as he looked to his secretary. Pav's secretary Drew was no stereotype, more of a cross between a cybergeek and track athlete. Drew was all wire and sinew. Five per cent body fat failed miserably in hiding Drew's ripped muscles. His lithe and glowing skin tone told its own story of hours in the gym. The geek look came from his nerd-like face, framed by square glasses and a questionable bumfluff goatee. Drew really was a strange concoction of a man.

"Yes sir," replied Drew.

"OK, what've you got?" Pav enquired as he led Wendy into his private office.

It was a very plush office. Thick carpets, a large polished mahogany desk and comfortable leather chair were framed by an expansive window to the left and a door to his private bathroom to the right.

The wall behind his desk displayed a myriad of photos. In every photo Pav was the central figure, pictured either shaking some dignitary's hand or standing shoulder to shoulder with them. The more powerful the person pictured with him, the more central the photo was positioned. Pride of place was Pav with the current president, although two to the left was a much younger Pav with the previous POTUS. Wendy was no stranger to the power struggle within government agencies though. She was a girl on the up, highly ambitious and earmarked for great things to come. She was building her own portfolio of photos with powerful people. She knew how things worked. Pav knew and she was learning from the best.

Wendy and Pav sat down. Making himself comfortable, he started. "So Ram's almost good to go. What have Drake and Kaspov got for us?"

"They're in situ, Pav. Kaspov has rendezvoused with the locals, Drake has comms up and running and they've completed a full recce of Knacc," she replied.

"What's the site like?"

"It's bigger than we thought; about 100 acres with a perimeter fence. There's only one way in and out via the main road and it's set back from the nearest building by about 1 km," she replied, her voice giving no emotions away.

Pav wondered whether Wendy ever let her emotions betray her. *Probably not*, he thought. Ice Queen was what the rest of his team called her. Although he liked and trusted her, he couldn't disagree with their nickname. Wendy was only ever 'on programme', she never let her guard down, ultra consistent was her middle name. He couldn't ask for a better number two and probably only needed to worry about her aspirations for his desk.

"What's the security?" Pav asked.

"The road in has a sentry box, although it's just for show. You know the story; it's mainly for deliveries signing in and so on. The real security is covert," she replied.

"Go on," he interrupted.

"The perimeter fence is silently alarmed; surveillance cameras are positioned every 30 metres and the entry gate has a state-of-the-art magnetic locking system. There is a 100-metre open clearing surrounding the entire village and the nearest obscured area is the forested area to the western perimeter."

"So, what's the plan then?" questioned Pav.

"Kaspov said the locals have two options. Option 1 is blunt, approaching via the main road. Take out the two sentries and rush the gates. They reckon they can go in two vehicles with a 30-second gap between. Mobile 1 would approach with a legitimate delivery, process the entry paperwork and proceed to the gate. Mobile 1 would be the 'Trojan'; their only aim would be to stop the entry gate closing. Whilst they do this mobile 2, the 'Breach Team', would follow, they would take out the sentries and rush the gate."

"Cons?" he asked.

"It's blunt, Pav. Internally they will switch to defensive mode immediately. If there are any safe rooms, then we may not be able to complete. Drake thinks the contact time will be over 20 minutes, which is likely to incur 'a response contact' with anyone they can get out to the village," replied Wendy with unwavering emotion.

"And Option 2?" came Pav, almost dismissing Option 1 without saying so.

Wendy knew though, she had needed less time than it had taken to read the options to assess and select the mission MO.

"In essence, there would be a threefold breach. The sentries would be deflected with our Trojan Team whilst the real entry would occur through the fence on the western perimeter."

"Through!" Pav replied, not so much a question than a statement.

"Yes, through. Breach team would go over the open ground from the western forest and cut through the fence. Trojan Team will take out the sentries and take control of the entrance. Team 3 would be where Ram comes in," she replied.

Giving Pav no opportunity to reply, Wendy continued with her report, "Ram will 'pick' the security system and immobilize the fence."

"But if he can do that, what's wrong with a main entry approach?" he quizzed.

"Nothing, Pav, but the escape route will be back through the fence and then the forest. Once Ram immobilizes the fence, he triggers an alarm in Omsk FSB HQ. They are 30 minutes away, but more importantly, he figures the comms response time from FSB HQ to Knacc will be 10 minutes," she concluded.

"Why so long? If this was us, it would be 30 seconds max," asked Pav.

"Knacc is a covert op. FSB don't know about its existence. There's a single FSB agent with the relevant clearance in the Omsk office. Ram can run a 'pick' that can block comms to the Omsk head, meaning he won't get the alarm notification until their field agent physically gets face to face with the head. Ram reckons 10 minutes minimum," she replied.

Wendy knew. She had known before she entered Pav's office what she would be doing next. It would be straight back to Drake and Kaspov with an Option 2 directive. No-brainer, Wendy always knew.

"So what do you think?"

"I think the same as you, Pav."

"Option 2 it is then. Get back to Drake and Kaspov," he instructed.

"On it, Boss," smiled Wendy. She was smiling because she had known and smiling because she knew the effect that simple word 'boss' would have on Pav. She always marvelled at the power of flattery. And with that Wendy left him to his plush, thickly carpeted office.

As the door closed behind her, Pav allowed himself a moment to drift off. He stared out of his expansive window and glazed over. Appearances can be deceptive though. In fact, where he was concerned, appearances were always deceptive. Pav wasn't fooled by Wendy's flattery. Did he like it when she called him 'boss'? Well yes, he did. He loved it, in fact. But it didn't sway him, he let her see his delight, but it was mainly for show.

Pav looked a thousand miles away, but internally he was alert and very much 'on programme'.

He sat there contemplating, only to be interrupted by his shrill ringtone.

Glancing at the caller display, he answered. "Yes, Ram."

"We're in, Pav. The 'pick's' inserted; I have full access," Ram replied.

"I'll be there shortly. Start the download, I want everything – EVERYTHING," he emphasized.

"Am on it, Pav, am on it," Ram replied and hurriedly put the phone down.

Back in the gloom, the monitors on Ram's desk where scrolling through files at a million miles an hour – or so it seemed. Files were downloading, lines of text and characters cascaded over and over on the left-hand side of the slave monitor above his head.

A series of green bars were continually filling up from left to right, once filled they would disappear only to be replaced by another empty bar, with the process repeating itself.

On the master monitor above Ram's head was 'класс' in large, bold font in the top left-hand corner, followed by a screen full of Cyrillic text – a mirrored image of Knacc's internal system. The slave was beavering away stripping the files out of Knacc's mainframe.

The door opened; Pav strode in purposefully.

"What's it look like?" he asked.

"Everything, Pav, we've got everything," Ram replied.

"Good job, Ram, real good job," and with no chance to reply, carried on. "Right, download everything, assign it to Steelhorse, code name 'chariot', and put my protocol on it," Pav finished.

"It's done. You have full access to it right now," Ram bounced back.

"Once it's completed, delete everything from the mainframe and all hard copy files, OK?" directed Pav.

"What about the 'pick'?" beamed Ram.

"Can it remain undetected?"

"Yes, Pav. No one will know, they won't know, and neither will we," said the IT expert still beaming as he spoke.

"You sure, 100%?" he quizzed.

"One hundred per cent, Pav. Would put my tablet on it," Ram replied.

Pav smiled. Just a small upturn of his lips, but it was there, a small, wry, little smile. Ram only valued two things in life and one of them was his tablet. Some people put their wife, mother or kids on the line, but not Ram.

No, Ram didn't care for his mum, and he didn't have a wife or kids. In fact, as far as Pav knew, he didn't really have a life beyond the virtual world he moved in. No, Ram's tablet was his prized possession. It was a statement; a statement that said, 100%, the 'pick' was secure and undetectable.

"Good job, Ram, really, really good job," and with that Pav left the gloom.

CHAPTER 3
STEELHORSE

Langley, Virginia
Thursday 29th September 2016

"We need to talk." There was no hello or other pleasantries. Brian O'Connor, the White House Chief of Staff, wasn't offended though.

O'Connor, as former director of the CIA, had recruited and promoted Pav as far up as assistant director of the CIA. It was only when O'Connor had left the agency that Pav's luck had run out. Stalled in the CIA and twice passed over for promotion to the top post, Pav had become a disillusioned, cynical Langley staffer.

O'Connor was standing in his plush office staring through the double doors that led to his PA's office. Overweight and with a ruddy complexion, it hadn't always been that way for the 65-year-old O'Connor. Too much time spent in the corridors of power had meant regular 14-hour days and a lack of personal time. In his early years, vim and vigour kept O'Connor trim and honed. Making time for a daily five-mile run every morning had been the secret. But in his later years, the knees had started to creak and eventually put paid to the running. It was downhill from there, Father Time had won, and O'Connor had gone to seed.

"My office in an hour," was O'Connor's short but by no means rude reply. Time was always in short supply.

"Gotcha," came Pav's single word response, hitting the end call button immediately. He leant forwards a touch and instructed his driver to head for the White House. Sitting beside Pav, Drew instinctively knew what to ask.

"Cancel your 11 o'clock?" more a statement than a question, quizzed Drew.

"Yes, and push back my 2 o'clock," responded Pav, it was going to be a long day. The news from the intel room earlier had made sure of that.

As Drew busied himself rearranging the day ahead, Pav returned to studying the brown Manila dossier resting on his lap. It didn't make for pretty reading.

Eyes Only: Martin Pawlowski
Ass Director, Clearance Level 5
Thursday 29th September 2016
Compiler: Sasha N'ganou, Asst Analyst (Level 2) ~ Washington Office

Deceased: Connor L Evans, DOB: 24.02.1997
Method: Shot. Two shots to the head. 38 mm bullets.
Location: Georgetown University Campus, Washington
Time of death: 18:22 Saturday 17th September 2016

Deceased: Sarah E Woods, DOB: 11.03.1997
Method: Shot. Two shots to the head. 38 mm bullets.
Location: Georgetown, Washington
Time of death: 23:16 Saturday 17th September 2016

Deceased: Rebecca L Schmidt, DOB: 17.03.1997
Method: Shot. Two shots to the head. 38 mm bullets.
Location: Fairfax, Washington
Time of death: 14:23 Monday 19th September 2016

Deceased: Joseph M Werner, DOB: 21.04.1997
Method: Shot. Two shots to the head. 38 mm bullets.
Location: Bethesda, Washington
Time of death: 07:12 Tuesday 20th September 2016

Insight:
MO – 98.5 % match

Suspected perpetrator: Professional lone killer, possibly two separate assassins.
Connection: Unknown. All parents are / were affiliated to the CIA.
Collateral: None
Witnesses: None
Leads: None

The report went on to expand further on the details of each victim. Details of the family contained a great deal of redacted material surrounding all four victims' parents. Pav could easily access this via his clearance but that would have been unnecessary.

It was unnecessary because he had been written in to the Steelhorse programme almost 15 years ago. What Pav didn't know about the families wasn't worth the proverbial paper it was written on.

Returning to the very top of the report, he glowered. The 29th September 2016 shone out like a lighthouse beam. Only now, eight days after Joe Werner had been fatally shot, was Pav sitting dissecting the facts – grim facts. O'Connor wasn't going to take this news well either; four dead MorphEns and a real shitshow to follow.

"Sorted, Pav," announced Drew, breaking Pav's silent thoughts as he concluded his calls. With his boss's diary replanned, Drew turned his attention to his laptop. Pav's mind was racing, briefing O'Connor was one thing but that was merely to bring O'Connor up to speed. His subsequent task was going to be much more painful. Wendy Angel was going to need to be 'written in'.

As Pav wandered deeper and deeper into the recesses of his own mind, the black sedan gunned towards the White House. Snapping out of it, Pav got back on track, he had another 40 minutes with which to address a few burning issues. He called Ram for an update prior to surprising him with his final instruction. Elevating Wendy Angel's clearance to FULL ACCESS to Steelhorse came completely out of the blue. Ram hadn't seen that coming, but then he hadn't seen the assassination of four of the 14 MorphEns coming either.

Next Pav called Wendy. With a conference meeting lined up for later that afternoon which asked more questions than it did answers for Wendy, Pav didn't give anything away. She would be beaming by the close of play, but she could wait for her good news.

As the gates to the White House approached, the driver brought the sedan to a gentle stop. Windows eased down, allowing security passes to be scrutinized, whilst a second guard scanned the underside of the sedan with a detector.

"Welcome sir," came the first guard's response as he handed the security passes back. The gates rolled open, a long entry road beckoned leading to a spacious and relatively empty car park close to the administrative wing of the White House.

Ten minutes later and Pav was seated in the Chief of Staff's private office.

"Drink?" quizzed O'Connor, playing the dutiful host to his underling.

"Scotch please," shot back Pav.

"A bit early, isn't it?" replied O'Connor.

"Not when I give you this," he said as he part placed, part dropped the dossier on O'Connor's desk.

O'Connor proceeded to pour Pav a drink but not before helping himself to bourbon.

"So, what am I reading?" Picking up the dossier, O'Connor started to leaf through it as Pav gave a general summary.

"Eight days ago, four of our guys were killed – identical MOs. It was a thoroughly professional job, identical in almost every detail. No witnesses, no CCTV, no leads. Exceptionally clean in every way."

"Done by us?" O'Connor enquired.

"It was very professional," Pav replied, his response a suggestion that the assassinations had all the hallmarks of any number of US-based agencies.

"You have anything?" O'Connor barked.

It wasn't a great start, but Pav had expected nothing less. "Not a thing," he replied.

A brief silence fell on the room as both men sipped their drinks whilst pondering their next thoughts.

"Eight days ago, Pav... WHAT THE FUCK...?" Giving no time to respond, "Why have you only come to me with this now?" boomed O'Connor.

"It just landed, Bock, I called you within 20 minutes of getting it," replied Pav, switching to Bock rather than sir to diffuse O'Connor's ire.

Brian O'Connor had always preferred his varsity nickname to 'sir'. In his line of work though, 'sir' was required a great deal of the time. It commanded deference and carried a certain gravitas that his nickname just didn't cut.

"Well, if it's not us then who? The Russians?" O'Connor continued to interrogate, not that any answers were forthcoming.

Pav offered a plan, admittedly a work in progress given the limited time since the news. A plausible explanation to each family was needed. A check on the remaining 10 MorphEns had already been instructed but a covert security detail needed doing too.

That would be costly, covert observations and security done properly required six members of staff in three teams of two to watch over a single MorphEn. That required 60 agents, not something Pav could muster. O'Connor agreed with Pav that two agents per MorphEn would have to do. Lastly was the Wendy thing. Writing Wendy Angel into Steelhorse clearance was a necessity. Did Pav like it? Not one bit and neither had O'Connor when he'd brought it up. But as Pav explained, there was no way he could carry out all the above without giving someone else oversight, and that meant writing in Wendy Angel.

Pav had one thing to check on before taking his leave. The thorny subject of Chloe Stephens, director of the NSA, a theoretical ally but the reality was quite the opposite.

"Keep me briefed if you hear anything from Stephens," asked Pav, more of an order than a request. "I don't know whether this will get caught in her radar or not, but she gets access to FBI daily sitreps."

Pav and O'Connor both wore visibly sour faces at the introduction of Chloe Stephens to their conversation. The director of the NSA was the biggest thorn in their side. They shuddered to think what would happen if Stephens got wind of Steelhorse.

With that Pav took his leave. Next stop was his meeting with Wendy: a meeting that would make her considerably happier than himself. Handing Wendy more knowledge and an elevated clearance meant handing her more power, something he could do without, but needs must.

Back at Langley HQ, Wendy Angel was purposefully going about her duties. She was intrigued by Pav's meeting request. It implied a great deal but had given nothing away. *Maybe it was the Knacc operation*, she pondered. *Something else?*

Sitting at her desk, her thoughts were interrupted by her PA, Mike Gratton.

"Pawlowski is back, Wendy, he's ready for you," came the assured voice of Mike as he leant through the door frame into her office.

"Let him know I'm on my way," she replied as she took to her feet.

Five minutes later and Wendy had arrived in Pav's office. Goosebumps prickled as Pav instructed Drew to stop all calls, whilst closing the door to his private office. They were all very promising signs she mused.

"I suppose you have been wondering what this is about," questioned Pav as he poured himself a Scotch. Offering Wendy a drink by way of a gesture, tipping a glass towards her got waved away. He knew she'd decline. In all the years Pav had known Wendy, he'd never seen her accept a drink. Why would today be any different?

"A touch maybe," she replied, playing down the level of intrigue she had been feeling all day.

Pav proceeded to inform Wendy of her promotion to a Level 5 CIA clearance for a covert programme called 'Steelhorse'. Now 20 years old, there were currently only four living people with knowledge of it. She wasn't surprised to hear that Ram was written in. Despite being Wendy's underling, Ram had a unique position within the agency and as such held a myriad of 'special clearance and access' rights.

One of the four being Brian O'Connor, though, was what really grabbed her attention. The current White House Chief of Staff still written in to a CIA Level 5 programme unveiled a bigger, more sensitive story.

"Operation Steelhorse was initiated in 1997. Louise Walsh, a British biogeneticist based in Geneva, created a postnatal gene therapy recoding procedure. The recipients, known as MorphEns, have a 20-22% enhancement in both physical and mental aptitude. These results, although emphatic, do not have clinical validity mainly due to the small sample data. The MorphEns programme and Steelhorse is completely covert." At this point in his summary, Pav paused. Staring intensely into Wendy's eyes, he took a sip of his Scotch. Wendy didn't flinch. Maintaining a poker face, she returned his stare.

"We created 14 MorphEns – 14 hand-picked babies from 14 in-house CIA lifers; all without their knowledge."

At this point Wendy interjected. "What does the procedure involve?"

Pav knew she was cold, one of her nicknames was Ice Queen, but even he was surprised by her first question. Not showing outrage or surprise at the news that 14 babies had been put through a medical procedure without parental consent, no, Wendy had only wanted to know what the procedure involved.

"It's a small, surgical stem cell implant that can only be carried out in the first four days postnatal," replied Pav.

Wendy nodded her head subtly whilst ever so slightly sinking a little deeper into her chair, body language intimating to Pav to carry on with his summary.

"Initially things went well. Testing and analysis was excellent. The programme was earmarked for expansion. But then we hit a snag."

"Snag?" she interrupted.

"Louise Walsh," replied Pav. "She went cold on us, initially demanding more money, which of course we agreed to. Initial funding of $14 m was increased to $37 m in 1998, but it didn't solve the issues."

"So, what was the real issue then?" quizzed Wendy.

"She switched sides," he replied.

"Sides?" she asked.

This is the master race question, the ultimate human being, and of course the highest bidder is king. And the highest bidder was the Russians.

"Why do you think a Brit came to us Yanks in the first place?" Pav retorted. "The miserly Brits weren't even interested," he continued.

"So, we created Steelhorse only to lose it to the Russians. They call it 'Knacc'." At this point Wendy finally dropped her poker face.

"Knacc," repeated Wendy. Her mind raced as she finally understood what she had been working towards over the last four months. The CIA didn't take murder lightly, despite popular opinion to the contrary. Although not having a green light yet, Operation Doorstop was enormous. If 'green-lighted' it involved killing over 200 Russians on home soil. Actions like that had enormous potential for escalation on a scale unimaginable.

"Knacc is an industrial-scale version of Steelhorse. Where we have created 14 MorphEns, the Russians have created an entire school."

"So why are you telling me this now?" she asked. The penny had finally dropped. Pav didn't give knowledge away freely. Something was missing.

"Last week, four of our MorphEns were assassinated," explained Pav. He passed Wendy a duplicate dossier to the one he had given Brian O'Connor earlier.

"They were contract killings, exceptionally clean hits. No leads at this point. Everything suggests this was a nation state enterprise."

"You think it was the Russians?" she replied, her train of thought swayed by Doorstop; hardly surprising given the energy she'd committed to this over the last few months.

"We aren't short of agencies closer to home," offered Pav with a grimace. Wendy curled a lip upwards too. The National Security Agency (NSA) and the Defense Intelligence Agency (DIA) immediately sprung to mind, but there was no shortage of suspect agencies.

"What…? Us?" Wendy responded, not with astonishment, but with something akin to surprise, nonetheless.

"It's a shitshow," continued Pav as he expanded further.

"We have ten MorphEns and they need observation, and they need security. We need to speed up Doorstop." A pregnant pause ensued. Wendy waited. She knew. She could sense something else was missing – again!

"Stephens needs managing." For the second time that day Chloe Stephens' name cast a shadow over discussions. Whether the NSA had been involved in the assassinations was a question mark that needed answering, but regardless, Stephens was a problem. A vehement opponent of almost every CIA initiative, Stephens was trouble.

Wendy sat stony-faced, motionless aside from her fingers silently tippy-tapping the brown dossier Pav had just presented her. Clearance levels elevated and a great deal of enlightenment too was a moment to savour, but the warm glow she was really feeling came from the very tangible costs incurred by Pav. Allowing Wendy into Pav's inner circle was the big prize, and she loved it in equal measure to Pav's discomfort.

CHAPTER 4
CHATEAU FORESTIER

Geneva, Switzerland

Situated halfway between Geneva and Lausanne was the stunning Chateau Forestier. Sitting in five acres of woodland, the chateau had a fully uninterrupted 300-metre lakeside frontage on to the magnificent Lac Léman. Idyllic didn't do it justice. Chateau Forestier faced a distant Mont Blanc and, as you approached the private jetty, its backdrop was the beautiful Jura Mountains.

The chateau was surrounded by an imposing three-metre-high wall to three sides, its remaining border being Lac Léman itself, the walls extending 15 metres into the water. Security was taken very seriously by its inhabitants.

The main and only gate was electronically controlled, with an intercom connecting any visitor straight to the main building. A closed-circuit camera system monitored the entire perimeter. The head of security was constantly moaning though, his concerns always about the barrierless lake frontage making a lot of what he did pointless.

Louise wouldn't buckle though. She wanted top-notch security, but her one luxury being her lakeside view. Every year that passed had seen a heated discussion during safety reviews. The last addition had seen two prowling Dobermanns let loose in the grounds. Louise didn't particularly like dogs, and neither did Xav, but she had relented. Dogs were better than a big wall, so dogs it was.

Louise Walsh was 56 years old and the chief executive of BioDS Industries. Attractive and slim, she was a lady with a healthy glow and an energy that belied her age. Yoga twice a week and a weekly session with her personal trainer paid dividends. Louise lived well. She worked hard but with that hard work had come the benefits. She wasn't married, but she may as well have been, she had met Xav a few years after an acrimonious divorce. Estranged didn't do her justice, Louise had left her husband with the children, unusual for a mother. She subsequently left New York, moving to Geneva in 1998.

Xav Picamole, a couple of years her junior, worked at BioDS and had been Louise's lover for over 10 years. He was head of R & D at BioDS and a fellow biogeneticist. Xav carried a slight excess in weight, but a full head of hair and alert, twinkling eyes still ensured he earned a second glance. He looked pretty good for his age, but looks were only secondary. For Xav, what counted, what mattered most was his mind, and his was a brilliant mind, second only to Louise's.

Louise descended the main internal staircase and stood in the spacious grand hallway. The hallway had an interesting mix of the French baroque with a modern twist. A large tiled floor was framed on both sides by stylish 18th-century sideboards and two enormous gilt-framed mirrors.

Xav was stood talking in German to Loic, their head of security. Dressed in a tuxedo, Xav looked every bit the high society Genevois. He turned to Louise reverting to French rather than English.

"Es-tu prête, ma chérie?" asked Xav.

"Bien sûr, mon amour," Louise replied.

Loic opened the main door. As they stepped out, the chauffeur-driven Mercedes crawled to a stop at the foot of the stone staircase. The only driveway into the grounds cut through the wooded area to the back of the chateau and then forked to both the front and the rear of the property.

At the front, the drive looped around in a large circle, a two-metre-tall stone statue helping to create a roundabout effect. Beyond the statue lay a well-manicured lawn leading to the water's edge. The grounds to the front of the chateau were immaculate. The lawn was edged with elegant stone troughs, broken every five metres by a series of high-backed iron benches. Adding to the very symmetrical feel, a generous three-metre-wide stone-paved path ran a full 50 metres through the middle of the lawn, ending at the jetty.

The jetty was approximately 10 metres in length and currently had two speedboats tethered to their moorings. His and hers maybe? There was ample space for another couple of boats; the two empty moorings demonstrated that fact.

Louise descended the small stone staircase, elegant in her shimmering black dress with matching heels and clutch. It wasn't difficult to look a million dollars when you were worth considerably more, but somehow she always seemed to look classy. By the time Xav had finished his final directive to Loic, the chauffeur had opened the Mercedes' rear door. Louise climbed in, whilst Xav rounded the rear, opening the opposing door himself, joining her in the back.

Six hundred metres distant, the black-clad operative adjusted his night-vision device (NVD). Robert Warner sat as still as was humanly possible on the RIB which rocked gently on the calm waters of Lac Léman. Rob was at the limit of his NVD's recognition capability, but being at their limit was very comforting. On a dark, autumnal night and only just coping to recognize his target, Rob knew that he was completely concealed, hidden in the darkness in the middle of Lac Léman.

"Departing now," whispered Rob into his throat mike. Sound travelled over water; tonight's mission was all about leaving no trace.

"Roger that," came the response.

Rob continued to observe. He watched the Mercedes pull away. He could barely hear the purr of its engine or the sound of the gravel crunching under the tyres. He switched his attention to the large figure standing in the arch of the main entrance. Rob couldn't make out the features, silhouetted as he was against the bright lights within the house, but he knew who it was. It was Loic Dubois, head of security and a former investigator with Interpol. Rob had a complete dossier detailing Loic's entire background.

Just prior to closing the door, Loic appeared to stare directly at Rob, it was just after 8 p.m. on a very dark and very cold night. A chill ran down Rob's spine as he continued to observe Loic, his

NVD giving everything an eerie green glow. Loic couldn't see him, that was for sure. He was probably just staring out across the lake, a force of habit. Humans are all creatures of habit. Rob had spent an entire week studying the psychology of 'humans and habit' as part of his wider training programme. MI6 had recruited Rob directly from 'The Regiment', which was what the SAS was usually referred to. The SAS had taught Rob how to survive, how to kill and how to go unnoticed.

At MI6 though, a whole new world had opened up. Rob had been introduced to a myriad of topics to learn and appreciate. He had been recruited because of his existing specialist skills, that had been made very clear at the outset, but immediately upon starting, he had been put through a vast array of specialist courses. Having been headhunted, Rob had gone in thinking his new job would be straightforward, almost easy in fact. He had been surprised though, very surprised. His first year had been difficult to say the least. Combative driving, mixed martial arts, close urban surveillance and the more hands-on programmes had been fine, fun even, but some parts had proven to be a real challenge. An IT basics had turned out to be anything but 'basic' and a series of case studies requiring an understanding of politics and geopolitics hadn't been a breeze either. Now though, after six years with MI6, Rob had found his feet, proving to be a real asset. He formed part of a specialist four-man unit. Jack Thomas, or JT to his mates, was the team leader, Dominic 'Nic' Smith was second in command and Mika Kimura was the newest member, having joined just a year ago.

Tonight's operation had taken weeks of planning. Jonno, their boss, had personally selected the entire team two years earlier, adding Meek a year later following a request for more field operatives from JT. It felt very good, special even, to be part of Jonno's 'team within a team'. Chris 'Jonno' Johnson was a bigwig within the UK's intelligence service. He attended JIC meetings on behalf of MI6, meaning he had sway with 'Five' (MI5), the Home Office, Foreign Office and the PM's personal adviser, which meant he had eyes and ears directly to the PM if and when required.

None of them were allowed to call him 'Jonno' though; there was a strict protocol in place. It was 'sir' to his face, but behind closed doors his special operations team referred to him by the shortened form.

"How's it looking, Meek?" came JT's voice on comms. All four of the team were hooked into the same open VHF frequency. The entire team could hear every conversation via a small, discreet earpiece.

"Just accessing the mainframe now," came her reply.

"How long?" he asked.

"I'm in, movement sensors to the southern perimeter disabled," came Meek again.

"First floor alarms too?"

"Roger that, switching to the drone's now," replied Meek instantly.

"Green light then, Meek, you're good to go." JT was always amazed at the speed with which Meek ghosted through highly secure firewalls.

"Roger that, drone up," came Meek's response.

Sitting in the rear of a chocolate brown VW Transporter just over 1 km from the chateau, Meek stared at her laptop screen. It displayed an aerial shot of the top of her van getting smaller and smaller as the drone ascended directly above her.

Using the attached joystick, Meek deftly navigated the drone towards the chateau.

Ten minutes later and the drone was hovering above the wooded grounds to the rear of the chateau. Meek could see the main buildings, front and rear driveway, trees and shrubbery and, most importantly, both Dobermanns.

One of the dogs was prowling around the front lawn close to the water's edge and the other was to the side of the property.

Meek positioned the drone directly above the first dog. Pressing a key on her laptop, the drone released a small projectile. It fell within two metres of the dog, a small thud, barely perceptible to a human, alerted the dog immediately. The drone hovered above, providing a perfect bird's-eye view. Meek kept watching as the

Dobermann wandered over, sniffed the item and then snaffled it up. Job done, the clock was now ticking.

The drone relocated to the second Dobermann and repeated the process. Now it was simply a matter of time – 10 minutes to be precise.

"Dogs should be clear in 10 minutes," instructed Meek, breaking the silence.

"Roger that," JT replied. "How're we looking, Rob?" he continued over the airwaves.

"Quiet, no movement. All clear at present," returned Rob.

JT and Nic looked at each other and nodded. Nothing was spoken, it wasn't needed. It was time to go. Both men zipped up their drysuits then checked each other. Slinging their rucksacks on, they completed the look with a black mask and snorkel.

The two men slipped quietly into Lac Léman's icy-cold waters. They only had a short distance to swim, a few hundred metres to round the wall jutting into the lake. That was the easy bit.

Slowly and quietly, JT and Nic glided through the darkened waters. Upon rounding the wall, they used it as a guide, like a handrail to the shore within the grounds. The two shadowy figures had so far gone unnoticed.

"All clear, JT," came the first of Rob's many sitreps. Rob currently had eyes on via his gloomy green world and continued to keep the team abreast of what he could see. Or rather, what he couldn't see.

Without responding, they crept slowly out of the waters, moving along the southern wall. To his right, JT spotted the shadowy form of a dog on the furthest edge of the lawn. The tranquilizers were clearly kicking in now. He could never understand the use of guard dogs in the modern world. Unless accompanied by their handler, dogs were never reliable. Sure, they worked well for common thieves, but for anything of a high value it was barking mad. He grinned to himself as he considered his 'barking mad' analogy.

As soon as they reached the first set of shrubs, they ducked behind and started to undress. Under their drysuits both men, all in black, were wearing a full body climbing harness. Nic put his rucksack back over his shoulders, whilst JT rummaged through his, pulling out a grappling hook gun. Resembling a crossbow, the device was constructed of lightweight aluminium and fired a barbed bolt with a trailing line.

JT looked to Nic and nodded, no words, just an 'O' made with finger and thumb to say OK. Nic mirrored the signal, silence was paramount. JT led, moving slowly to the southern wall of the building. The chateau was a classic Swiss alpine structure, meaning it had large overhanging eaves, great for giving shelter from the elements as its occupants walked around the perimeter and even better for what JT and Nic had in mind.

Taking aim, JT fired the bolt, aiming for the underside of the protruding supporting beam. The bolt buried itself into the thick wooden support leaving the cable trailing to the ground. It had made a dull thud upon striking the beam. Both men had been concerned about this part of the break-in during their numerous run-throughs in previous weeks.

"Any movement?" whispered JT through his mike. The question was for Meek back in the van rather than Rob. Meek was sat motionless watching the security team on their own closed-circuit feed. Having hacked into the chateau's mainframe, Meek had access to all but the 'safe' room within the site. Loic was sitting in his office watching TV, whilst his underling was leaning back in his chair reading a book. Every so often he would glance at the bank of monitors showing the various camera feeds throughout the house.

They didn't reveal anything though. Why would they? Meek had shut the feed to the southern perimeter wall, the jetty, the southern side of the chateau and the entire top floor, replacing it with a 30-second loop showing absolutely nothing.

But before Meek could speak, Rob managed to return the broken silence with an "all clear."

Meek reported in the instant Rob got off comms. "You're good, JT. Both are in the office."

JT pulled on the cable, testing the strength of the bolt. It stood up to his yank, but he repeated the action for good measure. Finally, he twisted the cable clockwise; it rotated no more than 90 degrees. This was the mechanism working within the head of the bolt. He was highly impressed with the boffins. Initially he had doubted the technology, but numerous drills had proven it a very simple and effective system. The bolt was hollow with an internal screw socket. The head of the cable screwed into this socket thus allowing the cable to be unscrewed after use and therefore leaving virtually no sign. The only thing showing would be a small, circular hole where the discarded bolt would remain within the beam – very clever.

He reloaded and discharged a second bolt and trailing cable, the same dull thud and the same outcome. They were now good to go.

Nic had already clipped himself to his cable via an ascender and lanyard to his harness, his right foot sat in a stirrup attached by a separate ascender also similarly attached. Known as 'single rope technique', Nic started to SRT up the cable. SRT-ing was a slow process involving a lot of grunt work. The ascender slides up the wire and small teeth then stop it from slipping back down. Nic moved his chest attachment up about 30 cm whilst his weight was on his right leg then, sitting in his harness, he transferred all his weight to his chest attachment, allowing him to slide his leg 30 cm up the wire. Nic then repeated the process – weight on his leg, he slid his chest attachment a further 30 cm up the wire, slowly inching his way to the window ledge on the first floor.

Nic made the ledge first, JT a minute behind. As JT finished his last shimmy up his cable, Nic was staring at the bolt entry into the beams.

"We may have a problem," he whispered. His whisper was for JT, but both Meek and Rob heard it too, over their comms.

"What's up?" came JT's reply.

With an upward nudge of his head and a flash of his eyes, Nic indicated the bolt entry to JT. Rather than the bolts being flush in the beam, or even better, slightly sunken, JT's bolt was proud of the beam by a centimetre. Would it be seen? The beam was 10 metres from the ground on the underside of dark eaves, but having said that, the chateau was immaculately maintained. Now wasn't the time though, it was out of their control. Training kicked in, control the controllable, so JT acknowledged it and cracked on.

Quietly and deftly, he retrieved a small power screwdriver from his rucksack and proceeded to unscrew the plate on the external side of the sash window, placing the contents carefully in a pouch, the plate and the screws. Revealing the window locking mechanism, JT changed the head of his driver and undid the internal screws. Once removed, he eased the internal barrel of the lock forwards, taking care to stop it from dropping into the bedroom.

JT gestured an OK with a nod of his head, giving Nic his approval to slide the sash window upwards. Slowly, silently, the window eased up a metre. Only the slightest of squeaks could be heard as wood sliding over wood allowed the window to open further.

Although sound had been minimal, this was without doubt the most dangerous point of the whole night.

Most people underappreciate the quality of their senses. Within the animal world examples, such as dogs and their amazing sense of smell and the ability of an eagle to see the smallest of rodents a mile away, are well documented, but humans are much more perceptive than they realize.

Opening a window causes a slight change in pressure, then there is a flow of cold air too and the addition of external noises, all tiny, but they can all add up and create 'a feeling' in someone of a change, a difference. The bedroom door was closed, though, and that helped immeasurably, helping to dampen down any changes that the inside of the chateau might be feeling.

JT and Nic climbed through and into the room, then left the window open. Swiftly, both men gathered up their lines, rapid hand over hand movements worked to pull the dangling ropes from the ground, setting them down neatly in the room.

With great stealth, they navigated out of the bedroom and down the long, broad corridor. The bedroom was carpeted, allowing for super sound dampening, but the upstairs hallway was tiled. *Better than floorboards*, thought JT as he crept timidly down. At the third door to their left, they both stopped, looked around to check and double-check. They knew it was the correct room, but the training was kicking in again – be sure, be very sure.

JT eased the door open, entering the room, Nic filed past him and JT closed the door behind them both; training again. Opening a door gives the person a feel for it, for how it swings, how the handle and catch behave, all tiny details helping the entrant to close it carefully too. On exiting the building, it would be JT that opened and closed this door too; training.

The room was dimly lit, its only lighting coming from a single lamp sitting on a large mahogany desk in the far right-hand corner. A leather-clad, captain's-style chair was tucked in place at the desk. A much smaller and neater single seat was placed on the opposing side, presumably for guests.

To the left, a comfortable-looking, brown, three-seater settee was located opposite two matching chairs. A low coffee table sandwiched between them completed the picture, very much in the style of a chic city coffee shop. Halfway along the right-hand wall was a door – a very solid-looking door. Solid was an understatement, this was the door they were here for and it was no ordinary door.

Weighing 250 kg, the door in question was special. With an 18 mm steel structure, and a 10 mm solid steel welded plate protecting the door leaf skin, the external oak cladding was solely for aesthetics. The door set was designed to deter the most determined of 'professional criminals', but JT and Nic wouldn't be using the battering ram method, their entry was to be a strictly covert and unseen visit to Chateau Forestier's inner sanctum.

The door came with a state-of-the-art electronic key code entry, supplied by a very low-profile German 'panic room' company. Munich-based Stockinger was a market-leading company in the world of safety and security. Meek had been surprised at how difficult it had turned out to hack into their internal IT system. In her first year working for Jonno, Meek had been put to work on several very high-profile systems. It had only taken Meek a day to get past the FBI's firewall and two days to break the primary and secondary firewalls of Interpol's internal mainframe. Other notable success included several leading banks, the London Met and British Petroleum, all had taken no more than a couple of days, whereas Stockinger had taken almost two weeks. They really did take security seriously.

Once in though, Meek had identified the exact locking mechanism and its functionality. She didn't have the code, only the end user would have this, but knowing which system had been used meant that she could pre-programme a 'cheat' onto a handheld tablet that, once linked to the control pad, would allow her programme to enter via a back door. All systems had such options, they had to, otherwise the chance of the client getting trapped in their own panic room was a very real possibility. All JT and Nic needed was access to the front panel and a little time.

Nic arrived at the door first. Unshouldering his rucksack, he took little time to access its contents. Laying out a set of slender driver bits, two electric drivers and a small amp / volt reader with crocodile clips, he proceeded to investigate the stainless steel surround housing the keypad. JT had donned a head torch and strained his eyes to see the screw head types before selecting the correct bit for his driver. The pair were well rehearsed, as JT started to carefully remove the front housing, Nic had fired up a small handheld tablet.

With the screws removed, JT very carefully eased the face off the keypad. The neon lights, initially discreet with the fascia in place, became brighter as he allowed the fascia to hang about 5 cm down the front of the door. It was connected by two small blue wires which served to prevent an intruder from simply smashing the front fascia off. Breaking the circuit would trigger the alarm – not an option.

The guts of the electronic mechanism were now exposed, a spaghetti junction of wires surrounded a circuit board and the window display which was able to be seen when the fascia was in place. A micro USB port was subtly located upper left of the circuit board, almost hidden in fact, but this was why Meek had spent the time and effort hacking into Stockinger. This port served two purposes – firstly, it didn't access the mini mainframe housed within the locking system, it was there as a decoy, and secondly, any attempt to run a current through it would trigger a silent alarm; simple but clever.

Underneath the circuit board a small diode protruded. Nic clasped his thumb and forefinger on to the end and pulled on it. It came out making a tiny popping sound as it did, caused by breaking the suction. Removing the fake diode revealed another micro USB port and access to the keypad's hard drive. Nic inserted the cable from his tablet to the port and fired up the application Meek had installed on his device.

The tablet's screen immediately changed from its bland grey background to a kaleidoscope of activity. Numbers raced across the screen, initially almost too quick to read. They started to slow a little before pausing. A box popped up prompting an action. Nic tapped the button, the box vanished and the numbers proceeded to scurry from left to right.

Meanwhile, JT had moved to the door to check for signs of movement, knowing Nic would be a few minutes. Rehearsals back in London had taken between four and six minutes. They had run Meek's 'cheat' on four different Stockinger doors; practice made perfect.

A few minutes later and Nic was done. The tablet was proudly displaying an eight-digit number: 8 0 3 3 2 1 9 5. He tapped the number into the pad, an asterisk concealing each entered digit. There was no 'validate' button, once eight digits had been entered the asterisks vanished, replaced with the word 'öffnen'. A faint mechanical click could be heard as the pins within the door frame slid open. The door had twelve pins in total, four along each side and two on the top and bottom. Each pin welded to the steel door, 50 mm in diameter and 100 mm in length, penetrated a steel housing running the entire perimeter of the door.

Nic turned to JT, nothing was said he just made the 'O' for OK sign. JT opened the door and entered the room with Nic following close behind. The room was large and windowless and matched the luxury of the larger outer office. A single expensive-looking teak desk was framed by two paintings, one of the Matterhorn and the other of the Eiger. Someone clearly liked mountain vistas thought JT.

A desktop PC sat on the desk along with a lamp and a few items of stationery. Behind the desk was a single high-backed, brown leather office chair, with a matching one in black resting on the right-hand wall. His and hers?

To the left of the desk stood a tall, dark cabinet, possibly teak, with a pair of identical lamp tables standing sentry to either side, although neither had a lamp sitting on them. The left-hand table had an expensive-looking tribal mask mounted on a stand. On the right-hand one sat a stone sculpture, it very much looked like a Rodin, JT was no expert though. He had attended a course a few years ago aimed at giving him an overview of art. The three days had been more like a crash course in bullshitting; he had needed it for an undercover operation in which he was required to befriend an art gallery owner. The boss had sent a couple of JT's team on the course. They had rocked up and expected to hate every minute of the course, but JT surprised himself, he had thoroughly enjoyed his time in bullshit-land and learnt quite a lot in the process.

Whilst JT weighed up the other parts to the room, Nic retrieved a camera from his rucksack and took photos of each aspect. The digital display presented each captured photo, a bright flash emitted after each shot of the room was taken.

"Good to go," whispered Nic as soon as the final photo was taken.

Each man proceeded to open and close each drawer and cupboard. They both started shoulder to shoulder and worked concentrically, moving away from each other around the side of the room. Only once they had completed their lap would they have covered the entire room. They left everything as they found it, the photos were just to double-check at the end – leave no trace.

JT reached a large sideboard, finished in a dark polished wood; it looked like something designed to house crockery and other such household items. Opening the large double doors revealed a smartly presented sliding filing system. He couldn't help but admire the mechanics of the system itself. It must have been expensive, but in his opinion it had been money well spent. The slides were smooth and strong, as he slid the extending arms outwards there was no lateral rocking at all. A very fine construction considered JT and he was no stranger to the world of filing cabinets. He allowed himself a slight smirk as he considered his expertise and appreciation of 'all things filing cabinet'. He and Nic had a standing joke that they should go into filing cabinet design after they left the service. In their line of work, they had both built up a healthy level of appreciation and understanding of what made a good and a poor filing cabinet.

JT started leafing through the files, each hung like a bat suspended in air, hanging on the two side rails. The files were conveniently labelled, although most of the labels didn't mean a great deal to him.

As JT continued his probing, Nic had located a hard drive in the right-hand drawer of the desk. It was a large box and had a second drive connected to it. Presumably a backup storage drive or maybe Louise needed more storage than a single drive could contain. The hard drive system was contained neatly within the desk; the desk had a discreet USB socket flush with the side wall. Internally the hard drives were connected in series into the internal side wall of the desk. She obviously sat a laptop on the desk and then connected to the drives – a neat system, very neat.

Nic connected his tablet to the USB port and immediately started interrogating the drive. His tablet showed two drives within the system, Q drive and S drive, the S drive was a mirror of Q; Nic assumed S was for 'shadow'. Nic drilled down into the Q drive, a myriad of files sat alphabetically, one on top of another on the left-hand edge of his screen. He scrolled down the list searching for references to BioDS, none were apparent, but then why would there be a reference? He was moving within the CEO of BioDS's personal hard drive, everything was probably BioDS-related. The Q drive must contain some highly sensitive information; why else would a hard drive be located in a secure, vaulted room and unconnected to the net? Firewalls weren't foolproof, Jonno had Meek on their team for that very reason, and Meek often told Nic and JT stories about hackers better than her.

Louise was a prudent person, very prudent, but her cautious actions hadn't taken MI6 into account. The very best that MI6 had to offer, hence the fact that he and JT were currently rummaging through the inner sanctum of Chateau Forestier. Nic continued scouring through the folders, drilling down methodically, folder after folder.

JT was applying a similar method to the hard copy folders within the cabinet. Labelled '1st Gen', he started leafing through the papers contained within it.

The second page instantly attracted his attention, headed '*CIA Select Gen*'. As he scanned the page facts jumped out at him, alarming facts.

Paragraph two started with a summary of a selection process: '*...parents **must** be serving members of the security service... this can include NSA, FBI and other security agencies in addition to CIA*', on the fifth paragraph it mentioned a vetting process within the agency: '*Martin Pawlowski, Assistant Director approves Steelhorse...*'

Flicking over the page, a list of names, dates of birth, hospitals, home addresses and parents were listed.

Connor L Evans, DOB 02.24.1997, Howard University Hospital, Washington
Address: 1501 Valley PL SE, Washington 20020-5715
Father Henry J Evans / Mother Susan D Evans

Sarah E Woods, DOB 03.11.1997, George Washington University Hospital, Washington
Address: 8190 Randoph Street NW, Washington 20020-5896
Father Robert K Woods / Mother Martha P Woods

Rebecca L Schmidt, DOB 03.17.1997, Providence Hospital, Washington
Address: 2510 Hartford Street Washington, 20020-7970
Father Carl H Schmidt / Mother Paula J Schmidt

Joseph M Werner, DOB 04.21.1997, George Washington University Hospital, Washington
Address: 1842 Anacostia Rd, Washington, 20020-2123
Father Rudi B Werner / Mother Heidi Werner

Henri M Wagner, DOB 06.18.1997, Providence Hospital, Washington
Address: 1583 Rhode Island Avenue, Washington, 20020-3025
Father Dieter K Wagner / Mother Sandrine A Wagner

Alan T Schwinn, DOB 02.22.1997, Gracie Square Hospital, New York
Address: 21 Belmont Place, Amsterdam NY, 12010-3707
Father Thomas H Schwinn / Mother Annette R Schwinn

Sascha B Pavel, DOB 05.10.1997, St Mary's Children's Hospital, New York
Address: 1834 New Utrecht Avenue, Brooklyn NY, 11219-4154
Father Jurgen S Pavel / Mother Elaine S Pavel

Zia L Patel, DOB 04.04.1997, Staten Island University Hospital, New York
Address: 1264 Cordell Road, Schenectady NY, 12303-2702
Father Arjun T Patel / Mother Saanvi K Patel

Anastasia J Sokolov, DOB 07.18.1997, Bellevue Centre Hospital, New York
Address: 2310 Stonebrook NY, 11794-1604
Father Dima V Sokolov / Mother Maria S Sokolov

Jay B McMath, DOB 08.14.1997, George Washington University Hospital
Address: 102 Nortonia Road, Fort Valley VA, 22652-3054
Father Simon C McMath / Mother Helena T McMath

Charlie G Donaldson, DOB 05.17.1997, Buchanan General Hospital, Virginia
Address: 822 Three Chopt Road, Henrico VA, 23229-5935
Father Richard R Donaldson / Mother Margaret Donaldson

Catherine L Blake, DOB 03.28.1997, Gracie Square Hospital, New York
Address: 1442 Delaware Avenue, Commack NY, 11725-5017
Father Gregory N Blake / Mother Alice S Blake

Wasim D Khan, DOB 06.25.1997, Children's Hospital of Richmond at VCU, Virginia
Address: 908 Liberia Avenue, Manassas VA, 20110-1742
Father Adi M Khan / Mother Sri L Khan

Alfredo M Sainz, DOB 01.14.1997, Inova Fairfax Hospital, Virginia
Address: 1034 Jeffers Avenue, Portsmouth, 23702-2430
Father Alberto J Sainz / Mother Marissa O Sainz

JT was gripped; the file had his undivided attention. Further down the same page, the document referenced '*Steelhorse*' again and '*Brian O'Connor, CIA Director sanctions the programme for fourteen 1st-generation Morphs… non-disclosure to the parents*'. *Could this be true?* thought JT. Fourteen first-generation Morphs created without their parents' knowledge. Reading further confirmed it; Louise had been paid by the CIA to create fourteen Morphs unbeknown to their parents. Incredible. Jonno was going to be speechless.

JT started to copy the document, his camera flashing vividly within the vault, page after page copied. Once finished, he continued moving through the folders, one marked 'prototype' stood out. Pulling out its innards, the very first page caused his jaw to drop. It wasn't so much a document as a personnel dossier, similar to what a HR department might have within a large company. The dossier was titled '*Daniel Fletcher, DOB 09.12.1985, Leeds LGI, England*' containing a few photos of a young Daniel Fletcher with a clear timeline leading to present day. The dossier was a little eerie as a great deal of what it contained had been collected covertly.

Similar dossiers sat behind Daniel's, containing complete profiles of his siblings. Benjamin, Rachel and Samuel Fletcher stared back at him. JT started copying their files too, his flash kicking back into life.

Nic looked over. "You got anything?" he whispered.

"More than you can imagine… How long will you be?" JT replied.

"Five minutes," he responded.

JT carried on, five minutes wasn't long, which meant he was going to be the slowest link. He still had about eight folders to trawl through, time was pressing.

Nic reverted to his tablet screen, he was copying dozens of files while an egg timer depicted how long was left to complete the action. Meanwhile, he was poring over an open folder headed '*2nd Generation*', a complex introduction explained the importance of the change in coding '…*2nd-generation coding essential for the long-term future of BioDS…*' making references to Knacc, Omsk '…*successful trials at Knacc, Omsk on 200 (TWO HUNDRED) volunteers…*'. Nic took a double take at this last line. Did it say 200 hundred volunteers? He glanced across at the egg timer, a minute more maybe two maximum he thought. He carried on reading. Knacc appeared to be some sort of Russian agency-cum-school with what appeared to be made up of 200 hundred second-generation MorphEns.

He wasn't sure what the difference between first and second generation was, but that could be looked at in detail once back in London. The priority for now was to covertly extricate themselves from the vault with the information intact. Leave no trace.

The timer emptied itself then disappeared. Nic checked the drive on his tablet. It showed the folders he'd copied. Check and double-check. Happy with his work, Nic prepared to leave. Securing his tablet in his rucksack, he closed the desk drawer, referring to his photos to ensure everything was as he had found it.

"Done," came his one-word report to his team leader.

"One minute, get on comms with Meek," instructed JT, with just two files left to check and copy.

"Status Meek? We're about to exfil," Nic responded.

Meek broke her silence and proceeded to give the two men an update on movement downstairs. Once updated, Rob reported in too, all was clear outside and the security team hadn't moved a muscle in over 40 minutes. Things were going to plan.

JT finished up and started the careful process of vacating the room; leave no trace. The two men retraced their steps, exited the vaulted room and started to replace the fascia to the door. They made their way stealthily to the bedroom, nothing said between the men, hand signals and eye contact was all that was needed. Once at the window, the last bit of their extraction was the part JT had had concerns about. Descending the cables was easy; removing them from their sockets was what worried him. In training, they had encountered a lot of difficulties and on several occasions they'd been forced to reascend their lines and loosen the cables a little prior to returning to the ground.

Nic was first to the floor, freeing himself from his line he started to twist the cable anticlockwise. At first the cable twisted along its length without movement within the socket itself, JT had now started attending to his own cable. Suddenly though, Nic felt the screw tip free itself from its socket housing and start to undo. JT was now slightly ahead of him, having encountered no problems with his line. Now almost synchronized, the lines came free of their sockets and dropped to the floor, making only the slightest of sounds. Quietly coiling up the cables, JT took a moment to inspect the eaves, this was the first time he'd seen them with just the bolt and no trailing line. Satisfied with the result, he turned to Nic and motioned with his head to move. Things were going to plan.

At the water's edge and back in their drysuits, they melted into the inky black Lac Léman, leaving no trace. All the while, Rob maintained his vigil, switching between the front of the chateau and the last visible signs of JT and Nic entering the lake.

"OK, Meek, they're out, get the drone up," came Rob's instruction.

Meek responded before getting the drone back in the sky. The final part of the operation was possibly the smartest. The boffins had spent hours discussing how long the Dobermanns would be 'out' for and, with no absolute answer forthcoming, another solution had been required. Smelling salts were the simplest of solutions. So simple, in fact, that at first it had been rejected, only to be revisited after another heated discussion. The problem being that they couldn't risk the dogs not coming round prior to one of Loic's team doing a grounds sweep.

Meek now positioned the drone over the first of the dogs and released a small squirt of gas; the dog jerked its head up immediately. Salts arouse consciousness by irritating the membranes of the nose and lungs. This in turn causes an inhalation reflex, a vigorous one that is often likened to being punched by Mike Tyson – very effective. The drone moved to the second dog and repeated the process – leave no trace.

"Mission complete," came an almost jubilant Meek over comms. JT and Nic were currently making their way back to the van and Rob had started his journey over the water back to Geneva.

Twenty minutes later and three of the team were reunited back in the van; no trace left bar for a couple of semi-groggy Dobermanns and a slightly protruding bolt head. Jonno would be pleased.

"Good job team," came JT's open response, as much for Rob as the other two within the van.

"Roger that," Rob responded from his RIB as he sped across the calm waters of Lac Léman. "I'll see you in an hour," as he signed off.

In the back of the van, "What've we got?" quizzed Meek.

"I think we're going to BioDS," JT replied. "London first, though, the boffins need to look at what Nic's got," he concluded.

CHAPTER 5
THE APFEL PART 2

Yale University, New Haven, Connecticut

It was deep into 'fall' as the Yanks liked to call it. Harry and Bush were for once in complete agreement, the Yanks were dumb shits! Dumb because they'd felt the need to change autumn for an elementary school 'describing word' – WTF!

It was beautiful though, no arguments on that score. Red, gold and yellow foliage all added to the charm of New Haven, home to Yale University. Taking in the sights though wasn't on the agenda.

Harry and Bush had a schedule, none of which allowed time for sightseeing. Alongside two other kill teams, they had delivered a trio of highly clinical, extremely professional contract killings at MIT, Boston. That was 11 days ago. Today, though, was going to be difficult. On the last job the 'marks' had had a single, covert angel watching over them. Their angels weren't even 'round the clock'.

Today things were different. Anastasia Sokolov sauntered gracefully along the block-paved road that bisected the campus buildings. Hand in hand with her boyfriend, she seemed oblivious to the 'minder' casually walking 20 metres back. A second minder had disappeared, skulking in the almost leafless trees that adorned both sides of the road. It was a crisp, clear Connecticut day; blue skies, practically sub-zero with a touch of wind. Although almost unseen, leaning against a tree, minder two's every breath was visible in the biting temperature.

Watching the watchers had become Harry and Bush's new game. Three miles away, Henkl and Zebra were playing a similar game, as were Gruppe Drei. Harry and Bush were Gruppe Zwei, the German for Group 2 and, of course, Henkl and Zebra were Gruppe Eins. Today, though, required all three kill teams to act against Henkl's strict protocol. Co-ordinated assassinations required an element of risk and a large degree of 'ad lib'.

Success today, or rather tonight, required precise timing and the probability of some collateral damage – collateral meaning innocent casualties. The fact his 'mark' was a 19-year-old, innocent young lady wasn't lost on Harry. Anastasia was the very definition of innocent. Bush, on the other hand, had smirked as Henkl had covered the rules of engagement for today's mission. Bush was a cunt. Harry fucking hated Bush.

The time was 4 p.m. Harry dutifully reported in, hitting the green call button on his mobile.

Just a single ringtone before Henkl picked up.

"Harry," in a clipped Germanic tone came his one-word greeting; German efficiency at its very best.

"We have eyes on, Boss…" from a hushed Harry. "…As far as we can tell she has two minders," he continued.

Bush stood silently by Harry's side; he could just about hear Henkl's tinny voice.

"Stick to the timings, Harry. Report back in at 7," instructed the German.

"Yes, Boss," he replied, hitting the call end button in quick time.

"Fucking 'YES BOSS'," muttered Bush sarcastically. "You're such a fucking suck-up," he carried on as he grinned at Harry.

Harry glanced towards his companion, instantly chastising himself for showing a reaction. *What a cunt*, he thought for the second time in less than 10 minutes. *Wanker.*

"Fuck off, Fish," the words spilt uncontrollably from Harry's mouth. A great response, nonetheless; sharp, acerbic and guaranteed to hit Bush right where it'd hurt him the most, his very brittle psyche.

Bush seethed. One of these days he'd just slot Harry. He had rehearsed it in his mind's eye many times. A quiet, secluded location, the two of them would be just wandering alone. He would slow up a little whilst quietly and carefully retrieving his Glock. Then, no hesitation, just a simple double tap to the back of Harry's head – simple. For once, though, he managed to suck it up. His eyes raged, but he stifled any utterance in return.

Anastasia, with boyfriend in tow, and her CIA shadows, made slow but steady progress north through the campus grounds. Harry and Bush curtailed their personal hostilities and slowly headed in the same direction – carefully though; very, very carefully. The stakes were high today. The slightest cock-up and it wouldn't just cost their hit; all three hits were on the line.

Having ended the call with Harry, Henkl turned to update Zebra.

"It's the same for Harry, the girl has two on her," he explained. The CIA had clearly doubled their efforts. It had been relatively easy in Boston. A simple distraction had bought just enough seconds to carry out the job. A true pro only needed a few seconds. Two agents though were an entirely different kettle of fish mused Henkl. He grinned to himself as he recalled the moment he had learnt this quaint English metaphor. He loved metaphors, for Henkl learning English, a language rich in strange, quirky metaphors, had been so rewarding.

Zebra was sitting in their nondescript black hatchback sporting a Yale University baseball cap and slate grey hoodie. In the near distance, he had a great line of sight on Alfredo Sainz. Called Freddy by his mates, Sainz was chucking an American football to a couple of friends. Goofing around in the park, the three lads were utterly oblivious. Why wouldn't they be?

Sat just 50 m across from Freddy, on a conveniently located park bench, was a couple. They could have been any couple. Zebra guessed late twenties or early thirties and reasonably well matched. The male CIA agent wore a scruffy stubble that partially hid a strong, square jawline and had alert blue eyes and a healthy shock of brown hair up top with a sporty, muscular physique to match. The female agent was easy on the eye too. A slim, lithe-looking physique indicated she was a frequent gymgoer. Long blond hair and a near perfect complexion belied her probable age.

Sitting arm in arm, the female agent was lolling her head on her partner's shoulder. Going for the romantic couple look was working. They were good too, very thorough. Now clad in a red jacket and scarf, the female agent was noticeably different to earlier in the day. In the morning, she had been sporting a white beanie, matching scarf and a grey dress coat, whilst the male agent had also switched his brown leather bomber for a distinctive red with white-sleeved baseball jacket.

The male agent hadn't been able to hide his very distinctive gait though. Henkl would zone in on that immediately if he were to be recruited to the Apfel. At a distance, clothes became indistinct but gait didn't. Once recruited to the Apfel, the first thing Henkl had taught Zebra was two very different styles of walking. Who'd have thought? He hadn't.

Walking is a fundamental human activity, most people take it for granted, but walking is an intricate biomechanical process that involves the co-ordination of various body parts. Whilst everyone walks, not all walks are the same and many of us have a clear and distinct style. In the murky world the Apfel moved in, being 'distinct' was a bad thing.

Zebra's natural style was to strike heel first and toe second, a quite heavy and distinctive contact with the ground with every step. He had adopted two methods to dramatically alter his human gait. The first was simply walking with a deliberately longer stride length. This visibly slowed his step pattern and made him strike the ground flat-footed. Zebra's third gait was to 'bounce' on his toes. With every step in his 'bounce gait', his hips, and consequently his centre of gravity, would rise and fall.

The male CIA agent had a toe-heel strike with a pronated action. In layman's terms, every time the agent's foot landed, he was turning his ankle inwards. The agent almost floated, his walking looked effortless yet energetic. Zebra figured he would be a good runner.

As he mulled over the finer points of human gait, his attention was dragged back into the here and now. Freddy's mate had misthrown the ball, sailing comfortably over Freddy's head. Pitching 10 metres beyond Freddy, it continued to bounce along before coming to rest just a few metres short of the seated agents. Zebra watched with interest, Henkl too.

Freddy dashed over, single-handedly scooping the ball up with a great deal of panache, turning to his mates but not before catching a glimpse of the female agent. Zebra grinned. A great-looking girl will always catch a man's eye, regardless of the fact she's sat with her guy. The agents were thorough professionals though. Not a flinch, they just sat calmly maintaining their cover.

The low winter sun had started to disappear below the horizon. Pale blue sky quickly turned to a gentle darkness. Campus street lights twinkled; students walked with a more obvious hustle than earlier in the day. Perhaps it was the cold. Freddy had walked a mile off campus and entered a local bistro with his mates. The two agents had split now, one on foot and the other in a car. At a distance Henkl and Zebra had followed suit.

Meanwhile, Anastasia was holed up in her boyfriend's campus room. Harry was sitting in the car, whilst Bush had gone for a walk-by. It was 8 p.m. now, still three hours till they were to make the hit. Gruppe Drei had the easiest hit. Catherine Blake was at a music festival; a nightmare scenario for the agents watching her and a dream for Apfel's third kill team.

Henkl and Zebra weren't complaining either. Freddy Sainz, having started the night in a local bistro, had now moved on to a lively New Haven bar full of twenty-somethings determined to have a loud night out. Harry and Bush, though, had big problems. Anastasia appeared to be holed up for a cosy night in. To make matters worse, outside offered no cover within 100 m of the residents building. Only the fact the two agents periodically sat in the car together offered a slight positive to the job in hand. It was a cold night. Probably the reason the agents had opted for their current MO. Frost was forming. Underfoot the ground crunched tellingly.

The residents building had a rear entrance, but this was a fire escape. Bush had skirted the building an hour ago. Having located the door, he'd failed to make it budge. It was well made, secure and designed to only allow egress not ingress. He hadn't come up with an alternative. Harry had, though it wasn't ideal – far from it in fact. But as Harry had outlined, 'needs must'. Bush begrudgingly agreed.

The left side of the residence had a couple of ground-floor apartments, both of which appeared to have inhabitants preparing to go out for the night. Breaching the first one to become vacant was the plan, via the window. Walk out of the apartment to the first floor and hit the boyfriend's room. The slicker part of the plan was buying the pizza. Harry figured a pizza delivery guy would be less obtrusive once within the residence corridors. It would ultimately result in two deaths, but he couldn't see any other way. Bush though – the twat! – didn't give a shit. Killing the boyfriend had seemed like a bonus rather than an inconvenience. What a cunt he was, Harry had surmised, but then, what was new.

With the plan agreed, Harry nipped out for pizza, leaving Bush with eyes on. Now all they had to do was wait. Waiting was what they were great at.

As the evening ticked by, things had started to look promising for Harry and Bush. At 9:30 p.m. the furthest apartment had become vacant, confirmed when the two guys seen clowning around in the bedroom window exited the residence block. Clown one, sporting a very distinctive red and blue New York Rangers jacket, with his clown for a buddy, sporting a distinctive red ski jacket and matching red and white beanie, were hard to miss. They had exited the residence block within 90 seconds of the lights going off in their apartment. Game on thought Harry.

There was still 90 minutes till 'the time'. Harry and Bush had wrestled with the thorny issue concerning a precise execution. Carrying out their job earlier than planned could risk alerting the other 'protection teams', but right now felt 'right'. Theirs was clearly the tougher assignment and, as such, Harry had made the executive decision to 'action it'.

Unusually, Bush had agreed with him. Unusual because even when Bush agreed, he'd usually revert to type and argue, but tonight, Bush had listened and got right behind Harry's plan. Bush the twat thought Harry. He'd still be a twat if he agreed with Harry for the rest of his miserable existence.

"Right, let's go," came Harry's low tones as he looked across to Bush. There was no one remotely within earshot, but start as you mean to go on was Henkl's mantra. Years of working with Henkl had instilled great instinct and even better habits.

"Roger that," Bush shot back as the Apfel duo quietly exited the black Chevrolet, a super car, as common as they came in the most popular colour.

Both killers looked like they'd shopped together; Harry in black cargo pants and a dark grey jacket, whilst Bush in black jeans and grey sports jacket, matching black rucksacks and black leather gloves completing the ensemble.

The two agents still had eyes on the residence, presumably feeling happy with the single entrance to the accommodation block. Harry wondered what kind of a bollocking they'd get after this was over. Knowing Henkl, it'd be one hell of a fiery debrief.

Approaching the left side of the building, all was eerily quiet. The pair crept along the wall, ducking down as they went past the only lit window. The alternate apartment appeared to be empty, but with lights left on. A further 10 metres and Harry was stood to the left of the window frame, Bush to its right.

Care was taken to check and double-check. The apartment was empty. Harry stood sentry, looking beyond Bush to the main thoroughfare. This was potentially the riskiest part of their evening's work, time was critical. The duo, although in a darkened ginnel between two buildings, were utterly exposed should a passer-by walk down the street, not to mention a walk-by from one of the two agents.

Bush unshouldered his rucksack with a carefully practised efficiency. Just as quickly, he was wielding a solid-looking flat pry bar, like a crowbar, but with a pair of flat teeth at the business end of the tool. His method of entry was a little crude, opting for speed over subtlety. He eased the pry between the frame and the housing, the plastic composite frame yielding to the force he exerted. The almost inaudible noise, as the frame gave way, felt much louder to Bush and Harry.

Just 30 seconds and, with the window agape, the two killers swiftly clambered inside. Harry gave the room a once-over whilst Bush pulled the window shut, the forced entry compromising its seal, but it wasn't something either killer had concerns over.

Harry retrieved the empty pizza box from his rucksack whilst mentally rehearsing the route from their apartment door to Anastasia's boyfriend's. He'd figured it was the second to the right at the top of the first flight of stairs. Get the wrong apartment and a shitshow would commence.

"Are you good?" whispered Harry as he looked searchingly into Bush's eyes. He knew the response he'd get, but protocol was protocol.

No words in response, just the international symbol for OK; silence was a virtue tonight.

More habit than necessity, Harry tweaked the peak of his baseball cap down a touch. Bush followed suit adjusting his cap too. Discussions earlier had resulted in the decision to wear caps within the residence. Neither had been able to see an internal hall camera on their earlier walk-bys, but why chance it. Would a pizza delivery dude have looked odd in a cap?

With Glocks to hand, concealed in their jacket pockets, Harry, with Bush in tow, exited the ground-floor apartment. To their left, the corridor led to a single door, it had all the hallmarks of a caretaker's cupboard. To the right, the corridor led directly to the main entrance doors with two apartment doors to the right-hand wall and a single apartment door to the left. Five metres shy of the left-hand apartment door stood a broad set of stairs. Not slow, not fast, the duo headed directly to the stairwell, Harry taking the lead, pizza box outstretched.

The stairwell was well lit and featureless. Eight steps led up before it turned 180 degrees via a broad, flat platform before presenting a further eight steps. As the duo reached the final step, a couple of girls exited the first apartment door, brushing past Harry in a flash. Giggling as they went, he instinctively dipped his head a touch to avoid eye contact. Bush played it well too and closed the gap to Harry, concealing his face as best he could.

The sound of the girls exiting the stairwell dissipated, leaving the first-floor corridor in total silence bar the dim hum from an overexuberant extraction fan overhead. Approaching the door, Harry stood left and centre of the spyhole. Bush hugged the wall, firmly out of sight.

A quick look to Bush, followed by a nod of the head; no words were necessary, they both knew the plan. Harry knocked on the door, trying to make his knock sound bored and unenthusiastic. Then he waited. He just stood there, staring at the spyhole with the best bored face he could muster.

Steps could be heard as someone approached from inside the apartment. Harry stood still, pizza box visible. The inhabitant responding was the boyfriend. Instinctively peering through the spyhole, Anastasia's boyfriend just opened the door.

"Pizza," blurted Harry in his best attempt at an American accent.

"Wrong room buddy, try…" came the response from Anastasia's boyfriend. Mid sentence, he was interrupted by two 19 mm suppressed rounds from Bush's Glock; two rounds delivered with deadly accuracy from less than one metre.

Blood splattered the wall to the left of Anastasia's boyfriend as he crumpled left and backwards. Bouncing off the left-hand wall, he slumped to the floor with an audible thud.

"What is it?" a female voice called out from the living room. The killers had 'lucked in', a double '*psst*' of a suppressed Glock and a crumpled dead body thudding to the floor had been masked by the TV.

Harry took to the living room as Bush secured the apartment door. Anastasia, in even measures of astonishment and fear, froze in her seat as Harry advanced into the room. Without hesitation, he raised and shot Anastasia in one economical movement right between the eyes, death almost instantaneous, the second shot a mere centimetre from the first. Anastasia hadn't managed to utter a single syllable.

She sank into the sofa. Her head lolled back and sideways as blood trickled down her face in two neat lines, splattered blood and brain matter visible on the sofa behind her head. It was 9:50 p.m., well ahead of the agreed schedule but the job was done. A clean exit was needed, but the risky bit was over.

A couple of miles away, Henkl was sat nursing a beer. The Gryphon was pumping. Exuberant young Yalies were in full party mode. The jukebox bellowed out the latest tune, largely irrelevant such was the chitter-chatter from the clientele.

Zebra was sat at the bar, periodically nudged by customers squeezing to the counter to place their orders. Freddy, a mere 10 metres away, sat at a table with a large group of mates. Drinks were in full flow, the entire table swamped with a mixture of half-empty glasses.

Freddy though, oblivious to the impending peril he faced, wasn't the issue. One of Freddy's shadows had been able to locate themselves within five metres of Freddy for the entire evening. Such was Freddy's level of merriment, it had been easy for the CIA agent to park himself unnoticed in the busy bar. With the other agent sat in their car street side, what initially looked an easy assignment had become increasingly more awkward.

Henkl and Zebra had come off comms prior to entering the Gryphon. As subtle as their throat mikes and earpieces where, in a bustling bar they hadn't wanted to risk it. Not that it would have mattered, such was the volume inside. Texts via their burner phones would have to make do.

Zebra had scoped out the rear of the bar, the toilets and the back room of the Gryphon. Nothing had screamed out. The bar was heaving; an open kill simply wasn't an option. The toilets offered a possibility, but on the two occasions Henkl had visited them they had been busy. Zebra's trip had been no different. Henkl was running out of options and, critically, time. It was 10:30 p.m., Gruppe Drei was almost good to go and he had received an alarming but understandable two-word text from Harry.

Txt: "*Boxed off*" 30 minutes ago was as much a warning as it was a report, immediately followed by "*Sorry Boss*". Henkl understood. He knew there would have been a very good reason for Harry to have actioned his assignment an hour early. Still, it didn't help matters for him and Zebra. A covert and well-timed op was critical.

Henkl had decided. Their job was going to go loud. As soon as Freddy took to the toilets, it would be his last trip. If it went well, he figured they'd have five to 10 minutes to exfil. If it went bad, then maybe a minute.

Texting Zebra, Henkl explained. "*Strike in the toilets, you're on the door, I am on point.*"

"*Roger that,*" Zebra responded. Now they would just wait. It shouldn't be too long. Freddy was six rounds of drinks down and his seventh beer was sitting almost three quarters drunk. Two toilet breaks already; his entire table had been making regular trips for the last hour.

As the killers patiently bided their time, the agent watching over Freddy made a move. Henkl's pulse elevated, his skin prickled slightly, externally though, nothing changed. An ice-calm persona from years of training kicked in. No panic, no reaction, as agent 'brown hair' walked in his direction. As the agent squeezed through the melee, agent 'blond hair' appeared in the bar, the agent passing without a hint of recognition. Sharing the warmth, Henkl figured. Or simply protocol. Who knew? Freddy certainly didn't.

Zebra texted, "*Swapping out, chief?*"

"*Ja, think so,*" Henkl texted back.

Suddenly the killers had movement. Freddy, with a mate in tow, had both clumsily taken to their feet – not incapable but clearly not sober – heading towards the bar; drinks maybe? No. Freddy and blue hoodie bypassing the bar meant one thing only.

No texts, no gazing around the bar. Henkl, with just the subtlest of glances, checked the agent out – still seated – the game was on. Except this was no game. Zebra had done similarly. Squeezing slowly but surely through the party-going clientele, the two assassins made their way through the crowd.

Zebra loitered outside as Henkl entered the restroom. To the left of the door, three quite ornate, white ceramic urinals hung from the wall. Ample space behind allowed for plenty of standing room. To the right, a corridor led to two toilet cubicles on the left with two countersunk sinks in front of a large gilt-framed mirror.

Freddy was stood in the middle of three urinals, blue hoodie to his left. A third guy was stood mid piss. Henkl instinctively moved to the two sinks. Were the toilets empty? He started to wash his hands as he tried using the mirror to check for occupants. He couldn't tell. Thoughts raced through his mind as he stood scoping his kill zone. The restroom door must be solid he thought. The room was quiet enough he could hear Freddy and blue hoodie pissing.

The third guy had finished, ambling to the sink to wash his hands. As he did so, Henkl turned to try the toilet cubicles. Neither gave way – occupied. *Bugger*, he thought. Things were going to be messy. Freddy was just finishing off as the guy washing his hands exited the room. It was now or it was never.

Blue hoodie started to zip himself, Freddy had made it to the washbasins. Steely-eyed and with no hesitation, Henkl unsheathed his Glock 19 mm. Freddy, wide-eyed, had seen something sinister in the mirror, but it was too late, far too late. At two metres, the first of two shots went through the back of Freddy's head and exited his forehead. The slugs embedding themselves in the wall the mirror had been attached to, shattered glass, blood and brain matter scattered the washbasin countertop.

Arcing round in less than a second, Henkl aimed and shot blue hoodie, two further shots to the forehead killing him instantly. Blue hoodie crashed to his right, hitting his head loudly on the side of the nearest toilet cubicle. A muffled "What the fuck, dude?" could be heard from within.

In comfortably less than 10 seconds, two human life forms were extinct. Remorseless, Henkl moved with speed. Exiting the toilets, no words to Zebra necessary, his facial expression told Zebra exactly what was required.

The duo started for the exit. It wasn't quick. The bar was pumping. The killers squeezed through. Exiting the bar, separated by a five-metre gap, Henkl turned right and Zebra left as they entered the street. The clock was ticking.

Now they both walked casually, heads down, resisting the urge to run. It was 10:55 p.m., the mission completed, barring a clean exfil. After 200 metres, Henkl took a left off the main street, quickening his stride a touch as he retrieved his phone.

He suppressed a half smile as he read the message from Gruppe Drei. Just four words: "*Boxed off and clean*". Xav would be pleased.

Henkl continued his loop around the Gryphon and what he could only imagine would be a state of bedlam right now. It was just 12 minutes since the kill had been carried out. Police sirens, clearly audible, grew louder with every stride he made away from the scene. A minute later and the first of three police cars breezed past him, neon blue lights flashing alarmingly in the cold, dark New Haven night.

Less than 15 minutes after hitting their mark, Henkl and Zebra plotted a steady 30 mph course out of New Haven. The calmest of appearances masked the job they had just concluded. As Zebra drove, Henkl discarded their burner phones bit by bit out of the window. Cold, bitter air rushed in, causing Zebra to stir his head a little. As Henkl put the window up, he retrieved a third phone from his pocket and proceeded to check up on his teams.

Gruppe Drei had successfully taken out Catherine Blake with no collateral. Theirs had been the easiest of the three assignments. A busy music festival had allowed for an easy kill. Harry and Bush had done well too. Out of sync, though, a thorough debrief would ensue, but importantly their job was done cleanly, and they were an hour's drive south of New Haven.

Henkl called Xav. It was 11:30 p.m. Eastern Standard Time, making it 5:30 a.m. in Geneva. Xav would answer it regardless of the time of day or night, but at 5:30 a.m. Henkl knew he'd already be up.

"Are you good?" A terse-sounding Xav, bordering on irritation, answered. He was usually succinct and to the point, but on this occasion he sounded annoyed. It couldn't be anything Henkl had done, could it?

Dismissing the thought, "Ja, Xav, all three neat and clean," he replied, wrongly assuming the news would perk him up.

"Get back to DC. You'll get the last four files tonight," replied Xav in his perfect accentless English. The two native German speakers could have reverted to their mother tongue, but they hadn't.

"We're on the way," Henkl replied, opting to keep it short and to the point too. Xav was in a mood and Henkl wasn't inclined to spend time asking why. With that Xav ended the call, and Henkl turned to Zebra to fill him in.

CHAPTER 6
JONNO

Vauxhall, London

Jonno stood at the end of the imposing boardroom table. At over four metres in length, Jonno's four-man team made the most of the space provided. The table sat centrally in the cavernous vault deep inside MI6 HQ. At level minus three, the aptly named 'Crypt' was a secure, near breach-proof haven for Jonno's clandestine briefing.

Bright overhead lighting bounced off the whitewashed stone walls. An entire wall of glass provided for a single door into the Crypt. The opposite wall featured a stone arch, a throwback to a disused London Tube thoroughfare. An enormous LCD monitor hung from the end wall, a pair of matching corner tables standing sentry.

The Crypt had a clean, surgical feel. Devoid of clutter, the room was Jonno's strategy hub. His entire 'special operations' team sat impassively, but attentively, as Jonno got down to business. Within the Crypt, JT and his team were allowed to refer to their boss as Jonno – formalities removed, replaced by analysis and critical thinking.

Rob Warner sat to JT's left whilst Nic and Meek sat across the table. JT's team focused on the LCD screen as Jonno tapped it into life.

At 55, Jonno's appearance belied his age. A trim, honed physique had been acquired through countless hours in the gym and a meticulous diet. His chiselled jawline, full head of hair and bright, alert eyes were the envy of any thirty-something. The creases to his forehead and a couple of lines emanating from each eye only served to enhance, rather than detract from, Jonno's good looks. He commanded a room. His mere presence was felt by those around him.

"Good job, guys," Jonno began as he kicked off his debrief, referring to the breach at Chateau Forestier.

"Any blowback on those eaves?" quizzed Nic. As clean as the job had been, both JT and Nic still harboured concerns.

"As far as we know, it's all good," replied Jonno. "Interject as necessary," the boss continued as he proceeded with his briefing.

Nic sank back in his seat a smidge as he averted his eyes from Jonno to the LCD.

"In 1996, Louise Walsh approached the government of the time. She wanted a funding stream and secure, private laboratories to help advance her work. She is a leading light in biogenetics. We turned her down, maybe foolishly now, but at the time it wasn't the funding that was the problem. She had gone rogue. At first highly unethical, Walsh went further."

"Further how?" asked JT, breaking Jonno's monologue.

"She was pioneering a groundbreaking genetic recode, a postnatal, invasive procedure that can only be done within a few days of birth. The programme was code-named 'Morph'."

"Is it safe?" enquired JT as he shifted his weight slightly, quietly tapping his fingers on the table as his mind ran computations.

"Well, that was the million-dollar question back then, JT," Jonno responded as he resumed his briefing. "The procedure is time critical, her early work led to several deaths including her own firstborn child." The room fell silent as that fact sank in. Walsh had tried and failed on her own child.

"So, it's working now then?" more a statement than an actual question from JT as he broke the sombre feel to the room.

Jonno switched his gaze from the LCD, initially looking JT in the eyes, before giving the entire team his focus.

"Yes, it is," he responded. Giving extra gravitas to his response, Jonno drilled into the details of Programme Morph.

"The recipients are highly intelligent and physically stronger. Walsh has pioneered a technique to enhance human beings at birth.

The data we have suggests 20% improvements in both physical and mental attributes, although the sample size so far is limited. In essence, she has found a way to create super humans; a medical procedure to unlock a potential inside all humans. Undetectable once scarring dissipates.

"Before she approached us, she had made some attempts that went badly wrong. Efficacy was questioned, and her early results cost lives. She wanted to offer human enhancement to the highest bidder. Essentially, she wanted to sell her product to the ultrarich, a kind of one-million-pound baby thing. The BMA instantly shut her down, which is why she came to us. We subsequently turned her away. She went to the Yanks; their medical set-up provided more options to assist her. We loosely tracked her work, but nothing tangible ever came to light. The more time that passed, the more we took our finger off the pulse." Jonno frowned as he outlined this, a damning indictment of his own government.

"What are we missing?" Meek interrupted, her steely eyes boring directly into Jonno. Mika Kimura was the most striking of women. The second of two daughters to a Japanese dad and Norwegian mum, with Baltic blue Norwegian eyes, perfect skin, and a vibrant, glowing face, Meek radiated intelligence and an enquiring mind.

Native in Japanese and Norwegian, Meek was a languages expert. Adding Russian, Swedish, German and passable Italian had come relatively easy for her. She was British though, born and bred in the UK, her parents had met in Aberdeen, both of whom worked in the oil industry. After completing a degree in languages, Meek switched her focus to a master's in communication technology.

Sitting quietly minding her own business in a café, midway through her final year, Meek met Jonno – not by chance. Initially it had been a little spooky. A strange yet charming man hadn't been cause for concern. The personal dossier that Jonno had slid across the coffee table that day had. Quickly, though, Meek's initial fright, as she leafed through the myriad of details covering the last five years of her life, was replaced by excitement. A week later and Meek had agreed to join a very special part of MI6. That had been a year ago. Extensive training had ensued, and right now Meek was showing her worth as she interrogated Jonno's briefing.

Jonno smiled, a momentary reflection that he'd recruited wisely. Instantly on the money, Meek had got straight to the point. Up till now, alarm bells wouldn't ordinarily have been ringing, but now they were!

"What if the Yanks created an undetectable super race?" Jonno asked rhetorically. Without allowing for an answer he continued. "A 'have and a have-not' society? A place where the rich bought designer babies? Olympic medals, Nobel Peace Prizes to the highest bidder?" As Jonno's words reverberated around the room, JT's team stole glances at each other.

"That's not it though…" interjected Meek, "it's far worse… isn't it!" Meek continued.

This time Jonno didn't smile. Proud as he was of Meek's sharp inquisitive mind, the grim, dark details he was about to spell out suppressed his pride.

"Russians." Jonno's one-word response was chilling, almost throttling the oxygen in the room. "We aren't sure why but, for some reason or other, Walsh's relationship soured. Maybe the Russians offered her more; maybe the Yanks wanted more control. Who knows?

"The files you retrieved from Geneva detail 18 MorphEns. It's the term she has detailed on the hard drives copied from Chateau Forestier. It's a hybrid of morph and enhancement," explained Jonno, giving no opportunity for questions. "Four British MorphEns and 14 Americans, none of whom have any idea who or what they are."

He turned back to the LCD. Tapping a tab revealed a long list of names with a neat and concise summary of each person. It could easily have been a 'long list' for a recruitment selection meeting, but it wasn't.

Daniel R Fletcher, DOB 09.12.1985
Manchester, United Kingdom
Current status: IT Consultant

Benjamin P Fletcher, DOB 16.02.1987
Leeds, United Kingdom
Current status: Civil Engineer

Rachel L Fletcher, DOB 14.06.1990
London, United Kingdom
Current status: Doctor

Samuel D Fletcher, DOB 17.04.1995
Edinburgh, United Kingdom
Current status: Edinburgh University, studying Applied Mathematics

Connor L Evans, DOB: 24.02.1997
Georgetown, Washington, USA
*Current status:**DECEASED–Shot at close range. Contract killing***

Sarah E Woods, DOB 11.03.1997
Georgetown, Washington, USA
*Current status:**DECEASED–Shot at close range. Contract killing***

Rebecca L Schmidt, DOB 17.03.1997
Washington DC, USA
*Current status:**DECEASED–Shot at close range. Contract killing***

Joseph M Werner, DOB 21.04.1997
Washington DC, USA
*Current status:**DECEASED–Shot at close range. Contract killing***

Henri M Wagner, DOB 18.06.1997
Princeton University, New Jersey, USA
Current status: Student

Alan T Schwinn, DOB 22.02.1997
MIT, Boston, USA
*Current status:**DECEASED–Shot at close range. Contract killing***

Sascha B Pavel, DOB 10.05.1997
MIT, Boston, USA
*Current status:**DECEASED** – Shot at close range. Contract killing*

Zia L Patel, DOB 04.04.1997
Harvard University, Massachusetts, USA
Current status: Student

Anastasia J Sokolov, DOB 18.07.1997
Yale, New Haven, USA
*Current status:**DECEASED** – Shot at close range. Contract killing*

Jay B McMath, DOB 14.08.1997
Virginia, USA
Current status: Student

Charlie G Donaldson, DOB 17.05.1997
Harvard University, Massachusetts, USA
Current status: Student

Catherine L Blake, DOB 28.03.1997
Yale, New Haven, USA
*Current status:**DECEASED** – Shot at close range. Contract killing*

Wasim D Khan, DOB 25.06.1997
MIT, Boston, USA
*Current status:**DECEASED** – Shot at close range. Contract killing*

Alfredo M Sainz, DOB 14.01.1997
Yale, New Haven, USA
*Current status:**DECEASED** – Shot at close range. Contract killing*

As Jonno's special ops team scanned the list, the most alarming of facts leapt out. Of the 18 listed, 10 were marked DECEASED. An icy chill tingled throughout the group. Scanning through the details, they were all young, highly intelligent, fit and healthy.

"In the last four weeks, of the 14 American MorphEns, 10 have been assassinated. We don't have the precise details, but obviously we're working on it. What we do know is they were all shot at close range. Very clinical and, right now, the Yanks don't appear to have a lead."

"Do we know why?" JT broke the silence, beating Meek to the punch.

"No."

Jonno's abrupt reply achieved the effect he wanted. His entire team now had a laser-like focus on him.

"The Yanks don't know we know, and we can't ask them," he continued. "We don't know who, either, but it was extremely professional," as Jonno regained control of the briefing.

"The killings were almost identical in every way and if not for the timings, it would have been safe to assume they were carried out by the same team. The hits in New Haven occurred within 30 minutes of each other."

"Team not assassin, Jonno?" questioned Rob. Other than a few pleasantries as JT's team had entered the Crypt, Rob had remained stony silent. Rob hadn't missed a beat, he'd hung on Jonno's every word and had memorized every tiny detail emblazoned across the LCD.

"Bang on, Rob," Jonno couldn't have been clearer in his response as he continued to explain.

"Every hit had the hallmark of a two-man team, but in a couple of them a distraction had been employed. The timings of these distractions suggest two killers. Added to this, several of the hits were carried out in tricky locations. If this had been us, that's exactly how we'd have worked. Right now, our immediate concerns are twofold; the safety of the Fletchers and why this is happening. We've sifted through every detail of the info taken from Walsh's chateau, our intel suggests everything she has of importance was stored there and not at BioDS offices."

BioDS hadn't been mentioned till now. JT's team already had a complete dossier, giving chapter and verse on Walsh's company. BioDS was a relatively small biogenetic company, listed in

Switzerland, employing a little over 40 people. Louise Walsh, CEO, and Xavier Picamole, head of research and development, were listed as the two primary members of staff. BioDS's website did a great job in masking its more sinister work. It portrayed an ethos that cared for the planet and humanity using sympathetic green plant motifs, blue skies and watery images alongside images of human love and empathy for others. Details of the biogenetic work BioDS were involved in were all deliberately vague and carefully worded. The website asked more questions than it gave answers.

"Any questions?" asked Jonno as he broke from his briefing, throwing it open to the room. JT, Nic, Rob and Meek all glanced around the room, a politeness, as they looked to ask without over-talking.

"Do the Yanks know about the Fletchers?" quizzed JT, Nic and Meek nodding heads in unison suggesting this was a question on their lips too.

"The answer is we simply don't know," shot back Jonno.

"And the Russians?" JT interrogating further on what the Yanks knew.

"We're in the dark on this too," Jonno replied.

Taking back the room, Jonno continued to expand on JT's questions. "It's safe to assume the Yanks must have some intel on Walsh's early work whilst she was in the UK, but nothing in the files we retrieved suggests so. Official channels and back channels between 6 and them have not once mentioned her, MorphEns or anything connected." Jonno referring to MI6 as just '6' and the CIA as 'them'. "In the last 15 years it's very much been a case of 'they know we know they know' with regards to Walsh.

"Regarding the Russians, it's a little murkier. We assume the Yanks are aware, suspect or are working on understanding where she has gone to, but we don't know."

"Do we have options with the Yanks?" interjected JT, suppressing a wry smile as the words tumbled from his lips. Half a grin appeared on Rob's face too, as the pair initially glanced at each other before returning their focus on their boss. Jonno had a very good back channel at his disposal. The mischievous looks from JT and Rob were all about the personal cost to Jonno. Nothing in life was free and, in the information game that they played, the price could be hefty, very hefty indeed.

The back channel Jonno would utilize would require him giving something in return. Quite what that 'something' was was way above JT's pay grade, hence his smile.

"I'm weighing this up right now," Jonno replied as he stepped away from the LCD. He pulled the chair back from the head of the table, gracefully sliding into it. Jonno had his team's entire attention, four pairs of eyes penetrating his mind as he continued, now seated, his briefing achieving a much more personal effect.

"We need intel on the Russians, and we need overwatch on the Fletchers. They're our citizens. They might be 'our assets'." Jonno rapped his knuckles sharply on the desk to accentuate the point. "We need Walsh back in the fold and we need to know why the Americans were killed." The questions spilt out in quick succession.

"And who killed them," interjected Meek, Jonno shot her a glance of approval as she verbalized her thinking.

Silence descended across the entire room, a pregnant pause but not an awkward one, the silence reflecting the gravity of the situation. As much as the team had done incredibly well in harvesting a ton of intel from their covert raid on Chateau Forestier, it now felt like they knew less rather than more. Awkward questions hung around unanswered.

Jonno had deliberately thrown the questions out there. He knew they would dwell in the recesses of their minds over the coming days. As quickly as Jonno had fired out the problems his team faced, he regained his control with instructions for his team.

"JT, get lines tapped and overwatch on the Fletchers," he barked.

"How far, Jonno?" JT replied. What he was referring to was the depth of monitoring of the Fletcher siblings' friends and family.

"Just direct family for now," Jonno shot back. The remainder of JT's team kept silent. Right now, Jonno was in total charge, his instructions were going down the chain of command. JT first, with tasks to be delegated by JT once Jonno was done.

"I want intel from Moscow, speak to Tyverskaya," Jonno continued. Tyverskaya was a suburb of Moscow, but in reality, was a reference to a MI6 satellite hub. JT nodded as the chief continued to spell out his instructions.

Concluding his team's orders and with his briefing over, he opened the floor to any final questions.

"Why Jonno, what are we really worried about?" Meek asked. "Are they dangerous?" she carried on, before Jonno could respond.

Staring directly at Meek, he hesitated slightly before he replied. The slight pause wasn't intended for effect, but it achieved exactly that.

"The 'master race', Meek, it's about the 'master race'. Are we bothered about 'designer babies' to the rich?" A rhetorical question from Jonno. "No. The 'higher-ups' are shitting themselves over nation states taking this to a place none of us can imagine right now."

Jonno's 'higher-ups' were indeed high given his contacts list was a 'who's who' of the people running the country. Meek remained silent, her mind whirring as Jonno's words resonated.

"In the wrong hands, YES." Jonno rapped his knuckle once more on the desk as he spoke. "These MorphEns are highly intelligent, extremely capable. If they are trained, who knows what they can do!"

The room felt icy-cold once more. JT's team felt it. A chill ran down Meek's spine as she took on board Jonno's warning.

With that, Jonno wrapped things up. JT nodded his head towards the exit, indicating it was time to go. With smooth efficiency, the team filed out in the direction of JT's ops room. Jonno remained seated. Having immediately retrieved his mobile, he was already forging plans.

CHAPTER 7
OPERATION DOORSTOP

Knacc, Omsk, Russia

Drake and Kaspov sat motionless in their very nondescript car. The car in question was a dirty white AvtoVAZ, the Russian car maker better known around the world as LADA. No branding was noticeable on the car though, its badge had probably dropped off at the same time the car had taken on its dirty white sheen. A bit like a chameleon Drake thought, the car seemed to have adapted to its surroundings.

Kaspov shifted in his seat breaking the silence. Drake glanced over for a brief second, his line of vision taking in the silhouetted outline of Kaspov's face in his foreground and the densely forested trees outside. It was just after 10 p.m., the dark forest was reasonably well lit due to a crystal-clear sky and almost full moon. Waiting for their meet with the 'locals', Kaspov started tapping his fingers ever so lightly on the steering wheel. Almost as if he had music in his head, he would every so often alter the frequency of his tapping, like he was playing his own private tune.

He had a classic Russian name. Anatoly Kaspov was a first-generation American; he had grown up in Chicago to Russian parents. Speaking Russian at home meant he was fluent. In his early years, he hadn't realized the advantages his parent's mother tongue would give him. He just saw the problems it had occasionally caused in the schoolyard, a hybrid, inland, northern accent with a Russian twang had set him apart. This had also given him an edge that he would later rely on. He had been in his fair share of skirmishes, rarely his fault. Being picked on wasn't nice, but it had served to toughen him up. Learning to street fight from an early age had its uses, as too did his skill for observing. He called it his 'streets', meaning that whenever he was out and about, he was alert and wary of everything around him.

He had learnt and adapted to his environment as a young kid and that, in turn, helped keep him out of more trouble. Later, having left school, Kaspov had joined the marines. A fine athlete, he hadn't excelled at school despite a highly intelligent and inquiring mind. In and out of trouble at school and the neighbourhood he'd grown up in hadn't made for a good academic environment.

Once signed up, though, he was on a level playing surface. He impressed his superiors from the off. Physically demanding tasks came easy to him and when shoulder to shoulder with the average marine, Kaspov was a genius in comparison. A smart genius, though, bright but also savvy. Lacking the string of academic qualifications the officers had meant he didn't talk in an elitist, highbrow fashion. He stood out for all the right reasons.

Kaspov moved through the ranks quickly before going through the gruelling Navy SEAL selection process. He had aced it and as soon as he passed, he was put to work. Training and more training was the SEALs' way. It was all exciting and he had finally found a life that suited. During his time with the SEALs, he was seconded to several joint operations assisting the CIA in South America. Excelling as always, Kaspov was singled out for outstanding work in 'OBSCOM'. Recruited directly by the CIA field director, he had joined the CIA aged 32. OBSCOM stood for observation and communication, something he had been trained to do with the SEALs. Although an expert in technology-based communications, this wasn't his strength. Where Kaspov really excelled was in the much murkier world of 'search and destroy'. Better known as assassination, he was a legally approved 'dealer in death'.

Drake knew all about his current partner's qualities, in part because they had been on several training programmes together over the years and partly because Drake was technically his senior. Neither man had an elevated title – both were field agents, pure and simple – but he was 'on point' for this operation and had been on their previous four operations together.

Drake had taken a similar route too. Although he had started life as an officer recruit in the army, he later passed selection to the Green Berets. The US Army Special Forces had a healthy dislike of the SEALs; both special forces outfits considered themselves the best the US had to offer. Their thorny relationship often led to more internal casualties through fighting than injuries sustained in the field. The two specialist units seldom worked together for this very reason. Drake and Kaspov got on, though. Their similar yet antagonistic backgrounds were very much a thing of the past, helped in part because both men now considered themselves 'above and beyond' their former units.

Years of experience within the CIA had taken both men to the brink of being outstanding in their field. There were probably only a handful of men on the planet with their particular skill set. Both had the unique combination of trained killers, highly proficient telecoms technicians and with an ability to become ghosts – not just grey men, ghosts.

Kaspov shifted again, his seat creaking slightly as he adjusted his weight. The 'locals' would be here any minute. Called the 'locals', it didn't mean the guys they were meeting were from Omsk though, quite the opposite in fact.

The 'locals' were the ground force team Ms. Angel had put together, 12 special forces operatives who all spoke Russian as their first language or were fluent Russian speakers. Operation Doorstop was a black op, complete deniability was the directive that had come straight from the Mega Bitch's lips. Mega Bitch was a reference to Ms. Angel. Drake had always thought a better surname would have been 'Angle' rather than 'Angel', as she always appeared to be playing the angles. He didn't trust many people, after all, in his line of work, trust was something they traded in rather than gave out, but in Ms. Angel's case he really didn't trust her.

Wendy Angel was going places though, so Drake played the game and did as he was told – and did it well. He couldn't tell if she liked him or not, she rarely gave anything away, but he was part of a select division within the CIA and, although not enormous, there were plenty of choices for Ms. Angel to choose from. Yet she consistently chose Drake, so he figured he must be doing something right. She was still a bitch though – Mega Bitch!

None of the team were to wear anything for the op other than local Russian clothing, no ID and certainly nothing that could link them to the US. Being taken alive wasn't an option. In death, the only proof of them being US citizens would be the state of their teeth. Eight years of clandestine ops around the world had opened Drake's eyes to what a dead body will and won't reveal. Great teeth didn't necessarily say 'American', but 14 sets of great teeth would. Drake just hoped that all 14 of them wouldn't get killed running 'Doorstop', mainly though because he was one of those 14.

Kaspov noticed first, nudging Drake with his right elbow, he gestured in the direction of the approaching car with a small upward nod of his head. It was dusky dark, but the car looked to be a similarly dirty white one. It pulled up five metres from where they were parked, the headlights turned off signifying its dormant status.

Two men got out and approached their car, Drake and Kaspov followed suit. Kaspov walked over and immediately fist-bumped the larger of the two men. Dmitry and Kaspov were close; they had a lot in common. Both had come from the SEALs and both were first-generation Russian Americans. In the tiny covert world they moved in, the things in common were almost too much of a coincidence.

Both men had grown up in the northern states, Dmitry came from Boston, and each had a mother called 'Ulyana', a relatively uncommon name for women of their mother's age. It was quite uncanny, but what really made them bond was their sense of humour. Maybe it was the shared backgrounds or just a quirk of nature, but in their line of work jobs could involve spending days together. Some field agents said very little, and others were quite the opposite. Dmitry and Kaspov were chatters. The banter between the two men would be endless, as a pair of tough Russian American immigrants they just did not revert to type. Trained killers they may be, but the world wouldn't have known it. More like a couple of lowbrow afternoon radio DJs, yapping on about all sorts, always with a comment or opinion that would generally end in a laugh or a giggle.

The shorter of the two men was Pyotr, pronounced Peter. Although bearing a Russian name, Peter was an all-American, boy-next-door type. A fluent Russian speaker in part due to a Russian grandfather of the same name, but a languages degree specializing in Russian and five years based in Moscow as part of the US embassy staff had made the largest contribution. Peter was a trained spy, recruited at university and fast-tracked from the age of 22. Intelligent, good-looking and athletic, Peter appealed to the ladies yet was liked by the men. People had always wanted to be Peter's friend ever since he could remember, lads wanted to hang out with him and girls wanted to marry him.

Drake cut to the chase, breaking up Dmitry and Kaspov's reunion.

"This way," he said, nodding towards a small path that led into the forest on their right.

Kaspov made for the path with the others trailing in his wake. It was a quiet, deserted area of the countryside about eight miles from Omsk, no one was around, but the four men didn't speak. In single file, Kaspov leading, they walked through the dense forest for over 20 minutes. Finally, they could start to see light in the distance, the night was a bright one, but walking through the forest things had quickly become very dark and gloomy. Now though, as they neared the edge of the forest, it was starting to brighten up.

The four men drew closer and closer to the edge of the treeline. Using the trees as cover to crouch behind, they stared across the open ground to a seemingly unending fence line. At six metres tall and angled outwards at the top, it told its own story. The fence was designed to keep people out not in. Cameras too, positioned at 50-metre intervals, scanned only outwards.

Peter pointed towards the top of the fence line, identifying the cameras. He then clarified their intended entry point. The fence had an upright every 10 metres, each upright linked with heavy-duty, wire mesh, electrified fencing. The fence went straight for more than 200 metres before making a 45-degree turn away from the clearing. Peter counted 14 uprights before pointing out the fifteenth.

"There," he said pointing between the fourteenth and fifteenth upright. "We go in through the section between those two," Peter said.

On the other side of the fence line sat a large, imposing building, with a pristine, manicured strip of lawn sandwiched between the two, no flower beds or shrubs, just open space. Good for security maybe, but this was no show garden.

Drake's team all knew the plan; they had been to this exact spot a week earlier and spent the last seven days formulating the precise details. This was their final recce. All they were waiting for now was the green light from Langley.

A two-man Trojan Team would drive to the sentry office and take out the guards, at the same time Langley would immobilize the fence and comms.

Meanwhile, a 12-man Breach Team would enter through the fence. At that point, the team would split into three – two teams of two to cover the external door and eastern perimeter door, whilst the remaining team of eight would enter through the main entrance, with the Trojan Team left to cover that door. The eight-man Entry Team were to seek and destroy, leaving all exits covered in the event of escapees.

The plan was brutal. Trained killers were to enter then seek and destroy 200 young men and women. Collateral damage wasn't a concern either. Drake's team had been briefed that the staff team within Knacc could be as many as 28. He had carried out many 'kill missions' for the Mega Bitch, but nothing on this scale. Deep in a Colombian jungle hide, Drake and his team had once carried out a massacre involving the assassination of a drugs cartel and its small, private army. Although it never hit the newspapers, he knew that over 60 Colombians had died that day along with one of his team.

That had been very different, though, it had felt right. Drugs were bad and in Drake's world that made it OK to scrub out the very life form involved. Even assassins had a modicum of sense about right and wrong. After the Cordillera Mission, none of the team had lost any sleep over it. For most, it had felt like a good job, a righteous job even. Most had got an inner reward, like a 'pat on the back', their own justification for why they did what they did.

But this mission wasn't going to be like that. Two hundred and twenty-eight human beings felt more like genocide and less like assassination. Drake's team had all been warned: don't be fooled, don't let appearances sway your actions. Seek, identify, destroy, then vanish; let the training kick in, become ghosts.

As the four men continued recapping the mission, a vehicle approached – a blue or maybe black sedan, the dusky glow not helping to give clarity. Crawling to a stop outside the main entrance, the driver climbed out and opened the rear left door. Peter pulled out a pair of night-vision binoculars, whispering a running commentary of what he could see. His world had become green, but it didn't stop him identifying the two figures clambering out of the back of the car.

The very upright form of Vitaly Urinov, the head of Knacc, was so distinctive Peter reckoned Dmitry would recognize him from his silhouette alone. As always, Urinov was accompanied by Sergei Asmov. Urinov's file said he was 1.9 m, his tall, angular frame a stark contrast to Asmov. A bull of a man, Asmov had the appearance of a battle-hardened dwarf from *Lord of the Rings*. Standing together, the two men 'stood out'.

Urinov was a 54-year-old ex-Russian Army major with 10 years spent working for Russian intelligence as a technical analyst. Langley had suggested that most of these file notes were a cover. Army majors rarely took positions as analysts, they were too far up the chain of command to start taking on research work. An addendum to the file hypothesized that Urinov oversaw FSB recruitment and training. Although unconfirmed, if it was in the file, it was more than likely true.

Sergei Asmov was also somewhat of an enigma. Described as 1.56 m tall and 95 kg, these were just about the only accurate details about him. After a brief spell working as a mechanic, his file detailed a blurred picture of a life spent as a low-level criminal before working his way up the ranks of a dangerous Ukrainian mafia family. The Boiko crime family were based in Kyiv and made their money from trafficking. Originally they trafficked drugs, mainly heroin from Afghanistan to Europe. The House of Boiko then diversified, running arms, following the breakdown of the former USSR into smaller states, and then more recently human trafficking.

Asmov started as a Boiko enforcer. The Russian for barrel, 'Бочка' as he was known wasn't just a tough guy though. Бочка was smart, Бочка knew when to use brute force and when to keep his head down, be subtle and use subterfuge. In the House of Boiko, these were the skills needed to keep you alive. Life and death in the Ukraine's second most powerful mafia family was a possibility with every decision made – as much peril came from within.

Yet the file outlining Бочка's turbulent past didn't tell the true story. It wasn't even close. Special Agent Sergei Asmov had never been in the army and, although a member of the Boiko crime family, Бочка had spent eight years leading a double life. Бочка had left school to join the army. He had excelled during the recruitment process, so much so that even as a green 18-year-old the recruitment panel earmarked him instantly for an elite path through the army ranks.

Officially Бочка was rejected, the army citing poor discipline and an inability to follow orders as the reasons for failing selection. But this had been a cover, a very good cover, in order to recruit Бочка as a special agent of the interior, but more importantly this meant he was a 'clean agent'. He had no history, and if he had no history, he didn't exist.

After training, Бочка was put to work in a world where the only rule that applied was to survive. He had spent his entire career working undercover. Other than staying alive, Бочка's secondary role was to provide human intelligence, humint, to his superiors. Aged 24, Бочка had already got his hands dirty within the Russian underworld. Smuggling drugs, working as an enforcer at several Black Sea ports and blackmail with violence had become part of his daily life. Then, during a spell running arms out of Chechnya, he crossed paths with a member of the Boiko mafia. This was his 'in'. For the last eight years, Бочка had spent his time moving up through the ranks, by day trafficking guns, people and drugs and by night feeding humint back to superiors.

It was a dangerous game though, some undercover operatives burnt out and some were ratted out. The Ministry for the Interior had leaks, the army had leaks, and even the FSB couldn't keep everything covert. This, for Бочка, was his biggest concern, the higher he climbed the ranks, the more aware he became of the corruption. The payments made to high-ranking officials in return for information scared him very much, but this was the life Special Agent Sergei Asmov had signed up for and so he continued his rise to power within Ukraine's second most powerful mafia family.

Then, after eight bloody and depraved years, Бочка's luck finally ran out. Only his speed of thought and dense musculature saved his life. He was sent on a fictitious job with two juniors, his would-be killers had been ordered to kill him and dump his body into the Dnieper. Arriving at the river dock, things just hadn't felt right. It was nothing he could put his finger on, just a couple of tiny feelings that had made Бочка a little more alert. Walking to the meet point, one of his killers had looked twitchy, only for the briefest of moments, just a hint, but a hint was enough. Looking back to the start of the day, Бочка had got his instructions along with his team. Thinking back, he had felt that the other two had already seemed to know the plan, as if they had heard it before – just a hint.

When they arrived at the river's edge, the hints became alarm bells, loud alarm bells. Why the edge of the river? The meet would make more sense 50 m back, by the containers, they gave cover from would-be observers, they were nearer the exit point. Why?

Speed of thought. Бочка had always had clarity of mind and speed of thought. In fact, he worked better under duress, it seemed to help focus his mind and amplify his thoughts.

The two killers pulled their guns in unison. Most people would have run, but then most people would have died too, not Бочка. The double agent almost did the unthinkable, taking a bullet for his troubles. He moved towards the first killer, wrestling with his gun arm, the pair of them spun round, sandwiching Бочка between the two killers.

The gun fired, hitting him an inch below his left collarbone. The bullet, released at a distance of 5 cm from gun to body, flew straight through Бочка, leaving a large, gaping hole just above his scapula. But it didn't just stop, it continued, flying straight into the second killer's chest. Death wasn't instant, that would take 40 minutes, but death was a certainty, nonetheless.

The wrestling continued though. A short man but weighing 95 kg, The Barrel had an accurate nickname. Bleeding profusely and in a lot of pain, Бочка fought for his life. But Бочка won. Biting his killer's nose off in the process, the fight was anything but clean. With his cover blown, a period of his life was now concluded.

Special Agent Sergei Asmov took up his position as Head of Centre, Knacc, Omsk working as Director Urinov's second in command. All references to his involvement, first in Chechnya and then Kyiv had been redacted from his file. The move from Ministry for the Interior Intelligence to a special division with the FSB had been made in order to ensure Бочка would be safe from his previous life.

"It's Urinov and Asmov," Peter whispered.

He kept his NVD trained on the men as they walked towards the main entrance. The driver returned to the car, driving it around the far side of the building.

"Entering now," Peter continued in his low hush.

Three minutes after arriving, the front of the building was calm, quiet and empty once more.

Peter lowered his NVD, and the kill team went back to their hushed discussions. Thirty minutes later and the four men had seen enough. Happy with their final check, they returned through the forest to their vehicles. All they needed now was the green light from Langley.

An hour later, Drake and Kaspov were ensconced in the comms room within their base. A dreary hotel room in Omsk, cheap and with virtually no facilities worth mentioning, the hotel provided the two important elements they needed – power and solitude. Drake had a serious satellite-tracking system booted up and connected in series to two laptops and an additional LED monitor.

Great kit, but it all required some significant juice. They could operate in the field, but the battery requirements would limit them to no more than a couple of weeks. They had now been in Omsk for three weeks and counting, waiting for their green light.

Drake, staring at his laptop screen, called in their daily sitrep to Mega Bitch. Kaspov, taking a slug from his can of Coke, sat opposite, grinning at Drake. He didn't like Ms. Angel any more than Drake and was grateful for not being on point. It was Drake's duty not Kaspov's to call in each day. Perk of the position, he taunted Drake daily.

Drake could hear the phone's low tone. After the third chirp, Wendy Angel picked up.

"Yes," she answered curtly.

"We're good to go, ma'am. Just waiting for the green light," he responded.

"How is the door?" Wendy asked. Door was the code word for Knacc, whilst 'stop' was self-explanatory.

Operation Doorstop was the largest kill mission the CIA had ever planned on Russian soil. Tension was running high, but the stakes were higher still. Drake's 14-man team had to breach a secure compound, locate and kill 200 residents and then vanish. Getting in wasn't the difficult bit, Knacc was secure, but it wasn't Fort Knox, and vanishing afterwards should be fine too. Vanishing was Drake's primary skill. He was a ghost.

The real difficulty was going to be locating and killing 200 people in a 12-minute time frame. Twelve minutes was very tight, very, very tight. This was all in a building they had no exact knowledge of. Their only intel had come from schematics hacked from the FSB mainframe with 12 unidentified rooms; unidentified because they had no title and no reference to them. These rooms concerned Drake, but there was something else gnawing away in the deepest recesses of his mind.

He had been warned by Wendy not to underestimate these trainees. She had told Drake and his team that the hit was for 200 Special Trainee Agents. Described to him as a specialist Russian school for assassins, his team was to kill all 200 assassins, but aged only 17 or 18, how dangerous could they be?

"It's all good. Nothing new. Urinov came back tonight. No sign of Natalia but Asmov was with him," reported Drake.

"Good. Keep on Obs, call in same time tomorrow," and with that Wendy ended the call.

Drake didn't get the opportunity to sign off, the line already dead. He wasn't offended though; this was business not a social call. No description of the fabulous holiday hotel and sights of Omsk were needed, which was handy because the hotel was crap and Omsk was a dump.

Interrupting his thoughts, Kaspov asked, "Anything new?"

"No. Sit tight and 'keep on Obs' is all she said," Drake replied.

"It's a shithole, mate. Shithole," Kaspov replied.

What he really meant was he wished the job was on. The sooner they got it done, the sooner they would be out of there.

"I'd rather be in the jungle, man!" he came again, lacking his usual chirpiness. Drake knew what he meant though. They were both used to long, drawn-out jobs, ones that were all too often called off, weeks on end in solitude, skulking in rural hides or urban crap holes, but for some reason Omsk seemed drabber and more miserable than most places they'd ever been to.

CHAPTER 8
DAN AND BEN'S ANNUAL RACE

Alpe d'Huez, France
Wednesday 4th January 2017

Crystals, not quite snow not quite ice, swirled off the surface, kicked up by the wind. Both men had their heads dipped, in part to look down as they adjusted their bindings, but lowering their heads a little gave some protection from the biting wind.

Dan Fletcher sat in the snow composing himself. The older of the two brothers, he was an incredibly gifted athlete yet still the lesser of the two. Ben had surpassed him in his late teens and now, aged 30, Ben was at his zenith. Still, it was a close-run thing, it always had been, but Ben had the edge, and he knew it.

Not that he minded. It was a challenge. Beating Ben, or at least trying to beat Ben, was his own personal yardstick, his private measure of how he was doing.

Today though was more complicated. Since young boys, the Fletchers had spent hours shredding the slopes of the French Alps. Initially as skiers, Dan and Ben had turned to the 'dark side' as their sister put it. Snowboarding was their winter passion. Today was more complicated though, more personal than usual, it was their annual 'race of brothers'.

Since their switch from skiing to boarding, Dan and Ben had at first tried to beat the rest of the family down the Pic Blanc. They had failed miserably, so they'd created their own personal competition as the only snowboarders amongst the family.

The Pic Blanc was Alpe d'Huez's highest peak. At 3300 metres, it paved the way down the Sarenne Glacier, a 17 km black run. The rules were simple. Last year's winner got to say 'allez', and at that point, anything went. Cross the ice road first and you get a year's worth of bragging rights – simple.

Dan had won, but only twice. Ben had now racked up a very annoying eight victories over the last 11 ski seasons. Ten races plus the year they missed due to Dan's broken leg had seen a near total dominance from the younger of the two brothers. Dan was ever grateful that Sam hadn't made the switch from skiing too. Although only 22, Dan knew that both he and Ben were physically inferior to their baby bro.

Dan caught a glance at Ben, who had just finished his bindings and was taking in the breathtaking vista. The low winter sun made everything look sweet. Brilliant pale blue sky contrasted with pristine white snow. Glittering diamonds appeared to shimmer as the wind blew snow dust off the cornices. Far below, the last few skiers were making their way down the run. Dan and Ben were waiting for a clear piste. They had got the last lift, only the pisteurs would be following them down now.

Ben switched his attention to Dan, a big grin visible beneath his goggles. Dan returned the grin, he didn't mean to, but some actions were just involuntary. Dan needed his 'race brain' and that meant game face time. Steely-eyed concentration had just lost out to Ben's inane grinning. Dan averted his gaze. Look at anything but Idiobro was his mantra; Idiobro being Dan's personal nickname for Ben.

"Watcha," blurted Ben, breaking his concentration once more. Dan knew what he was up to, a tried-and-tested formula over the years of brotherly rivalry. Ben had the edge physically, but Dan could just about redress the balance with a slight mental advantage.

"Yeh, mate, almost shredding time," he replied, doing his best to keep conversation to a minimum. He needed the mental rehearsal more than Ben. It was close. It always was. Approximately 12 minutes of muscular endurance, about 150 turns, jumps or drops and, fingers crossed, 'no crashes'. A crash would be fatal, race over. That was for sure.

"Give it another minute," came Dan. "Should be clear by then," he continued, leaving no gap for Ben's reply.

"Yeh, mate, works for me."

Dan nodded his head in reply. No need for words. They both stared down the mountain; the last few skiers had turned into tiny black specks. The brothers wouldn't be catching them up now. The slope to themselves, they both just sat there – motionless.

Dan's thoughts jumped to their evening to follow. Rachel was coming out and that meant her best friend Kate too. Shit. Bugger, shit, bugger, what was he doing? He scolded himself internally and got back into game-face mode. There would be time to think about Kate later, but now wasn't the time to be weighing up his best strategy for chatting up his sister's best mate.

Ben leant forwards and ratcheted his bindings secure once more, doing his utmost to get his boots locked in tight. Instinctively, Dan did the same. Minimal movement between boot and bindings was critical.

Both brothers rocked forwards, stood up, and then stopped any forward momentum with their heel edge. Their boards bit into the snow, knees slightly bent, they just stood and stared. In front of them was an open slope, criss-crossed with tracks. An almost 60-degree black run stared back at them. Steepness wasn't the issue, though, being both highly skilled boarders, the sharp right-hand turn 400 metres down was the first major problem. The turn led to a rat run, a small alley of snow and ice that fed into the main part of the lower slope.

Slower in and quicker out of the turn. Slow in, quick out, Dan kept it foremost in his mind.

"You ready then, buddy?" Ben asked.

Slow in, quick out. Dan kept running through his rat run entry over and over.

"Yeh, mate, am good to go. You to start it, Ben, make the call," he replied.

Dan glanced over at Ben, mirrored goggles obscured his eyes, but he could tell; the slight facial twitch gave him away. Ben's eyes were smiling.

"What about Helen, mate. Tonight?" said Dan, unable to suppress a grin.

It was Dan's turn to use a mind game or two. Helen was fit and Ben hadn't talked about much other than 'how fit' she was for the last few days. Their sis had told Ben to keep away from her, though. Ben had a terrible track record with girls and Rachel didn't want him messing another one of her friends about. Mess with his mind was Dan's only remaining play.

"I reckon Rachel won't mind really," came Dan again – mess with his mind.

"On your marks," replied Ben, doing his best to ignore his brother. "Get set," he came again – no pause, no opportunity given. "ALLEZ," he screamed, as he flipped his board 90 degrees, his left leg leading the way down the slope.

Dan reacted as quickly as possible. A similar 90-degree twist saw his board land a fraction of a second later. Ben's line was marginally better and with the slightly quicker start, gave him a five-metre lead. They picked up speed at an alarming rate. Dan covered the first 50 metres before needing to turn. It was a breaking turn; too much speed would lead to disaster. Ahead, Ben kicked up snow as he initiated his breaking turn too. Visibility was superb, always a blessing as skiing blind was never nice and when racing it was horrendous. Ben had got a 20-metre lead now and was nearing the critical turn into the rat run.

Dan hit a kicker, bending his knees to soak up the upward propulsion. Barely skimming the surface, he returned to the slope 10 metres later, forced to break turn as soon as he could. Control was everything, hence the need to check his speed. Ben rounded the corner and was screaming along the rat run, no turning, just straight-lining it, tucked as low as he could. Dan followed; knees bent as low as his quads would allow. They weren't burning yet, but they would be, that was a certainty. Ben, although still ahead, wasn't making ground any more. Dan dug in and maintained his crouch.

"Woo-hoo! YEH," screamed Ben ahead, his yelps resonating across the valley.

"Have it. HAVE IT!" Dan replied back, in part an answer to his brother's enthusiasm but mainly an involuntary response to the adrenaline coursing his veins. "YEHHH MATE," he screamed. Yet more automated shrieks came from him.

Ben had just entered the main face of the Sarenne Glacier. A vast glacier coated in snow opened below them both, its sheer slope leading into the Sarenne Gorge. Ben put a breaking turn in, scuffing his turn and wobbling slightly, a tiny error, costing a couple of seconds. But two seconds at just over 60 mph equated to 30 metres lost. Dan was now a mere 20 metres behind and, with the extra momentum, the gap was closing further still. Turn after breaking turn, Dan's legs were starting to feel it, but he was level with Ben. The pressure was on Ben now. Dan knew it. Did Ben?

Riding serenely, Ben aimed for a kicker, catching it beautifully. Soaking up the upward propulsion, travelling at speed, he didn't touch the slope for more than 15 metres. Dan risked a slight glance across to see Ben nudge ahead. Ben turned as soon as he could after his landing, checking his speed slightly before shooting yet further ahead. As he put his turn into the left, Dan made a right-hander. The brothers were within two metres of each other, the danger of crashing into the other becoming very real. Snow sprayed up in front of Dan from Ben's turn. A momentary loss of vision was instantly replaced with the Sarenne Gorge beneath him. Dan didn't waiver, his full attention given to the bumps and drops under his board. The only sounds came from Idiobro, an occasional whoop, wahey or whoa.

The silence was broken on each turn the brothers made.

They were over halfway now, it was close, but Ben was ahead and making further progress. He had eked out a lead of 80 metres and it was getting dangerously close to 'race over' time, save for a crash.

Dan risked a longer run before his next break turn. The slope was running out, now wasn't the time for taking it easy. The extra speed had the desired effect, quickly eating into Ben's lead, but this came at a cost. The bumps and kickers creating a rougher ride, Dan struggled to hold his line as the extra bounce strained every muscle in his legs. The ice road came into sight as the brothers rounded the neck of the next fold in the slope; just a kilometre below them, but very, very steep. The finish was a killer, so, so steep, breaking turns necessary every 20 metres.

Ben crept ahead; muscular strength just as important as technique now. Dan dug deep, grimacing with the effort. The final technicality of the race quickly approached – a false summit, which was really a sickening drop, running across the centre of the slope. Steady skiers would negotiate it with a couple of turns. On *Ski Sunday*, the pros would be seen taking it head-on, tucking legs to reduce the height gain in return for speed and length of landing. Ben and Dan did likewise, both brothers taking off and landing a healthy 25 metres further down the slope. But landing wasn't the problem. Everyone landed. It was what you did next, and Dan knew it. Ben was neat and tidy, he landed, kept straight until he could get a break turn in, kicking up snow as he did so. With enough speed checked, he straightened his line and ploughed onwards to victory. Dan landed pretty well too but couldn't quite turn as he wanted to. Picking up too much speed, he momentarily caught Ben up before being forced to scuff his break turn – quick in, slow out – the reverse of what was needed. It wasn't much, but the difference was two seconds or 30 metres.

"YEHHHHH," screamed Ben as he crossed the ice road. "FUCKING YESSSSSS," came another scream from him as he checked all his speed, coming to a stop 50 metres lower than the finish.

Dan caught Ben up, spraying him with snow as he stopped.

"Ya bugger, Ben. Ya big, ugly bugger," retorted Dan, but it wasn't with malice, no envy or hatred in his voice. He had lost, lost by a smidge, but lost he had. The two brothers had always had an intense rivalry, they would burst blood vessels to beat each other, but it would only ever finish with congratulations, a 'big hand' and a heap of 'piss-taking'.

"Well done, buddy, well done. I thought I had you too. You almost fell after the rat run and again a bit after," said Dan.

"Yeh, mate, proper close wasn't it! I caught an edge; thought I was toast," grinned Ben, his grin turning into an enormous smirk.

"But I didn't, mate. That's four years now! FOUR YEARS!" exclaimed Ben holding up a four-fingered hand, the glee practically jumping out of him. And before Dan could get the next word in, Ben piped up, "Ya may as well change sports, mate, this one ain't for you."

"Don't bet on it, Benny Boy, just don't bet on it," Dan replied, reverting to his childhood nickname. "You may have won, but you are still I D I O B R O," he continued, spelling out 'Idiobro' to make his point. He added, "You're still the family thickie, a poxy engineer playing *Bob the Builder* with concrete planks all day long."

"Line 1 – Dan is a knob. Line 2 – Go to Line 1; Line 3 – RUN," returned Ben. It was his default barb to 'all things Dan'. Dan called himself an IT consultant, a relatively bland, nondescript title. In truth, Ben had no idea what Dan actually did. To be fair to Ben, the term IT covered a magnitude of roles within the industry and Dan never helped either. He always fudged his explanation. Whenever anyone asked him what he did, the phrase IT consultant got rolled out followed by an explanation consisting of a bit of RAM, a bit of ROM and ending in a joke.

Annoyingly though, Dan was seemingly an expert in his sector whilst having none of the appearance of a computer geek. His not quite perfect face, handsome but ever so slightly rugged, caught the attention of most girls. Dan had the kind of face that could get away with skipping a shave; an ability to jump out of bed without doing his hair also vexed Ben. Then, to make matters worse, he had a honed body. A ripped physique was the training term. The gym, mountain biking, and rugby had all given him a very non-IT physique.

Dan had done a degree in electrical engineering and the way Ben saw it, this meant the two of them were the same. After all, how different could electrical and civil engineering be? They both ended in 'engineering', right?

Dan was 'a man in demand'. He had left university and started work immediately for a large blue-chip IT firm in London. Only two years in, though, and he had been headhunted by a competitor.

It didn't last. Dan had simply been too good. His next two years had seen a multitude of offers and requests for his services. None were successful. He had very quickly recognized that, given his talents, he would be better off becoming a self-employed consultant, picking his work and hence his workload. Choosing who to work for and when. At 31 years young, Dan Fletcher commanded seven-figure earnings and a generous work-life balance. Life couldn't get much better, and if he could finally snare Kate, then life really would turn into perfection.

Dan bent forwards and started to unclip his bindings, as Ben followed suit, mischievous thoughts entered Dan's mind. Ben was seated as he unfastened his bindings. No sooner had Dan freed himself from his board, he sprinted to Ben wielding his board as a makeshift shovel. Digging as much loose snow as he could, Dan did his best to shower his seated brother in a furious snowstorm. Giving up after six or seven of his best shovels, he flung himself on top of Ben, screaming "SUMO TIME", as he crashed on top of his brother.

The pair of them grabbed each other, rolling over several times like a pair of fighting alligators in some weird form of 'snowy death roll'.

"Well done, bud. Well done. Beat me fair and square, buddy," came a breathless and laughing Dan.

"Shit a brick, mate, you been putting on weight?" Ben replied.

"Fuck you, ya cheeky twat," retorted a smiling Dan. "It's all bought and paid for, that's just the extra muscle," he continued.

"Yeh, yeh bro, whatever… Felt flabby to me. Soft and weak, like," teased Ben.

As the piss-taking continued, the brothers, kneeling in the snow, buckled their boards to their rucksacks before hoisting their bags to their shoulders. The sun was setting, another 20 minutes or so till it disappeared behind the distant ridge. They had a 1 km walk back to town along the ice road; this was the price they paid for getting the slope to themselves. The bottom lift had closed for the day.

As they walked down the ice road, the only sounds coming from their crunching steps, Dan's thoughts drifted to the evening to come. To be precise, they drifted to Kate.

Unlike his brother, Dan had got the 'OK' from his sis, meaning Kate wasn't off limits. Dan was a catch, not that Ben wasn't, but he didn't mess girls around and, as such, his sis wasn't anti Dan's interest. It was Rachel herself that had accidentally deliberately shared their mobiles a couple of months back. Since then, a healthy amount of flirting had commenced. The only stumbling block being the fact Kate lived in London and Dan lived in Manchester, but that could change. Dan worked where he wanted to, meeting his clients up and down the country and then mainly from home. His laptop was his office. He was mobile, very mobile, whereas Kate was a junior doctor at University College London Hospital (UCLH) and tied there for at least two more years. He had gleaned that much from Rachel. After that, who knew?

But that was a long way ahead. More pressing matters were just around the corner, tonight, in fact. They were meeting the girls for a meal out followed by a night in Dan's favourite bar, The Underground. It was going to be a fab night, beer, live music and three awesome girls, not forgetting Idiobro.

Along with Kate would be Rachel's other bezzie. Helen was cute, funny and single and didn't he know it. All Ben had done for the last week is bang on and on about Helen this and Helen that. The problem wasn't Helen though, it was Rachel. Dan didn't doubt that Helen would fall for Ben's charms – no, that was almost assured – but Ben's charms needed to work on Rachel too and their sister was a totally different animal. Although four years younger than Dan, Rachel was the boss. Clever and enigmatic, she had taken on the part-time role as the family matriarch until their dad had remarried.

In the Fletcher household, what Rachel said 'went'. Their dad and the three brothers all did as they were told and for the most part it worked out. The occasional conflict would usually be resolved with Rachel taking a more dictatorial stance. No, tonight wasn't going to be a smooth passage for young Benny Boy, thought Dan.

The peace and quiet was suddenly broken by Ben's ringtone. Wearing gloves, he fumbled in his salopettes' pocket before giving up and throwing a glove to the ground, managing to get to his phone before it rang off.

"Hey up, sis," answered Ben.

"Where are you?" quizzed Rachel.

"Top of the scare chair," he replied. "We'll be back in about 15 minutes," he continued.

"Cool. We're just off out now for an 'après'. See you in the O Bar, yeh?" she replied.

"Of course, sis. See ya there. What's she wearing?" asked Ben cheekily. It didn't help his cause, but that was always his problem. He just couldn't resist pushing and it was always a push too much.

"I told you, Ben, keep away. OFF LIMITS!" growled Rachel as she ended the call.

Dan was smiling. He hadn't heard any of his sister's conversation until the last two words uttered, but Rachel hadn't held back. In fact, she had been that loud there had barely been a need for a phone.

"Can you hear me?" teased Dan. "Can you hear me now?" he carried on with his joke.

"Yeh, yeh, yeh… I hear her," Ben replied, although hearing was one thing, listening to his sister was another. "We're meeting them in the O Bar. Sister's orders," he continued.

As they trudged on, the lights from the chalets and bars twinkled against the backdrop of a silhouetted mountain ridge. Pale blue sky mixed with an array of electric-coloured lights made for a classic winter alpine village feel. Dan drifted back into his Kate-filled world.

CHAPTER 9
RACHEL AND KATE

Alpe d'Huez, France
Wednesday 4th January 2017

The three girls could pass for sisters or a girl band trio, slim, attractive and full of energy. They had a zest for life, a vibrancy that came from their passion for working hard and playing harder. Rachel, Helen and Kate had met at university and ever since that first fateful day they had got on like the proverbial 'house on fire'.

Sharing the same student house had gone a long way to firm up their friendship, but similar passions were the cement that had glued them together. All three had played hockey for their school and college before making their university hockey team. That alone had helped forge a strong bond, but there was more, the girls were all runners too. Rachel had represented her county in the 800 m, whilst Kate and Helen were 1500 m runners. Although not quite as good as Rachel, the other two more than held their own.

Uncannily, the girls had all come from a similar home life too, and it was probably this fact more than any other that had really unified them.

From the north of England, Rachel Fletcher came from Leeds. At 5 ft 8 inches and with long, blond hair and deep blue eyes, the slim, athletic junior doctor really turned heads.

Rachel had three brothers and, quite unusually, had been brought up by her father and then, in her early teens, her stepmum too. More often than not, when parents divorced, the mother usually became the prime carer. Not for Rachel, though. She barely knew her biological mother, she was only six when her mother had upped and left – too young to really understand or even notice the breakdown in her mum and dad's relationship. One day Rachel had a mum and a dad, the next it was just Dad. She did have a mum though, and a fabulous one at that.

Rachel and her brothers all called Sarah Fletcher 'Mum' and they meant it. Sarah had met Tom Fletcher through work. Sarah was the head of the Hospital Trust, effectively Tom's boss at work. After a couple of years together, she had moved into a bustling, noisy and energetic family. A year later, Tom and Sarah had married. Life in the Fletcher household continued at a hectic pace and Sarah cemented her position as mum, a fabulous mum. She managed being 'Mum' with style, panache and humour, and humour more than anything else was an essential requirement in the Fletcher clan.

In the early years though, after their mum had left, their dad had been brilliant. A consultant at Leeds General Infirmary, Tom Fletcher had held down a job for seven years whilst single-handedly bringing up four children. As the eldest, Dan had helped of course, but really it had been Rachel, the sensible girl amongst three daft boys that had been their father's go-to assistant. Tom Fletcher called her his '2iC'. Rachel had relished the title and, although four years junior to her eldest sibling, she had really stepped up to the mark.

Age was just a statistic. In the Fletcher hierarchy, Rachel was second behind their father. That was until Sarah had come along. Sarah Fletcher hadn't barged her way into a closed-off family, though; not at all. She had joined a very happy family unit, complementing and adding to it. Demoted to third in command hadn't been a negative in Rachel's eyes. In many ways, she had seen Sarah's introduction as the cavalry arriving to help finish the job she had started.

Kate Harper, tall for a girl at 5 ft 8, was toned and slender. Shimmering light brown skin, shoulder-length black hair with intense jade green eyes, she was utterly striking. From Manchester, her parents were also divorced. Although Kate had lived with her mum rather than her dad, they had a lot in common. Kate was the eldest of her three siblings, which had seen her take more responsibility within the family home too. She was on the same course as Rachel, both graduating at medical school before accepting positions as junior doctors in London, not quite mirroring each other, but close. Kate and Rachel were the best of friends, rarely an argument between them in nine years, but they weren't inseparable. Strong and independent alike, both girls had a blast when they were together, but they didn't feel the need to lean on each other.

Attractive and vivacious, a good career opening ahead of her, life appeared to be perfect for Kate. One thing was missing, though, and that was to have someone to share it with. She had ended a long-term relationship a couple of years ago. She had had a few dates since then but not one of them had led anywhere. This was mainly down to Kate, who hadn't felt the flutter in her stomach for any of the matches.

Recently though, she hadn't been able to stop her thoughts drifting to Rachel's brother Dan. Kate had known Dan for years; they'd initially met in her first year at medical school. As the years had passed, the pair had met many times. Rachel was close to all her brothers and Kate was Rachel's best friend. There had been parties, large group weekends and even two holidays where Dan and Kate had both been there at the same time. But, on each occasion, the timing hadn't been right. The spark was there. It always had been, just little signs over the years, but nothing had ever been spoken – just eyes that shined and smiles reciprocated between the two of them.

First Kate had had a boyfriend whilst Dan was single. Three years into university life and Kate became a single girl just as Dan had entered what became a two-year relationship with a girl called Zoe. Now though, they were both free and very available.

Text flirting had been going on for months now; the chemistry between them was electric. Only work commitments and a messy diary had stopped them from meeting up till now. Excited as she was about a ski trip with her best friends, the cherry on the cake was the fact Dan had called to say he and Ben were going to join them for the second half of the week. Kate's state of happiness was off the scale and tonight was the night, she just knew it. Rachel and Helen knew it too.

Weekly updates made their way directly to her two best friends – what Dan said, what Dan intonated, what Dan was doing. From Rachel's point of view, she was both elated and nervous that her eldest brother and best friend might finally be getting together. Excited because Dan was a catch and Kate was sassy, they would make the perfect couple. Nervous because what if they split up?

Helen though was just excited. Helen Waters had less to lose should a split ever occur. She knew and was friends with Dan, but her loyalties were for Kate alone, unlike Rachel's divided feelings. Blond, slender and just an inch shorter than both Rachel and Kate, Helen was utterly stunning. She radiated beauty as did her two best friends, yet Helen had a little extra.

Where Rachel and Kate had cornered the girl-next-door market, Helen exuded sexuality. Whilst her friends favoured no make-up, Helen would wear provocative, red lipstick highlighting fabulous lips and striking cheekbones. Helen knew men found her tantalising and she liked it. She loved it.

Books shouldn't always be judged by their cover, though. Helen was a prime example of this. Outwardly, she came across as a carefree, risk-taking, provocative young lady. For the most part this was true, but Helen's true friends recognized a more fragile, delicate person, someone wanting to love and be loved. The playful and sexually provocative Helen was really a girl trying to find a pain-free route through life, her mischievous and impish mannerisms merely a defence mechanism.

Ben didn't see this side to Helen. All he saw was a cheeky glint in her eyes, a naughty and seducing smile and a very sexy and very single friend of his sister's. Helen was off limits to Ben; this had been spelled out in clear and very definitive terms by Rachel. The problem with this was that the more his sister told Ben that he couldn't go near Helen, the more he wanted to.

Rachel had just ended her call with her brother. Kate and Helen had both sat listening to the conversation, doing their utmost to work out the other half. They had known immediately that it was

Ben not Dan she had been speaking to. Just her tone gave that away but was confirmed as she finished the call "I told you, Ben, keep away. OFF LIMITS!" said in a loud and commanding voice.

Helen grinned to herself; she knew the call had been about her. Ben was cute and she quite liked him. Kate had a thing for Dan, so Helen thought, why not with the other brother? Rachel hadn't said much, her quietness about Ben had been telling though. Where Rachel effused over Dan, almost championing him to Kate, there was a silence, almost a vacuum when it came to Ben. Helen wasn't stupid, mind. She knew he was happy-go-lucky, always the one taking the easier, less serious route through life.

But what was wrong with that? Where was the harm? Plus, he was a total hunk; charming, great-looking, smart and articulate with a good job and better prospects. He couldn't be as bad as her last boyfriend. As Helen drifted through thought after thought, she quickly concluded that Ben probably couldn't be as bad as her last three boyfriends combined.

Kate interrupted her thoughts though. "He likes you, he likes you..." came the initial tease.

Rachel glowered at Kate, nothing spoken but the frown was saying loud and clear 'STOP'. She didn't want any encouragement from Kate, or anyone for that matter, about Ben and his current obsession with Helen.

Helen tried to suppress a smile, but the more Rachel glowered at Kate, the more the pair of them struggled to quell their fun-loving side. Erupting in giggles, both Helen and Kate alike had tears in their eyes.

"Come on, Rach, he's nice. He's your bro..." responded Helen, in part a vocalized response to Rachel's frown, but also as a statement of intent too, indicating a possible reciprocation to Ben's advances.

"He's not right for you 'H'... He's a clown..." replied Rachel. And with no chance for a reply, she carried on. "He'll hurt you, he won't mean to, but he will. He's a clown. Life's a laugh in Ben's world," said with the sternest face she could muster; the impact couldn't have been less effective had she been talking Swahili. Helen and Kate fell about laughing.

"You're NOT helping, Kate!" boomed Rachel, this time though her face finally cracked. Twinkling eyes and a broad grin replaced her previously growling features.

"OK, OK you win…" giggled Rachel between breaths. "Do what you want. Don't say I didn't warn you," she advised. The girls' laughter continued unabated.

"Are we off then?" Helen asked, clearly excited by what the evening had to offer.

"Fletcher dating service ready," joked Rachel, referring to the fact that her two best friends were both going out with designs on her brothers.

The three girls stood to leave. An early winter evening in Alpe d'Huez, the night was crystal clear but icy-cold. Putting their ski jackets on, the three of them looked like the Italian flag as they walked up the street arms linked, Helen and Rachel's long blond hair flowing over their green and red coats respectively. Kate wearing a pure white coat had her black hair concealed under a matching white beanie. The girls were dressed to kill.

Giggling and laughing as they made their way through the town, carefree and happy, the bar beckoned.

Standing in the shadows, the killer tracked the girls' movements as they made their way down the main high street. Wearing a black ski jacket and beanie, Bush melted into his surroundings. Nondescript was the required look and he had managed this to perfection. He looked like just another holidaymaker looking for some après-ski action.

But the action he was intent on was anything but après-ski. The sun had well and truly disappeared now behind the distant ridge line. Of the three girls Bush had been tracking, it was still easy to identify his target. Wearing the same coats from earlier in the day, Rachel's blond hair and vivid red coat were easy 'key identifiers' (KIs). Identifying her friends was easy too. Blond-Green coat was Helen Waters and Brown-White coat was Kate Harper. He kept 'eyes on'.

The girls were closing on him as they strolled up the other side of the street. As they neared to within 30 metres, he turned away from them, pretending to window-shop. With a variety of different-sized stuffed toys, mainly marmots, the shop was a classic alpine tourist gift emporium. In the reflection, Bush monitored the girls as they walked by.

As they passed him, he slowly and casually turned around, staring in the direction they walked.

"Got visual," he whispered, his throat mike picking up his comms clearly.

"Roger that," replied Harry.

"They're entering a bar," he returned as he tracked the girl's entry into the bar about 80 metres up the Route d'Huez from where he was standing.

"Keep visual, we wait," came Harry's curt response.

"Roger that," and as he signed off, he started a walk-by of the street and bar. As he passed the bar, he stole a glance through the windows. Full of skiers enjoying the après, the bar was already three quarters full.

Two of the girls had managed to squeeze on to the end of a table, already attracting the attention of some 'would-be suitors'. A couple of fresh-faced ski bum types were seated at the same table each clutching a Corona. White coat was stood at the bar getting served. Bush continued walking, navigating past the bar entrance, a mass of skis and boards sticking out of the heaped snow. Didn't the Alps have thieves he thought to himself as he carried on walking? Once he had made a safe distance beyond the bar, he checked himself, finding another store to continue his window-shopping. Appearances were everything, even in a bustling ski resort where the people were pretty much all new to the place.

A lone man wandering aimlessly amongst thousands of others doing similarly was the perfect cover. Bush blended in perfectly. Rarely had he been given an easier assignment. All he needed now was the green light from Harry.

Kate returned from the bar carrying three Desperados, a healthy glow to her face in part from the warmth of the bar but also the after-effects of the last few days skiing.

"Despes girls," said Kate as she stood over the seated Rachel and Helen. She placed the drinks on the table and, like her friends, she doffed her coat, hanging it on the back of her chair.

"Cheers chicas," toasted Kate as she raised her beer, clinking it against her friends'. In unison, Rachel and Helen chorused the word 'chicas', smiles all around.

Ever since their first holiday together, a summer break to Mallorca, the three girls had adopted use of the word 'chica', Spanish for 'girl'. No matter where they were in the world, when the three of them were together they were the 'chicas'. And tonight, the three chicas were going to have a great night. A night to remember thought Kate. It would be a night to remember, but for very different reasons.

Bush had relocated himself to a darkened doorway with a good line of sight to the bar. He just stood waiting. He was good at waiting. The ability to watch and observe whilst drifting into his own thoughts had always come easy to him. Standing in the shadows, the only drawback was the cold. Six o'clock in the middle of winter, high in the French Alps, the temperature was well below zero. He reckoned it was already minus eight and it would plummet further as the night drew on.

One quick drink and on to the next bar was what he hoped was the girls' plan. Then all he needed was the 'go-ahead' from Harry. He didn't know why Rachel Fletcher was his 'mark' and he didn't really care. Henkl had sent Bush and Harry on the job and that was that. What he did know, though, was that this evening's merriments were about to be Rachel Fletcher's last.

Almost an hour later and the girls were just finishing their second beer.

"My round," said Helen, not so much a question as a statement of intent, standing to make for the bar. Helen negotiated her way through the throng of people all similarly clad in ski salopettes and jackets, most of the bargoers having come straight off the slopes and into the bars of Alpe d'Huez. Five minutes later and she was back at the table clutching three more Desperados.

"CHEERS chicas," boomed Helen over the noise and hubbub coming from the rest of the bar.

"CHICAS," chorused Rachel and Kate, clinking bottles as they spoke.

"What're we toasting?" asked a smiling Kate.

"You know," responded Rachel, an enormous grin appearing ever so slowly across her face.

"Dan, Dan, you wan him ta be your man," mispronounced Helen in an attempt to make a rhyme. The girls all burst out laughing at Helen's cheap poem.

"Anyways… check you out in your red lippy," Kate replied looking directly at Helen. "We know your game, Ms. Waters, we know…" she continued. "Red means danger…" leaving a slight pause for dramatic effect, "so is Ben in danger?" grinned Kate.

Rachel smiling as she listened to the banter, pondered whether to join in or keep her council. It was tricky; she hadn't changed her opinion one bit. Ben would hurt her best mate, of that she was certain. But it seemed that Helen was intent on some fun with her 'other brother' and she had warned her, so what more could she do?

"Well, if red means danger, then I guess I'm having your jacket chica," smirked Helen, playfully yanking Rachel's red coat from the back of her chair. "Red lips, red coat…" she stated, "…means my night… my night…" repeating her words for effect.

Helen jumped to her feet and put the jacket on before Rachel could stop her. It was hers now, possession being nine tenths of the law considered Helen.

Rachel and Kate sat laughing whilst Helen started fishing through Rachel's pockets. Piling the contents on the table, she placed a Lypsyl, a red and black buff and a crumpled piste map on the table.

"Vanilla Lypsyl… don't think so," came Helen's running commentary, "cherry all the way…" she continued.

The girls continued the banter, the alcohol was kicking in nicely now. They weren't drunk, they were just in that happy, 'merry' stage where everything felt warm and fluffy. The world was a good place.

"Time chicas," voiced Kate as she took a final swig of her beer. She stood and started to dress for the short walk to the O Bar; food and Dan awaited. With coat and beanie on, Kate made her way to the exit, standing just outside amongst the hotchpotch of skis protruding from the snow.

"Someone's keen," smiled Helen noting the rapidness of Kate's exit.

"It's Dan, H, she really likes him… she really does," Rachel replied as she stood putting on Helen's jacket. It wasn't a bad fit either. Helen made for the exit whilst Rachel was a little slower as she turned her attention to zipping up her coat.

Bush perked up as soon as he saw Kate standing outside. White coat, brown hair gave up her identity easily, a halo of light surrounded her profile, the glow of the bar lights serving as a neat and stylish backdrop.

"We've got movement," he said breaking comms silence to give Harry an update.

"Roger that," Harry responded.

Thirty seconds later and red coat, followed by green coat, exited the bar too.

"They're leaving now… Am I good?" he asked over comms.

He hated having to ask permission from Harry. Harry was a tosser and he should be leading the job. They were all tossers pondered Bush; Xav, Henkl, Zebra and especially Harry. Still, the money was good. The money was very good. Prior to landing the job with Henkl, he had been earning 100k per annum plus expenses. Far better than his days in the Paras, but he was on triple that now, his expenses alone added to more than his previous salary. Why would he leave?

"Green light. Repeat, green light," replied Harry.

Coming out of the shadows, Bush started towards the direction of the girls – not slow, not quick. Red coat was in the middle, arms linked in a chain with her two friends. All three girls had their hands back in their coat pockets such was the bitterness of the night. The girls started down the street before turning left into a ginnel. He followed, slowly but surely closing the gap. The ginnel led to a set of steep steps that descended to a lower-tiered section of the town. A single street light, acting like a sentry, stood at the top of the ginnel where it joined the street, the only other light coming from the clear night sky. Perfect he thought. No need to roll his balaclava down, looking up the ginnel would only show a human outline. Bush could have smiled as he considered the irony of not using his ski balaclava in a ski resort. He could have, but he didn't.

He adjusted his pacing, getting his timing right to catch the girls as they went beyond the first of three horizontal paths that crossed the ginnel creating a grid-like effect serving the access needs of the chalets and other buildings. The dark and gloomy alleys shimmered underfoot, the moonlight bouncing off the snow.

As he got to within 10 metres of the girls he drew his gun, with suppressor attached his silhouette created a frightening image as his dark form emerged from the shadows. Could a black-clad man in a dark alley be more sinister? Suddenly aware of the proximity of the killer in their midst, the girls looked over their shoulders, but it was too late – much too late.

Their meaningless chit-chat and the sounds of snow crunching underfoot stopped immediately. The momentary silence was instantaneously interrupted, initially by the double *psst, psst* of two high-velocity bullets travelling eight metres from gun barrel to human and then by the screams.

The two deathly projectiles hit Helen Waters in the centre of her upper back. Being in the middle, she had been the only girl to have not turned around. The second bullet was the one that killed her, penetrating her heart before tearing a large exit hole out through her chest. The bullet continued its deadly flight, finally coming to a stop embedded in a wooden railing lower down the alleyway.

Helen fell to the floor. With arms still linked, the other girls fell with her. Kate, to her left, landed in the snow and ice with only her left arm free to break her fall. She was lucky too; the recent heavy snowfalls had supplied a healthy snow berm that railed the ginnel from top to bottom.

Rachel, with her left arm linked to her dying friend's right, was dragged left and forwards down the ginnel's path. Landing half on top of Helen, she hit the hard, ice-packed ground with a thud, instinct and adrenaline causing Rachel to move towards her friend, no thought process just an involuntary action.

Bush tracked the girl's fall and then, not slow, not quick, he adjusted his aim, firing two more shots both to the head, Helen's prone and motionless body making an easy target. The second bullet, though, hit Rachel in her left shoulder as she struggled to disentangle herself, before finally burying itself in Helen's skull.

He wheeled around 90 degrees to his right and took off along the horizontal pathway. Leaving the screaming girls in his wake, he ran as quickly as was safe to on the dimly lit, icy surface. One hundred metres further on and the path joined another of Alpe d'Huez's side streets.

It was well lit and contained several people walking in both directions. Bush didn't panic though – or run. This was where his training kicked in and this was why he trained. Turning left, he simply started his long walk down the street to where it joined the main road that twisted and turned though the old quarter. Talking quietly to himself, his running commentary came through loud and clear to the waiting Harry.

"Boxed off," whispered Bush.

"Roger that. Your location?" Harry replied.

"Underpass above the tourist info," came Bush again as he continued walking in that direction – not quick, not slow.

"Roger that. Any problems?" Harry quizzed.

"BOXED OFF," Bush responded again, said as loud as he could given his situation. The friction in his two words was clear, though, very clear. He didn't like being questioned; he saw it as an insult or criticism. In his eyes, the job was done and there was no need to analyse it or go through it. Job done, move on and that was all that was needed.

But Harry saw it differently and, ultimately, that was the difference between the two men. 'Fish' was arrogant, he believed he was the best, in fact, he knew he was the best and that was his weakness. Harry had passed selection, and Fish hadn't, and there was a reason for that.

Having failed selection, Fish had rewritten his own history. His sorry tale was one full of excuses, shifting the blame on to others. An inability to listen and take instructions was why Fish had failed. It wasn't a trait that always came to the fore, but it was there, nonetheless. And selection to the SAS was gruelling, maybe the hardest thing on the planet to pass. Eventually the assessors 'found you out'; they stripped your personality back to the bare bones, layer by layer.

No one could stop them; it wasn't even the point of selection to try and stop them. The selection panel wanted to see each and every layer that made up the men they had running around the Brecon Beacons. And if they wanted to see those layers, they would. Fish though had tried to fight it, but that was a fight no man could win. Getting 'stood down' from the process had had an adverse effect on Fish. Rather than listen to the feedback, he buried his head in the sand, choosing to disagree with their feedback just because he didn't like the critiques presented to him.

Now years later, and Harry was spending much more time than he cared for working with Fish. Fish, the utter twat, pondered Harry. A total wanker and yet most of the work he did was spent with this knobhead. His boss, Henkl, had just recently consulted him about two new members joining the Apfel. Harry had spent the weekend scouring through every detail of the two possible new recruits. In the line of work he was in you didn't get a two-page CV with a covering letter applying for the position.

Harry had a 20-page dossier on each man containing a warts-and-all profile from childhood to professional career to present day. He was a studious man who relished the detail and was Henkl's go-to aide for sifting through crap like 'new recruit' dossiers. This task had put a larger grin on his face though. An extra two men would mean an extra team. The maths was simple, Henkl knew it and so did Harry. One of the existing teams would be split to create an additional team leader and this represented a great opportunity to get a new partner. Fish could fuck off thought Harry.

"Pick up at the underpass," Harry replied.

"Roger that," as Bush continued walking down the Route d'Huez.

Back in the alleyway, Bush had left a scene of devastation, a world suddenly shattered, destroyed even. Clad in Rachel Fletcher's red ski coat, Helen Waters was lying face down in the snow and ice.

She would never know, never understand why she was dead. Killed by a shot to the heart, the additional three shots were the telling facts. Any good investigator knew this was a professional hit.

The blood was pooling on the ground underneath Helen's head and chest, looking more like a black oil slick in the low lighting. A few people were grouped around Kate whilst two bystanders were helping to staunch the bleeding in Rachel's shoulder. Within five minutes, a local gendarme arrived and started to create a sense of order.

For Rachel and Kate, their sense of order might never return though. A truly happy holiday had, in the blink of an eye, been turned into a living hell. Tear-stained eyes and dishevelled hair didn't tell the full story. Whilst Rachel was being tended to, Kate had managed to call Dan. It had been a terrible call, full of tears, swamped in pain. At one point, the call was interrupted due to Kate's crying, but she had stoically carried on.

'They're taking us to Grenoble' had been the central message. 'Helen's dead' and 'they're going to the hospital' had pretty much been the only detail Dan had gathered from the distraught Kate.

Bush climbed into the black Audi A3 parked just short of the underpass. Harry pulled out and started their route past the tourist information and the last of the chalets that formed Alpe d'Huez.

"Well?" came his one-word request for a full report.

"The girl's dead, no collateral," replied the mistaken Bush, unaware that his final headshot had first passed through Rachel's shoulder en route to the wrong target's head.

"Certain?" quizzed Harry, who knew that if Bush said the girl was dead then that meant she was dead. Fish didn't miss from 10 metres, he might be a twat but he was an expert marksman, a deadly agent of death.

"Good job," continued Harry, it would have been churlish not to congratulate Bush. There was an upside to his positivity though and it was what motivated him to say nice things to Bush even though it was a personal struggle to do so. Bush hated feedback, even good feedback, and Bush particularly hated feedback from Harry or Henkl. Every 'good job' comment reminded him who was boss, and he hated that. He thought he was better than Henkl and

Harry alike, in fact, he knew he was better. Every reminder as to who was in charge was a slap to his face.

Harry was an expert human psychologist; in his line of work you had to be. Pushing Bush's buttons at every opportunity was his own little perk of the job, sort of like his reward for having to work with 'Fish' the knob-twat-tosser. Harry grinned wryly to himself as he weighed up his personal thoughts on Bush.

In silence, Harry drove on, making his way down the famous 21 hairpins. He didn't cycle but he had seen fleeting glimpses of the Tour de France over the years, and he had heard of the 'mythical ascent' prior to arriving in Alpe d'Huez. Every hairpin bend was numbered with a large sign containing cyclists' names and the altitude. The road snaked down and down, the town of Le Bourg d'Oisans could be seen in the valley far below, its lights twinkling against the inky dark backdrop of the valley floor.

In the distance, the electric blue lights of an ambulance could be seen flashing frenetically as it made its way up the pins. A minute later and it whooshed past them, no sirens just its lights on. Five minutes later and Harry was almost at the bottom, another ambulance and two gendarmes had since flashed past too.

Once on the valley floor, the road opened up. He gunned the Audi, speeding up to 80 kmph, within the speed limit though – never quick, never slow.

Harry called in, his mobile on speakerphone as its shrill tones came through the car's sound system. On the fourth ringtone the phone picked up.

"Is it done?" Henkl asked.

"Yes, Boss," Harry replied as he glimpsed the side of Bush's face as he said the word 'boss'. *Tosser*, he thought to himself. Henkl was the boss, respect and the chain of command dictated you called the boss 'Boss'.

Henkl interrupted his thoughts. "Come back to Geneva now," and with that he ended the call.

"He's a boss, Fish, and you'll always be a tosser," Harry blurted as soon as the call was finished. The stupid little smirk had got the better of him.

"Fuck you," retorted Bush, angry at being called 'Fish'. Bush, as always, struggled not to react. It was Harry's personal button and no matter how much Bush got under his skin, Harry always had his 'get out of jail free' card. Just calling Bush 'Fish' was enough.

"You'll never get it, Fish… ya just don't get it," replied Harry.

"Fuck you," came Bush again.

Harry didn't reply and silence resumed as the car sped towards Geneva.

CHAPTER 10
HOSPITAL INTERPOL

Grenoble Hospital, France
8 p.m. Wednesday 4th January 2017

Dan's phone started ringing. Vibrations in his pocket initially grabbed his attention. He was stood waiting for his brother who was currently spraying himself in every flavour of aftershave he owned. Ben was clearly taking tonight very seriously indeed.

Fumbling in his pocket, he retrieved his phone and took the call. A distraught Kate had immediately started half crying, half waffling through a devastating and mind-numbing story. Disjointed and confusing, she had seemed to relay something that couldn't possibly be true. Could it?

Between the tears and a great deal of fright, Kate seemed to be telling him that Helen was dead, and Rachel was on her way to hospital having been shot in the shoulder.

What? Was this right? No one would make a joke like that. No one could even or would even begin to know how to make such a joke.

Amidst the immediate shock of hearing her news, Dan had felt a certain amount of guilt. His first thought had been about Rachel's shoulder and Kate's well-being before actually weighing up the fact that Helen was dead. Shit, how was he going to tell Ben? Currently trying to make himself smell nice for Helen, his brother was going to take the news hard.

Dan burst into the bathroom, but before he could utter a word, Ben knew something was wrong. It wasn't the lack of a knock or the door getting barged open, the look on Dan's face told a frightening story.

"What's up?" Ben asked.

Dan's sombre story unfolded, his usual smiling eyes filled with angst, smile lines replaced with a taut and grimacing jawline.

"It's Helen, bud, she's dead! Helen's dead!" blurted Dan, unsure of himself and how to say it. He hadn't had training in how to tell someone about a death. He had never done it before. He was in new territory and, with no time for rehearsals, he had just burst into his brother's bathroom and uttered the worst news imaginable.

"Helen's dead and Rach has been shot," Dan carried on.

"What?" Ben replied. "What… What…? …What d'ya mean?" Ben wittered on, struggling to comprehend. He knew this was no joke, he knew. But the news still didn't add up, didn't make sense, couldn't even be possible or true, even though Dan wouldn't be wrong.

But Dan must be wrong thought Ben, he must. Shot? How, why? This couldn't be right, they were in the Alps on a ski holiday, this wasn't the movies, this wasn't war-torn Africa. What was his brother on about?

"We've got to go… now. NOW. NOW, BEN, NOW," boomed Dan, speaking louder in part to spur on his very shocked brother, but it was just as much a self-motivating prompt to get himself shifting.

"Grenoble Hospital, we need to go right now… Grab your coat… Come on," Dan continued as he placed both hands on his brother's shoulders, squeezing them tightly, half as a prompt to move but equally as a reassurance. They were together, this was his brother, and they were united.

Dan wheeled around and exited the bathroom with Ben in tow. Within a minute, the pair were in the car, navigating the twists and turns of the descent down the mountain.

As soon as they hit the open road, Dan called Kate back, the in-car speakerphone helping to keep the call more informative and a little less emotional. But her voice had still wavered, both brothers could feel the strain in her words as she told them where they needed to go.

Kate was currently sitting alone in a small examination room off a long corridor in the casualty ward. Rachel was next door in a similar cubicle with a nurse and a doctor attending to her shoulder.

The gendarmes had taken a statement from both girls and then explained that their superiors would be back shortly to go through a few more details. Kate was a mess, dishevelled hair and bloodshot eyes that were now dry of tears. Could you run out of tears she wondered.

Her clothing was bloodstained, and she was unsure whether it was Rachel or Helen's blood. Did it matter?

Having ridden in the ambulance with Rachel, she had been amazed by how calm Rachel had been in comparison with herself. After all, it was Rachel who had been shot not her. Yes, they were both grieving the loss of their best friend, but add Rachel's gunshot wound too and the pain that came with it and it ought to be Rachel in the biggest mess. But she wasn't, she was a rock, dishing out instructions like a normal day at work, 'Call Dan and tell him where we are', then 'Tell Dan to call Mum and Dad', 'Don't call Helen's parents until we know a bit more of the facts'. Rachel really had been a rock.

As soon as they ended the call to Kate, the brothers rang home. Mum and Dad were just about to have their evening ruined.

After what seemed like seven very quick ringtones, their dad picked up. It was a Wednesday evening and the lads both knew what their dad would be up to. He would almost certainly be sitting in their local pub with friends waiting for the pub quiz to kick into life. Tom and Sarah Fletcher made it most Wednesdays, only ever missing it for the odd work commitment and holidays. If any of the kids were ever at the Fletcher family home, then they would be roped into the quiz team too.

"I thought you'd be too busy to call your old man," answered Tom; the line wasn't very clear, the background noise confirming his location.

"You're on speaker, Dad, I'm with Ben," instructed Dan, as he continued, Ben broke into the conversation, "Hi Dad."

"Something bad's happened, Dad," Dan replied, the conversation lacking clarity due to the noisy pub, their car speaker system and the three-way chatter.

Giving his dad no time to respond, he carried on. "It's Rach, she's been shot. She's alright, but she's been shot, Dad!" Dan hadn't got any better at delivering his message, he just couldn't see any other way though. "We're on our way to the hospital right now. She's in Grenoble," he carried on, the silence on the end of the line was telling.

"What? What did you say?" Tom replied. Maybe it was the noisy pub or the startling news, but Tom wasn't quite sure what he was hearing.

"She's been shot, Dad, in the shoulder... And it gets worse, Dad... Helen's dead," Dan replied.

"WHAT?" came Tom's raised voice, now very clearly hearing Dan's words. The background noise had started to disappear; Dan assumed his dad was moving somewhere quieter as the gravity of the news made its full impact.

"Helen's dead, Dad. We don't know what's happened, but she's dead. Shot. Shot dead," repeated Dan. His news was shocking and was taking some time to sink in.

"Have you spoken to her?" asked Tom.

"Not yet, Dad, we're on our way now... We'll be there in 40 minutes... Tell Mum, Dad, we'll call you as soon as we know more... She's alright, though... she's alright," replied Dan.

"I'll call you back, let me tell your mother," and with that Tom Fletcher hung up.

The two brothers looked across at each other as they raced towards Grenoble. Dan had a soul-searching look in his eyes, whilst Ben, seemingly lost for words, was still trying to compute what was occurring.

"You alright, bro?" Dan asked. It was a stupid question, he knew, unplanned and lacking thought it had just come out, almost involuntarily. He wasn't trained for this, who could be? He had seen the shock still glued to his brother's face and felt compelled to say something.

"Sorry, mate… this is fucked, bro… it's fucked. It makes no sense!" Dan carried on, maybe to fill the silence he wondered. "Say something, mate, talk to me," he carried on as Ben sat staring straight ahead.

"I don't know what… I don't get it… This is mad…" uttered Ben more rambling than coherent thoughts, but speaking, nonetheless.

Thousands of thoughts swirled through Dan's mind; nothing made sense, though – nothing. His sister had been shot and her best friend was dead. Terrorists in a ski resort? What else could it be? Dan's cortex was racing through thought after thought, but nothing was logical. Nothing computed. The satnav said 35 minutes to Grenoble Hospital, he was driving as fast as he dared, switching his focus to driving faster might help he thought. Accelerating slightly, he put his energies into getting to the hospital quicker, which wasn't lost on his brother. Ben had glanced over, peeking at the odometer it read 130 kmph which was as quick as the car could handle on these roads.

Rachel had been very fortunate, the examination had revealed a small entry wound, but more importantly, an exit wound. Albeit larger and messier, the exit wound was still relatively superficial. The bullet had missed all bones and ligaments. A flurry of activity had followed Rachel's X-ray, morphine via a cannula into her good arm followed by a thorough cleaning of the wound and stitches.

Kate had joined Rachel, sitting by her hospital bed, the girls silent in their own thoughts. Kate had called Dan, briefing him on the news so far. All she had really known was the room and ward Rachel was to be kept in overnight and that they were yet to be interviewed by Interpol. Time seemed to be moving slowly.

The silence was suddenly disturbed as the door to Rachel's room opened. A nurse led the way tailed by a rotund, grey-haired man with a younger lady in tow. The bespectacled man looked in charge, his demeanour and the way he walked gave off an aura.

The nurse presented the man to the girls in clumsy English, her words, though technically correct, were a little out of context.

"Here the girls are," stated the nurse, gesturing with her right hand in the direction of Kate and Rachel. Before the nurse got an opportunity to say anything, Monsieur Louis Blanc dismissed the nurse in French before turning his attention to the girls.

"My name is Monsieur Blanc from Interpol," voiced Louis Blanc introducing himself to both Kate and Rachel. His English was excellent, slightly accented but perfect, nonetheless, "...and this is my colleague Mademoiselle Barruol," he continued as he nodded his head towards the diminutive lady stood to his left. Greta Barruol at 5 ft 5 wasn't short, but stood next to Louis Blanc it appeared that way. Towering over his colleague, Louis Blanc was well above 6 ft and at least four stone overweight. Lead investigator with Interpol for the last 20 years, Blanc looked like he hadn't seen a gym in years, choosing red meat and wine before a run round the park hadn't helped.

"...And you are Kate Harper... is that right?" Blanc continued as he looked Kate in the eyes. Greta Barruol remaining silent looked towards Kate too.

"Yes," came her single-worded response.

"And you are Helen Waters..." said Blanc, more a statement than a question as he turned towards Rachel.

Rachel was sat up in her bed sporting a hospital gown with her shoulder and upper arm dressed in bandages.

"What...? No, I'm Rachel... Rachel Fletcher," she replied almost startled by Blanc's question. "She's dead... Helen's dead... He killed her," she carried on. The mere statement seemed to upset both the girls; tears had already started to well in Kate's eyes.

"Désolé, désolé... My apologies. Sorry, I meant Rachel... Please, accept my apologies," Blanc started in French before reverting to English. His gaffe causing consternation; Blanc embarrassed a little.

Greta Barruol looked on, her eyes silently resonated the same apology on behalf of her boss.

"Helen Waters, your friend, was killed, you have been shot in the shoulder," stated Blanc, recovering from his mistake as he continued his dialogue with Rachel. The two girls, visibly upset, still in shock, didn't notice a thing. To them his gaffe seemed like a tiny 'faux pas', just a simple mistake people make every day. Greta Barruol wasn't in shock though. Greta was Blanc's lead detective, his underling with eight years' time served working alongside Blanc. She knew Blanc, knew his mannerisms, the way he carried himself, how he thought and how he behaved.

Blanc had been surprised by his own error; a bit startled even. It could have been embarrassment, but it felt different to Greta, more like a discovery than a mistake. Whatever it was, it was a little strange, weird even. Her train of thought was broken though by the 'here and now', as Blanc continued his questioning of Rachel and Kate.

The girls in turn collectively filled Blanc in with as much information and detail as they could, but it hadn't been much, ambushed in a quiet, dark alley in the early evening in Alpe d'Huez by a man in dark clothes. It had all happened devastatingly quickly. One minute the girls were amid a perfect ski holiday and the next their lives had been shattered by death, destruction and mayhem. It was mind-boggling, it didn't make sense, and the two surviving girls were totally and utterly confused.

As the interview started to conclude, the door to Rachel's room opened again. Dan and Ben rushed in almost knocking into the two members of Interpol, Ben, half apologizing to them both as he went straight to Rachel, whilst Dan almost crushed Kate to death with the biggest bear hug he could muster.

"How're you, Rach?" Ben asked as he knelt on the floor. At first not wanting to touch her, he rested his right arm on her bed before stroking her hair with his left hand.

Rachel, having just about managed to keep the tears at bay for the duration of her interview, broke down. Her eyes closed to try and stem the flow, but it didn't help. She quietly sobbed as her body shook ever so slightly.

"She's dead, Ben… she's dead…" her voice wavering so much her words were difficult to decipher.

Almost two minutes passed with nothing said. Ben held Rachel as gently as he could whilst Kate stood crying in Dan's arms.

"Ahem… excuse me…" A slight but voluntary cough broke the near silence as Blanc, having stood observing the reunion, brought the interview back on track. "…I am Monsieur Blanc, chief inspector at Interpol," he said as he extended his hand towards Dan, "…and you are?" he quizzed as he looked at Dan directly, his eyes unflinching.

Blanc was a natural reader of people and had honed his skill during his 30 years as a detective. Initially a gendarme working in Marseille, he gained promotion to the Special Investigations team ahead of moving to Paris. After 10 years as a detective he switched to Interpol, his kids had grown up and, although still married, the passion and interest between him and his wife had vanished. Interpol had offered Blanc the chance to work in Belgium, Sweden, Germany and many other parts of Europe. Where some viewed working away from home as a chore, Blanc saw it as a mini adventure, almost a paid holiday.

"Dan… I'm Dan, Rachel's brother," he replied as he broke apart from Kate. He took in the portly figure of Chief Inspector Blanc before averting his attention to Greta, giving her a polite nod of his head. Blanc clearly commanded the room, but it had seemed only right to acknowledge in some way the other person in what was now a crowded space.

"And your friend, Monsieur Fletcher?" enquired Blanc, motioning with his eyes towards Ben.

"This is our brother Ben," interjected Dan before either Rachel or Ben could say anything. Dan's answer seemed to catch Blanc off guard a little, not that the brothers noticed, but Greta did, a small puff of the cheek and an ever so slight twitch of the eyebrow were the only 'tells', but nonetheless a couple of subtle signs that Greta took in. The motionless Greta silently observed a scene being played out, not quite understanding what she was missing. Yet she was clearly missing something, Blanc was her superior; maybe a 'need-to-know' was occurring. Now wasn't the time but later she would push Blanc on this, after all, how could she really solve a case if she was missing some of the facts?

Blanc continued his questioning of Dan and Ben and, having established they weren't witnesses and with no idea what had happened in the town, he concluded his interview. Blanc made his excuses and left, leaving Greta Barruol to deal with the official pleasantries, contact details and a promise of a follow-up as soon as they knew anything. Barruol had never come across as the most empathetic human being and she wasn't winning any awards right now either, but she was diligent and methodical, and she always ensured that the correct protocols were carried out.

Blanc hastily used the five minutes it took Greta to conclude her pleasantries to report in, but the HQ Blanc was calling wasn't Interpol's. He exited the main hospital atrium and entered the cavernous stairwell to the upper levels of Grenoble Hospital. The stairwell was gloomy and gave the impression it was rarely utilized which, given the fact the hospital had six lifts and a service lift, probably wasn't too far from the truth. Blanc looked up to check for people, but it was clear. Retrieving his mobile, he put his call through, the line answered before the third tone was completed.

"Yes?" came the clipped response from Xav Picamole who sounded slightly irritated. Xav, so often glued to his phone, was usually quite even mannered, almost tolerant of others, yet Blanc, in his haste to make his call, had missed the initial signs.

"We have a problem…" Blanc started, pausing slightly before continuing, "…she's not dead… The girl isn't dead!" reiterated the Interpol man.

"What…? Are you certain?" Xav replied tersely. This wasn't what he had been expecting to hear and it wasn't improving his mood.

Blanc jumped in and began to explain the facts as he knew them. In essence, the wrong girl was dead and the news that, although injured, one very alive Rachel Fletcher sitting up and looking quite perky didn't go down at all well.

"Who is this dead girl then?" interrogated Xav, having processed the news. Although caught off guard, he wasn't the sort of person to remain on the back foot for long. Xav Picamole would establish the facts, redefine a plan and move quickly to implement it. This would certainly involve some 'blowing off of steam', but that wasn't a problem for him. Never one to shy away from conflict, he was already working through the tongue-lashing he would be dishing out.

"The girl is called Helen Waters, a friend of the Fletcher girl…" Blanc replied and there was more, giving Xav no opportunity to respond, "…Two of the brothers are in the hospital too."

"What are you talking about…? They are in Manchester! Henkl is there now, he has eyes on!" he barked, the frustration building in his voice by the second.

"No, Xav, you're wrong… They're here… I've seen them… spoken to them…" interrupted Blanc. The conversation was going from bad to worse. Blanc was feeling clammy whereas Xav's usually cool, calculating exterior was beginning to boil over into a seething pile of molten lava.

"One hundred per cent… you are 100% sure?" quizzed Xav, not wanting to compound their mistakes.

"Certain, Xav, completely sure," Louis Blanc replied.

"I'll call you back, stay near the phone," and with that Xav abruptly ended the call.

Blanc pocketed his mobile before looking up, more out of habit than because of any sense of being observed. The stairwell was still empty, but checking didn't harm. He exited the stairwell, squinting as he entered the brightly lit atrium. There was no sign of Greta which was a blessing. Blanc had a healthy respect for Greta Barruol and didn't underestimate her investigative instincts. Keeping Greta in the dark was a constant challenge that wouldn't be helped if he presented any odd behaviour.

A minute later and she appeared from the elevator doors to his left. As she drew nearer, Blanc nodded in the general direction of the hospital exit and turned to head for the doors. Greta followed a step back still mulling over her boss's behaviour. Should she bring it up now? The investigator in her said she should. The psychologist in her told her no though. Timing was everything and so the psychologist in her won through. Now wasn't the time!

Rachel's hospital room seemed calmer, and a great deal more tranquil, once Greta Barruol had departed. Reality had well and truly started to sink in. The expenditure of all their nervous energy was now taking its toll. Kate and Ben sat quietly staring into space, whilst Rachel lay in her bed resting her eyes, not asleep, unable to sleep, but no longer fully awake.

Dan though, standing at the window, was restless. His mind was racing back and forwards through the events of the last few hours. His mind, uncontrollably wired to a seemingly vast mainframe of thoughts and ideas, ticked over. Turning from the window, he broke from his cluttered subconscious and tried to be practical. Rachel could leave the hospital in the morning and, with their ski holiday well and truly over, plans needed making for getting home.

Dan and Ben agreed to return to the chalet, pack the girls' belongings and collect both Rachel and Kate in the morning. Kate opted to stay with Rachel overnight at the hospital. Rachel had insisted she was fine, but Kate was having none of it. As the brothers left, Dan gave Kate a lingering hug and an even more meaningful squeeze of her hand. The traumatic evening had done little to dim the obvious connection they both felt. Kate searched the depth of his eyes, he reciprocated with a telling look of his own, both giving and receiving a supportive half smile which, in the circumstances, was as much as they could muster.

"I'll call Mum and Dad," said Rachel breaking the silence, "and tell them we'll be home late tomorrow night."

"Love ya, Rach," Ben replied.

"Ditto," came Dan, leaving barely a gap from the end of Ben's response.

It had been a bad day. Xav Picamole was in a dark mood before the call from Louis Blanc, now though, he was seething. Mistakes were made, he could accept that, but to not know a mistake had been made! Well, that was a little different. In his world this wasn't acceptable.

First though, Xav would have to 'fight the fire', the enquiry and reprimands would come later. He needed to abort Henkl and get him back to France and then he needed to turn Harry and Bush around.

Hitting speed dial, his smartphone displayed 'H' as the dull ringtones rang in his ear. After three rings, Henkl answered.

"Ja, Boss."

"Have you had eyes on yet?" Xav enquired.

"Not yet, Boss, no sign at all," came Henkl's sitrep.

"They aren't there… they're in France with the sister." He paused as he delivered the news giving it extra gravitas. "…Get back to Geneva ASAP."

"Ja, Boss, on our way," and with that he ended the call and promptly disassembled the phone, snapped the SIM card in half and discarded the bits out of the car window.

"Problem, chief?" queried Zebra, who had been sitting quietly behind the wheel of their very plain-looking black Renault.

"The job's aborted, they're with the sister. Xav wants us back at base," Henkl looked to his right and caught Zebra's eye as he motioned to start driving.

Zebra started the car, checked it was clear and pulled out. The two killers took one last look at the chic Manchester apartment as they started their long drive south.

Xav delved back into his speed dial list, his smart phone displaying '*H2*'. Harry answered after the third ringtone.

"Yes, sir," came Harry's deferential reply.

"Where are you both now?" asked Xav, his clipped mannerism sounding more curt than usual. Harry knew instantly that something was wrong. Reading people was his strength, added to this he knew Xav well enough to know most of his external 'tells'.

"Just approaching Geneva," replied Harry, as he glanced over at Bush. He was driving and, although out of earshot, had picked up on Harry's change of mood.

"She's not dead… you killed the wrong girl!" informed Xav.

"Are you certain?" questioned Harry, instantly regretting his response.

"COURSE I AM SURE," boomed an ever-angrier Xav.

The line went silent, but Harry thought better of interjecting. Ten long seconds ticked by, Xav allowing himself some time to return to his usual calmer self.

"There is more, the brothers are also there, so turn around and get back to Alpe d'Huez and finish the job," Xav snarled.

"What, all three brothers in Alpe d'Huez?" quizzed Harry, back on safer ground now they were discussing further work.

"No, not all three, the elder two... Dan Fletcher and Ben Fletcher," came Xav's long-winded response. It always bemused Harry when Xav would list two full names rather than say 'Dan and Ben Fletcher'.

"What about Henkl and Zebra, do they know?" asked Harry.

"Yes, they should be back here tomorrow... so just turn around and finish your job. NO MISTAKES," came Xav's barbed reply.

"Yes sir," replied Harry, which fell on deaf ears, Xav had ended the call.

"What's up?" asked Bush.

"She's not dead," came Harry's short response. There was never any love lost between Harry and Bush, but right now the feeling between them was practically defcon 5.

Bush continued driving and remained silent whilst trying to process what Harry had just said.

Breaking the silence, "Two to the chest, two to the head, Harry, no way she survived... no way," said Bush.

"You killed the wrong girl... You fucking killed the wrong girl," boomed Harry, "and Xav is fuming!"

"Impossible... she's dead... I saw it," Bush interjected, but before he could go on Harry exploded.

"That's the fucking problem, that's YOUR FUCKING PROBLEM, when you're wrong 'you aren't wrong', you are never fucking wrong, are you?" screamed Harry. Bush pulled the car up to the side of the road and cut the engine.

It was late and very dark outside, only the glimmer of suburban street lights offering any hope of vision. Inside the car the atmosphere was darker still. Bush turned sideways, in part to help diffuse the tension and in part for self-protection.

Harry started to calm down; screaming at Bush had certainly improved his mindset. Observing a little deference in Bush's demeanour helped to make serious inroads into his state of mind. He would still have liked to wring Bush's neck, but now wasn't the time. He talked Bush through the reassignment; a return to Alpe d'Huez to complete the kill on Rachel Fletcher whilst also make the hits on the brothers too. They were going to be very busy and there was little time to prepare. Logic told them they only had tomorrow to get this done. The family were bound to start heading home after their recent ordeal.

With that Bush turned the car around, heading back to where they had been just a few hours earlier.

Pounding the treadmill, Chris Johnson was deep into his workout. Sweat was pouring off him, he was 30 minutes into his run having already completed 5000 metres on the rower. At 55 Chris Johnson could have passed for 40 facially and 30 on physique alone. As head of MI6, he mixed with the 'fat cats' of Whitehall, but he didn't share their waistlines. Five gym workouts a week, for the last 30 years, had ensured Chris Johnson kept a taught, honed body that would be the envy of anyone 30 years his junior. Tonight, though, would be one gym session he wouldn't quite complete, as his phone interrupted his workout.

"Yes, what is it?" quizzed Johnson, still breathing heavily as he responded to his call.

"Sir, you need to come in. We've just intercepted a call to the Fletcher house." Concise intel delivered succinctly.

"And?" he asked.

"Rachel Fletcher has been shot in France. She's OK, but her friend was killed," came the reply from the other end of the phone.

"Roger that, am on my way in. Call JT, I want him in. I'll see you in 30," and with that he ended the call.

CHAPTER 11
ALPS FLIGHT

Alpe d'Huez, France
8:30 a.m. Thursday 5th January 2017

The surreal events of the day before were whirring though Dan's mind. Staring at the ceiling for the last hour, his alarm brought him sharply back to reality. They had a long day ahead of them. Drop the girls' rented skis back off, load the car, collect Rachel and Kate from Grenoble and drive across France. Thankfully, the French péage autoroutes were nothing like the British motorways.

He could hear Ben stirring in the next bedroom. The chalet seemed very quiet, almost eerie, and not just because there were no girls bustling about the place. With classic Fletcher efficiency, the two brothers cracked on first with breakfast, before completing their packing and loading the car in readiness for the journey north.

Both clad in blue denim jeans and winter ski jackets, the lads looked every bit brothers. A tough 24 hours hadn't impacted their lithe, rugged good looks. Alert and with a spring in their step, they stepped out of the chalet and started making their way into the town centre. Mid January in Alpe d'Huez was generally cold with clear blue skies, today was no different. It was 9:30 a.m. and minus four, a thermometer was unnecessary to know how cold it was. Heavy, icy breaths and a stinging feeling on any exposed flesh told its own story. Dan and Ben gradually made their way steadily up the icy path from the chalet to the town centre clutching three pairs of skis and poles whilst trying to do their level best not to lose their footing.

Three hundred metres distant, Helen Waters' killer stood as still as a statue, staring intently down the road towards the chalet, suddenly alert to movement as Dan and Ben exited and started making their way up towards the town centre.

"We've got movement…" reported Bush through his comms. "…Both in blue jeans and black jackets," he continued.

"Roger that… Am moving down the opposite side to loop around," replied Harry.

Bush had been on stag for over an hour now and was really feeling the cold. Usually, a surveillance operation like this would have been shared, but Harry had made it very clear. Bush would start and only when Harry was ready to join the party would he do so. It was a punishment and Bush knew it. But what could he do? He still didn't think it was his fault. After all, how could it be his fault that the girls swapped jackets?

Seeing movement was a relief though, an opportunity to move and to finally get the job done. Today was going to be different, requiring a great deal of ad-libbing. No time to create a thorough plan and two hits meant two on the job and no one running an OP.

In the distance, Bush could see Harry making his way down the opposite side of the road, the same side as Ben and Dan. In two minutes, they would do a 'pass-by'. He kept eyes on and watched as Harry casually walked past the brothers and continued on his way. Two hundred metres later, Harry stopped, crossed the road and started making his way back up. Ben and Dan had now gone beyond Bush's position, making headway towards the top part of town.

"Follow them… I am right behind you," came Harry's instructions over his throat mike.

"Roger that," Bush replied and started up the road.

The brothers finally made it to the uppermost part of town, entering the ski hire shop. Although sub-zero, Dan had still managed to break a sweat carrying the girls' ski equipment a kilometre uphill. The hire shop was bustling with skiers browsing the clothing aisles and queuing to return or collect ski equipment.

As the brothers entered the hire shop, Harry pulled up 100 metres short on the roadside; a bus stop conveniently located giving him the perfect reason to be standing still. Bush carried on 30 metres beyond, only stopping once he got to a suitable ski boutique to use for cover. Window-shopping was a favourite tool in the observation game, a great reason to be stood still and nearly a guaranteed reflection to assist with indirect vision. And then the killers simply waited. Waiting was what they were good at. No, waiting was what they were great at.

Ben queued, juggling three sets of skis and poles whilst Dan unzipped his jacket and moved to the shop doorway to cool down. The sweat quickly started evaporating in the sub-zero air, his body giving the appearance of breathing to onlookers. An eerie feeling tickled his subconscious as he gazed across the road towards the slopes. He had seen the man earlier walking down the mountain, hadn't he? Weird. Now stood at the Trans-Isere bus stop rather than the town circular didn't make sense. Maybe he was waiting for a friend?

Dan averted his gaze and focused back on the skiers getting their first runs of the day in, but the nagging feeling wouldn't dissipate, it hung there, gnawing away at the darkest recesses in his mind. Maybe he was tired? Or paranoid even? He turned and re-entered the shop to see Ben, now third in the queue.

Paranoid or not, though, the events of last night couldn't be explained rationally. Helen killed and Rachel shot by a terrorist in a ski resort. It didn't add up no matter how Dan rectified it in his head. Turning to Ben, his look more than anything was compelling.

"Bro, there's something odd. It might be just me, but I think we're being followed," whispered Dan more for effect than because he may be overheard.

"What you on about?" asked Ben with an unusually serious face. He mostly wore a permanent grin on his face, even at the worst of times, now though he was looking very solemn, reassuring his brother of his full attention.

"Take a peek through the window, try some of those sunnies on," motioned Dan with a nod of his head towards the Oakley's carousel. "He's across the street in a blue beanie and jacket stood by the Isere bus stop." He collected the skis, freeing Ben up, who wandered towards the sunglasses stand by the window.

Casually, Ben picked a pair to try on and looked down the street. Stamping his feet to keep warm stood a man in a blue beanie seemingly waiting for someone. Ben tried a few other pairs on, continuing to watch the man – not a man though, a killer.

He rejoined Dan, who was now first in the queue.

"What you think?"

"He's still there, just standing… Maybe he's just waiting for someone," replied Ben unconvincingly.

Both tired and a little spooked, maybe it was all just paranoia, considered Ben.

"Are we just being para?" he asked. The brothers looked at each other and then went silent. Their silence was broken by the ski technician, extending his arms to collect the returned skis. Ben dealt with the technician leaving Dan lost in thoughts.

It wasn't wasted time though, Dan rarely wasted time. Thoughts swirled around his head; were they being followed? If so, then who would follow them? Police? He didn't think so. And how could he be sure?

He leant over Ben's shoulders and proceeded to spell out a plan. If they were being followed, they had to be sure. Rather than walk back down the street to the chalet, they agreed to walk to another shop, a gift shop and buy some tat. If the man was still there then they'd know.

Back outside, Harry was also weighing things up. Bush was in a great location, no way could he be pinged, but Harry, although at a bus stop, was stood in the open ground on his own. Was it odd that the Fletcher brother had stood outside? Or was he just cooling down?

Was he taking one last look at the mountain view or was he staring right at him? Whichever it was, he needed to fill Bush in. Over their comms, Harry gave Bush the full account. Bush had seen Dan's breath of fresh air too, albeit from a different aspect.

"You take the lead next, Bush, just in case," directed Harry.

"Roger that."

As the brothers exited the hire shop, they walked purposefully back down the street, careful not to look across towards the bus stop. Harry remained motionless, whilst Bush took the lead. Dan and Ben continued down the street, taking the third right onto one of the main high streets, lined with clothes shops, gift shops and expensive-looking chocolatiers. Five hundred metres later, they stopped and entered a gift shop selling T-shirts, postcards and key rings amongst other tourist tat.

Bush walked on and stopped just beyond, whereas Harry remained out of view, a good few hundred metres back and well out of sight. Through the window, the lads saw no sign of blue beanie, not a trace. Three young girls walked by clutching snowboards and a family struggled past, walking uncomfortably in their ski boots, and then a single man, uncannily wearing a similar beanie, but red this time, but it wasn't the man.

"One more shop?" suggested Ben. Dan nodded in agreement. Exiting the shop, they worked their way down the high street, stopping at the final gift shop before the retail outlets became accommodation units. Repeating a similar pattern, Dan and Ben rustled through various tat all the time watching intently through the shop window. More skiers and boarders sauntered by all clutching their equipment, but no blue beanie man.

"I think it's clear, bro. Guess we are just being paranoid..." said Ben, more a statement than a question. "...Head back?" he continued.

Dan nodded and made his way towards the high street with Ben in tow. Turning right, they headed back up the street, now forced to walk past another man in a red beanie. Had they seen him earlier too? Shit thought Dan, either he was really paranoid, or the world was following him. He looked across at Ben, a frowning Ben, a knowing Ben. The 'knowing' part was that Ben had literally just had the same thought.

"Walk faster," whispered Dan under his breath and with that the two brothers picked up their pace a little. As they walked, Dan desperately started looking for ways to turn around and peek behind, but nothing presented itself. Stopping, he took his phone out of his pocket, pretending to answer it. He stood street side, just aimlessly glancing around, as he talked to no one. Clever thought Ben.

Sure enough, down the street, looking into a shop window was red beanie man. Three times now, not a coincidence. It couldn't be. Without breaking his call, Dan started to speak to Ben, filling him in on what he could see.

"Don't look, bro, but red beanie man is three shops down… he's following us… You feeling like a run?" and with that Dan ended his call as they continued their journey up the street.

Walking briskly, they turned off the high street into a small ginnel, a big mistake. The quiet back street, more a path than a thoroughfare, felt lonely and dangerous, nowhere to hide if you were trying to covertly follow someone, but equally nowhere to hide if you were running for your life.

The ginnel took an almost straight line for 80 metres, offering left and right-hand turns every ten or so metres. They were halfway down as red beanie made his entrance off the high street. Bush had been made and he knew it. He had walked off a bustling high street into a deadly quiet alleyway and, as he had done so, the two brothers had turned and stared. The game was over.

"They've made us…" alerted Bush over comms. "…In pursuit, heading towards the slopes," he added as he retrieved his silencer and took two shots.

The lads had already turned on their heels and were now 60 metres from Bush, quite a distance to make an accurate shot with a handgun. Two bullets whizzed past and ricocheted off the walls beyond them. Adrenaline coursed through their veins, fight or flight kicked in and this was very much 'flight'.

Sprinting for their lives, Dan and Ben exited the alleyway, meeting a steep, broad stairway leading to the wrong side of the ice rink. Taking the deep steps two at a time, Dan was ever grateful the steps had been cleared of snow and recently gritted. The killer had taken chase, the gap closing as the lads climbed the steps. Another shot taken and missed, very close this time though, the bullet embedding itself in one of the steps to the left of Ben's foot. Reaching the top of the steps, a 1.5 metre barrier encircling the ice rink stood imposingly. With no second breath, both Dan and Ben half climbed, half vaulted over this wall, dropping to the ice on all fours as another bullet flew into the solid wooden wall.

Back on their feet, the lads sprinted across the middle of the rink, barging through a throng of morning skaters. Bush was scrabbling over the wall as they exited the rink, entering the last high street before the piste. Looking up the street, Dan could see blue beanie man about 100 metres away running towards them.

"Blue beanie man!" he screamed, Ben fleetingly glanced as they both continued their sprint towards the slopes.

The brothers were fast and fit but so were their pursuers. They had a gap, but it wasn't growing, and the foot race was starting to become attritional. Dan and Ben neared the slopes, lots of open space now and nowhere to hide. *Shit*, thought Dan, *where do we go? Keep running, keep running.*

Bush was 100 metres back with Harry a further 20 metres behind. Both killers looked menacing, pumping their arms with silencer-fitted handguns drawn. They were committed now, their 'op' was completely overt, they had both made the cardinal sin in their line of work. Now everything was all about the kill.

Ahead, Dan and Ben were running down the side of the piste, a freshly groomed slope aiding traction. Glancing behind, Dan estimated they were 150 metres ahead, but more worryingly, they were running into vast open space.

Down the slope, a bunch of snowboards and skis stood upright, speared into a snow bank. Two skiers hurtled past them and then a boarder. One of them appeared to shout abuse, probably about being on the piste, but Dan wasn't about to stop to explain.

"The boards, Ben... go for a kid's," screamed Dan motioning towards the various ski kit stuck in the snow. Clever thought Ben, small boards or, more to the point, smaller bindings would sort of work with normal shoes.

Without breaking stride, first Dan and then Ben grabbed a board each as they ran past. Almost jumping into the boards, they hinged the back plate of the bindings and took off. Initially, the gap closed to the killers, but they very quickly picked up speed, accelerating away down the slope. Looking back up the mountain, though, and the killers weren't just standing still in despair. They had already turned around and were making good time back to the road.

"Rachel," shouted Dan, whilst looking back across to his brother. Ben was on his wavelength. Shit, if they were in danger, if they were being shot at, was Rachel safe?

Hurtling down the piste, they hung right in the direction of the chalet. One very long minute later and both had discarded their borrowed boards and were running for the chalet.

Dan jumped behind the driver's seat of Rachel's Golf, never more grateful than now that his sister always drove sporty hatchbacks. There weren't many better-suited cars for haring around the tight and twisty alpine roads. Ben had barely got his seat belt on as Dan gunned the car out of the driveway. Tight switchbacks in the road came quick and fast and he did his utmost to both keep the car on the road and his speed up.

"Call Rachel," barked Dan, not in a rude way, just the need to concentrate on driving causing such an abrupt demand. Ben was already on it though, and hadn't needed the prompt, not that he minded. There was something very reassuring about their synchronized thought patterns.

Ben relayed to Rachel what had just happened. He did his level best to sound calm and reassuring, but he didn't feel like he'd achieved it. Initially hurrying the story across, he adapted a little and tried slowing things down a bit. It certainly helped, but the adrenaline was still coursing through his veins and with that came a certain amount of haste. They knew the journey to Grenoble Hospital very well now, an hour or maybe 50 minutes at best the way Dan was tearing down the hairpins.

"Be ready, Rachel," was Ben's final instruction. "Be ready!"

Back up the road, the two killers had just made it back to their car. They hadn't wasted time with recriminations or a post-mortem as to why their 'kill' had gone wrong. Only amateurs behaved that way. There would be time to analyse later. For now, they needed to vacate the town as quick as possible. Reports of two men running through a sleepy ski resort in daylight, firing handguns, albeit with silencers attached, would soon get out. Added to this, they still had to finish the other half of their job. Right now, matters were taking a turn for the worse as it would be hard to imagine that the Fletcher girl wouldn't have been warned. Harry opted not to update Xav immediately. They would only get a tongue-lashing, and it could wait. In fact, it might not even need to happen. Find Rachel Fletcher and it might lead to finding the brothers too! No, there was nothing to be gained for calling it in, that he was certain of.

Screeching into the car park, Dan selected the parking bay closest to the main entrance, still 60 metres shy of the doors, though. Running where possible, Dan and Ben made good time along the ground-floor corridor. Two flights of stairs and another long corridor beckoned before they reached Rachel's room. Practically smashing the door off its hinges, the brothers virtually fell into the room. Rachel, sitting on her bed, initially startled, relaxed a touch as she took in her brothers' crude entrance antics. Kate shot bolt upright from the chair in the corner, her anger at getting a fright subsiding instantly as recognition kicked in.

"Is everything OK?" blurted Dan in the general direction of both girls, whilst still gasping for breath. "We need to leave... right now... NOW," he carried on.

"We should call the police," replied the two girls almost in unison.

"No, leave now... NOW," reiterated Dan assertively. The command in his voice was part reassuring but part terrifying too. He knew it too, but now wasn't the time to discuss better bedside techniques. He and his brother had just been chased and shot at by two assassins, Helen was dead, and his sister had been wounded the previous day. Grave danger, they were all in seriously grave danger!

Bush and Harry pulled into the car park, shoehorning their car between a large black people carrier to their right and a beaten-up old Citroen to the left. Parking spots were becoming a much scarcer commodity now. Debussing, the killers made their way purposefully towards the main entrance. Harry led the way as they entered the large hospital atrium. He spoke passable French, but he didn't intend on using it. The reception desk was a large, curved, wooden feature accommodating four workstations behind it. Three staff members sandwiched between the desk and a filing cabinet-clad wall busied themselves answering phones and tapping on keyboards. Harry stood patiently waiting to be attended to, whilst Bush hung back, skulking as best as he could to avoid passers-by connecting the two of them as being together.

A minute later, a rotund, middle-aged lady grabbed Harry's attention. In slow English, as was often the way for Brits abroad, he explained he was Rachel Fletcher's brother, not the best cover story but he was pressed for time. Right now, he was compromising covertness for expediency. Room 212 Harry repeated back to the receptionist. He hadn't needed to double-check for his sake though, his reply was for Bush, currently standing 20 metres away. Bush was scanning the plan of the hospital, a large red pin marking the spot they were currently in. Room 212 was located on the second floor in the adjacent wing to the main building. There were several ways to access the ward all taking circuitous routes around and through the myriad corridors and wings of the hospital. Harry started towards the east wing which led directly to the upper level, a long corridor led to a meeting of wards at a featureless crossroads of hallways, whilst Bush headed west towards Orthopaedics, a longer route but ensuring he would enter Rachel's ward from the only other exit. Both killers set off purposefully, steely eyes concealing their sinister intentions.

Harry made slow but steady progress through the hospital. They had both swapped beanies for baseball caps, but keeping a bowed head helped immeasurably in reducing exposure to the internal security cameras. Xav would be using his Interpol contacts to try and redact any video footage, but it was always better to take as much control of the situation yourself.

Rachel and Kate grasped the gravity of their situation in an instant. Following Dan's lead, the two girls fell in line behind the brothers. Dan exited the room, glancing both ways before heading towards the entrance to the ward. The internal corridor stretched for 50 metres, broken every 10 metres on either side by doors and with an occasional noticeboard. In the distance, the corridor fed into a generous atrium accommodating three lifts, two large plant pots stood sentry either side of the lift doors.

Ben hurriedly pressed the down button commanding a green down arrow to appear on the lift display accompanied by a soft chime. Whirring cog sounds and heavy cable noises were just audible coming from within the lift shaft as one of the lifts made its way to floor two, slowly though, very slowly.

Dan stole a glance down the long, sterile corridor from where they had just come. A doctor and her underling stepped spritely in his direction, whilst an old lady was inching her way in the other. Right at the very end, though, strode a man in a cap. At 100 m, too far to recognize, it wasn't his face that caused alarm. Way too far to appreciate facial features, it was the man's silhouette and gait that resonated. Purposeful steps, strong yet light footed, Dan pinged the man immediately. Standing in a huddle, motionless whilst waiting for the lift, didn't attract Harry's attention. If the quartet remained calm, had they not flinched, then maybe he might have missed them. Remaining calm, though, isn't something that comes naturally. Human instinct doesn't function that way. Only meticulous training and hours and hours of practice can eradicate such reactions.

"Look, Ben," prompted Dan, indicating with a nod of his head towards the silhouetted man a good 100 metres down the corridor. Rachel and Kate instinctively turned their heads too and this was the only 'tell' Harry had needed.

"It's him," retorted Ben urgently, one of the lifts' whirring sounds now starting to soften as it approached the second floor.

Harry had broken into a run, arms pumping as he weaved around several hospital patients ambling slowly in either direction. The central lift doors opened and, with no hesitation, the quartet piled in. Pressing the close door button violently, Dan watched anxiously as the door closed with Harry still 20 plus metres short.

Sighs of relief were very short-lived though; the lift was going up!

"Shit, shit, shit… what do we do? …Shit, shit, Dan," shrieked Kate as the lift started its speedy ascent. Floor three quickly came and went as did floors four and five. The lift came to a smooth stop at the sixth floor as the doors slid open. An orderly with an empty wheelchair was waiting to enter.

"Get out," yelled Dan. Ben moved first as the girls and Dan followed suit. Jogging down the corridor, the white walls were bathed in an eerie yellow light. Doors on each side labelled '*Salle d'Opération*' were all accompanied by a number. Kate and Rachel knew immediately, they hadn't needed to translate. The red or green light above each door was an almost identical image of the operating theatre wing in their own hospital back in London.

Passing the first four theatres with red lights, the fifth door was green, signifying it was empty. Unspoken, Kate dashed in, with Dan, Ben and Rachel in close attendance. Quickly taking in their environment, the room contained double doors leading to theatre. To the sides, sterile work surfaces accommodated a variety of monitors, a couple of flat-screen VDUs and trays of more crude medical items. In the opposite corner stood a portable ECG machine, neatly housed in a white metallic frame on wheels. The room was bathed in the same yellow lighting.

The group moved with haste through the double doors, the girls first followed by Ben and Dan. As Dan exited the room, he checked himself. Turning on his heels, he grabbed the mobile ECG and wheeled it in front of the doors before entering the theatre.

The theatre was vast in comparison with its reception room. Two enormous circular lights hung above the central operating table, both anchored to the ceiling. The opposing wall was almost an entire window, presumably a students' viewing gallery. The walls either side were once again lined with sterile work surfaces containing a myriad of medical instruments.

Another ECG on wheels stood sentry to the left of the operating table and an even larger machine on wheels stood to the other side. Tubes protruded from its guts and cables trailed across the floor to the left-hand wall.

More of the same dim yellow lighting afforded reasonable visibility and certainly didn't offer any dark recesses in which to hide.

Kate and Rachel instinctively zipped behind the operating table. Ducking down below its upper edge, the girls sandwiched themselves between its sturdy legs and the mobile anaesthesia machine.

Dan and Ben stood to either side of the double doors but not before grabbing the nearest medical implements adorning the work surfaces. Ben had found a stainless steel implements tray about the size of a tea tray, whereas Dan grabbed a hefty-looking metal briefcase. He had no idea what it contained, but it was heavy, so it must be something solid. Motionless and as quiet as they could, the brothers stood anxiously, just waiting.

Harry hadn't wanted to attract attention, far from it. His dash down the corridor had put paid to that though. Falling short of the elevator doors, he didn't panic. Training kicked in, tried-and-tested training. Startled bystanders stood by looking puzzled. To dissipate their concerns, he stood pointing at his watch, as if to indicate he was late for something, all the while fixing a stare on the ever-increasing numbers displaying the journey the elevator was taking.

"Sixth floor, Bush… Get up to the sixth," whispered Harry subtly into this throat mike.

"Roger that," came Bush's instantaneous response.

Harry didn't move though, choosing to concentrate on the central elevator. The elevator display kicked back into life again having paused on the number six. It continued now, stopping on the eighth floor.

"There are four of them, Bush, two girls and the brothers…" Giving no time to respond, Harry continued, "…The elevator's gone to eight now… I'll take eight," still talking in hushed tones.

"Roger that," came Bush's curt response. Harry wheeled around to his left and gunned it towards the adjacent stairwell.

Bush made good time up the northern stairwell, concrete stairs well lit and strangely quiet. Arriving at floor six, he found himself in a quiet and peaceful atrium. To his left and right were two long, featureless corridors, green or red lights above every door. In the distance, two hospital staff were ambling along clad in green operating gowns. Instinct dictated turning right, good instincts too. Bush, unknowingly, was making his way towards the Fletcher siblings.

Approaching the first door, 'Salle d'Opération 12' presented itself, boldly marked with a large red light. With his Glock to hand, he proceeded to enter, poking his head and shoulders through the doorway.

"Qui es-tu?" enquired a startled-looking clinician.

"Désolé," Bush shot back as he retreated quickly from the 'prep room' re-entering the soulless corridor. Ahead were a further 11 rooms; all were marked red except for theatres seven and five.

He advanced down the corridor, bypassing those with a red overhead light, glancing over his shoulder as he made his way towards theatre seven, ever nearer to his prey.

Approaching the operating room, he entered to find an empty prep room. A dull humming sound emanating from the theatre itself, Bush crept forwards. Right-handed, he pushed the doors open with his left allowing his right to keep his Glock pointing forwards. Theatre seven was vacant.

Retracing his steps, Bush was interrupted. "Anything?" came Harry's voice in his ear.

"Not yet," he replied as he moved towards theatre five.

"Nothing here so far," Harry shot back.

Bush stood inches from the door to the prep room of theatre five. Stealthily, he moved inside. As before, only the same dull humming sound could be heard. He pushed forwards towards the double swinging doors to the theatre itself, just metres from his prey.

Inside the operating room, Ben first and then Dan heard the prep room door open. It wasn't loud though, much more of a subtle entry, and it was this fact that really heightened the brothers' state of alert. Ben and Dan braced themselves, pupils dilated, muscle and sinew tensed, their breathing slowed.

Bush moved on with the same MO, left hand pushing the doors open, his right hand wielding his Glock. His killer's instinct twitched inside, gnawing at his conscious. His sixth sense nagged. Edging half a metre further, Bush was almost entirely within the theatre as Ben lunged forwards with a high-arcing swing of his arm, clutching his steel tray. He clattered into Bush's gun hand, discharging a shot as the Glock dislodged from his grip. Bush, spinning 90 degrees to his right, delivered Ben a crunching lateral uppercut, clenched fist contacting mercilessly into the side of Ben's head. He crumpled into the wall, down but not quite out.

Dan seized the initiative, smashing Bush in the back with as much force as he could muster with his metal briefcase. Bush fell backwards, only the theatre wall catching him from a complete fall to the floor. Dan swung his weapon again, but slowly, too slowly. The untrained would have backed off, and this would have been fatal, but years of close combat training told. Bush moved towards him, closing the gap, reducing 90% of the impact. Seizing the impetus, Bush landed a telling blow to Dan's chest. Stumbling backwards, he clutched at Bush to no avail. The Glock lay on the floor as Dan sailed backwards past it, crashing into the ECG machine. He lay sprawled on the floor as the machine rolled across the theatre, coming to a stop against the work surface.

With Ben still prone on the floor, Dan helpless too, as he scrambled to get to his feet, their very existence was looking bleak. Bush bent to retrieve his Glock.

Screeching, Kate flew from behind the operating table, part wrestling, part piggybacking on top of Bush. The pair crashed to the floor. Bush rotated, elbowing her in the face with a sickening blow to her right cheekbone. Loosening her grip due to the blow, Bush was almost free of Kate as the one-armed Rachel threw herself into the fray. Her single arm and body weight helping to knock Bush back to the floor, the girls were bravely doing their utmost in a fight for their lives. Dan, now on his feet, charged too. Half of his momentum was in part checked by Kate but the other half hitting Bush, arms and legs twisting together as the three of them fought with all they had. Body weight and determination started to make progress against their deadly assassin.

Ben, still very groggy, was returning to his senses. Seeing a mass of bodies writhing on the ground, bridging the gap, he charged across the floor, kicking Bush's exposed face with all his might. Blood spurted from his nose; the single kick had knocked their would-be killer out cold.

"Fuck... fuck are you alright?" blurted Dan as he looked up at his brother. Dan was sprawled across the floor, partly tangled up with Bush and Rachel. Ben, towering above his brother, the girls and an unconscious assassin, was sporting an angry-looking lump to the side of his head.

Kate wasn't looking her best either, signs of a black eye coming, but the blood splattered across her face though wasn't hers.

"What the fuck...? FUCK..." rasped Ben, breathless as the adrenaline dissipated.

"Bush, anything?" came a small, tinny voice from the loose earpiece now hanging on the assassin's collar. "Bush, come in," came the squeaky voice.

"Shit. Go, come on go. Let's go," ordered Dan assertively.

As Dan, Rachel and Kate made for the doors, Ben turned to the killer. Swinging his foot back, he dealt Bush another almighty kick to his ribcage before heading for the door.

"That's for Helen... you fucking animal," he grunted as he exited the theatre.

On the eighth floor, Harry knew immediately that there was a problem. He had heard a scuffle, nothing of clarity but he knew. The confirmation came when he heard the very recognizable 'psst' of a gun with attached silencer being fired. Abandoning the eighth, he ran with urgency to the nearest stairwell, descending the flights in leaps and bounds. Entering the sixth floor presented a calm, almost tranquil environment, no sign of Bush or the Fletchers. He started to search door by door. He had joined the floor from the opposite end to Bush and had 12 theatre doors facing him down the corridor, their green or red lights still unwavering.

Upon entering theatre five, Harry came across an almost unconscious Bush. Still prone, he looked awful. Drenched in blood, his nose was almost flat to his face, each breath making a rasping sound. Quick thinking, Harry grabbed some gauze which lay amongst a variety of other debris strewn across the theatre floor, carnage from the recent scuffle. Mopping Bush's face garnered a few groans, but it wasn't till he propped Bush upright that the real wincing began. Each movement sent an electric bolt through Bush's torso, several broken ribs courtesy of a brutal kick whilst he lay unconscious. For now, the hunt was over, the need to exit as inconspicuously as possible took precedence.

Outside the main entrance, the quartet sprinted across the car park, diving into the sporty black Golf. Dan had taken the wheel allowing a one-armed Rachel to tend to both Ben and Kate. Without considering where, he gunned the car, tyres screeching over rough tarmac as he exited the hospital.

"Take the péage, Dan, the péage," barked Kate, the urgency not lost on him as he motored down the main thoroughfare in the direction of the slip road. A large blue sign with arrows denoting Lyon / Paris in the two right-hand lanes, Geneva remain in the middle and Marseilles / Sud in the left-hand lanes. Instinctively, Dan aimed for Lyon and Paris, heading homeward felt right, felt safe.

Cruising down the péage, a weird calmness descended on the four of them, not dissimilar to the anticlimax following a festival or grand party. Sadness, fear and despair hung over them rather than relief. Should they feel relieved? Who knew?

Discussions began, plans formulated. Drive directly to the UK versus hole up immediately in some cheap, nondescript hotel was hotly argued. After all the exhilarations, they all needed the rest.

The péage, as always, was free of traffic. Dan, having initially raced out of Grenoble, had slowed to a steady 130 kmph. Unlike the UK, the French Gendarmes were rarely seen on the péage, but he still figured it sensible to stick to the limits. Each little town and péage junction seemed to zip by. They cruised past Lyon, turning directly north in search of a hotel to hole up for the night. Sure enough, a few junctions later, they came across an Ibis Hotel, more of a traveller's hotel than a holiday destination, but perfect for what they needed.

The dishevelled-looking group got out of the Golf and booked two rooms. With everything they had experienced in the last 24 hours, Dan hadn't given much thought to Kate. It was only when the lady at reception assumed two couples that he returned to romantic thoughts of Kate. She stole a look, trying but failing to suppress a small smile which Dan reciprocated. Now wasn't the right time though. Déjà vu! Unconsciously, Dan extended his arm and gave Kate a tender squeeze of her hand, the briefest of contact, not quite lasting a second, but probably the most meaningful and heartfelt action between the couple in over three months of phone flirting.

Although subtle, his action wasn't lost on Rachel. More than anyone, she knew exactly what Dan and Kate thought of the other. A ski trip in the Alps was meant to be their union. A race for their lives through France would only delay the inevitable. Dan and Kate's attraction remained undimmed.

Back in Grenoble, a usually calm and considered Harry was more hissing than pondering. Having to tend to Bush was an automatic action. Years of training drilled into Harry afforded him the luxury of simply patching Bush up without any thoughts as to how much he couldn't stand him. Bush was a mess too. Like the Fletchers, the killers had also holed up in a cheap, local hotel, not before a stop at a chemist. A broken nose requiring copious dressings to staunch the bleeding was the least of Bush's problems. Although it looked awful, it just hurt, and the painkillers Harry had bought would help a lot. The ribs, though, were another matter altogether. Every movement made him wince, even lying completely still with the shallowest of breaths wasn't comfortable. He was still operational but only just.

Worse still for Harry was the phone call he now had to make. With Henkl and Zebra currently returning from the UK, it meant calling Xav, no enviable task.

Xav picked up almost immediately, like he was sitting waiting for the call.

"Is it done?" came the perfect, accentless English – no formalities, no small talk, not that there ever was. Xav getting directly to the point added weight to the bad news Harry was about to dish out.

"No, Xav, sorry. No, we've had a problem," he replied.

He could almost feel him raging. When Xav was angry his nostrils flared a little, but his eyes were the most telling. They focused directly like an eagle zooming in on its prey. His eyes felt like lasers when he entered a state of anger.

"Tell me," barked Xav, not wasting words, "and don't spare the detail," he continued.

Harry brought him up to date with the escape from the hospital. He conveniently left out the bungled chase through Alpe d'Huez, but he had no choice but to detail the state of Bush and the fact that he and Bush had been 'pinged' by the Fletcher brothers prior to getting to the hospital.

The conversation hadn't gone well. He received a thorough tongue-lashing, made worse by the fact that it was Bush's stuff-up in the theatre room. He reminded himself that this was why he was paid more. It hadn't helped. Right now, money wasn't a priority; Xav had made that very clear. Sit tight, wait for further instructions and when the Fletchers are next located DO NOT FUCK IT UP!

Bush had heard Harry's side of the call. Remaining motionless didn't just alleviate his pain, it went some way to calm Harry down too. He usually wouldn't have cared about Harry, but this was his cock-up and he knew it. His first cock-up, but nonetheless, it was his fault.

"We sit tight and wait for instructions," as Harry passed on Xav's orders.

Harry exited the room in search of food and more medicine for Bush. In part, though, he needed some time to cool off and reflect. Xav had incredible resources at his fingertips; he had known this for years now. He had known about the direct feed into Interpol and the Russian FSB, not who, but that Xav had someone in both agencies, but this was the first time he'd got a twitch about information coming from the UK. He mulled it over as he walked in the direction of the local high street for more supplies. The London Met maybe? It couldn't be either of the intelligence agencies, could it? MI5 were a notoriously 'closed shop', but that didn't always prevent leaks. Whereas MI6 were even harder to penetrate, not helped by their departments within departments structure, a deliberately designed set-up to ensure that even if breached, only so much information could be stolen. Harry walked on as he pondered. He didn't arrive at any kind of conclusion as he reached the high street.

CHAPTER 12
BIODS

Geneva, Switzerland
4 p.m. Thursday 5th January 2017

Smooth, blemish-free tarmac curved neatly away from the main road to form the entrance to BioDS. The entrance had a barrier overhead that looked like it was rarely in the closed position. Modern, contemporary stone gateposts bookended the entrance which led directly to an expansive car park to the front and right-hand side of the main building.

Geneva in January, it was a cold, crisp day. A beautiful, cloudless blue sky framed by a backdrop of white-capped mountains in the distance added to BioDS's wholesome appeal.

The building had a very clean, clinical, almost futuristic appearance. Clad almost entirely in mirrored glass, the visible steel frame elements were painted a metallic blue to complete the very chic and stylish finish.

Above the main entrance doors the 'BioDS' logo took pride of place. The letters 'i' and 's' formed artistically with a double helix, the first clue to the company's background. Through the automatic sliding doors, the main atrium was light and airy. Granite flooring and clean white walls adorned with contemporary artwork didn't initially scream 'biogenetics'. The welcoming feel was probably aimed at impressing visitors, and it was working.

In the dead centre of main reception stood an island desk, operated by a single attendant. The desk was neat and tidy, a computer monitor, phone and a few items sat on top. The attendant was a smartly attired, mid-thirties lady, sat staring intently at her monitor as she tapped rapidly on her keyboard. Over 30 metres in length, a cluster of shabby chic leather chairs and low coffee tables were grouped together at the far end, presumably for visitors to make themselves comfortable as they waited to be seen.

As large as the main reception was, only one exit was evident, large double doors positioned symmetrically in the middle of the rear wall. The ceiling was double height, affording a long line of windows along the length of the rear wall. Overlooking the main reception atrium, some of these windows had their blinds closed, the open ones giving a sneaky peek into the private world of BioDS.

The furthest window to the left was the largest. A five-metre expanse of glass offered a commanding view of BioDS's main atrium. Inside her office, with the blinds open, was Louise Walsh. Xav Picamole, his back turned away from her, stood staring down at nothing as he contemplated.

Sitting comfortably on a brown leather chesterfield, Henkl nursed a coffee in his hands. Zebra sat impassively to his left on a matching single chesterfield. Since their arrival, Zebra had barely spoken. Summoned to BioDS HQ, Zebra and Henkl were there for instructions not small talk.

Having concluded his report on the Americans, Xav was happy and Louise was almost beaming. Only four MorphEns remained alive, and all 10 jobs had gone ultra smoothly. Henkl had positively glowed when he caught her satisfied nod of approval. Zebra hadn't missed it, he knew Henkl as much as anyone, but Zebra was poker-faced, unwavering, as Henkl gave one of his visible 'tells'. Louise hadn't missed it either. She knew he had a soft spot for her, and she made it work to her benefit.

The atmosphere in the room darkened considerably, though, when Xav moved on to the news from Grenoble. The mess Harry and Bush had caused was the single reason Henkl and Zebra had rushed back from the UK. Xav was almost growling as he spat out the news, not that Henkl was at fault, but at that moment in time it didn't matter. Henkl was at BioDS and Harry and Bush were holed up in Grenoble licking their wounds.

"How did this happen?" hissed Louise, adding to the fervour emanating from Xav. Zebra sat motionless, thankful he wasn't on the obvious receiving end of a combined Louise and Xav dressing-down.

"Bush got jumped at the hospital, he was…" Henkl started to explain, but Louise had already jumped in.

"YES, but how did they know?" she screamed, her notoriously thin patience already eroded to nothing.

He had discussed chapter and verse the debacle in Alpe d'Huez with Harry. He knew exactly what had gone down. Henkl could have stuck the knife in and hung Harry and Bush out to dry, but what purpose would that have served? He'd had the last eight hours in transit to consider his words. Harry and Bush were good operators; great operators, in fact, after all Henkl had trained them. Getting pinged in Alpe d'Huez by the Fletcher brothers was the root of the problem. In Henkl's murky world, the watchwords were covert, surprise, subterfuge, but the two brothers had proven to be very problematic.

Not only had they demonstrated exceptional observation skills, but they had also shown an ability to think on their feet when under extreme duress. This skill set was usually only possessed by those with special training; special forces or clandestine agency staff.

Henkl chose a middle ground. He needed Harry and Bush. After all, how could he replace them?

"They were very good… different even…" he explained, as he described Dan and Ben Fletcher. "They pinged Harry and Bush and verified it too. They were incredibly clever. If I didn't know better, I would have said they worked for an agency," he carried on.

His reference to an agency suggested MI6 or similar. He explained the run through town, justifying the brothers' escape due to their skills on snow. Louise sat behind her desk, initially seething, but as Henkl explained Dan and Ben's speed of movement and thought processes as they made their escape, her face visibly softened a touch.

Henkl could see a pride in her at the ability of her MorphEns, Zebra too. They were her creations. She wanted them dead, and he didn't know why, but they were still her creations.

"You get yourself to Grenoble immediately," barked Louise.

The softer edges of her face had once again disappeared. Xav glowered at Henkl as she continued spitting out orders. Louise was angry because it was required, Xav was angry because he enjoyed it.

"You four find the Fletchers and get it finished," she hissed.

Henkl didn't respond; he didn't need to. Louise hadn't once broken her direct eye contact with him. Eye contact meant a lot, more than most people really understood. In the intelligence world, communication started with eye contact, followed by hand and body movement, lastly with verbal communication. This was because verbal comms was often a luxury you didn't have on ops.

So Henkl stared back at Louise not once averting his gaze. Once she was done, he just nodded his head, motioned with his left hand in Zebra's direction to leave and headed for the door.

"Update me when you get to Harry," ordered Xav as Henkl pulled the door open.

"Ja, Boss," came his clipped reply. With Zebra in close pursuit, the two members of the Apfel filed out of Louise's office.

Xav waited for the door to close. With Henkl clearly out of earshot, he turned towards Louise. Returning the gesture, she gazed intensely into Xav's eyes. Making plans, he agreed to call Urinov, an update from Knacc was overdue – Sitka too. Knacc was everything she had desired when she had first approached the British government, a facility solely designed to further her work, answering to no one in the pursuit of excellence in the world of biogenetics.

Back in the 1980s, all Louise had wanted was to push the boundaries of what was and wasn't possible in human development. The BMA hadn't understood, neither had her country. Even the Americans hadn't got it. For years, she had battled, argued and ultimately despised first the Brits and later the Americans too. Finally, she'd found the right people, a sympathetic biosphere and the perfect cultural ideals. The Russians got it as much as the Western world didn't.

If Knacc was to be Louise's utopia, then words failed to do Sitka justice. BioDS's new facility, Sitka, was located deep inside the Russian interior. Mirny had been selected by Urinov because it had the perfect site, an old disused military training school, discreet and anonymous, hidden in plain sight 10 miles from the urban sprawl. In the Russian, she had the perfect partner; well connected, bottomless funding and the desire to see things through. He always went the extra mile to ensure the detail was right.

Louise flipped her laptop lid open, the screen instantly flickering into life. As Xav placed his call to Urinov, she pored over the figures on her screen. It was very early days, the data she scanned was not large enough in sample size to be trusted, but for now, it was all she had to go on. It didn't stop Louise from smirking, a very big, self-satisfied smirk.

The tall, angular Urinov had been sat overseeing the recruits' gym training session. The gymnasium inside Knacc's facility was a large, rectangular sports hall. In the far corner, an open-plan weights area offered an array of free weights and machines. The bulk of the area though was a large, cavernous space. Бочка was screaming at them, 40 young men heeding his every word. By his side, Natalia was as equally demonstrative. Urinov knew how hard Бочка would push the recruits. He'd push them as close to exhaustion as was humanly possible, of that he had no doubt, but Natalia? He'd always figured she'd push them beyond if ever given the chance. Natalia was no one's shrinking violet. As Бочка screamed and shouted, Natalia, visibly red in the face, almost frothed at the mouth. The recruits were being made to 'run the lines', one of Бочка's favourite failure tests. Legs and lungs burnt as the recruits were forced to run back and forth between lines 30 metres apart. Natalia was almost doing as much as the recruits, half running alongside them, as she thumped a clenched fist into her open hand.

The call from Switzerland had been timely. Urinov gave Xav an updated report on the recruits. New data would be winging its way later that day, a dark, wintery, cold Omsk day.

As soon as Xav had signed off his call to Urinov he'd just as quickly dialled again, this time to France.

Just a single dial tone and Louis Blanc picked up – impressive.

"Oui?" came Blanc's soft French accent. Xav elected to converse in French rather than English. Blanc spoke good German, better

English and of course his mother tongue, but Xav's French was better than Blanc's English.

"Tu as des nouvelles?" Xav, as ever, was straight to the point. Blanc didn't mind the directness though. Physically, Blanc was a big, lumbering man, his days running around quickly were long gone – dining out, too much wine and an aversion to the gym had well and truly put paid to that – but his mind, sharp as it ever had been, was calculating, incisive and lightning quick.

"Les Fletcher sont au nord de Lyon," Blanc delivered the news, pinpointing exactly where the Fletchers were holed up, one of two hotels just off the A6, one hour north of Lyon.

"Bien. Votre compte habituel?" asked Xav. Intel came at a price. Xav had great sources of information from a myriad of agencies. The price for Louis Blanc's eyes and ears at Interpol wasn't cheap, but it was worth every cent.

"Bien sûr," Blanc replied. It wasn't implied rudely. Louis Blanc saying 'of course' was more a turn of phrase, a way of signing off, than it was a sarcastic comment. No figure was mentioned but he needn't worry, Xav was generous. He'd never received a payment less than €10 000 and those payments had been for trivial bits of intel. Blanc returned the phone to his pocket as he allowed a smile to break across his face.

CHAPTER 13
VAUXHALL
SITUATION ROOM

Vauxhall, London
10 p.m. Thursday 5th January 2017

Three technicians were seated on their own stretch of a horseshoe-configured desk layout. Soft lighting in the windowless room helped make it easy on the eyes. Above the desks, LCD screens adorned the walls, all displaying discrete information relating to a myriad of geopolitical issues. Details of people and geographic locations were laid out concisely.

Each technician also had twin computer screens on their desk; these were connected and allowed their operator to move the mouse cursor from one screen to the other. A large phone set, files, a laptop and mobile phone helped to clutter the desks too. It was 10 p.m., but you wouldn't have known it. Informally referred to as SitRep, the Situation Room at Vauxhall was a hive of activity.

Details of a mobile intercept were emblazoned across the monitor above the smart-looking female technician. Dressed in black suit trousers with a brown-yellow fitted cardigan, Jane Simmons was the model professional, a young, diligent member of MI6's intelligence-gathering department. At 5 ft 9 Jane was tall for a woman. Long, platinum blond hair was tied back neatly, although pretty, Jane half ruined her natural good looks with her overexuberance on make-up. She didn't need it. Anything she did to enhance her face detracted from a far nicer-looking, late twenty-something young lady.

Working the late shift didn't mean it was quiet though. MI6 worked across the globe, and 10 p.m. in London meant daytime all over the show. The SitRep room was almost always lively. No one ever clock-watched in SitRep.

On Jane's screen a red-flagged individual had popped up. *Tom Fletcher, Leeds* was flashing gently. His name repeated twice more as the header.

Tom Fletcher, Leeds. Tom Fletcher, Leeds. Tom Fletcher, Leeds.

Underneath his name, details of the call were itemized. A word-for-word transcript displayed the call between Tom Fletcher and his son Dan. After the transcript, protocols itemized a course of action to take.

Contact Jack Thomas ~ overwatch.
Special Operations ~ Team Leader

Notify Chris Johnson ~ overwatch.
Chief of Operations

The transcript was time stamped 20:34 Wednesday 4 January 2017. Something wasn't quite right; this was 24 hours ago. Then a second transcript followed, time stamped 22:08 Thursday 5 January 2017.

Jane's monitor flashed angrily. Not that she would have ignored the protocols, but the system had been designed to flag loudly. Jane reread the transcript, double-checked the protocol request, and immediately called Jack Thomas.

On the fourth dial tone JT's phone picked up. Answering without giving his name, JT just offered a 'Hello', a carefully trained response.

"Verify please. This is X-ray, Kilo, Tango, 3 9 5," as Jane read from the code underneath JT's name on her monitor.

"I'm going to the match tomorrow," he responded, the current phrase as always designed to be an everyday 'thing to say'.

"Verified," replied Jane. With formalities completed, she started to brief JT. He'd get the transcript very shortly, but time was pressing and right now JT needed to act. Jane wasted no time, concise and efficiently talking him through the relevance of the intercept. Helen Waters shot dead, Rachel Fletcher in hospital and two of the three Fletcher brothers in the Alps too.

JT ended the call, leaving the SitRep office to update Jonno. He would speak to his boss shortly, but for now he had three calls to make – urgent calls. His team was going to Grenoble and JT was about to ruin their weekend plans. He called Nic first; the furthest to travel, JT figured giving him five minutes head start helped a little. Calls immediately followed to both Meek and Rob. Next he called logistics; the crew needed alerting, the jet required a flight plan filing and equipment and vehicles needed sorting on arrival.

MI6 had a logistics hub in Lyon, so landing at Lyon Airport, although 30 minutes further to drive than Grenoble Airport, was the better entry. Two cars, medical equipment, guns and comms including burner phones would be needed on landing.

JT was 'on it'.

As soon as he finished his calls his speed of movement increased. A quick change of clothes and a double-check of his go-bag were first up. Not running, but with haste, JT left his flat. Further calls would be made en route to the airstrip. Calls needed making to Jonno; a check in with his boss to let him know the course of action. A call to Lyon was also needed. JT's logistics guy was way ahead of him, but double-checking the details might save time and hassle when his team landed. The clock was ticking, and JT could ill afford to lose time due to logistical errors. Finally, he needed to deal with his personal admin. His own weekend plans needed amending. That was a personal tragedy. Would Emma forgive him? It wasn't a done deal, but a dinner date this weekend had given him much optimism. But this would be the second time he would be cancelling a first date with the luscious Emma Walker. JT had a feeling he may have just blown his chances, or rather his career choice had blown them!

CHAPTER 14
IBIS FIGHT

3 a.m. Friday 6th January 2017

The shrill tone of Harry's iPhone broke him from his slumber. Bush heard it too, wincing as he sat up in bed. It was 3 a.m. The two members of Apfel, having only a few hours' sleep, were now listening to Xav bark out orders.

Bush shovelled a bunch of painkillers into his mouth, gulping water from a glass on his bedside table. The instructions had stipulated two tablets every four hours, but he had ignored it. His nose had stopped bleeding hours ago. It looked a mess, as did the black eye that had grown angrier and angrier since his meeting with the Fletcher brothers, but his face wasn't his concern. His ribcage, though, well that was another matter altogether. His every movement screamed. He had managed to breathe slowly, shallow breaths really helped. Every large movement was excruciating, fuelling his burning desire to finish the job. Killing the Fletchers was now something he'd gladly do for free.

Harry signed off his call with Xav with his usual 'Yes, Boss'. What a wanker pondered Bush, keeping his thoughts to himself though. Ordinarily he would have instantly spat out an insult towards Harry, on this occasion though he guarded his thoughts. A combination of gratitude, Harry had sorted his drugs and dressings out last night without comment, plus it had been his cock-up. For once, he was slightly less bullish. Harry was aware too of the more subdued Bush. It certainly helped alleviate their frosty relationship.

Xav had received good intel from his source inside Interpol. Rachel Fletcher's car had been flagged exiting the péage an hour north of Lyon. Number recognition had located her car, pinpointing two cheap travel hotels sat conveniently off the motorway junction. The Fletchers were there now. Almost three hours' drive, Harry and Bush had to get a wriggle on. The hunt was a GO.

Apfel's Gruppe Zwei grabbed their stuff. In less than three minutes, Harry was gunning their car towards the péage. A little after 3 a.m., the roads were completely clear. Harry ran computations in his head; he figured they could get to the Fletchers around 6:30 a.m.

Two hours later, Harry and Bush were making good time. It was just approaching 5:30 a.m., and they'd whistled around the outskirts of Lyon. Now on the charge directly north, a collision course with the Fletchers was a mere 60 minutes away.

Their route had taken them within five miles of Lyon Airport. Nestled in a corner, far from the commercial airlines, stood a medium-sized airplane hangar, a small jet parked centrally, sandwiched neatly between a couple of matching black SUVs. A large, white van was parked up at the far end of the hangar. JT stood silhouetted in the large hangar doors as he stared across the vast expanse of tarmac, phone to his ear. Nic and Meek were unloading the last of their bags, whilst Rob was carrying the remaining holdalls from the van.

JT ended his call, with Jonno up to speed his team needed to get on the road. Cell site analysis had pinpointed the Fletchers to an Ibis Hotel a couple of hours north of the airport. JT had been surprised; previous intel had them in Grenoble. It was a stroke of luck, better logistics had meant his team had landed in Lyon not Grenoble, and he was 40 minutes better off. With cars loaded, JT and Nic jumped in the first SUV, Rob and Meek followed suit in the second. In formation, the SUVs exited the hangar. Making their way out of the airport complex, JT and his team aimed for the A6 péage north. They should be there in a couple of hours, forging the exact same path as the Apfel 'kill team', Fletcher bound but an hour back.

The Ibis was quiet – why wouldn't it be? – set back a couple of kilometres from the péage in open countryside and at 5 a.m. Dan lay motionless on his side of the bed. Last night had been awful and weirdly great. One of his sister's best friends was lying next to him. Kate Harper had been the only thing he had been fixated on for the last few months, and now she lay by his side. Perversely though, his sister's other best friend was lying dead in the morgue at Grenoble Hospital.

Nothing had happened between Dan and Kate. Sharing a bed had brought a certain level of intimacy, but comforting cuddles and a warm, long-lasting kiss goodnight had been the extent of their physical contact. It wasn't that the two of them hadn't wanted more – holding each other close last night was almost electric. They'd both felt it and had both squeezed each other tighter. Dan looked across to the sleeping Kate. A thick wisp of hair cut across her face, slightly stuck to the corner of her mouth. He reached across and, with the faintest of strokes, he cleared her face of the errant black locks. The heavy bruising to Kate's right cheek didn't detract from her beauty. Elegant cheekbones, beautiful brown face, long eyelashes and perfect nose, Dan was well and truly smitten.

Kate stirred a little, adjusting her head as she moved ever so slightly. She didn't wake though. She looked so peaceful; sleep was what she really needed. Dan, though, was wired. Yesterday's events had been on a continual loop as his mind ran through every bit of detail he could recall. He could recognize both killers, but particularly the one Ben had kicked in the ribs as they had fled the hospital theatre. Both men had always worn a hat, but Dan had got a very good up-close-and-personal view of one of them.

Why were they being chased though? This was the question that nagged him the most. Helen Waters' shooting had felt like a weird mistake, maybe a mentally unhinged lunatic? Now, though, it was clearly not a mistake, this was premeditated intent. The killers were 'miked up' too. That tinny voice he'd heard last night coming through the killer's 'earpiece', Dan, not an expert in the military, knew enough to understand that this was extremely professional – scary even. He ran the numbers, analysed, reassessed and circled back what he knew. Two assassins, trying to kill his sister, or was it Kate they were after? He looked across at the still sleeping Kate. But that couldn't be it. They'd tried to kill him and Ben too.

As his mind whirred, an uncomfortable feeling grew inside him. Glancing at his watch, it was just after 5:10 a.m. Suddenly that feeling became overwhelming, a sickening fear. They needed to leave. The killers had tried and failed at their second attempt on their lives. Why would they just stop now? His mind was racing. Leaning over, he gently shook Kate.

"We need to leave," Dan spoke quietly, gently even, as he did his utmost to sound calm whilst doing his level best to convey urgency. "Get yourself sorted, Kate, I'm getting Ben and Rachel," he continued.

She stirred, opening her eyes, initially smiling, her joy suddenly replaced by fear as she came to her senses. Dan's face wasn't hiding his thoughts. Fear was written all over him. Fear, though, not panic.

Kate shot up and started to collect herself as Dan exited the room in the direction of Ben and Rachel. Two doors down, he was quickly outside their door, rapping sharply. Inside there could be nothing misinterpreted, Dan's door knock conveyed a pressing urgency and nothing else. Opening the door, a fully dressed Ben didn't appear to have just woken either. Had he been running through stuff in his head too? Probably thought Dan.

"We need to go…" blurted Dan, "…we aren't safe…" he carried on as he strode past Ben.

Rachel was half asleep. She looked tired and uncomfortable. Shot in the shoulder, patched up and now on the run weren't conducive to sleeping well. She had slept badly.

"Rach, wake up… We need to go…" urged Dan as he stood over her bed. "We aren't safe, sis," he carried on.

Ben was in unison; he understood Dan's misgivings and had been having similar thoughts too. Moving swiftly, Ben stuck his shoes on; he'd slept in his clothes as had Rachel. Right now, this felt like the clever choice. Retrieving his phone and charger first, Ben started to chuck the few items Rachel had left on the hotel room table into her bag. Rachel was moving now, slower than her brothers, but to be expected – one functional arm slowed you down.

Dan darted back to his and Kate's room. In the two minutes he'd been gone Kate hadn't wasted time. Things just about all packed, she was just putting her shoes on. Dan chucked his few items in his bag and grabbed Rachel's car keys. All efficiency and urgency, he caught Kate's stare. Her eyes welled; he wasn't sure what she was feeling, what it meant, but he knew what to do. Dropping his bag, Dan closed the gap to Kate and just hugged her, pressing her tight to his chest, initially burying her head in it. He could feel her body shuddering, small, uncontrollable little shakes. Dan moved his arms upwards, cradling his hands around her face as he kissed her, a long, gentle kiss. Kate reciprocated as tears ran down her cheeks, the couple both experiencing a mixture of emotions, love blended with fear. At that moment in time everything was surreal, almost not real, but it was!

Standing intertwined, lovingly embraced, neither Dan nor Kate wanted to break their connection. Almost magnetically joined, pulling apart seemed to require an extra little force, but the fear inside Dan took control. As quickly as they had embraced, they now stood apart, a half smile on their faces.

The couple grabbed their bags and headed for Ben and Rachel. It was 5:30 a.m. Dan felt the strongest of urges to return to the UK. Somehow, he sensed this was the right call, the safe call.

Hurtling up the A6, Harry and Bush were 5 km from the péage turn-off. The last two hours Harry had gunned the black Audi, its engine had whined as he hit 100 mph for most of the journey. Quiet péages in France, made even quieter in the early hours, had afforded them the quickest of journeys. The Apfel 'kill team' were starting to smell their prey. Glancing across at Bush, Harry sensed a fire burning deep inside. Bush was hurting physically, broken ribs and almost flattened nose evidence of a fight he'd well and truly lost, but the pain Harry could see etched across his face wasn't physical. No, that wasn't what he could see as he looked deep into Bush's eyes, deep into his soul. Bush was suffering mentally. Was it shame? Anger? Something furious that was for sure. He was seething and right now all he wanted to do was correct yesterday's aberration; repair the damage, right a wrong – kill the Fletchers.

Dan pulled out of the Ibis car park. Ben, riding shotgun, started entering details into Rachel's satnav. They all knew the way, but there was something comforting about knowing the ETA. Five hours 40 to Eurotunnel, Calais read the display in the bottom left corner. Initially silent, the four of them started chatting as Dan made progress towards the péage. It wasn't small talk though, far from it. Directly to the police in Kent was top of the agenda, having dismissed the notion of reporting to the British Border Force in Calais. The four of them felt a strong desire to be on British soil as quickly as possible.

As the discussion continued, the entry to the péage grew closer; a single lane with an even tighter funnel to the péage, obstructed by a barrier blocking their way. Stop, take a ticket and the barrier would lift. As Dan pulled the car to a halt, Ben opened his window, reaching across to take the ticket. Across the road, two men in a black Audi had slowed as they exited the péage. They had a badge in their window, allowing them quicker access through the péage barriers, clearly heavy users of the French péage.

At 5:45 a.m. in winter, the skies were dark, almost entirely black, the only useful light emitting from the péage kiosk, but it was enough. Rachel's car stood out like the proverbial sore thumb. Although black, like the killers' Audi, it sported a bright white front number plate – a British plate! Harry saw it immediately. On the opposite side of the road and segregated by the péage kiosk system, there was no alternative – drive through the exit, U-turn and sweep round to re-enter the péage. Harry was good. He was great, in fact. He didn't speed up, he didn't overreact; his every action designed to remain unnoticed. It would have worked too. Dan wouldn't have noticed if it hadn't been for Bush. As Harry moved through the barriers, Bush leant forwards, his battered face looking almost demonic in the low lighting emitted from the kiosk. Dan saw it first as Ben, still focused on the ticket machine, shot upright.

"Shit… Shit, shit, shit… It's them…" screamed Dan as he gunned Rachel's Golf. The barrier was starting to rise, but too slowly. Dan smashed the plastic barrier to pieces; the brittle plastic showered the tarmac with shards of red and white fragments, while a large stump remained. As he made the Golf scream and whine, the girls in the back initially did their best to emulate the car. Panic had taken over. Dan floored it, asking Rachel's car to go as fast as it could. Behind them, the killers had wheeled around. Now in hot pursuit, Harry was flying back through the kiosk entrance, broken shards of barrier crunched under the tyres and some smaller pieces momentarily lifted from the floor such was the speed he was asking of the Audi.

Dan had a head start, but his initial gap, no more than 500 m, was quickly closing. A quicker car? Less weight? He ran computations in his head as he asked as much as he could of the Golf. It didn't matter, though, whatever the reason, they were quicker. The péage was deathly quiet, no cars visible ahead or behind. He kept gunning the car – what else could he do?

"What can we do?" he yelled, not really directing his question at anyone.

"People, we need people," Ben shot back a response. It was a good one too, but it didn't help. It was just shy of 6 a.m., the péage was empty, and they rarely had gendarmes on the French péages either. Dan continued driving as fast as his sister's car would allow.

Harry closed the gap, his prey almost within his grasp. Bush had his window down. Just 20 metres back, he aimed and fired. His first bullet shattered Dan's window, the bullet embedding itself in the dashboard, his second bullet lodging itself in the car door. At 100 mph, two cars swerving violently didn't allow for accurate shots. Bush's broken ribs didn't help either. Expletives and screams rained out of the mouths of Dan, Ben, Kate and Rachel. No longer just scared, panic had taken over.

Dan swerved wildly to the left, causing Harry to do the same. Bush's arm rocked violently in the window frame. Any shot right now would prove worthless. He retrieved his gun arm, holding the door frame for support. Dan swerved the car again, this time smashing into Harry. A grinding metallic noise, more felt than heard, belched out as the front end of Harry's Audi felt the full force of Rachel's Golf. Dan had the accelerator pushed to the floor as he willed the car to go quicker. It wouldn't though; the Golf was giving all it had.

Harry was drawing level now. Dan swerved once more, clashing again with the killers' car. At least they couldn't shoot whilst he smashed metal on metal. The Fletchers and Kate were doing all they could to remain upright as the Golf heaved dangerously to and fro, death by car crash the greater threat than being shot.

Ahead, a slip road came into sight – a slip road to an unmanned péage aire, essentially just a car park, some picnic tables and more than likely a toilet block. Common in France, these aires were interspersed with actual service stations. As the slip road approached, Dan went for it. Trying to leave it as late as possible, his thought process was as sharp as always. Turn off and allow the killers to sail straight on. It didn't quite work though; Harry was wise to it. As Dan turned sharply right to get on to the slip road exit, Harry followed suit. His apex was a little sharper though, as was his speed. Harry's Audi, struggling for grip, lost control. Initially keeping to his intended apex, the Audi veered violently right before swinging back left, finally departing from the tarmacked road and colliding head-on into a large tree. Dan too had struggled to maintain control of the Golf. He hadn't crashed, but the car now stood off the road amongst some small shrubs.

Dan instinctively looked to the killers and then to Rachel and Kate. They had a semi-beached Golf, but they were all seemingly OK. The black Audi was crumpled. Airbags had detonated and the driver wasn't moving at all. Harry was unconscious. A branch had smashed through his side of the windscreen; he wasn't dead, but out of the fight – for now. Remarkably, Bush appeared fine and was now attempting to open his door, with no joy. The crumpled Audi displayed a crease extending from the front right wing to the front passenger door. His door was not going to give.

Bush started to climb through his window, a slow process, made slower with shattered glass, a now deflated airbag and his broken ribs. His gun had dropped into the doorwell on his side. As he clambered out, both Dan and Ben recognized the danger. Dan had tried to get the car moving. The Golf screamed, but the wheels span wildly in ever-increasing muddy tyre grooves as the car merely wiggled left and right. Ben's presence of mind and blind bravery saved them. The Golf was going nowhere fast. He sprang from the car, sprinting towards the killer with every muscle fibre he could summon. Bush had already turned away, leaning through the window to retrieve his Glock. With gun in hand, Bush straightened as he made to turn in Ben's direction and shoot. It was too late, Ben's 80 kg at full tilt smashed into Bush, sandwiching him against the Audi. Dan now was in full flight too, recognizing the danger, understanding this was their only option, fight not flight.

With the wind knocked out of Bush, Ben had the upper hand, but it wasn't over. Wincing pain that shot across Bush's entire ribcage served his cause as he pushed back from the car, still clutching his Glock. Every muscle fibre twitched as he forced is gun-carrying arm towards a suitable firing position. His gun was almost pointing at Ben. A shot rang out as Bush squeezed the trigger, more down to the struggle than an intentional shot. At full speed, Dan's body smashed into the wrestling duo, Ben's body taking as much of the force as the killer's. Bush, though, suffered the most. The weight of the two brothers alongside a set of broken ribs started to take its toll. Dan had managed to grab Bush's gun hand, forcing his arm and, importantly, his Glock directly upwards.

Meanwhile, Ben took full advantage of the now exposed torso. With both of Bush's and Dan's arms pointing skywards, he didn't hold back. All the fury and anger Ben had ever harboured poured from him as he rained several sickening blows into Bush's stomach and ribs. Bush dropped the gun, his arms and shoulders relaxed. Dan felt the tension depart the killer's body. Releasing his grip, Bush crumpled to the floor, doubled up in agony, suffering and close to blacking out from the sheer pain.

Dan quickly collected the Glock from the floor, whilst Ben continued to kick the now unconscious Bush. In the distance, Kate and Rachel were now out of the car, fear still written across their faces, but at least the panic was starting to subside.

"You alright, bro?" Dan asked Ben, as he looked his brother square in the eyes. The pair of them were still breathing heavily, adrenaline coursing as they started to assess the situation.

"This is fucked, Dan, it's all fucked," replied the panting Ben. Looking first to the floor, the prone Bush wasn't moving. Inside the Audi, the other killer was still unconscious. Whilst Dan pondered what to do, Ben instinctively kicked Bush again, a barely audible, dull groan emanated from the man.

"He's got to die, Dan; he's got to die," grunted Ben. Barely escaping not once but twice, Dan and Ben had just fought for their lives, their would-be killer lying at their feet.

Ben kicked him again; this time no groan could be heard. Dan gave Bush an almighty kick to the head too, for good measure. Both brothers almost felt it, a soothing feeling. Maybe it was karma? Either way, neither Ben nor Dan walked back to the girls with any feeling of guilt. Neither checked whether Bush was dead, but something internal told them he was. Dan decided to keep the Glock. Returning to the car, he chucked it in his rucksack before looking at the next problem. A beached Golf was sitting well and truly stuck in its own muddy tyre tracks.

Dan didn't take long to get back on track. His mind was his single best attribute. Not only an adept critical thinker, he also had the ability to adapt, problem solve and at speed.

"Sheets, or clothing… We need something to go under the tyres," he blurted out.

Kate started pulling out some clothing from the boot, quickly inserting hers and Rachel's salopettes underneath the rear tyres.

"Pile in, we need weight… we need traction," ordered Dan.

The girls jumped in the back; Ben sat in the boot with the hatchback gaping open. Dan slowly released the clutch, inching the Golf forwards enough to allow the salopettes to get sucked under the tyres. With traction achieved, he didn't accelerate hard. Maintaining forward motion, Dan ever so slightly increased his speed. The Golf, having already discarded the now muddy salopettes, hit harder turf and eventually crept back on to the tarmac.

"Let's go, Ben," instructed Dan, as Ben leapt from the back. Closing the door, he climbed into his sister's now battered Golf; no front door window, a bullet hole in the door and the left rear wing was a state too. Rachel's car was a mess.

Dan started to drive, northbound, as before. As he entered the péage, a cold, wintry breeze rushed into the car as he picked up speed. It was going to be an uncomfortable journey home. Ben had retrieved his phone. He glanced towards Dan in search of a suggestion of who to call. It felt natural, right even. Surely, they should call someone, but who?

"Dad, call Dad," suggested Rachel. Although unable to see her brothers' faces, she also recognized what felt right. Ben and Dan nodded approval. As Dan continued driving homeward bound, Ben started tapping his phone. Speed dial four and 'Fatty Daddy' appeared on Ben's screen as the first ringtone, just audible inside the car, could be heard. Ben, ever the joker, had daft names for all his speed dial contacts. Fatty Daddy was Tom Fletcher's, not that he was fat, but that hadn't stopped his number two son.

As the third ringtone rang out, Dan reached across. Ripping the phone from Ben, he ended the call immediately.

"What's up?" Ben asked.

Dan jammed the brakes on, bringing the Golf to a screeching halt on the hard shoulder. Turning the ignition off, he swivelled 90 degrees, opening his face and body up for the benefit of Kate and Rachel in the back. He had a face of thunder, stern and serious rather than scared.

"This is wrong…" he started, "…it's all wrong… How did they find us?" he carried on. "This morning, how did they find us?" reiterated Dan. He had everyone's full attention.

The silence, broken only by a car as it whistled past them, was deafening. The last hour of their lives had been traumatic. Initially scared, the chase and then fight for their lives had gone a long way to hinder rational thinking. Dan was now back on track as his mind raced through the last 24 hours.

"Phones… throw them away… it must be our phones," he said as he looked his brother firmly in the eyes. "We're being tracked… it can only be our phones," he continued.

As he spoke, the girls furiously rummaged through their pockets, each digging out their mobile. Dan chucked Ben's out of the window followed by his own. Kate and Rachel followed suit.

"We should change where we're heading to," Dan suggested. Expanding, he outlined the fact that ever since the attempted murder in the hospital, they had been making an obvious straight line for the UK. This was wrong, Calais would be watched, maybe Dover or Folkestone too.

"What about Mum's?" suggested Ben. "It'd be a surprise, but it'd be safe too. Who would connect us with her?" he offered.

Rachel suppressed a growl, but the anger was all too evident. Splashed across her face, she struggled at any mention of their mum. To Rachel, her real and only mum was Sarah Fletcher, the mum that brought them up, not the mum that ran away, absolving herself of all family responsibilities.

Dan and Ben kept some kind of contact with their real mum. Both brothers had even met up with her a couple of years ago. Rachel wouldn't even open the present that landed every year for her birthday, neither would Sam. As the youngest two Fletcher siblings, Rachel and Sam could remember almost nothing of their biological mum.

"She's in Annemasse. It's quiet, out of the way. We could hide there whilst we work out a plan," suggested Ben.

Dan nodded; it made sense. Annemasse was in the exact opposite direction to the UK. With phones ditched, a change of direction made a heap of sense. With a gaping hole for a window and an obvious-looking bullet hole, they agreed a pit stop and another night in a cheap and cheerful hotel was needed first. With that, Dan fired up the Golf and set off. Getting off at the next junction, he headed south, Annemasse bound.

Eighty kilometres to the south, JT's two-car convoy was making good progress north.

"They're on the move," said Meek as she updated JT and Nic. Meek was tracking all three Fletchers via their phones, as Rob did his level best to keep on JT's wheel. Half an hour ago the Fletchers had left their hotel, clearly heading home. Meek was a little confused, though, because right now they'd stopped. It didn't make sense; they'd been on the road less than 30 minutes. Broken down?

It was good news though, the team were closing in and that was a good thing.

"Roger that," JT replied, reverting to radio comms language as he glanced in his rear-view mirror. He could just about pick out Rob and Meek's form in their car, dark as it still was.

Protecting the Fletchers, keeping them safe was within their grasp. MI6's Special Operations Team inched closer, Jonno would be pleased.

Back in the aire, Harry stirred. His head thumped, but other than a few cuts and bruises he seemed to be OK. How long he'd been out for was a mystery. The aire was deadly quiet. He figured it couldn't have been long though. Surely someone might have driven in by now.

Blood had trickled down his left cheek but was already coagulating. Showered in small glass cubes and the deflated airbag draped over him, Harry went to open his door. Where was Bush? Where were the Fletchers? His door wouldn't budge. The once compact Audi A3 was now even smaller. The front end and bonnet crumpled upon impact with the tree. With no windscreen, he clambered through the front, half sliding, half shuffling down the creased bonnet. As he did, he saw Bush's dishevelled body on the ground. Motionless, Bush looked a state. Approaching him, Harry feared the worst; the angle of Bush's head rang alarm bells. Kneeling, he gently shook Bush before checking the pulse in his neck. Bush was dead. Not a medical expert, but he was sure it was a broken neck or blunt head trauma. Not that it mattered. Dead is dead, mulled Harry.

He despised Bush – he certainly wouldn't be shedding a tear – the anger and remorse he now felt wasn't for his fallen comrade. He needed to call in. Henkl wasn't going to take this well. Business came first, though. Harry retrieved Bush's phone and wallet. Searching for his gun came to nothing. Grabbing the remaining first aid bits, he cleaned himself up as best he could.

Then he waited. Harry was good at waiting. He'd call Henkl once he was on the road. For now, he needed wheels. He should feel sorry for the next person to stop at the aire. He should, but he wouldn't. His need for wheels trumped the next passer's-by life.

As Harry patiently waited for some unlucky traveller, JT's team whistled past the aire. Meek was on speakerphone to JT's car as she walked and talked both cars to the Fletchers' location. Odd, very odd. JT slowed to a halt at the side of the péage. Meek was adamant, they were within five metres of all three Fletcher siblings, the cell site tracking was never wrong.

Nic spotted it first. A phone lay nestled in a clump of grass in the verge. As the team scoured the péage roadside, three more phones were discovered, the three Fletcher phones and an additional one – Kate Harper's.

"Fuck," voiced JT, vocalizing what his team were all thinking. He didn't wonder why the phones were there. That was obvious. In fact, he was comforted a little by the knowledge that the Fletchers were clever enough to discard such items, but why now? What did it mean? They couldn't have been killed, could they? The killers would just dump their bodies with their phones, right?

JT had more questions and no answers. Getting back in the cars, JT's team headed for the nearest town. Jonno needed updating and after that who knew where his team would be sent. For now, any kind of an eatery would do. It had been a long night; JT and his team needed a reset.

CHAPTER 15
SAM FLETCHER

2 p.m. Friday 6th January 2017

The match was nearing the end of the first half. Edinburgh University first XV played an uncompromising style of rugby, assisted by an exceptional crop of students, three of whom represented Scotland U20s. Sam Fletcher, arms on hips, stood on the wing breathing heavily. Icy plumes of breath emanated from his mouth. More steam escaped his body at the nape of his neck. Hot from the last 30 minutes of exertion, the match was in full tilt on a bitterly cold, Scottish winter's day.

At 6 ft 2 and 90 kg, Sam cut a dash. An incredibly good athlete, he could have been so much better had he decided to apply himself. Possibly a better 200-metre sprinter than rugby player, in an alternate life he might have made it as a pro. But Sam was a carbon copy of his older brother Ben; a happy-go-lucky guy, driven but fun-loving too. Finding both mental and physical challenges easy may have been his downfall. Sam had breezed through life, never really having to work hard to succeed. It was his only chink in a very sturdy piece of armour.

As he took off again, flying up the wing in the hope of receiving a pass from his outside centre, the two MI6 operatives casually shuffled on their feet. Both were sporting heavy winter coats, thick gloves and beanies, but they were still freezing. As soon as the game ended, they were under strict instructions; Jonno had been ultra clear.

Sam was to be taken in. A limited briefing would be required, sufficient to impress upon him the danger he was exposed to.

The match was being played on the main pitch. A moderate, seated stand ran along one length of the pitch with enough seats for maybe 400 spectators. At the far corner of the pitch, a run of netting a good 20 metres high served to prevent the ball getting kicked beyond the pitch and into the neighbouring field. Several small groups of spectators stood the other side of the netting, watching the match as they all shuffled from foot to foot too. No one appeared immune to the near zero temperatures.

Detached, a lone figure stood almost in line with the left-hand rugby post. Clad in blue jeans and black coat, they were another spectator just watching the game. Not just any spectator though, sporting a blue beanie served two purposes for the observant assassin. Drey was one half of Henkl's Gruppe Drei, his other half currently enjoying the warmth of their vehicle, situated in the car park by the changing rooms.

Drey's beanie was keeping him warm, but better still, it conveniently hid his earpiece. As he silently observed some occasional light-hearted banter would come through from Mex, currently themed around how warm Mex was whilst sat in the car – too warm in fact. The two Americans really got on. Apart from the East versus West Coast rivalry, Drey and Mex had a ton in common, similar humour and an uncannily similar upbringing too. Coming from blue-collar neighbourhoods, both had signed up at 16, in part to escape a shitty home life and in part to satisfy an urge to see what was out there, the 'out there' being a better life. Initially excelling in the marines, Drey and Mex passed selection to the best of the best, the SEALs. They crossed paths a few times, did a couple of special ops together and went on a few tough training courses too. Their friendship ran deep. Now in their late 30s, their once noble careers, protecting the weak, had taken a much uglier path. Neither had consciously decided to become 'killers for hire'. Both had landed decent 'private contracts' after leaving the SEALs. Earning five times their navy salary had led them to wanting more, more of the high life that required more money to fuel it.

Being headhunted by Henkl had made them both a little heady. In the navy no one blew smoke up your arse, it didn't work like that, quite the opposite in fact. In the navy, you got told you were shit when you were shit at something, then you got told nothing if you did something well. You never got praise.

Henkl had found them in their hotel bar in Baghdad. Concerns over morality had dissipated the second they received their remuneration offer, $500 000 per annum plus costs and significant 'add on' bonuses. It had been just too good to turn down.

Their current assignment had looked straightforward enough. Today had been observation and tomorrow, the 'hit'. Nothing is ever a constant though. Just now, Drey was stood in the near freezing cold watching his 'assignment' going south on him. At first unsure, he was now certain that Sam Fletcher was under observation.

The same two men now stood watching the match had been parked outside the changing rooms two hours earlier. Mex had seen them first thing in the morning outside Sam Fletcher's digs and in the café the Fletcher boy had gone to mid morning. Drey kept on point as Mex called it in, updating Henkl. The job would still go ahead, but this clearly complicated matters.

The match ended. It was another big win for Edinburgh. Two tries from Sam Fletcher hadn't quite won him the man of the match award, but he'd been close. As the players trooped off, the two MI6 agents nodded approvingly as they subtly followed suit. Adjoined to the changing rooms, a large bar and players' lounge provided a warm, comforting environment. They'd sit it out in there, warming up as they waited for Sam.

The bar was reasonably lively for a late Saturday afternoon. Spectators were now clientele, while players and coaching staff helped swell the ranks. Thirty minutes later and Sam appeared, shoulder to shoulder with a couple of teammates, boisterous and happy. No doubt about it, the match was well and truly over, festivities being next on the agenda.

Sam approached the bar, but he never made it that far. His happy, carefree world was about to be shattered, his night on the town too.

"Sam Fletcher?" asked Macky, as he stepped across Sam's path. It was a question, but a question the MI6 agent knew the answer to.

"Yeh, why?" Sam replied, not startled, just quizzical. He didn't know yet, but he felt it. He sensed the formality, the gravity of the man now standing in his way.

"We need to talk to you," Macky replied as he nodded to his fellow agent, Dec. As Macky responded, both agents had retrieved their IDs and were now proudly displaying them. Sam glanced at both, not really taking in the detail. The IDs were meaningless to him, he'd no idea what a real one looked like.

"You for real?" Sam asked, he wasn't really questioning their validity, just the fact MI6 wanted to speak to him.

As his mates watched on, Sam, indicating with a nod of his head, motioned the agents to a cluster of vacant chairs nestled around a low coffee table in the far corner of the lounge. Noticeably quieter too, it was as good as it was going get in the ever-busier sports bar.

Macky led the debrief, Dec providing the appropriate facial expression and low utterances to lend gravitas to the story. The story Sam heard was short on detail but incredibly compelling. His life was threatened as were his siblings'. When Sam had shown his disbelief, the two agents had been quick to whip out a horrifying dossier.

Several graphic photos showed the death of several young Americans. No expert, Sam could clearly see a pattern – executions. He was next. The single, central message spelt out by the MI6 agents was that Sam was next. Safe house though? His mind raced, momentarily lost in thoughts. How long would he have to hide? Could he bring his girlfriend? Not that Sadie was his girlfriend, more a friend with benefits, but that wasn't the point.

Sam had lapsed into silence as he worked through his thoughts, the almost permanent spark across his face lost, replaced by puzzlement. Why him? Really him? This mustn't be true.

"I don't understand... This can't be right..." offered Sam. "... Are you sure?" he continued, a hopeful look in his eye as he tried to contest, to interrogate the narrative he had just heard. The MI6 agents didn't flinch, didn't offer hope. In unison, both Macky and Dec remained grim-faced. The agents' togetherness, part of their professionalism, prevented the meeting from going off track, something all three of them could ill afford.

"We need to go now. RIGHT NOW," Macky asserted. Still stony-faced, he bored deep into the back of Sam's eyes. Not for a second did Macky glance elsewhere, eye contact was the most important form of communication. He had spent two days on a course in his early days at MI6. The course had an odd title *'Credibility and Dominance'*; essentially Macky had spent 16 hours learning how to use eye contact to assert control, to reassure and to both calm people down and to urge them to hurry. He'd learnt a lot, though some of the course had been hilarious too, bordering on acting at one point as he and his colleagues had been made to practise 'wild eye stares' and mood-lowering 'sad eyes'.

Now, though, the 16 hours spent exercising his eyes were paying dividends with firm words to Sam strongly backed by the most telling of glares. Sam was hesitant, devastated too. He had a slightly forlorn look as hundreds of thoughts swirled around his head, but equally, he became compliant. Macky had finally convinced Sam that they needed to go, right there and then.

With Dec leading, the trio exited the bar, oblivious to the watchful eyes. Dec took the driver's seat, Macky opting to sit in the rear with Sam. A minute later, Dec slowly negotiated the car park exit, turning right on to the main road, before accelerating away, the agents' car quickly disappearing into the distance, aided by the diminishing light.

Dec drove defensively, observing anything and everything as he navigated the 'priority' away from Edinburgh. As he did so, Macky had already called it in. The phone call with Jonno had deliberately been put on the car's speakerphone, in part so Dec could hear but mainly to help reassure Sam. Jonno was calm, reassuring, and masterful. The safe house address would follow, and Sam's parents were to be briefed face to face. As soon as Sam was safely ensconced in the safe house then he would be allowed to contact them over a secure line.

Drey turned away from the clubhouse, striding purposefully towards Mex still sitting in the warmth of their car. As Drey approached, he spoke into his throat mike.

"Call it in, Mex," said Drey, their report to Henkl wasn't going to go down well, but what could they do? It wasn't their fault, right?

"Ja, is it done?" came Henkl's clipped Germanic tones. Wrongly assuming the outcome hadn't helped his mood as he received the update from Edinburgh.

"No, Boss… we were compromised," replied Mex.

He'd fucked up; he knew it as soon as he said it. They hadn't been compromised, that made it sound like they'd made a mistake. *Fuck… fuck, fuck*, thought Mex as he replayed his own words instantly in his mind.

"Sorry, Henkl, my bad… I don't mean compromised… I mean…" Mex carried on, trying to right his wrong. He didn't get to complete his sentence though. An ever-agitated Henkl interrupted him in full flow.

"What do you mean…? Speak fucking English…" barked Henkl. Referencing 'speak English' was damning and Mex knew it. Henkl's English was perfect, but it wasn't his mother tongue, but it was Mex's!

Henkl's barb stung.

"EXPLAIN… and be quick," fumed the German, exasperated by the usually concise Mex.

Gaining some composure, Mex wrestled back control of his report. As he did so, Drey slid into the passenger seat, remaining silent, listening in to Mex's half of the conversation.

Fletcher was under Obs, reported Mex. Immediately after the game he'd been taken away by two men. Henkl quizzed Mex about the men, who they were, what they looked like, how they operated, more of an interrogation than a quiz. Not police had been the only common ground. Mex and Drey were certain it wasn't the police and Henkl had concurred. With that, Henkl rang off. Mex breathed a small sigh of relief, turning to Drey for solace. A beaming Drey took it up a notch at Mex's expense.

No sympathy was in Drey's opinion the price he'd paid for having the warmest seat in the house that afternoon.

"What's he said?" Drey asked, knowing full well that Henkl would have given the killers some parting instructions.

"We sit tight and wait," Mex replied and with that he turned the ignition, exiting the car park, to hole up and wait.

CHAPTER 16
JONNO S RENDEZVOUS

Jonno entered Waterstones, the hubbub of Trafalgar Square quickly dissipated, replaced by a soothing, whispery hum of voices. The bookstore offered a delightful, almost charming backdrop for a meeting.

Café W was a discreet, quiet place to meet, but prying eyes were always possible. Jonno understood, as did his opposite number.

Jonno, seated nestling an Americano, stared nonchalantly across the café, giving the appearance of daydreaming, lost in his own thoughts. To assume that would be entirely wrong. He was alert. He'd arrived 30 minutes early deliberately. Sitting patiently, Jonno had taken the time to observe and take in his entire environment. The mother and two kids in the corner, she'd have been the ideal spook with a cover like that, but she wasn't, of that he was confident.

The single guy in the corner reading a paper would have been more likely, had it not been for the fact he was already in the café with a three-quarter finished coffee. Jonno had similarly dismissed the other patrons already in the café. A couple, arm in arm, had entered five minutes after him. Smiling occasionally at each other, they'd caught his attention, but after 15 minutes he wrote them off too. The man fielded a call, causing the woman to visibly seethe. A couple of minutes into the call, the woman almost exploded creating a minor scene in such a quiet and tranquil environment. A bloke in trouble with his other half, Jonno allowed a small wry grin to himself.

It was secure; he knew it, felt it. Now he would just wait, Crystal wouldn't be late.

At exactly 2:59 p.m. Crystal entered Waterstones. A spritely forty-something lady, lithe and slim, Crystal Robinson was an interesting woman. Long, mousey brown hair, neatly tied back, green eyes and freckled face, Crystal still turned heads; she even got the odd wolf whistle. The girl-next-door look had served her well over the years. She looked after herself, ate sensibly, took the stairs not the elevator where possible and kept herself trim. It worked. She still looked great, impressive too given the world she moved in.

Still a man's world, skullduggery, politics, gentlemen's clubs were all things to contend with. Making London's CIA Chief of Station had been a big coup for Crystal. She'd been in London two years, cultivating important links with the various other agencies. Top of the list was her relationship with Jonno. Although almost 10 years younger than him, a thing existed between the two of them. Crystal liked Jonno, but she was too professional, too careful to let anything happen. Maybe it was Jonno just playing her? Who knew? It didn't stop her from reciprocating a smile here, a subtle touch of the arm there.

Crystal made light of the stairs to the first floor, entering Café W bang on time at 3 p.m. Seated in the far corner, Crystal picked out Jonno instantly. She almost glided between the tables as she made her way to the seated Jonno. Eyes smiling at him, she took a seat to his left rather than opposite him. It gave her as complete a view of the room as possible; spy craft never wavered. Jonno's eyes smiled back as he casually squeezed Crystal's arm as she sank in her seat. The pair exchanged pleasantries, in part to kill time whilst the waitress took Crystal's order, but equally because it was the 'dance they both did' each time they met up.

"Why am I here?" asked Crystal, dispensing with the pleasantries.

"Does there have to be a reason?" Jonno replied flirtatiously, an infectious smile aimed directly at her. It worked too, Crystal smiled back and, hard as she tried, she couldn't quell the warm feeling she now felt.

"There is always a reason… even when there isn't," Crystal shot back, still smiling as she eased back a touch in her chair.

"Ten dead Americans… what gives?" Direct and straight to the point from Jonno, no reference to who, where or what, but there didn't need to be. Ten was a precise number; a member of British intelligence wasn't interested in run-of-the-mill murders. Crystal knew exactly which 10 Americans he was referring to.

"You tell me, Jonno," replied Crystal, still playing hard to get, still deliberating in her mind as to exactly what to say, how much to tell.

"The school bus victims," Jonno replied sarcastically, still smiling though, not put out by Crystal's muted response. "Was it one of your own?" he continued.

Asking Crystal if someone from her own agency had assassinated 10 young Americans told her a lot. MI6 knew about the assassinations; they knew the exact number killed and here was MI6's top guy asking if the CIA had done it.

"Are we sharing on this?" Crystal enquired, the realization dawning that Jonno might not just be fishing, maybe MI6 had intel too – intel the CIA didn't have. He let slip a grin, a deliberate grin, one aimed at implying he knew more than he'd let on, a clever little 'tell' on purpose and designed to lure Crystal in. It worked too.

"Who did it?" Jonno had rephrased the question, but it was still there, needing an answer, requiring an answer.

Crystal had bought some thinking time as the two spooks danced around the subject, calculating what to divulge and what to hold on to. The Yanks and the Brits might have a so-called 'special relationship', and they shared a lot between their respective intelligence agencies, but they didn't share everything.

"OK, here you go," Crystal opened up, as she outlined what she knew. "It was professional, all killed with the exact same MO. Probably by kill teams with a minimum of two and it wasn't us."

As Crystal briefed Jonno, whilst listening intently, he scanned the room. It was clear, but he did it anyway. She was telling him what he already knew. Was she still dancing?

"Double teams, all using Glocks," offered Jonno, still on the charm offensive.

He smiled again as he looked Crystal directly in the eyes, the intel given to further demonstrate MI6 were still ahead, nothing new had been forthcoming.

"Come on Crystal, who are they?" asked Jonno, referring to the victims not the killers.

Silence descended. Crystal, motionless at first, leant forwards, reaching for her coffee. Jonno allowed a moment to reflect on what hadn't been said. He studied Crystal's lips as she sipped her coffee – a pretty tone of pink, no lipstick needed, considered Jonno.

"What do you know about genetic enhancement?" asked Crystal.

Till now she hadn't got a read on Jonno. The perfect poker face, a mixture of facial expressions and body language had disguised every single 'tell', but just then, he'd given away a single but very telling sign. He had straightened up ever so slightly, having initially averted his focus on Crystal he'd overcompensated to cover up, a clumsy attempt.

"Walsh," Jonno replied.

It was just one word but it was worth a thousand. Jonno's thoughts immediately leapt to the plight of the Fletchers. Gathering himself, he'd need to be careful how he played this out.

"Has she really done it?" he continued, firmly back in control of his poker façade. Not just in control, Jonno was already several steps ahead in the game of chess he was currently playing with Crystal. There and then he knew this was going to 'go well'.

He went into free flow, explaining to Crystal that Louise Walsh had come to him, the 'him' being the British government. Efficacy and morality had become problematic, then costs and finally the red line the government at the time couldn't get past. Walsh had crossed a line; she'd gone rogue, very rogue. Jonno elaborated a little; deaths of infants and 'experts of the time' confidently saying her work was of no value had been the final nail in her coffin. She had been cut loose, unshackled but watched from a distance for a while, and then finally forgotten about.

Jonno's openness worked a treat. Crystal had won, or so she thought. Falling for his change of tack, she finally gave information back. The two-way street was now up and running.

"Walsh came to us after you discarded her." Crystal deliberately chose the word 'discard', taking enjoyment out of the Brits missing a trick. "We ran with her; the programme was called 'Steelhorse'. It works, Jonno, it works. She has resolved her early difficulties; she has managed what she couldn't originally."

"Was called?" interrupted Jonno, picking up on her use of the past tense.

Crystal carried on, now in full flight she'd half forgotten the golden rule – give a little, take a little. The lifeblood of the intelligence service was 'information'.

"We worked with Walsh; we created them together, but then things turned sour. She demanded more money, bigger facilities, her own staff and finally her own security detail. We were on top of things, we had everything covered, but it wasn't enough. She left and went private. She's based in Switzerland," she continued to elaborate. "But you already knew that... didn't you?" abruptly ending her narrative.

Jonno was sat stony still, taking every syllable in. The sharp ending had slightly caught him out, but he was nimble, adept in any situation. Crystal had been very considered with her ending. He was only momentarily on the back foot, though.

"Them?" Jonno asked, clarifying what he thought. The 'them' referred to the 10 dead Americans, 10 of Louise Walsh's creations, 10 genetically enhanced human beings.

"She calls them MorphEns," Crystal responded. "They are everything she told your government back in the early days, the perfect human being. They are off the charts in every test they have ever done. All of them scored in the 99th percentile in every mental task, every SAT. Physically gifted too. One of them was heading for the Olympics; a couple of others could have done so too."

Jonno sat impassively, hoping Crystal would keep chattering away whilst working his next angle.

"So, I have shown you mine, now you show me yours," ended Crystal, the free flow of intel now on hold, scanning the room again before returning her gaze towards him.

"We don't have anything concrete," Jonno started, already in disinformation mode. "We had no idea about who your 10 dead ones were. We picked up chatter, collated it, put two and two together. They were all the same age, all killed with identical MOs. Our SitRep picked up on it and that's why I'm here."

As Jonno continued his story, oozing confidence, he replayed his own narrative back to himself. Believable? Yes, he thought so. Carry on then was how he figured it.

"Our office in Zurich has a connect with someone at Interpol. Some chatter came our way about a company called BioDS, Walsh's company. But we have nothing, just white noise, and that's why I am here, asking."

Crystal nodded her head, he wasn't quite sure if she was convinced, but she didn't seem too quizzical. That must be a good thing, he thought.

"Why? Why kill them?" Jonno finally asked the question, the question that neither knew the answer to; the million-dollar question.

"We have no idea," replied Crystal as she shuffled in her seat, casually sweeping a rogue strand of her hair from her eyeline.

In the 20 minutes the two had been together, a great deal of intel had been shared. But it hadn't, Jonno had been wily. He'd given little and gained lots, but he still had more questions than answers and clearly Crystal was in the same boat.

The meet started to draw to a natural end. Jonno had what he wanted and more. As the pair finished with more pleasantries, Crystal just started to wonder whether she'd been duped. Questioning herself, a tiny nag in the back of her mind started tapping away.

"Am I being played, Jonno?" she asked as she stood to leave, looking Jonno square on, hoping for a sign.

He looked Crystal directly in the face, not a flinch, not a single 'tell'.

"Why do I feel like I've just missed something?" suggested Crystal with a slight unease in her voice. The nag wasn't dissipating, she smiled, nonetheless. She couldn't stop herself. In another world, at another time, maybe she could have something more intimate, more concrete.

"If I knew, you'd know," replied Jonno reassuringly, touching Crystal's hand gently as he made to exit. The two spooks, scanning their environment, departed. Crystal headed for the toilets, Jonno directly to the ground floor. He exited Waterstones, Vauxhall bound.

Five minutes later, Crystal exited Waterstones, joining the throng of people bustling around Trafalgar Square. Walking at a brisk pace, she hit speed dial two, the single word 'Pav' appeared on her screen. Just a couple of ringtones completed before he picked up.

"Is this secure?" he quizzed, sidestepping formalities instantly.

"Yes, Pav, we're encrypted," Crystal replied. "Six knows about Steelhorse…" she continued, the 'Six' referring to Jonno's MI6.

"How?" came Pav's curt response.

"I'm working on that," she replied reassuringly. She'd anticipated Pav's question and had her answer pre-planned. Crystal expanded a little as she outlined to Pav the next steps she'd be taking. With Pav suitably satisfied, she rang off. Not once slowing her pace, Crystal disappeared into the crowd milling around Trafalgar.

CHAPTER 17
HOLED UP

Saturday 7th January 2017

Kate stirred, slowly coming to her senses, mixed emotions competing for headspace. Her eyes focused as the grogginess dissipated. Taking in her surroundings, the hotel room was basic but clean and functional. Waking up for the second morning running with Dan beside her was comforting. On the run from killers, discarding their phones, hiding in nondescript hotels was beyond surreal.

Looking across at Dan, she marvelled at him. He was good-looking, Kate had always thought so, but he was much more. As he lay there, eyes wide open, staring quietly at the ceiling, she could almost see his brain ticking. She was clever; she'd always done well in her studies. Highly intelligent, she had added to this with diligent hard work too, but Dan was on another level. Yesterday, after all the panic, a run for their lives and a fight to the death, it was Dan who had the foresight to discard their phones.

Having suggested heading to a safe haven, he had then come up with another layer of protection. Rather than drive back south, the group had headed west, not before stopping at a Mr.Bricolage for some provisions. The car needed some work to prevent it catching unwanted attention. Dan's DIY shopping list had included a screwdriver, tape, clear plastic sheeting, expanding foam and paint.

He wasn't finished. Having paid by credit card he'd instructed the entire group to rinse their accounts for as much cash as they could withdraw. Last night's westbound hotel was to be their final transaction paid for by credit card. As soon as Dan and Ben had the car fixed up a little, then their circular southbound journey to safety would begin; a journey with no breadcrumbs for anyone to follow. Kate wouldn't have thought up any of the plan. Dan's mind, though, thought things through, wading through the detail, analysing and computing at an incredible speed.

Dan, with Ben's assistance, had deliberately left the car untouched as they made their way westwards, deliberately stopping to fill up with fuel at one service station, stopping for coffee and food at the next. Then a decent-sized shopping spree at the Carrefour was the final stop prior to landing at their hotel, another Ibis, all deliberately leaving a credit card trail directly west.

Having holed up at their latest Ibis Hotel, Dan and Ben had busied themselves in readiness for the following day's 'about-turn'. Dan had been certain that Rachel's car would have been picked up on a bunch of CCTV images. The bullet hole clearly displayed in the door, British plates and no passenger side window were hard to miss. He had stolen a set of French number plates, with the aid of the screwdriver. Next, he'd sealed up the hole in the window with the plastic sheeting and filled in the bullet hole with foam, making a decent job of painting over it. It was by no means perfect, but good enough to limit any cursory attention paid towards his sister's Golf.

Dan was an utter hunk, and Kate was well and truly smitten. That was his initial appeal. Yet he made her feel safe. Currently in a terrifying run for their lives, she would have been totally lost without him. The same probably applied to the others too. Dan seemed to be the glue holding them all together, keeping them safe whilst doing his level best to stop events spiralling out of control.

As Kate, motionless, studied Dan's face, he looked across. Sparkling green eyes, leading the way, smiled at her, followed quickly with a broad grin. She felt a tingle shoot through her body. Dan rolled 90 degrees towards her. Gently cupping her face with his right hand, he part pulled her face to his, whilst closing the gap still further himself. As he kissed her ever so lovingly, the tingles Kate felt suddenly turned into goosebumps. Her entire body stirred, she felt her nipples harden as he ran his hand off her face, past her breasts and as far as her hip bone.

Kate longed for his hand to continue its direction; she was ready for him, ready to cement their unity. Reversing direction, Dan purposely brushed her left breast as he returned to cupping her face. She kissed him harder, the strongest of hints that when he was ready, she was all his. Dan broke off his kiss, pulling back a smidge to allow his eyes to focus on hers.

"Morning you," he said, breaking the silence. Kate loved Dan's phrase. He used it often, but only with those he was close to, a select few.

"Morning," she whispered back, not wanting their conversation to enter the real world, desperate to remain in their private, nondescript hotel room where no one could find them.

"We need to hit the road," Dan replied, bringing her back to reality with an enormous bump, exactly what she'd been hoping not to happen.

"I know," whispered Kate, still harbouring hopes of them staying put. It wasn't going to happen though, and she knew it. They had a plan, and they needed to crack on with it.

Today was all about changing direction without leaving any breadcrumbs – no trail whatsoever.

The plan was to make most of the distance towards Bordeaux, holing up en route for a third night in hiding. Then, if they felt it was safe and the trail had gone cold, they'd make a slow about-turn towards Annemasse. Kate got dressed before scurrying off to attend to Rachel. Her dressing needed changing and wound looking at.

CHAPTER 18
THE INNER CIRCLE

8 p.m. Saturday 7th January 2017

The meeting had been hastily convened. Ram hadn't needed a heads-up. Although early Saturday evening, he was still in his 'Arena'. Ram's life was work and nothing more. Wendy Angel wasn't dissimilar, although it had taken her 40 minutes to scurry over to Langley following Pav's call.

Ram despised Wendy, he knew her nicknames and he was equally a little frightened of her. Unsure why exactly, he just sensed a darker side to the Ice Queen. He was doing his utmost to hide his contempt for Wendy, hindered by the slightly smug look she had plastered across her face. She was now in the 'inner circle'. Written in to Steelhorse, a few other perks had followed, the biggest one being access to Ram.

Until recently, Ram had only answered to Pav, but now, he begrudgingly had to answer to Wendy too. Her smugness inversely matched his irritation, and she knew it. Still, there were always the specially designated programmes that she didn't have the clearance for. Ram's privileged position allowed him more access regardless of the fact he was the Ice Queen's underling.

"What do the Brits know?" Wendy asked with the confidence her lofty clearance now gave her. Previously she'd have waited for Pav to commence proceedings, but things were different now, a little more even. He recognized this too. In fact, Pav was almost as uncomfortable with her new clearance level as Ram, but he couldn't put that back in the box now. The old status quo was a thing of the past. Wendy had more power, and she was flexing it right now.

"They know about Steelhorse…" Pav replied, "…they know about the assassinations too," he continued. The already eerie room took on a gloomier feel as he explained further. Subdued lighting, a myriad of green LCD screens in the large, windowless room added to the ambience. "We think they know more than they're telling too," he outlined.

"What's the source, Pav?" Wendy almost grilling him wasn't lost on Ram either. Pav had to check himself before replying. She was beginning to irk.

"Do I need to remind you who's in charge here?" he snapped, finally tipped over the edge by her exuberance. Ram stymied a tiny smile as Wendy looked Pav full in the face a little sheepishly. Admonished but not silenced, though.

"You've put me on point," flashed the bullish Wendy, unprepared to wind her neck completely in.

The defiance in her brought about a momentary impasse as Pav evaluated his stance. He had almost instantly regretted his decision to bring her into the fold and right now that uneasy feeling was growing. He'd circle back to that later, now though actions needed discussing. Pav bit his lip and rose above Wendy and her mannerisms. Ram silently observed the power struggle; his fear of Wendy had just elevated a notch or two. Maybe this evening had been her first big mistake, pondered Ram.

"Crystal met with Johnson…" replied Pav… "…Head of MI6…" he continued, more for effect than detail. Both Ram and Wendy knew all about Johnson, although neither knew 'Jonno' personally. Pav did.

"Direct from the horse's mouth…" More a statement than a question from Wendy. "…Do we trust it?" she added, now very much a question. The Brits were good allies to the CIA, not an open book, but that was the intelligence game across the globe. But in the main, the CIA and MI6 were tight, very tight.

"Crystal says so," replied Pav. Placing Crystal Robinson's endorsement on the intel gave the intel validity. She was CIA

London Chief of Station; Wendy had beaten Crystal to the punch with the Assistant Director CIA job, but she had recognized at the time how much of a close-run thing it had been. Quite clearly Crystal was a rising star at Langley. She was 'tight with Pav' too, something that had always unsettled Wendy. The uneasy feeling she had about Crystal worsened once she learnt of her current CIA clearances. Crystal was written in to Steelhorse and Doorstop, amongst other Level 5 programmes, whilst Wendy was still playing catch-up.

Ram and Wendy remained silent as Pav expanded. "Somehow, the Brits knew about our dead MorphEns. They don't know who or why, at least that's what they're saying. London thinks they know more than they're letting on." Pav referencing London rather than Crystal was not lost on Wendy. He was protecting his asset, shielding Crystal wasn't necessary though. She was a fervent Pav acolyte and someone Wendy had recognized years ago as 'off limits' to Wendy's sphere of influence.

Ram swivelled left to right in his chair as he listened intently. None of the politics or power struggle was lost on him. He drifted off a little as he allowed thoughts of Crystal to take over. More than 10 years his senior, Ram liked Crystal in a very unprofessional way. As brilliant as he was in the murky tech world he lived in, outside of that, he walked unnoticed in real life. Sadly, for Ram that included Crystal. He knew he had no chance. Less than no chance given he would never even make an approach, but it didn't stop him dreaming.

"Do the Brits know about Knacc?" interjected Wendy deferentially. Pav noticed the easier tone in her question, a first step to making a more cohesive meeting.

"The short answer is we have no clue," he replied, puzzlement plastered across his face as he responded. "We have no one internal either, Johnson runs a tight ship." Pav had a mole in MI6, but his mole didn't have access to Jonno's special operations team. For now, he would have to rely on Crystal's ability to share and pry intel from Jonno. Pav's alternative, and not one he cared for, would be to 'write Johnson in to Operation Steelhorse' – almost unthinkable.

Silent, barring pleasantries, now was Ram's opportunity. He didn't provide human intelligence extracted via personal relationships. His way was via the back door.

"What if I could 'pick' MI6?" offered Ram, the smile across his face serving to accentuate his weak chin and gawky-looking face. Wendy smiled too, but not as Ram thought, in solidarity with him and his well-known hacking ability. Although appreciating the talents Ram possessed, she thought him to be a stupid, little boy with sad, inflated ideas about how the world viewed him. Insisting on everyone calling a hack a 'pick' was one of many of his sorry attempts to big himself up. Remaining silent though, she allowed Ram to shine.

"Can you get through?" questioned Pav, unable to hide the doubt in his query, for good reason too. Ram, as good as he was, didn't always succeed. He had previously tried and failed to access MI6's system.

"I don't know, Pav…" replied Ram, "…I have a new Trojan to trial…" he continued. "…First thing tomorrow, Pav…" Interrupted mid sentence, Pav's face glowed.

"Good job, Ram, start ASAP," Pav tipping his head in Ram's direction as he spoke. A small but deferential gesture as much designed to solidify their relationship given the 'Wendy problem' that now existed. Ram returned the gesture, much to Wendy's ire.

Now in firm control of proceedings, Pav started to lay out instructions for both Wendy and Ram. The two most pressing matters left to deal with were laid at Wendy's feet. Protective custody for the four surviving MorphEns was first up. Until now, they'd been under a heavy covert detail. Pav had been wrestling with this approach ever since the events in Yale. The report from Crystal had now brought matters to a conclusion. If the Brits knew about the assassinations, then what else was known? What else was going on? A haven for these four was needed and needed quickly. That brought as many problems as it did solutions. Explaining why they were in danger meant the truth or a bloody good cover story. He hadn't come up with the solution to that one.

Finally, Pav arrived at the main reason for ruining everyone's Saturday evening, Operation Doorstop and Knacc.

"You have THE green light." Emphasizing 'THE' and with no mention of Doorstop, Pav was speaking directly to Wendy. Clear engaging eye contact left her in zero doubt as to what he was referring to, Operation Doorstop.

"Doorstop, when?" Wendy asked; her team were in place and good to go. She suppressed a gulp as she asked. Doorstop was a big operation with serious ramifications if it went wrong. In fact, it had almost as many knock-on issues if it went to plan. The technical term was 'collateral', but the trio seated in Ram's Arena would all revert to a much more common phrase, 'shit'. No matter how Doorstop went, it was guaranteed that some 'shit' would follow.

"As soon as your people are able," commanded Pav.

Doorstop was a serious breach of another regime's security. Not just any regime either, Russia was mighty. Russia represented one of the world's genuine axes of power alongside the US and its allies, with China taking the third slot in the world triumvirate. Pav demonstrated his power, his leadership, as he took full ownership of Operation Doorstop. Wendy nodded her head solemnly. She wanted to smile but she didn't. Just there, at that moment, she had been given what she had wanted, the green light. Doorstop was a go.

She rose from her seat, no formalities, no goodbyes. Almost gliding through the room, she felt the energy surging through her. Pav had conceded knowledge and clearance levels. Now she was fully in his confidence too. As soon as she exited the door to the Arena, Wendy retrieved the first of two mobiles from her bag, not breaking stride as she marched in the direction of Langley's car park west.

The display on her phone showed a single word '*Dad*'. It took just three ringtones to be answered, but not by her dad.

"Yes, ma'am," answered Drake, with his typical military efficiency.

"You have a green light..." replied Wendy keeping the conversation to a minimum, "...tomorrow evening..." she carried on with her short but succinct instructions.

"Roger that, ma'am," he replied. The line went dead almost immediately, Wendy had already rung off, instantly pocketing the phone before pulling out a second mobile.

She trawled through her speed dial options, hitting number four. The screen sprang into life, *'Mike Gratton'* displayed neatly in two lines across the centre of her mobile. It was early Saturday evening, but she knew Mike would answer. Mike Gratton was both loyal and committed. As her right-hand man, he was privy to most of what Wendy knew too. Upon answering, she proceeded to relay instructions and fill Mike in.

"Are you home?" she asked, having finished her official business. Mike knew exactly what that meant, a boss with benefits – not a girlfriend, just benefits.

"See you later then," Mike replied before signing off, and with that Wendy continued marching purposefully towards her car.

Back in the Arena, Pav and Ram were still huddled together conspiratorially. With the absence of Wendy, both men had relaxed their guard.

"Whatever she asks you, Ram... circle back to me," Pav instructed. The nodding Ram hadn't needed telling. Wary of Wendy wasn't even 'the half of it', and for good reason too.

"And her permissions?" Ram replied, referring to Wendy's clearance access.

"Strictly Level 5..." answered Pav, "...all O'Connor designations are OFF LIMITS," he continued. A broad beam splattered across Ram's face with Pav's final instruction. He was now answerable to Wendy, but it wasn't a one-way street. Pav was still doing what he could to keep Wendy firmly in the dark. With that Pav departed, there was still a part of his Saturday evening worth salvaging.

Ram though remained. The Arena was his life, his entertainment. As the Arena door swung shut, the sound of Pav's footsteps disappeared. The Arena fell stony silent, just the tippy-tapping of Ram's keyboard audible. He was already immersed in his world, a world of code and of cascading characters across multiple LCD screens.

CHAPTER 19
GREEN LIGHT

10 p.m. Sunday 8th January 2017

Drake, crouched behind a large pine tree, had 'eyes on' the large building located ominously across the open ground. His team were all similarly ensconced in the forest, hidden within the treeline that encircled Knacc.

The CIA 'kill team' had been watching and waiting for over an hour. A few comings and goings had interrupted what was a quiet and bitterly cold night. The imposing building was silhouetted against a dark, winter skyline, while mild yellow, intermittent lighting helped to break up the darkness. The 6 m fencing had lights every 50 m directed onto the open ground between the forest and the fence line. The building itself had downlighting every 10 or so metres. This lighting was white, helping to bathe the walls and the path that hugged the building.

Between the main building and the sentry box, the road was lined with inset lights, helping to demarcate the tarmacked road from the tidy, well-kept lawn. The sentry box was manned by a solitary guard, seated and motionless. The sentry, head tilted down, appeared to be reading, anything to help while away the long, lonely night-time, Drake guessed.

To his left, Dmitry and Kaspov huddled together behind the same large pine, the best of buddies now in operational mode. Gone was their usual light-hearted and chatty banter. Crouched and motionless, both men scanned the entire perimeter through their NVDs. Their world was entirely a dull green.

Peter tapped Drake on the shoulder. He leaned back a touch, closing the gap to Peter to help reduce noise.

"Trojan Team two minutes out," whispered Peter. Drake didn't reply, instead giving him the 'OK' signal, touching the thumb and index finger together while the other fingers of the hand were held outstretched.

Drake looked to his left, catching Dmitry's attention. With silent use of hand signals, he held two fingers up before pointing a flat, vertical hand in the direction of the compound. Dmitry acknowledged him before turning to his left, passing an identical instruction to Kaspov. Drake's unit, professional and well drilled, passed the instruction precisely down the line, and then they just waited. All their preparation, training, rehearsals and yet more rehearsals were about to be put to the ultimate test. The 'kill team' did their utmost to quell nerves, minimising nervous energy expenditure was vital.

Drake's team all silently ran through their roles, the time sat waiting for their two-man Trojan Team to arrive spent wisely. Time seemed to have drifted into slow motion, each second felt like an hour.

Just as Drake glanced at his watch for what felt like the hundredth time, a pair of lights became visible in the distance. A small, indistinct van slowly approached the facility, as it neared the sentry box it slowed to a crawl before stopping completely.

Through his NVD, Drake could only see two forms in the van, a pair of dull green, unrecognizable human beings, but he knew who they were. The driver was Todd, and his accomplice was Siski; trained killers. The sentry approached the driver's side window, an arm outstretched; he'd clearly asked Todd for his paperwork. A couple of seconds later and another human life was extinguished. The green form of the sentry suddenly crumpled to the ground and with that Drake, from 200 metres' distance, saw a flurry of activity as Siski jumped out of the van, furiously dragging the now dead sentry back into his pillar box.

That was the 'GO'. Drake quickly stepped out from the shadows of the forest, running quick and low across the open ground to the fencing section that stood immediately between his team and their target. His entire team following suit, their dash across the open ground almost looked choreographed. The clock was ticking, his team had to get in and out in 10 minutes, 10 murderous minutes.

Dmitry surged ahead, a small handheld laser cutter gripped tightly in his right hand. Such was Dmitry's lightning speed, he had almost got half the breach cut before the last of the team had made their ground. A few seconds later, an aperture big enough to crouch through was complete. The 12-man 'kill team' filed through, all speed and efficiency.

Drake's team split as they sprinted towards the building. Two men had peeled off instantly, darting off around the northern perimeter of the building. Of the remaining 10 men, the two at the vanguard had made it to the front door ahead of Drake and his eight-man search-and-destroy team. Time was now the scarcest of commodities. The last hour, Drake's team had remained totally covert, out of sight and as quiet as a mouse. Now, though, things were about to get very loud, very quickly.

The main double doors, oversized and modern, were located 30 metres from the corner of the building. Drake's vanguard, plastic explosive and detonator in hand, arrived first. In just five seconds, a small putty-like circle of plastic explosives sat neatly surrounding the locking mechanism, the detonator immediately stabbed firmly into the explosive with a short det cord to its operator.

His eight-man team stood a couple of metres short of the door, automatic rifles in hands. It was an ominous sight. The det operator had worked wonders. Just three more seconds, slight pressure applied to his handheld detonator and the charge went off. It wasn't an enormous bang, but it would almost certainly be audible to someone inside the building. Not that this mattered any more. The detonation created a momentary flash of light as a puff of fire burst across the locking mechanism.

With smoke still swirling from the explosion, Drake planted a foot firmly across the left-hand door, kicking it wide open as he charged inside. His men scurried through too. Drake, instantly confronted by an occupant, aimed and fired without hesitation.

Releasing three shots in fewer seconds, the look of surprise on his victim's face was instantly replaced with fear followed by death. His first kill was so swift his victim didn't even manage to cry out.

His team split into two groups of four. Drake, leading team one with Kaspov, Dmitry and Peter in tow, went straight ahead and, according to the data Ram had sourced, directly to the ancillary facilities within Knacc. Leading team two, the sinewy Sascha and his team charged off in the direction of the sleeping quarters.

In less than a minute since the sentry had been overwhelmed, Drake's team were now wreaking havoc as their deathly mission really kicked in. His own team worked the building, in pairs they leapfrogged one another as they methodically went from door to door. With each door opened, a grenade was thrown in, the kill teams' guns held sighted to shoot as they followed each explosion. Occasional shots were released at the already prone bodies.

As Drake moved deeper into the bowels of Knacc, a great deal of gunfire could be heard from the direction Dmitry's team had gone in. Interspersed with the noise of flash-bangs and frag grenades, Dmitry and his team were clearly in the thick of it.

Drake and Kaspov, having re-entered the corridor, moved swiftly to the next door down. Kaspov, on point, opened the door, throwing a flash-bang, a grenade designed to stun and disorientate. The pair darted through the door, revealing a large room with low-level, comfortable seating, coffee tables dotted around, and furniture hugging the right-hand wall. It was a scene of mayhem and carnage.

A young man, prone across the floor, was clutching his head in both hands to cover his ears. To the man's left, an upturned coffee table had scattered its contents. Strewn across the floor, a chessboard and its pieces lay amongst debris from a couple of broken glasses. Kaspov hadn't wasted a second, a double tap to the man, instantly killing him, as he resighted his rifle. In automatic mode, he began to lay waste to the shrieking, terrified men and women as they did their utmost to make for safety.

Drake, shoulder to shoulder with Kaspov, did similarly. Shooting on sight, young men and women dropped to the floor. Drake was wide-eyed as he concentrated on his mission, adrenaline fully flowing, all his sensory organs operating in overdrive. In his field of view, a young couple came to the foreground. Assassination was often a quick thing, a rapid action designed to benefit by surprise. He had entered the room 10 seconds ago, surprise no longer his ally. As Drake adjusted his aim for these two new targets, first the woman then the man moved to close the gap on him.

With remarkable speed, Drake's prey had now become his assailants. Fighting for their lives, why would they go quietly? A myriad of thoughts whistled through his mind as he did his utmost to aim, shoot and kill. The eight-metre gap should have been enough for him to get his shots off, but it wasn't. Suddenly he was compromised, a single shot had released, hitting the woman in her left shoulder. As the blood spurted out on impact, the woman had continued her charge. Drake's second shot also found its target, the bullet passing directly through the woman's lung cavity, exiting and embedding itself in the man's right pectoral muscle.

Undeterred, the man smashed into him, neatly sidestepping the buckled over young woman. Drake was surprised. He was in the thick of the action, but clarity of thought, honed and perfected through countless hours of training, allowed him to take stock of his situation. Later it would be something he could review too, why, what and how he did and did not do something. In that moment though, Drake noticed, noticed that the young man and now dying woman had moved with alarming speed. They'd gone towards not away from danger. Although counter-intuitive, it had been the right call. The man was now wrestling with him. Bullet wound to his shoulder and easily 40 pounds lighter than him, yet Drake was struggling. The fight was not going Drake's way at all. Shots continued to ring out as Kaspov continued his murderous actions. Drake though was overwhelmed. Two vice-like hands gripped tightly to his wrists as the two men fought for control of his rifle. Drake, straightening his body, lent forwards heavily on his assailant. He might not have the upper hand physically, but fight craft could compensate. Engaging his core, he then pulled his opponent towards him as he thrust his right knee ferociously upwards. He felt the connection. It was a good one. Strong and powerful, it was a sickening blow.

The young man seemed unperturbed. The wrestle to the death continued unabated. Just as quickly, Drake pulled his head back as much as was possible, before brutally snapping his head and neck forwards, planting a headbutt firmly on his opponent's nose. He more felt than heard the crack, the familiar sound of a broken nose concealed by the mayhem within the room. Rather than fall away from him or loosen his grip, the young man returned the compliment. Learning quickly maybe? In what seemed like the blink of an eye, Drake received a brutal blow from forehead to nose. Blood splattered across his face, a mixture of his and his quarry's.

With arms still locked together, Drake's energy levels were wilting. He desperately needed something to unnerve his opponent. His future was beginning to look bleak. Two more shots rang out loudly, blood sprayed across Drake's already crimson face. The instantaneous death of his opponent didn't register immediately though. He felt it first, the grip loosened on his wrists and then his opponent's body crumpled inwards. Leaning on Drake, his opponent slid unceremoniously to the floor, a gaping hole in the side of the young man's head.

Drake looked to his right. Kaspov, staring down his gun sights, lowered his gun before nodding his head at him, a tiny piece of body language to check he was OK. Drake reciprocated.

Momentarily taking in the devastation within the room, 20 plus bodies lay amongst the debris. Tables, chairs, broken ornaments and books were spread haphazardly across the floor – utter carnage. Back on it, Drake and Kaspov took flight, exiting the room to continue their murderous path through Knacc.

The rat-a-tat-tat of automatic gunfire echoed around the corridor, emanating from the door 10 metres ahead. Drake quickly closed the ground, Kaspov followed suit. The corridor, broad and at least 50 metres in length, ended with a 90-degree, right-hand turn, presumably marking the internal building perimeter. As he advanced, a figure in the distance darted out of a doorway. Shots rang out, Drake felt displaced air as two bullets whizzed past him, high and wide – close enough though. Kaspov had instinctively ducked, now crouched on one knee, firing furiously at the lone shooter. His shots missed the target, as the shooter made his ground, disappearing into the right-hand turn in the corridor.

Drake marched forwards, crashing through the door to his left, with Kaspov in close attendance. The room was clear. Drake used the lull in the action to steal a glance at his watch. Almost three minutes gone. As he made for the corridor, he did some rough maths. In just three minutes, he figured he and Kaspov had made 40 kills. Quadruple that and they were 120 down; maybe, but maybe not!

As they re-entered the corridor, Dmitry and Peter rejoined from the door behind, moving in a two-man convoy. Dmitry led, Peter on his shoulder, drafting like a cyclist, gun pointing forwards as they moved swiftly down the corridor. Drilled and drilled to move like this meant they presented a smaller profile to an oncoming assault team.

Drake and Kaspov reached the next door in the corridor first, Dmitry and Peter trailing in their wake. The pair dived in, guns pointing forwards as they crashed through the door. A man and two women rushed at them, all three wielding makeshift weapons. Kaspov started shooting immediately. Drake though was unable to join the melee, his line of sight compromised as Kaspov lurched to the left upon entry. The woman closest to Kaspov crumpled to the floor immediately, dying almost instantaneously, the result of three deadly accurate bullets to her centre mass. The second woman, though, had managed to fling her weapon, a claw hammer, directly at him. Striking a sickening blow to his collarbone, the hammer then cartwheeled over his shoulder narrowly missing Drake before clanging into the wall behind.

Kaspov grunted in pain, before ploughing headlong into a screaming banshee for a woman. He spoke fluent Russian, but that didn't help one bit in understanding her war cry. Drake tried desperately to open the angle to get a line of sight, but the room didn't allow for this. Kaspov's situation worsened as the man drove forwards with gusto, brandishing a Stanley knife in one hand and a screwdriver in the other.

The second woman rushed towards him with such speed, his mind boggled, as did Drake's. Too slow to reaim and shoot, Kaspov felt the full force of the slight but very lithe young woman's body weight as she crashed into him. Less than a second later, the young man had doubled up as Kaspov lurched backwards. Drake squeezed to his left to avoid the trio of bodies as they thumped to the floor. Every gasp of air squashed out of Kaspov's lungs as he thudded onto the hard surface, sandwiched between the floor and two assailants.

He gasped as he hit the floor, suddenly feeling a searing pain in his left side. The young man had managed to embed the screwdriver deep into his left flank. Kaspov's arms, still clutching his rifle, were pinned to his body with the weight of the two assailants. Momentarily he felt the relief in his left flank, but it didn't last. The relief was the screwdriver, now retracted from his side. The young man, wild-eyed, violently managed to stab him twice more with it. As he did, the woman, weaponless and sandwiched between Kaspov and her accomplice, bit aggressively onto his right ear.

Free from the melee at his feet, Drake, unable to shoot for risk of killing Kaspov, reversed his rifle. Not quite quick enough to prevent the man from frenetically stabbing Kaspov three times, he smashed the butt of his rifle into the back of the young man's head. Drake felt the outcome of the blow. Kinaesthesia is the perception of body movements and detecting changes in body position and movements. He detected. The young man was fucked; a telling blow to the back of his cranium extinguished his life.

Just as quickly, Drake pounced onto the young woman. Banshee or not, she was about to get the good news. It wasn't good news though. He delivered a vicious blow into the dead centre of her shoulder blades. Such was the force, Kaspov, pinned underneath the woman's mass, felt it too. Not unconscious but rendered almost helpless, the vicious biting down on Kaspov's ear released. He shoved the woman off. In a flash, Drake took aim; a single shot to her head finished her off.

Drake pulled Kaspov to his feet. He looked dreadful. Missing an earlobe, his ear was bleeding profusely, his collarbone more than likely fractured too, but these were the least of his problems. His side was bleeding heavily. The three stabs to his torso had at least all entered the same hole to his flank, but that had served to enlarge the original puncture wound. Drake quickly grabbed a large field dressing from his webbing. As Kaspov stuffed it untidily into the hole, Drake grabbed another dressing and hastily pinned it on top. It wasn't army medic standards, but it'd do for now.

"Спасибо, дружище!" grunted Kaspov in Russian, expressing thanks, the first utterances between the pair since they'd entered the building.

"Давай двигаться," replied Drake, telling Kaspov to move, whilst ejecting a magazine from his Russian AK-74M. The covert protocol meant Drake's team were only using Russian weaponry. Some of his team always grumbled about that sort of stuff. Many of his men favoured certain rifles and handguns, he, though, didn't mind. Right from an early age, he had learnt to adapt and ad lib rather than be particular over anything. He inserted a new magazine as he exited the room. Kaspov followed; his movements noticeably slower.

Now 30 metres ahead, Dmitry and Peter had made good progress. Both men were hugging the wall besides the final door before the right-hander. Waiting to enter? As Drake and Kaspov advanced in their direction, a loud explosion rocked the corridor wall. Reverberations from the final room were felt the entire corridor length. In a flash, Dmitry and Peter disappeared inside the room. The grenade had done its job, both men reappearing seconds later.

Drake and his subteam were now a single unit as they finally reached the right-hand turn in the long corridor. The clock was ticking. With just five minutes gone, time was on Drake's side, or so he thought.

The Knacc facility had been carved into two sectors. Drake's team were tasked to clear all ancillary facilities whilst the other team were left to deal with the accommodation wing. Ram had pulled the schematics off the Knacc mainframe. These had been useful over the course of months of planning, but there also been some cause for concern too.

The schematics were very detailed, itemizing sleeping accommodation, workshops, office space, the gymnasium and more. The concern, though, emanated from what was not detailed. Several rooms, one of them reasonably large, were unlabelled. Why? What were these rooms? Safe rooms maybe?

As Drake carefully rounded the corner, his gut instinct kicked in. His instinct was bang on the money. Having only exposed half of his head, a barrage of bullets rained down on him. Quickly withdrawing, the wall spat plaster and brick fragments as it took the punishment. Several figures were well concealed within the door reveals about halfway down the extensive corridor, automatic rifles trained at the corner of the corridor Drake and his men were now stood at.

Resistance was to be expected. Drake stole another peek as the first flurry of bullets abated. He wasn't 100% sure, but the fourth shooter looked like Sergei Asmov. Bullets flew, shattering glass. Fragments of building spewing from the walls didn't allow for an easy ID, but he was confident, the distinctive shape of Asmov wasn't something he'd miss. Withdrawing to safety again, he turned quickly, gesticulating the number four to indicate how many shooters he'd seen.

Unpinning a grenade, Drake released it down the corridor. Seconds later, the entire corridor wall shook as the grenade did its best to put him in the ascendency. Now devoid of the four defenders, rifle sighted forwards, he made to advance, supported by his team. Just as quickly, the four figures re-emerged from their doorways 30 metres down the corridor. Drake's team sent a barrage of fire upon them, whilst charging as far forwards as possible. The suppressing fire did its job, just. Drake crashed through the door to his left, Dmitry and Peter to the door on the right. Kaspov though, moving a little slower, didn't fare as well.

Bullets spat out of the front two door wells, the surrounding walls and ceilings heavily pockmarked in an instance. Not all the shots were errant. The first of two bullets punched a hole in Kaspov's left shoulder, causing him to lurch dramatically to his right. Almost simultaneously, a second bullet thumped mercilessly into his left cheek, exiting the back of his head. Kaspov was dead before he hit the floor.

Drake had registered his death, but that was all. No time for sorrow or 'what-ifs', that could come later. The corridor was bedlam, the occupants of Knacc were putting up a fierce resistance and the clock was ticking down. In the opposite door well to Drake, Dmitry and Peter readied themselves. Each man, grenade in hand, worked to assert control. The first grenade was rolled down the corridor by Dmitry, exploding a few seconds later it helped to push the defenders back. Peter timed his grenade to go off as the shooters reappeared – clever.

It didn't work perfectly, but it did work. The figures in the closest two doorways re-emerged and then dived for cover a second time, recognition of the second grenade a little too late with both men injured in the blast. Dmitry rushed the corridor, Peter and Drake leapt to the fore too. Shots rang out from Dmitry, as he put suppressing fire on to the furthest two doorways, doing his best to persuade the concealed figures to remain concealed. Dmitry tore into the left-hand door, Peter following him. Drake bolted through the right-hand door, releasing a hail of bullets as he entered the room, the already injured occupant taking the brunt of his salvo.

In the chaos, Drake allowed a moment of calm. Taking in his surroundings, he was standing in one of the unidentified rooms. The left-hand wall was lined with four identical incubators. Various medical equipment was suspended from the wall in between each station. A couple of mobile ECG machines, one of which lay on its side, half pinned to the floor by the very dead young man, completed the scene. He was standing in a state-of-the-art neonatal unit. Amongst the carnage of a brutal firefight, he almost felt the shivers. It was eerie, creepy even.

The skirmish, far from over, dragged him quickly back to more pressing considerations. In the opposite door well, Dmitry was shooting furiously down the corridor. On one knee, Peter too was putting down yet more suppressing fire. Drake didn't need to think, instinct kicked in. He unpinned a grenade and launched it towards the remaining two door wells. Dmitry followed suit with a second grenade. Drake surged forwards, repeating the process, he charged through the now vacant door well to his left, shooting as he entered.

The room was empty bar a young man lying dead three metres inside the room. A bank of LCD monitors was attached to the right-hand wall, several laptops, keyboards and a couple of PCs sat on the worktop underneath. At the far end of the room, an imposing, metal-clad door stood framed in a sturdy-looking metal casing. Above the door, a dome-shaped CCTV unit blinked with a tiny flashing red light. Despite the scene of destruction in the room, half the wall monitors were smashed, the small, dome camera was intact.

Drake approached the door and tried to pull it open. It wasn't budging. Standing directly under the CCTV camera, he stared up at it then instantly regretted doing so. He was being watched. He didn't know it, but he felt it. Momentarily, he was sidetracked, losing direction caused by the sudden feeling of being observed. He glanced at his watch, eight minutes down. Time was running out. His team needed to be finishing this.

Drake's instincts were correct. Behind the steel door, huddled up in the safety of a fully provisioned safe room were five members of Knacc. Vitaly Urinov, the tall, angular Head of Knacc stood staring at a video screen. Бочка and Natalia stood to his left and right, both staring intently at the monitor too. The remaining two occupants were a pair of vigilant young women, both seated.

He had watched Drake charge into Knacc's Security and Communications room, gun blazing as he did so. Steely-eyed and stern-faced at the best of times, Urinov grimaced as he observed Drake take in the surroundings. Whilst the man stood no more than 30 cm from the camera, Urinov almost reciprocated Drake's action. Closing the gap to the monitor, he had done his utmost to transmit his entire being through the video screen and out through the camera.

He had never seen Drake before, but the man's face was now permanently etched in his memory, broken nose, blood-spattered face and all. Drake was a face Urinov would never forget.

Бочка took it all in too. It was Бочка that noticed Drake snap back to reality as he glanced at his watch. Caught on camera, the watch display presented a stopwatch rather than the actual time. Drake's stopwatch had shown 00:08:02. The unknown killer stood the other side of the safe room door had offered some intel. His operation was on the clock and that was telling. The killer knew enough to breach Knacc, but importantly, the killer knew enough to be in and out quickly too.

Drake rejoined the melee. Dmitry and Peter, now a couple of doors ahead, continued the room clearing. Shooting, now evident from the other end of the corridor, was friendly fire. Drake's two subteams had completed the sweep of Knacc. Now face to face with Sascha and his complete team, Drake's sense of relief fuelled his sadness. The seven men were now in full exfil mode, and it didn't have provision to retrieve Kaspov's dead body.

Sascha looked a sight too. A split forehead made matters appear worse than they probably were. Blood had constantly trickled down the left side of his face. His left eye was rinsed in blood, giving him the appearance of a Cyclops. All Sascha's team were carrying injuries, two of them had been shot but were both OK-ish. The fourth member of Sascha's team though was in a bad place. His neck, patched up with a blood-sodden dressing, was still oozing blood at an alarming speed. His right arm dangled tentatively by his side was also bleeding. Puncture wounds to both legs completed the picture. He needed immediate medical attention.

Moving as quickly as they could, Drake and his men headed back to the main front doors as the self-imposed 10-minute deadline drew near. Once outside, the CIA kill team reunited with the remainder of their men. The men tasked with guarding the sentry and the external doors had had it easy. Bar from a couple of skirmishes, they had barely seen any action. Fresh and uninjured, the six did the heavy lifting, making the exfil as quick as was possible.

Having made it through the woods, the kill team got trucking. Sat in the passenger seat, Drake ran through the assault – reflect and review. He had to complete his report for the Mega Bitch, but he'd have done a review regardless.

Was it a success? He didn't think so and he knew Wendy certainly wouldn't, but for different reasons. Drake had lost a man, maybe two depending upon how Sascha was getting on in the car behind. Sascha was his best field medic and a great deal now rested on his shoulders, the very survival of one of his team.

Wendy was cold though. She wouldn't give a shit about Kaspov's death, mulled Drake. A 100% kill rate would be all she'd want to hear, and he knew that hadn't been achieved. Fuck it and fuck her, thought Drake. Incomplete schematics and 200+ kills in less than 10 minutes, that alone had set him up for a fall. He checked out his nose in the mirror as his mind ran through the events. Fuck, it was a mess. Not quite flat to his face, the bridge was squashed flat, cartilage exposed through the broken skin. The middle to tip of his nose kinked significantly leftwards. Unsure quite what to do about it, he decided to leave it for the moment. Maybe Sasha could weave some magic once they got back to base.

The shitty AvtoVAZ rumbled on towards Omsk. Drake wasn't sure if it was the crappy roads or the car that made it rattle so much, either way, he'd be glad to see the back of it. Operation Doorstop had lasted months, most of which had involved eating shite food, bunked up in a crap hole. Doorstop hadn't ended well either and now all he wanted was to get out of Dodge.

He had an itch though, a metaphorical itch to his psyche. Something was wrong. Those people were wrong. Thoughts whirled around his mind. Drake's prefrontal cortex was racing. The brain was a fascinating and complex machine. He had spent time understanding the different elements of the human brain on a very intense psy-ops course. Psy stood for psychological and ops for operations. The course was designed to help the goodies fuck with the baddies on a mental / cognitive level. Well at least that's how the course had been sold to him. He hadn't cared too much for it, but he had quite enjoyed learning about the divisions within the brain on a purely academic level.

The prefrontal cortex, situated at the front of the brain, oversees anything that you learn brand new. He had a wry grin as he pondered that fact given the prefrontal cortex was essentially accommodated behind a skull wall used to headbutt people. His recent headbutt being the precise reason his face was such a car crash right now. With that, he returned to his itch.

Doorstop was a mission to kill trainee agents, that's what Mega Bitch had said. Something was off though, very off. He couldn't quite put his finger on it. They were all young, maybe 18 he thought, but clearly not older. Yet they behaved, or rather acted, strangely. Facing peril, death even, some people collapsed under the weight of fear. Others would run and some might fight, but not a single encounter had been anything other than pure aggression. His nose and Kaspov's earlier injuries, before he took a bullet, were testament to that. Then there was the other thing. Gnawing away, Drake had flashback after flashback of their speed of movement. It wasn't just that, strength too and speed of thought. A chill ran through him as he recalled events.

He would have lost a one-on-one fight to the death had it not been for Kaspov's intervention. It hadn't been bad luck either. He had delivered some telling blows, used all his fight craft including a few dirty tricks. He could have left it at that, put it down to a freakishly strong and brave young man, but it wasn't isolated. The girl that had chewed Kaspov's ear off wasn't crazy. She'd closed that gap in milliseconds, she'd acted not reacted. Kaspov would have lost too had he been alone. As the convoy rumbled on, Drake remained lost in his own thoughts as he continued his own internal review.

Urinov looked like he was about to spit fire. Holed up in Knacc's safe room, he'd witnessed the carnage through the safety of the camera lens. Initial assessments from Бочка weren't pretty. Of the 24 members of staff, just himself, Natalia and Бочка were alive and unscathed, their good fortune down to the fact they had been in that part of the facility when the attack occurred. A fourth member of staff was alive but badly wounded. Бочка thought he'd pull through, but Urinov was unconvinced.

Worse still, though, was the number of fatalities to his children. Natalia saw them as students, but the mostly stern-faced Urinov felt a greater warmth towards his MorphEns. Of the 200, only six were unharmed, but four of those six were currently over at Sitka, his special ones thankfully out of harm's way. The two that had escaped the carnage and sat out the attack in the safe room were fine too, but that still left 194 to account for and, so far, Natalia had only found two still alive, albeit fighting for their lives. He seethed. It had been a bloodbath. Almost all his MorphEns had been in their sleeping quarters. Many were either in bed asleep or drifting that way. Heads would roll, but whose head? He didn't know, yet!

Drake's tiny convoy finally made it through the dark Omsk night. His team was still up against the clock though. Drake had to quickly report in, then his team needed to be ghosts, but that was what they were good at. No, that was what they were great at.

As he dialled, Sascha caught his eye. Solemnly and silently shaking his head in Drake's direction, Sascha then nodded subtly towards the motionless form of a man lying on the bed. Drake had just lost a second member of his kill team. He felt a mixture of anger and puzzlement. He didn't know what the mission was about. Wendy had him on a strict 'need-to-know' and right now he felt anger at his lack of knowledge. Losing two men was bad enough, but not knowing doubled the ante.

It took two very quick ringtones for Wendy to pick up.

"Go ahead," came her instant response, small talk wasn't her strong point at the best of times.

"Two men down," Drake replied, deliberately starting with a brief regarding his team, rather than giving her the only intel she was interested in. For Wendy, it was only about the task, collateral wasn't her lookout.

"But have you completed?" she snapped angrily. Frosty didn't do it justice; she was in full Ice Queen mode.

"Who are they?" asked Drake defiantly. Making her wait for her intel report wasn't going to help matters but, in that moment, he was pissed, really pissed. He'd lost two very good men, and in Kaspov he'd lost a good friend too, a man he'd spent time with, in shitholes across the world, a good man, a true warrior.

"Don't try me…" she snapped… "now isn't the time," she carried on. Drake could feel the frost from 5000 miles away. "Intel NOW," boomed Wendy.

Maybe he had pushed too much, but at that moment he had the upper hand. She wanted her report, whilst Drake wanted knowledge.

"If I'm running Doorstop, I need detail," he persisted. At that moment, as Drake sat staring at his dead team member, a tongue-lashing from Wendy was an irrelevance. She could screw herself thought Drake. She probably did screw herself in fact, as Drake allowed his mind to wander a touch.

"FUCKING NOW!" she screamed, her tinny voice almost audible to his entire team through his mobile.

Dmitry, breaking off from packing the comms kit, looked over at Drake. His best friend had died, and matters made worse, the team hadn't been able to retrieve Kaspov's body. Dmitry had been listening to Drake's half of the conversation and had guessed the elevated degree of angry responses from Wendy. His look had been that of support for Drake. It helped too, serving to shore up Drake's defiance.

"You want your intel, then you're gonna need to give me some answers," grunted Drake.

Suddenly, his job didn't feel that important. Admittedly, getting on the wrong side of Wendy might result in something far greater than getting fired, death maybe, but fuck it, if the Mega Bitch wanted info, then she could share a bit too. As enraged as she now was, the penny had finally dropped. Drake was pissed and threats alone weren't going to cut it.

"Get yourself back, you'll get full disclosure," Wendy replied, softening her voice as she reeled back, the strategist in her recognizing the need to change tack.

"We didn't fully complete," Drake replied, having got his way. He'd get a dressing-down later, that was a certainty, but he'd also get answers, and that was a price worth paying.

He did his best to detail events. The kill count was the biggest issue. He knew the job wasn't 100% completed. The safe room alone accounted for someone. Running out of time had compounded his problems. His team had to exfil rather than circle back and do a count. Wendy was less than ecstatic as he gave her a detailed account.

She interrupted Drake several times, keen to know if Urinov and his thug Asmov had been taken out. Drake recounted his almost certain sighting of Asmov and, although unsafe to assume anything, he had felt certain it was Asmov sitting securely on the other side of the safe room door. He finished his report with his concerns, deliberately so. He wanted Wendy to have total clarity about what he wanted to know, to understand. Full disclosure needed to be exactly that.

"Their behaviour, it wasn't right…" Drake tried to explain, "… unusual… like different…" he carried on.

"Example," she barked, not aggressively just direct, almost impatient to understand what he was referring to.

He explained, as best he could anyway. The movement was one thing and some quite remarkable examples of strength too. Uncanny speed, but Drake had been far more engrossed in the pure aggression and their speed of thought. He could remember how he had been at 18. A fine athlete, extremely capable, he'd excelled. When he trained with the special forces he'd learnt quickly, mastering an array of skills, but he wasn't like them. The 'them' being the young men and women he'd just been assigned to kill.

Their decision-making had been scary. They'd instinctively made the right decision, and it hadn't been luck. They'd shown aggression and adaptability, all under immense pressure, and not once had any of them buckled. Drake completed his report, leaving Wendy to stew over the detail. All being well, he'd be face to face with the Mega Bitch in a few days. More pressing matters lay ahead as his team needed to become ghosts.

"And the unidentified rooms?" quizzed Wendy.

Drake could feel a relative calmness in her voice now, the debrief had gone a long way to pacify her. Sitting 5000 miles away, she was back in control. Satisfied with Drake's initial briefing, it was now her opportunity to drill down on the details, on aspects Drake had missed off, not deliberately, just natural and normal omission. No human being had perfect recall. Most sitreps would miss info because the 'reporting agent' lost their sense of priority. Adrenaline and high anxiety levels always exacerbated this. The gunfight Drake and his team had just experienced was just about as extreme a set of conditions as you could get.

Wendy's question suddenly jarred his memory. The safe room had already been explained. Drake knew he was being watched on camera, but by whom? Well, that was a question without an answer, but the room had made sense. He was aware of many facilities with a safe room, why would Knacc be any different! But the other unidentified room, that was weird, eerie even. A neonatal unit in what was effectively a young person's training school was odd, wrong in fact. When he explained this to Wendy, she had paused, a momentary silence that had become elongated – too elongated. Drake didn't push, but he knew, he sensed this piece of information had put her on the back foot. He made a mental note to ask specifically about this when he got back to Washington.

The debrief had taken 15 very expensive minutes. Mega Bitch was as happy as was possible. Much more pressing matters jumped to the fore. His team needed to disappear. They needed to melt into their environment. A search-and-kill order would almost certainly have been initiated by now. Knacc's surveillance footage would identify exactly how big Drake's team was. His team's exfil plan was complex but perfectly thought through. Several groups of ones, twos and threes all assigned to exit via all points of the compass, some by air and others overland or via sea.

"How was Bitch Face?" asked Sascha, aware of Drake's side of the conversation. Sascha's question wasn't asking for an answer, more a message of support.

"Like a bug on shit," he replied sarcastically, grimacing as he did so. He'd fill Sascha in later, but right now wasn't the time and both men knew it.

CHAPTER 20
WAS THIS YOU?

Louise sat upright staring at her laptop, engrossed in a screen full of data. Although it was Sunday evening, her work took precedence. For her a relaxing evening in was hours spent going over the detail, analysing and forming an action plan for the next day.

Across the room, Xav was similarly ensconced in a world of work. Louise momentarily broke off from her screen, initially glancing towards him before directing her gaze out of the window and across the lake. Although dark outside, the view was still beautiful.

The inky black lake shimmered, moonlight reflections in the distance and a couple of splashes of light, emanating from the jetty in the foreground, made for a hypnotic view. As she sat transfixed on her picture-perfect vista, the shrill ringtone of her phone broke the tranquillity.

She checked the display prior to answering. A single letter '*U*' sat centrally across her iPhone. She answered it straight away, choosing not to look in Xav's direction as she did so. He had looked up once he saw Louise electing to take the call, an unusual action for her late in the evening.

"Yes, Taly," she answered warmly. Only a select few people had the relationship that allowed Vitaly Urinov to be addressed as 'Taly'.

"Was this you?" growled the man in his heavily accented but perfect English.

Louise was unaccustomed to Urinov's ire. She had seen him bark orders and scold his underlings, but not once, not ever had she suffered his rage. Taken aback, she stumbled for a response.

"Taly?" Repeating Vitaly's name was her limited response before being interrupted.

"Knacc… it's gone…" Urinov blurted out, cutting Louise off. "Is this you?" the rage in his voice undiminished.

"What? Knacc what?" she quizzed, managing to gain some level of composure whilst attracting Xav's attention from across the room. He could see in her eyes that whatever the conversation, something was up, something serious. Closing his laptop, he walked over to her as she placed the call on speakerphone.

"Knacc has been compromised – attacked," Urinov spat out, his thick Russian accent weighing heavier in his every intonation.

"How bad?" she asked. "…And you think this is me?" snapped Louise, his initial accusation now sinking in. "Are you deranged?" she carried on, now almost as angry as the angular, erudite Russian. "Why would I attack everything I have worked for?" she continued, looking her partner in the eyes, searching for support.

"Xav then, is this Xav?" Urinov was more snarling than talking.

"Va te faire foutre, Taly." The always thoughtful Xav entered the conversation, mixing strong words with a calm, dispassionate voice.

"Cut the accusations and tell us what's happened," demanded Louise.

A silence ensued, a telling silence. Telling because it was clear the news to follow was not going to be good. She had known Vitaly Urinov a long time and he'd never been at a loss for words.

Several seconds ticked by before he spoke. On a phone call, several seconds added gravitas to the conversation. Urinov didn't waste time with minor details, he didn't need to. The summary made for a sombre tale. Knacc, as a facility, was a bullet-ridden war zone, but Knacc wasn't a building, it was a programme and its most valuable assets were the 200 second-generation Morphs. In fact, the only thing of value was its 200 Morphs.

"They're dead, my children are dead," he explained, the rage in his voice still evident although the intonation was no longer aimed at Louise or Xav.

"All of them…!" This was more a statement than a question from Louise, interrupting his account of the attack on Knacc.

"Eight are still alive," Urinov replied, at which point a second silence ensued.

Xav looked her in the eyes; all he could see was fire, a raging fire.

The room fell silent once more as they both took in the news. On the other end of the line, 1000 miles away, Urinov, still seething, in that moment understood. He knew; he knew it wasn't a double-cross. Breaking the silence, he regained his composure as he formulated an action plan.

He had already started with moving everyone to Sitka, which didn't amount to much given the level of destruction he was currently looking at. Бочка had already been dispatched to start chasing up leads, Natalia too. The Americans, Germans and the Brits were discussed. The sacking of Knacc had been highly organized. Other than nation states, there was barely an organization capable of carrying out an attack of the magnitude and clinical efficiency anywhere in the world, let alone at a location deep inside Russian territory.

Intelligence assets would all need to be put to work. Бочка was already looking into several clandestine agencies within Russia. Everything was not as it appeared to onlookers outside Russia. Power struggles existed between various agencies and two very high-profile oligarchs controlled a couple of very secretive, clandestine organizations. Although run and staffed by a myriad of former politburo staffers, both agencies were completely independent of the Kremlin.

Both Бочка and Urinov had constant suspicions over infiltration of Knacc by members of GRU. GRU was the Russian armed forces' intelligence wing, currently under the control of Sergei Fedorov. Fedorov and Urinov shared a long and hateful past. No love was lost between GRU and FSB, and although Urinov didn't officially answer to the FSB Chief of Staff, Fedorov didn't know or see it that way.

Xav was assigned to work both the German and French angles. His moles within Interpol and the German BND were the best-placed assets to hand. Urinov, although outwardly happy with Xav's input, was privately irked and jealous that he had better-placed moles with a proven ability to access intel from deep inside both the German and French intelligence service. He had, over the years, tried unsuccessfully to gain an insight into Xav's network, but the Swiss national was no one's fool, shutting down every attempt.

That left the Brits and the Yanks, and therein existed the problem. Louise and Xav had no asset of worth in either London or Washington. Urinov, having initially gone on the front foot, dishing out directives for both Xav and Louise whilst all along assuring his partners that no stone would be left unturned within the Russian interior, had suddenly clammed up a little when it came to discussing the Brits.

Louise listened intently as Urinov and Xav bounced off each other. The usually attentive Xav hadn't picked it up, but she had. Urinov had skirted across the issue, not denying but certainly not admitting to access to intel within the British camp. Yet something gnawed away, an itch, just a tiny little nag in the furthest recesses of her mind. She couldn't quite put her finger on it, but she felt Urinov was covering up. He seemed just a bit too OK with the lack of a clear plan to tackle the Brits.

Louise allowed the conversation to move forwards, making a mental note to discuss her thoughts with Xav later. Finally came the Yanks. The Americans presented a different problem altogether. The trio all had assets within the USA, the issue, though, was that none of them had a mole within the CIA.

Stephen Bell worked in the New York office of the FBI. Known to his friends as Hop, due to a high school nickname emanating from the term 'bellhop', Hop was married, happily married. At least that was the image Hop liked to portray, and that was Hop's downfall, a weakness that Louise had cruelly exploited for over a decade. Xav didn't like it either, he knew most but not all of the details, how she had lured Hop to her hotel room for a seedy one-night stand, the covert cameras recording every lurid detail of Louise and Hop's tryst.

She hadn't gone rogue, 10 years previously she had planned immaculately, got approval begrudgingly from Xav, in order to exploit the obvious attraction that Hop carried towards her. But even now, 10 years later, it was still a play that stung, a wound that never truly healed. Right now, though, Louise could make use of her FBI mole, but the issue was the FBI to the CIA was like oil to water, they didn't mix and the FBI really didn't have sway over the CIA.

Xav had a slightly better asset, although even this was debatable. Where Louise used guile, he used money. Where Louise used persuasion, Xav used coercion. He had cultivated a career NSA staffer for many years. It hadn't come cheap, but in his eyes 'you got what you paid for'. For 15 years, he had paid Rex Williams a healthy retainer. He had even fed Rex useful intel in order to help him climb the greasy NSA pole.

Rex Williams eventually made it to head of Technology and Systems Directorate. Aged 63, Rex was unlikely to climb any higher, but Xav didn't mind that too much. As head of one of the five NSA directorates, there was only the assistant head and head of the entire NSA above him. Rex had access to very high-level intel, much of which had benefitted Xav and his beloved Apfel. Sadly though, the quality of 'intel sharing' between the CIA and the NSA was appalling. It was that bad that most of the time each agency spent more time working on disinformation rather than what, in theory, should be a relatively harmonious existence. Xav agreed to tap Rex up for intel, but internally he knew the results it would harvest.

Urinov's best asset was code named 'смазка' which was the Russian for 'grease'. Neither Louise nor Xav knew why, but if they knew who 'Grease' was then they might have figured it out. Urinov didn't play cards, but if he did Louise figured he'd be good at it. He kept all his cards close to his chest. His asset 'Grease' was a good example of this.

Grease was a high-level White House staffer with direct access to briefings from the director of the CIA, the NSA Chief of Staff, the FBI director and the list went on. The only problem was these various heads didn't play ball or give full insight in their briefings to the politicians. Still, it was another angle that might lead to something tangible.

Having agreed to a division of labour, the conversation circled back to the state of Knacc. The surveillance footage Urinov sent through showed exactly what he had outlined, a very professional and well-drilled team of men. The assailants were all masked, using standard Russian-made weapons and were very clearly from a military background.

The single dead assailant had revealed nothing; his face had already been put through the FSB's facial recognition software and drawn blanks. So far, Anatoly Kaspov's dead body had revealed nothing other than a thirty-something Caucasian with no distinguishing features or tattoos. He could be Russian, possibly even Belorussian or Ukrainian, but Бочка didn't think so. Urinov trusted Бочка's instinct and had been inclined to agree.

It was still early days, the assassin's body wasn't going anywhere fast, dental records and a full post-mortem might reveal more clues. With that, the conversation ended. Louise and Xav's quiet Sunday evening had been ripped apart, almost 20 years of work close to near complete destruction.

The room fell silent the second the line went dead. They sat silently pondering. As she reflected on the gravity of the situation, her gaze wandered from Xav's face to the shimmering lake view. The room was so quiet she could almost hear the water lapping at the lakeside. Xav broke the silence, snapping her back to attention.

"He has someone... did you hear it?" he stated. "In London," he continued before Louise had the chance to clarify.

She was surprised, she had thought he hadn't picked up on it, but weighing things up, she shouldn't have been. After all, when did Xav miss a trick, she mused.

"I felt it too, cheri," Louise replied affectionately.

Urinov was clearly holding back on something or someone he had in London. The various British intelligence services had been a tough nut to crack. Over the years, Louise and Xav had tried and failed on several occasions, but the Russians had historically had more success post WWII, more success, in fact, than the Yanks. So why should she be surprised?

London was a closed shop to Louise and Xav. Try as they might, they had both drawn blanks with any meaningful access to intelligence. For now, they'd have to rely on Urinov, a big 'if' of course. Control the controllable was the conclusion she had come to, so both she and Xav started to work on the intelligence assets they both had, leaving Vitaly Urinov to do the same.

With the Fletchers still alive, the Apfel down a man and Knacc destroyed, the current outlook for BioDS was bleak. Louise was almost smouldering, a deep rage burnt within.

An angry Louise Walsh was a very dangerous human.

CHAPTER 21
DAN AND KATE

Toulouse, France
Sunday 8th January 2017

Kate looked across the table, giving a half smile to her best friend in the world. Rachel returned her smile. Without a word spoken, Kate reached across the table, tenderly sweeping an errant wisp of hair from Rachel's face, tucking it behind her right ear.

As Kate retracted her arm, Rachel grabbed her hand, squeezing it lovingly. As she did, a solitary tear ran down her face. Kate wasn't sure what the tear was for, so much had happened to the girls in the last four days. She tried as best she could not to cry too but seeing Rachel's tear also set her off. As tears rolled down her face, the silence remained unbroken.

Kate's thoughts drifted to their dead amiga, Helen, and then to their hair-raising escape from the hospital in Grenoble and the car chase in Lyon. Her world had been blown apart on what was supposed to have been a relaxing week skiing with her two best friends. But right now, she was sitting for a fourth night in another nondescript hotel, on the run from murderous assassins.

She noticed some movement at the far end of the dining room, a figure silhouetted against a highly lit atrium strode purposefully in the girl's direction. Initially alert, Kate relaxed immediately as Dan's form came into focus. Emotions and nerves had been constantly heightened since Wednesday. She guessed this was normal; the human being in 'fight or flight' mode was an edgy animal.

Dan squeezed Rachel on her good shoulder as he took his place at the table. Noticing the dried tears on both girls' faces, he broke the silence.

"You OK?" Dan asked, not really directing his question at a specific girl.

Neither Rachel nor Kate answered at first. An awkward silence ensued. His sister finally eased the tension with a half smile as she first looked across the table at Kate before focusing fully on her brother's face.

"Yeh, Dan, we're good," Rachel replied softly and, with that, she stood to leave, not before giving Kate a huge, one-armed hug. Expressing a warm 'night night' to Dan and Kate, Rachel left the dining room.

Initially tracking Rachel's route exiting the hotel dining room, Dan returned his gaze to Kate. "Did I miss something?" he asked, reassuringly taking her hand in his as he looked her in the eyes.

"Just a girly cry," she replied as she lolled her head on Dan's shoulder for comfort.

She suddenly felt incredibly vulnerable, the emotions she felt seemed overwhelming and Kate in that moment yearned support. She longed for protection, a loving and caring force to envelop her. Oddly, Dan seemed to recognize this, Kate reflected. As she rested her head on his shoulders, Dan wrapped a strong but comforting arm around her. Squeezing her closer to him somehow made her world a safe place.

For over a minute, Kate just let Dan sit quietly by her side, silently hugging her. Finally, she pulled away enough to allow space to focus her eyes directly into his. Softly smiling, she took both hands, cupping Dan's entire head and face as she pulled him towards her. She locked her lips on Dan's as she kissed him lovingly. He reciprocated, turning the kiss from a loving one into something much more electric, more sexual. Eventually pulling apart, she broke the silence.

"Take me to bed," asked Kate, part plead, part instruction.

Until then, Dan and her hadn't done anything more than kiss and cuddle, the tension of the last four days on the run hadn't made it feel right, but now, in that moment, it felt more than right. It felt needed.

Dan and Kate exited the dining room. Hand in hand, they made light work of the 60-second journey to their hotel room. He retrieved his room key, swiping the door entry and unlocking the door, the two of them filed in.

As soon as the door closed, Kate pounced on him. Sexual electricity and desire swept through her entire body as she half embraced, half undressed. He was no different, Dan juggling, trying to kiss Kate, undress himself and rip her clothes off too. The couple, so sexually charged, almost tripped over as they fumbled to remove their clothing as they kissed each other passionately whilst journeying the six metres from door to bed.

Both naked, a trail of clothing items in their wake, they crashed onto their bed. Kissing each other with both passion and ferocity, the couple rolled together in a tangled loving embrace, Dan eventually ending on top of Kate, taking some of his weight on his elbows, kissing her with all his passion as he entered her. She pulled him towards her; her hands gathered around the small of his back. In and out, Dan's body worked as Kate's pulsated.

As he climaxed, so too did Kate. Her entire body quivered, goosebumps appeared on the back of her neck, and she let out an uncontrollable whimper of delight. She lay motionless under the weight of Dan's handsome form. A mixture of euphoria, elation and gratification consumed her. She held him in her arms, not letting him move, as she felt his chest contract and retract with every breath. The heat from his body, the smell from the nape of his neck, Kate took in every tiny detail of the man she was falling in love with. She savoured the moment.

Since entering the bedroom, neither Kate nor Dan had spoken a single word, both had been lost in a world of passion.

"Fuck me," uttered Kate, as she cracked the biggest smile she was capable of.

"I thought I just did," he quipped, causing both of them to laugh uncontrollably.

"Oh yes, you REALLY did!" she replied, accentuating the

'really' to ensure that he understood.

Dan had understood though, he knew. He'd felt Kate's every shudder, her body tensing, the extra hard squeeze. Most importantly of all, though, the smallest of tells was the loudest sign of all. Her skin around her shoulders and neck had tingled as she climaxed. Prickly goosebumps, cold skin and the smallest of hair follicles all standing on end had confirmed it.

He rolled over and lay on his back, grinning upwards as he took in the moment. Across from him, Kate lay half straddling his naked body. Perfect pert breasts adorned her beautiful glowing brown body. Erect nipples, taut, lithe skin stretched across a slim yet athletically muscular body, she could have been a model.

She stroked Dan's chest as she lay beside him in wonderment. She'd known him for nine years and had probably been in love with him most of that time without ever realizing it fully. Finally, the moment had arrived, bizarrely under the most awful of times; a best friend dead and four days on the run from a team of killers without a clue as to why. Yet in that moment, holed up in a hotel on the outskirts of Toulouse, none of it seemed to matter. Kate was able to embrace the moment for what it was, Dan was finally her man; a brave, intelligent and gifted man, maybe the only man capable of saving the four of them.

Dan broke his stare from the ceiling, half turning his head towards her. Marvelling at her stunning form, he ran his eyes down the length of her body and back, finally focusing again on her face.

"You seen enough?" teased Kate, enjoying the spectacle of being looked over. A huge grin splashed across her face as she waited for his response.

"Better just check again," quipped Dan as he overaccentuated another scan of her naked body, unable to stymie a smile as he did so.

She playfully smacked him on the chest as he did, before leaning across to plant a long and loving kiss on the lips. She was 100% well and truly smitten and, for the first time in four days, felt safe. A sense of security and comfort in Dan's arms washed over her.

Kate and Dan joyfully played around for 20 minutes, making the very most of each other. Maybe it was the nine years of never quite getting together, or maybe it was the last four days of heightened emotions, either way, the couple embraced every second they had together, culminating in another electrically charged and passionate act of love. This time Kate took the lead, straddling Dan as he lay obediently underneath her.

He allowed her to ride him, compliant to her every need. This time they both took longer, feeling the pleasure together. The sex the second time around was even better than before as Kate, finally satiated, rolled off Dan in an exhausted but enraptured state.

"Fuck me," blurted Kate once more… "Don't you dare," she continued, a futile attempt to stop Dan's inevitable joke.

"I thought I just did," he replied, refusing to let the opportunity for a joke go begging again.

She laughed loudly as she caught his wild-eyed smile. He acknowledged her thoughts; the second time had been better, raw passion first off followed by tender pleasurable love the second time. Dan and Kate both felt it. They both felt the other one's love.

She enjoyed the warm, fuzzy feeling as she lay half across his body. Her breathing adjusted, almost matching the rise and fall of his chest, as the couple drifted off to sleep.

Tomorrow would be another step in the direction of a safe harbour. Dan's plan was to spend another night in a final hotel, somewhere near Montélimar. If everything went smoothly, if they felt certain they had got their would-be killers off their trail, then the next day they would push on to Annemasse.

CHAPTER 22
ANNEMASSE BOUND

Monday 9th January 2017

Dan and Kate entered the dining room together, almost but not quite hand in hand. The choice of staying in the Mercure had been discussed at length the day before. On the run over the last four days, the group had stayed in cheap, budget hotels immediately off the péages. Dan had argued that a change in tack would be sensible and so it was that they plumped for the four-star Mercure, much more of a tourist hotel than a traveller's stopover.

The dining room was a large, expansive room. The breakfast set-up was an efficient and comprehensive offering of cooked and continental items, all neatly laid out on a large, elongated self-serve island. Beyond, stood a myriad of tables, chairs nestled neatly around each.

In the furthest corner of the room, Dan spotted his siblings seated. Ben was munching his way through a couple of pains au chocolat, whist Rachel watched on, hands cupping a coffee mug. Dan and Kate weaved their way through the tables, both having grabbed a coffee en route.

As the four exchanged morning pleasantries, Rachel trained a laser-like focus on her best friend. From the moment Kate had entered the dining room, Rachel had noticed a difference. She'd seen the closeness of the pair as they walked to the coffee station, almost arm in arm, but even more tellingly, she saw the glint in Kate's eyes as she took a seat at the table. The confirmation came when Kate was unable to suppress a broad grin as she said 'morning' to Rachel.

Ben hadn't noticed, but he was a big, daft dope, more concerned with shovelling copious French pastries in his mouth. But Rachel had. She aimed a second 'morning' back to Kate, looking her directly in the eyes as she did. No words spoken, Kate just smiled back and then ever so subtly nodded her head. A nod just for Rachel, one that not even Dan noticed. Rachel was in the direst of situations, a gunshot wound to her arm, one best friend dead and on the run from her killers, yet at that moment at least, her other best friend had finally found the love she had craved.

Her 'chica' and her brother were one. Rachel glanced across the table to her brothers, Ben had been oblivious to the girls' subliminal messages and Dan too hadn't picked up on Rachel and Kate's near telepathic ability.

Pleasantries over, Dan wasted no time as he turned the discussion to the plan for the day. An overnight stop in Montélimar, stopping en route for some more supplies, had been the agreed plan. Then if all went well, they'd push on to their mum's place in Annemasse on Tuesday.

Rachel glowered at the mention of the word 'mum'. It was an instinctive reaction, an almost involuntary one. She hated her mum. Rachel Fletcher was six when her mum left home, leaving Tom Fletcher to bring up four young children. Aged six had been an awful age for her to lose her mum. The only daughter and old enough to really remember her mum, she grew up despising her mum for the betrayal of leaving her family. What mother could truly do that? Growing up, she became determined to never be like her mum. She had lost a bit of her childhood, maturing quicker than she should have as she filled some of the void left by an absentee mother. This, in part, was a reason for hating her mum.

Worse still, every year Rachel received a birthday present through the post. As a teenager, she used to open the parcel before smashing, breaking or ripping to bits whatever the gift was, but as she matured she recognized this wasn't good for her, psychologically speaking, so she moved on and merely put the gift in the bin without so much as a flicker of emotion.

Now, in a terrifying run across France, chased by deadly, murderous assassins, she was having to 'suck it up'. Dan had argued that 'needs must' and that Rachel simply had to lump it. Begrudgingly, she acquiesced.

The plan was a good one though. The Fletchers had almost no connection to their estranged mum. Annual birthday presents aside, the four siblings never really met up with their mum. They just needed a haven. Cash was running low, and Dan was convinced that under no circumstances could they leave a digital trail of any sort.

So, like it or not, Annemasse and their mum's house was the only logical and safe place to aim for.

CHAPTER 23
KNACC DEBRIEF

Tuesday 10th January 2017

Drake touched down at a remote airfield in Virginia. A smooth extraction from Omsk hadn't helped reduce his ire. It had taken two days to get stateside; his emotions in that time had gone 'full circle'.

Having had the luxury of time to go over the breach many times during the transit, Drake had some conclusions, some theories and a heap more questions for Wendy. He was calm though, having reassessed the mission he was satisfied that he'd done all he could for the best of his men. It wasn't on him, that was the conclusion he'd arrived at. Kaspov's death stung, but it stung because he was a mate, a fallen colleague, but he had known the risks. Kaspov had done what they all had; he'd weighed up what the company offered versus the risk of it all going fubar.

The black ops missions paid well. They paid very well in fact, as they should, given these were deniable missions sanctioned by 'the company'. The company, being the CIA, and the deniability effectively put Drake et al. in the same boat as paid assassins; no payslips or insurance, no uniform and certainly no recognition. Clandestine deniability paid exceptionally well but it did so for a reason.

As Drake alighted from the plane, he immediately recognized the silhouetted figure of Wendy Angel, framed neatly in the centre of the hangar doors. The Mega Bitch stood impassively, with her PA Mike Gratton to her right. As he strode towards the pair, they turned on their heels, making a beeline back inside the hangar.

To the rear of the hangar two brightly lit, office-type rooms were located. The one to the left was unoccupied. Wendy and her PA entered the right-hand office and took a seat at the solitary table. A stern-looking man, athletically built and clad in a Secret Service regulation dark suit, stood outside the door, presumably the Mega Bitch's driver cum security detail.

Drake strode confidently past the guy without giving him a second look, acutely aware of the fact the guy in question gave him an eyeful. *Fucking rent-a-thug* was the single thought that went through his mind.

He entered the room and took a seat, as he did so Mike Gratton jumped to his feet and closed the door behind him. Clearly, Mr. Rent-A-Thug wasn't in the loop.

Wendy dispensed a few pleasantries, slightly unusual for the Mega Bitch mused Drake, but they were more housekeeping issues than niceties, updating him on the successful repatriation of his entire team, whilst her PA planted a coffee on the table in front of him. Mike Gratton hadn't offered the coffee; he'd just done it. Pleasantries concluded in less than 60 seconds, typical Wendy Angel efficiency pondered Drake.

She opened with a run-through of the mission again. The luxury of time allowed for no details to be spared, whereas in Omsk Drake had had to juggle, giving Wendy a quick overview whilst doing his utmost to 'get out of Dodge'.

Of the details Wendy wanted, Drake was able to give a great deal of insight with the single exception of the hits. The original plan had included a sweep back to accurately record the extent of the kill count. Body cam footage from his team revealed a great deal, but it wasn't as comprehensive as he or Wendy would have liked. Of the 200 targets, 188 clear and obvious hits had been made, but 'hits' were not necessarily deaths. Members of Knacc staff hit totalled 16, but conspicuous by their absence were both Asmov and Urinov.

Wendy was clearly disgruntled, her usual poker face had 'gone wanting' as she relayed the news relating to Urinov and his bulldog, Asmov. Drake's own body cam footage confirmed what he had thought he'd seen mid firefight, the very distinctive figure of Asmov scuttling down the corridor and almost certainly to a haven inside the safe room.

She grilled Drake for over an hour, drilling down on the minute detail. Drake finally took the initiative; he'd been promised full disclosure two days ago and he was damned if he wasn't going to get it.

Who were they? Or rather, what were they? Trainee agents didn't cut it. He had spent the two days in transit back stateside going over and over the edict about his mission to assassinate 200 trainee agents. Something didn't add up. He'd lost two good men, one of whom was his friend Kaspov, and now he was ready for some answers.

"What are they?" he asked bullishly, unable to dress it up, pent-up rage combined with a genuine inquisitive thought pattern fuelled his approach. Mike Gratton raised an eyebrow at Drake's forthright intonation and was even more surprised by Wendy's relatively soft reply. Under normal circumstances, Mike would have expected a tongue-lashing to be forthcoming.

"They're trainee agents…" she replied, "…just as we said," she carried on. "They're special though," she continued, staring directly at Drake as she spoke.

Mike Gratton didn't flinch, clearly this wasn't news to him mulled Drake as he took in Wendy's every word.

"Special how?" Drake enquired.

"A couple of decades ago, a British biogeneticist approached us. She had developed a technique to enhance neonatal human beings. The enhancement can only be carried out within the first few days of birth, a kind of human gene recode process.

"Are you with me?" quizzed Wendy.

"So far," Drake shot back.

"The process isn't without risks; some babies didn't survive, some mutated for the worse."

"Mutated?" asked Drake, the gravity of the intel was sinking in as he listened intently to Wendy's every word.

"The British didn't want to know, and this is why we got her," Wendy expanded. "Her name is Louise Walsh. She calls them MorphEns, the hybrid for 'morph' and 'enhancement'. Each successful MorphEn has shown a 20-22% increase in physical and mental aptitude versus their expected profile. Essentially, she's developed a programme to create a master race, a route to creating the perfect human."

"You said we got her..." Drake asked, the implication of his question understood by her immediately.

"We lost her," she replied, "...to the Russians."

Drake fidgeted slightly in his seat as she expanded. As Wendy finished her sentence, the room fell silent. Drake had a myriad of thoughts swirling around his head. Over the course of his flight from Russia he'd had some wild ideas about what he'd encountered, but nothing remotely close to what he was now being told.

"So these things, these MorphEns, do we have them too?" asked Drake.

For the first time during the debrief, Wendy looked uncomfortable, slightly edgy. Another pregnant pause ensued whilst she considered her response. To his left, Mike Gratton shifted ever so slightly in his seat, causing Drake to avert his gaze momentarily.

He returned his attention to Wendy, his eyes trained on hers. The tension in the room was palpable. As the silence continued, Drake maintained his stare, eyes fixed on hers. For a few seconds, it was like the pair were playing a game of chicken, both holding out to see who'd break first.

"It's called Steelhorse..." Wendy finally breaking the silence, "...that's its code name.

"We took Walsh under our wing when the Brits didn't want her. We gave her everything she desired, a private facility, a team of staff, the financial resources and, more importantly, the access." She stopped her summary at this moment as she fumbled for clarity on this final point.

"Access? What access?" asked Drake, almost reminding Wendy what full disclosure meant.

"To... to the babies..." The way she said this, or rather the way she tripped over her words, left more questions than answers.

"Are you saying she, we didn't have consent?" quizzed Drake as he glanced across to Mike Gratton, who for the first time had dropped his poker face. Gratton, looking slightly uneasy, shifted his weight once more in his seat.

"We selected babies with a connection to our intelligence community, ones born to at least one parent that worked for us. These babies came from 'good stock', their parents were already highly intelligent and so it stood to reason the outcome would be greater." The atmosphere in the room felt heavy as the intel left her lips. The use of the word 'outcome' wasn't lost on Drake. Try as she might, she had failed to make Steelhorse sound like a run-of-the-mill educational procedure, and it was anything but 'run-of-the-mill' – far from it.

"We figured with the candidates we selected, their natural attributes and their parents' background, that our recruitment of them would be straightforward. Only they were too good, too talented. We were, in essence, 'beneath them'."

Drake searched the room as she spoke. The lighting hummed ever so slightly, whenever the room fell silent its tinny pulse audible. There and then the room was like the proverbial mouse – quiet as.

"Too talented…?" he quizzed. "…And how many are we talking about…?" shooting a double question right back at Wendy.

"Of the 14 MorphEns, one was a shoo-in for the US Olympic gymnastics team, two others were very close to the US Track and Field Development Programme, a couple were music prodigies and all bar two scored top of their class in the very best universities going." Her use of the past tense wasn't lost on Drake as he took in the long list of accolades.

"Was a shoo-in?" he asked.

"Of our 14 MorphEns, 10 are dead, assassinated with the exact same MO. Extremely professional hits. We have nothing to go on; zilch."

"Russians," interjected Drake as she carried on.

"It might be the Russians, but it's just conjecture, although of course it's the obvious explanation."

As he sat listening, he went to take a slurp from his empty coffee cup, quickly returning it to its place mat. Gratton, on cue, jumped to his feet, refilling both Drake's and his own. Wendy held out a hand, waving off her PA as he leant over to recover her mug too.

She moved on, addressing Drake's other query. "Steelhorse selected highly capable human beings for its candidates." Drake allowed a wry smile to crack at her use, once again, of the word 'candidate'. "The babies came from parents who already presented an array of physical and mental attributes that placed them in the top one percentile. When Walsh came along and boosted them, her enhancement programme created starlets." He was getting it, but she drilled the point home. "Ask yourself this, are you going to take a job in the CIA over a career as a world-class athlete or earning millions creating your own tech start-up company?

"This is what she created – geniuses. They were simply too good for us."

"Is that why we lost her?" interjected Drake again.

"No, that wasn't it," Wendy snapped back quickly, not angrily, just a rapid response to bring the conversation back under her control.

"She constantly wanted more. More resources, more money and, ultimately, she wanted the one thing we couldn't give her." She paused, allowing the room to fall silent and the tension to rise. Drake sat impassively, choosing not to break the silence; he didn't twitch a single muscle fibre. Stony still, Drake sat and waited for her to carry on.

"Walsh wanted more candidates. Her desire to carry on her work far outweighed her moral and ethical responsibilities. We failed to satiate her and so we lost her. At first it appeared she'd gone solo. She created a start-up called BioDS based in Switzerland. BioDS fronts as a biogenetic company, we kept tabs on it and on Walsh. But nothing ever cropped up, BioDS is squeaky clean. It's a front, but it's a good one.

"The Russians weren't spotted initially. She and Urinov were extremely clever and even more cautious. She threw us off the scent because she spent her early years trying to get approval for what was effectively a 'recode your baby' product. All behind closed doors, she had been seeking government approval to no avail."

"So that's Knacc," Drake asked, although it was more a statement than a question. "You're telling me Knacc is an industrial scale MorphEns farm, more akin to a USSR-style human conditioning programme."

His reference to the USSR was a good one, insightful and a decent attempt at drawing a comparison with some of the programmes the former Soviet entity had created.

"So that explains the neonatal unit," prompted Drake, jumping to a conclusion that Wendy shot down in a flash.

"That's not it," she replied, before continuing a long, uninterrupted explanation.

"We don't have the answers, but we have some conclusions, and they aren't good ones. First, Walsh doesn't travel to Russia, so if the neonatal unit is there to work on her MorphEn procedures then that means she has trained others to do her work, but we don't see that. She has the proprietary knowledge, training others would cost her. The Russians would no longer need her.

"We think Knacc is a baby farm. The body cam footage showed bedrooms for two. The breach at Knacc happened late evening, most of the agents were in their sleeping quarters. Every bedroom your team entered encountered a couple, one male and one female agent. We think Walsh and Urinov are creating MorphEns specifically to mate with one another." Drake looked across at Gratton, who for the first time chipped in. He didn't speak but he nodded his head to reinforce Wendy's point.

"The impact, the gains, they'd be massive – off the scale. Her procedure is scoring a 20%+ uplift in mental and physical capabilities. Factor that enhancement on to a baby born from two MorphEn parents and we're talking near superhuman abilities. Think humans running sub-three-minute miles, the ability to comprehend algebra only a computer can calculate. The scope is endless. These people would be running the planet before they even reached adulthood."

Drake studiously listened whilst nestling his coffee, steam still rising from it. He took a big slurp as he cogitated the facts.

"So now you know," stated Wendy almost triumphantly. As she did, she glanced across to Mike Gratton, giving him a subtle yet telling nod.

"Yes, ma'am," he replied. Rising from his chair, Mike Gratton walked to the rear of the office to retrieve a small black suitcase.

"Your arm," directed Wendy as she motioned to Drake to present his arm on the desk.

Gratton laid the case on the desk, opening it up revealed a stumpy-looking syringe gun. Drake knew instantly what it was; the gun housed a microchip within its cartridge.

"What the fuck…?" voiced Drake. "…Not fucking happening…" he continued.

"You wanted full disclosure… YOU GOT IT," she boomed, raising her voice for the first time that afternoon. "Disclosure wasn't for free," she carried on. She expanded, "You're now in the inner circle, there's no going back, no leaving it. Do you understand?"

Drake listened but didn't react, adamant not to visibly acquiesce to her demanding overtones.

"Your fucking arm," Wendy repeated herself.

Reluctantly, Drake presented his arm on the table. Gratton took a firm grip of his forearm, pressing it into the table, whilst he manhandled the microchip gun in his right hand. Gratton pushed the gun nozzle into the underside of Drake's forearm and lightly squeezed the trigger. The gun made a small clicking sound as it plunged the microchip into the fleshy part of his forearm. Drake's face growled, but not from the physical pain. Chipped like a dog irked. The Mega Bitch now had full knowledge of his every movement.

"Are we done?" snapped Drake, glowering at Wendy as he pushed Gratton's hands off his forearm angrily.

"For now," she replied coldly. Emotionless as ever, she stood up as she watched Drake turn on his heels to exit the room.

Like it or not, Drake had just accepted a new job. He was now one of the Mega Bitch's personal agents.

Drake made the six metres to the door swiftly and was

about to exit. As he put his hand on the handle, he paused before withdrawing, turning to face Wendy.

"Why not take Walsh out?" Drake asked as he searched her face.

It was a calculated question, the timing and the execution. Drake had almost asked it earlier in the debrief, but he'd wanted to put Wendy off guard, if that was possible. She was caught out, surprised by the question. In fact, surprised that Drake had even paused at the point of his exit. In her mind, the meeting had concluded.

She paused; silence ensued as she considered an answer, weighing up the best answer.

"You want her back." Breaking the silence, Drake answered his own question. Still Wendy said nothing, but her eyes told him what he wanted to know.

And with that, without waiting for a reply, Drake turned and exited the room.

CHAPTER 24
THEY WEREN T MUPPETS!

Tuesday 10th January 2017

JT sat across the table from Nic, who was munching through his breakfast, nestling his second cup of coffee in his hands as he pondered what the day ahead might entail.

Ever since Friday, JT and his team had been one step behind finding and securing the Fletcher family. Initially they'd made good ground, a promising dash north from Lyon up the péage had ended with nothing but a handful of discarded mobile phones.

The discarded phones had helped JT a little. As much as he and his team had grave concerns over the safety of the Fletchers, the phones dumped roadside suggested a level of intelligence amongst the Fletcher group, and if JT and his team now had a cold trail, then hopefully the same applied to their would-be killers.

Initially, JT and his team had stuck together. Both teams, JT with Nic and Rob with Meek had followed the trail westwards across France. Clever enough to have discarded their phones, the Fletchers continued to use their credit cards. Not that clever after all had been JT's initial conclusion. Now, though, he had fully reassessed his summary of the Fletcher clan.

They weren't muppets! That had been the expression he had used in his last report to Jonno. On the run, the Fletchers plus Kate Harper had paid for hotels in cash, yet they'd bought various supplies on credit card in supermarkets and fuel stations. JT had only learnt which hotel they'd stayed in after copious legwork from the local gendarmerie. That hadn't been quick. The time delay for 'intel' from Interpol to MI6 via the local gendarmes had meant his team had been five hours behind the Fletchers' last known layover.

But the final most telling piece of evidence, the bit that really highlighted the level of competence amongst the Fletcher family, had been the moment the entire group had rinsed as much money from their accounts in cash as their daily limits would allow. JT hadn't seen that coming. It had been exceptionally clever from a quartet on the run, presumably scared for their lives.

That was the point when the trail had gone cold; western France and with no clear and obvious direction to head in. JT had reasoned that heading north to Caen would be the most logical, given that offered a ferry crossing home, whereas turning south only left Spain. Back in Vauxhall, Jonno had his minions scouring the quartet's possible options in Spain but nothing obvious and concrete had come to light. The strongest link had been a good friend of Ben Fletcher's who now lived in Barcelona.

But JT just didn't feel it. Social media contact between Ben and his buddy in Barcelona had been cold for several years. But that wasn't it; he didn't feel it because it didn't match 'his itch'. The Fletchers were in full flight mode, seeking safety at home. This was extremely common; he knew all about this. He even schooled others in it.

MI6 put a great deal of time into training its agents in its 'track and capture' programme. Training was broken down into several elements. The practical parts, often considered the more glamorous section, involved tearing around streets in cars and running down escapees on foot, but the electronic and digital elements were really the main cornerstone of modern hunt and capture. JT had thoroughly enjoyed discovering all about every aspect of a digital trail, scary as it was. Yet a more nuanced and subtle element of the programme existed, a thorough and comprehensive unit in human psychology, all about 'fight or flight'.

As much as modern humans are 'learnt creatures', they all fall back to a very standard and basic few principles unless they are incredibly disciplined and well trained, the 'fight or flight' principle being a great example. Under acute stress, all humans undergo a physiological reaction to a perceived threat, this is known as the 'fight or flight response'. It's a very immediate response with virtually no cognitive bandwidth utilized to decide what to do. In other words, it's almost automatic.

Once on the run, in what the MI6 training officer had coined as 'full flight' mode, humans then start to use cognitive reasoning. In other words, the control centre takes over and pre-learnt thinking and concepts start to have sway over decisions any human may or may not take. Being at home is a comfort, a feeling of safety and, as such, becomes an overriding emotion for almost anyone on the run. But at the same point, logical thoughts counteract, such as 'my home will be watched'. So, humans on the run will look for something close to home, the best version of what they can achieve to give them the safety they crave.

The Fletchers getting back to the UK made the most sense to JT. His team had all concurred. That had been a couple of days ago, so JT dispatched Rob and Meek north to cover the Calais-Rotterdam corridor, Jonno had sent a team to monitor the ports at Portsmouth and Plymouth, whilst he and Nic had backtracked to cover the main north-south route from Lyon to Paris.

JT's phone broke his thoughts, the mini vibrations causing it to gravitate across the table with every tremor. He glanced at the display, consideration made as to whether he should take the call or not. It was his boss, Chris Johnson calling, his iPhone displaying a single word '*JONNO*' all in capitals proudly across the centre. Not a call he would ever field.

"Jonno," answered JT with quick efficiency as soon as he hit the green 'receive call' button.

"Still nothing our end," returned Jonno, straight down to business. The two men knew each other well; a friendship existed built out of respect for each other's professional capabilities. Small talk or other aspects of life would be easily discussed over a beer in a multitude of social settings, but right now they were both 'on the job'. The clock was ticking and pleasantries could wait for another time.

Jonno proceeded to give JT an update, although the update basically said nothing. In the intelligence game 'no news was bad news'. News or information was the only currency that existed. The Fletcher parents knew nothing, the phone taps to both Tom and Sarah Fletcher had drawn a blank. All their close friends were being monitored too, but nothing was forthcoming.

Interpol had also drawn blanks, made more irksome considering Rachel Fletcher's car was both damaged and had a UK plate presumably still being driven in continental Europe. If it had been dumped, then where in hell was it? The only comfort came from knowing how hard it must also be for their assailants to track them down, but that was starting to wear thin.

Jonno ended the call in a little less than three minutes. Nic hadn't heard Jonno's words, but the half conversation he had heard was enough.

"Nothing new?" Nic asked, more a statement than a question, as he glanced towards his boss. JT shook his head, resigning the pair to another day hanging around on the outskirts of Mâcon.

Their waiting game continued.

CHAPTER 25
HELLO MUM

Wednesday 11th January 2017

Rachel Fletcher's Golf crawled through the large, imposing gates, gravel crunching under the tyres, as Ben inched it close to their mum's front door. Parked up, Rachel looked out of the rear window, the door appeared to be dark blue or maybe black, it was difficult to tell in the early evening dusk. At 6 p.m. in winter, the only light emitted from the pair of subtle wall-mounted lights straddling the door frame.

Dan twisted his body sideways to give Rachel the attention she needed. He knew her feelings about their mum; blimey, the entire world knew her feelings.

"Rach, we need her," he spoke softly and reassuringly to his sister.

Dan and Ben didn't feel a great amount of love for their mum, but neither brother hated her, whereas Rachel had never forgotten or forgiven her, but 'needs must' and right now she had to suck it up, bite her lip and be nice. Her best friend Kate and her brothers' lives depended on it.

The quartet got out. Dan, leading the way, approached the front door and gave the knocker a confident, loud double thump. Standing waiting for their mum to answer, the Fletcher group looked a lonely and sorry sight. On the run for almost a week and off the grid completely all added to their exhaustion. Fraught nerves and heightened levels of arousal were incredibly taxing.

Footsteps could be heard internally as someone approached the door. Dan braced himself to say 'Hi Mum, surprise' as the door opened, but he needn't have bothered. The door was opened by a smart-looking man, who looked slightly nonplussed. Dan was a little taken aback; he didn't recognize the man standing in the expansive, tiled hall.

"Is my mum in?" he blurted out as he took in the obvious splendour of his mum's home. Not bringing up four kids had clearly helped the finances. As other initial thoughts shot through Dan's mind, he looked back to check on Rachel's well-being. She was failing to conceal a glowering face.

"But yes," came the reply in perfect but accented English as the man took a step back, extending his arm by way of offering entry.

The quartet stepped inside and followed the man into the cavernous hallway. Large black-and-white chequered tiles adorned the floor, a few stylish artefacts sat on a handsome sideboard, presumably French antique. As Dan took in his surroundings, Ben and Rachel started chit-chatting. Ben was fuelling the fire by giving Rachel a running commentary on the opulence in front of him, not on purpose; he just didn't quite get it. The more happy-go-lucky Ben didn't get wound up by his mum's obvious success in life.

Highly audible, the noisy chatter, whilst they waited for the man to find their mum, did the job. Dan looked up to see his mum standing framed in the door to the left of the main stairwell.

"Daniel!" came a very obviously surprised, one-word response from his mum as she stood looking at her three children, mouth almost agape.

Louise Walsh was rarely lost for words, but at that moment, standing in her own house, she almost was.

"Xavier, mon chéri, viens voir," she said, reverting to French, as she beckoned Xav from the living room.

He appeared in almost double quick time. None of the siblings had ever met him, but they knew he existed, knew what he was.

"Welcome, welcome," came his near accentless English as he smiled warmly at the quartet whilst placing his hand on Louise's shoulder warmly, Xav consciously playing the charade, a warm and welcoming house a haven for his unwitting house guests.

Louise approached Dan. No hugs or kisses, she offered her hand in an attempt to squeeze Dan's hand affectionately. He retracted his hand a touch, just enough to emit the correct signal to his estranged mother. Louise took the vibe and pulled back too. Her own children in her house were one thing, but sentimentality wasn't about to start creeping in, that was instantly clear.

"Hi Ben, Rachel," directing her conversation towards her other two children, standing together a couple of metres back. Ben replied, whilst Rachel just stood staring Louise down. Kate, meanwhile, remained politely steadfast as she took in the Fletcher reunion. Dan looked on as a slight unease took hold of him. He had been harbouring doubts about how his sister would handle the situation, and it now appeared with good reason. She looked prickly with body language to match.

"Hello Mum," she replied politely.

It was a start at least thought Dan, as he relaxed a little given Rachel's slight softening. Finally, he introduced Kate to Louise, as Xav ushered the entire quartet into the living room. As the quartet filed through Xav, unnoticed, stole a telling glance at Louise.

Dan hadn't given too much thought as to their approach with their mum. They needed a safe place to hole up whilst they figured out how to get back to the UK. That really had been his single consideration. It would of course worry his mum, but telling her the truth was the only option, although neither he nor his siblings were close to his mum.

He proceeded to explain to Louise, relaying the events of the previous seven days. Ben interjected too, sharing the awful burden the story telling entailed. For the main, Rachel sat silent, as much a tactic to stop herself from biting the hand that was feeding them, because right there and then, the quartet desperately needed a haven. Unbeknown to them, Louise Walsh, who had returned to her maiden name, their estranged biological mother, had unwittingly landed her prey.

Louise and Xav listened intently, playing their parts perfectly, aghast at all the right moments, Louise looking her most concerned as she heard the details of Helen's death and Rachel's gunshot wound. They were both astounded as they heard of the quartet's dramatic escape at the péage. Xav hadn't even had to act at that point, a natural look of surprise spread over his entire face as he sat almost enthralled by the high-speed car chase and the gory details of how Dan and Ben had effectively dispatched one of his highly trained Apfel pairings. His face positively glowered as Ben, with anger and defiance in his voice, described the final boot delivered to the prone Bush.

Dan clocked Xav's reaction, not quite anger, maybe closer to disappointment. Dan didn't know him; everyone had their own facial expressions. Maybe this was his face of pain, mulled Dan. Either way, he didn't give it any more thought as the story continued.

Once completed, the room fell silent. Rachel had done her best to keep quiet, whilst Kate had been her dutiful best, supporting her best friend by staying hushed too.

"What do you need?" Louise asked as she broke the silence.

As she did so, Xav got up and summoned someone from the hallway. Speaking in French, Dan picked out the word 'boisson' and figured he had suddenly thought to offer some refreshments.

"Somewhere to stay..." Dan replied, "...and some money... cash..." he continued awkwardly. Awkward not because she lacked for money but because asking for cash felt a great deal more symbolic. Rachel noticeably squirmed in her seat as Dan outlined what they were asking for. The hatred she felt for her mum wasn't dissipating, despite how nice her mum was currently being. From her point of view, this was just an act. No matter what, Rachel wasn't about to forgive her.

"But of course," Louise replied in English although sounding almost French, the years in Switzerland having a noticeable impact upon her choice of words.

The smart-looking man who'd originally opened the front door arrived carrying a tray of drinks. Maybe he was a butler mused Dan as he watched on. Coffee and tea were the sole offerings, all gratefully received by impromptu house guests. Xav took control of proceedings, shooing the man away as he poured coffee and milk as requested by Dan et al. Louise, meanwhile, excused herself, explaining her need to address the quartet's bedroom needs, raising an eyebrow in the process as Dan suggested three bedrooms not four were required. A smiling Kate was all the explanation she required.

Whilst Xav played the host, mixing small talk with a show of concern, Dan took in his surroundings. The chateau his mum lived in bordered on opulence, tastefully furnished with a mixture of classic pieces of furniture and some very expensive-looking contemporary items. Fine gilt-framed art adorned most walls, with a luxurious-looking matching gilt-framed mirror commanding the centre of the longest wall in the living room, handsomely located above a beautifully tiled fireplace. Across the living room, at the far end, stood a large window, broken into three separate frames, staring out across the inky black lake. Dan figured the daytime view would be magnificent; it looked pretty good there and then as the moonlight shimmered across the water.

His mum wasn't hiding her wealth, that was for sure. A different man, presumably another member of staff, walked past the open door frame. How many domestic staff did they need pondered Dan. Louise returned, having made suitable arrangements, and suggested the group get their bags and freshen up whilst she attended to an evening meal. Dan suppressed a smirk as his mum mentioned the meal, a safe assumption it wouldn't be her doing the cooking. Still, they were all hungry and a quick shower wasn't the worst idea either.

"Is half an hour enough?" asked Louise, suggesting a mealtime. "We can sit down then and work a plan too."

His mum offering help with a master plan wasn't what Dan wanted, but maybe it was what he needed. Either way, he wasn't churlish enough to reject his mum's offer.

"Yes, Mum, that would be great…" he replied, "…and thanks…" the first real show of gratitude from any of them.

The quartet was shown to their respective rooms via the broad staircase which stood imposingly in the centre of the hallway. Reaching the first-floor landing, a generous corridor extended both left and right. The guy leading the way directed them left, first Ben and then Rachel offered the rooms immediately to the left. Dan and Kate finally reached their bedroom, with what Dan assumed was a fourth bedroom further still down the corridor.

Kate entered first, dumping her bags down as she and Dan took in their surroundings. A large double bed, maybe a king, took pride of place centrally in the imposing bedroom, to the right stood an open door leading to a spacious en suite. A matching pair of bedside tables nestled either side of the bed, both accommodating a pair of stylish-looking bedside lamps. Dan had spent many nights in great hotels, almost none of which came close to the bedroom experience he was confronted with. He caught Kate's eyes as she did the classic action many people did when they arrive in a new bedroom. She sat playfully on the end of the bed, bouncing ever so slightly up and down as if performing a mattress test. He returned her grin.

"Blimey, Dan, you didn't say," stated Kate in reference to the incredible house his mum owned.

"News to me too," he replied as he reaffirmed the fact that none of his brothers or sister ever had contact with their mum. "You jump in first," suggested Dan, nodding his head towards the shower.

Aware they only had 30 minutes, he started to take a few things out of his bag in readiness as Kate took to the en suite.

As the quartet freshened up, Louise sat impassively in her private study, the private, inner sanctum used by both. Xav was prowling along the side of the sturdy desk as the two conspired.

"Get Henkl here immediately…" ordered Louise. "…Where is he now…?" she continued.

"North of Lille…" he replied, "…a good eight hours' drive…" Xav detailed.

"Demain alors," she responded, reverting to French as she suggested the Apfel carry out the kill the next day.

"D'accord, ma chérie," he replied as he grabbed the phone resting in front of her.

Henkl picked up almost immediately, a look of surprise splashed across his face the instant Xav relayed the intel. Not that Xav could see Henkl's face as the head of the Apfel sat in his hotel bar almost 800 km from Chateau Forestier. Instructed to make a beeline for Geneva, Henkl jumped to it. He and Zebra had a long drive ahead, Harry was slightly nearer, but not by much, and his third team were currently returning from the UK. Still, his mission had suddenly become remarkably easier, having his prey almost handed on a plate to him. He allowed himself a wry grin as his call from Xav came to an end.

After dinner, the quartet retired to the living room along with Louise. Dan stood peering through the windows across the lake. It was almost hypnotic, a mesmerizing view, as he allowed his eyes to search in the distance. As he stood there transfixed, his attention averted to the foreground.

The grounds between the chateau and the waterfront were spectacular, a beautiful, circular gravel driveway made ever so slightly untidy courtesy of Rachel's Golf. Ben's parking had left a lot to be desired. Beyond the drive, a neat, manicured lawn led to the waterfront, while a couple of speedboats bobbed up and down ever so slightly on their moorings as the water lapped around their bows.

On the lawn, the silhouetted Xav stood talking to another unknown staff member. A pair of Dobermanns sat obediently on their haunches as the two men chatted. The dark night concealed the man's status, but the dogs' presence suggested security. Why did his mum need this many staff? Security too? Dan didn't reach a conclusion as he took it all in.

He turned back round to face the room, rejoining the conversation. A few awkward moments had come and gone over the course of the evening, Louise immediately regretting asking after Tom Fletcher. Rachel, unable to keep quiet, reacted in a flash before leaving the room. Kate went after her, not to return, as the two best friends remained in Rachel's bedroom for the remainder of the evening. It was probably for the best mused Dan as he and Ben spent the time explaining to Louise what they intended to do.

Safety and cash had been Dan's original plan along with some time to weigh things up. It became very clear that staying at his mum's for a long period of time wasn't going to work for Rachel. Fortunately, his mum had offered them a lifeline, a car with French plates was a big help. He had wanted to hire a car days ago but without a safe credit card he'd been unable to resolve this. Louise arranged for a car to be brought over mid morning, €10 000 in cash too. It wasn't the plan Dan had originally had in mind, but adapting in a crisis was critical. Both he and Ben figured a clean car to be the biggest win even if it meant they were back on the road, on the run again, the next day.

With that, both Dan and Ben retired, leaving Louise alone with her thoughts; dark, murderous thoughts.

Deep in the bowels of MI6 HQ in Vauxhall, an alert splashed across the LCD monitor. A couple of technicians sat impassively as they stared at several monitors within the SitRep.

19:08 CET (18:08 GMT)
Contact Jack Thomas ~ overwatch.
Special Operations ~ Team Leader

Notify Chris Johnson ~ overwatch.
Chief of Operations

Followed by a transcript and a highlighted watchword. The watchword "Daniel Fletcher" flashed intermittently. The technician wasted no time, glancing at his watch it was just after 7:30 p.m., over an hour since the call had been intercepted, information transference still agonizingly slow from Interpol to MI6.

The technician, ever efficient, completed his calls in less than four minutes.

Dan retrieved Kate as he went to bed, the relief on his sister's face palpable as he confirmed they'd be leaving their mum's house by mid morning.

"I fucking hate her," hissed Rachel as Dan parted company for the night. "I wish we'd never come," she continued.

He tried to placate his sister, but his attempts were futile. He stopped short of saying they were screwed without their mum's help. He knew Rachel enough to know the battles to compete in and the ones to leave. Healing the relationship gap between his sister and their mum was a bridge too far.

"Night sis," as he took his leave. Hand in hand, he and Kate retired for the night.

CHAPTER 26
FIREFIGHT

Thursday 12th January 2017

Dan lay awake, a shaft of light squeezed through the gap in the curtains, crossing the room like a laser beam. As he contemplated the day ahead, Kate stirred as she started to come round from her slumber. Transfixed on her face as she slowly woke up, Dan marvelled at his girlfriend. Was that what Kate was he pondered, his girlfriend? Maybe. No matter her official title, she was beautiful and seven days on the run from a bunch of maniacal killers hadn't detracted from this. He stretched across and swept an errant strand of hair off her face.

As Kate's eyes finally opened, Dan's face came into focus as he lay just inches from her.

"Morning, you," she whispered, aware that Dan, just lying motionless, was gazing at her.

"Morning back," he said as he leant across and planted a tender kiss on her lips.

Maybe being on the run wasn't too bad after all he mused.

"Time to crack on," he suggested, sadly bringing them both back to reality with a bump.

It was just after 8 a.m. and there was a great deal to do. His first mission was to try and extricate Rachel without any more animosity. He jumped out of bed, hurriedly getting dressed. He figured she wouldn't come out of her room till he knocked her up en route to breakfast. There was no way she wanted to be alone with Mum.

Dan, with Kate in tow, tapped on Rachel's bedroom door as

they made their way to breakfast. To his surprise, she wasn't there, and neither was Ben. Presumably Ben had beaten him to it and chaperoned her downstairs.

Dan followed the noise, as he and Kate arrived downstairs, he could hear Ben's voice coming from a room they hadn't seen the previous night. Entering, Ben and Rachel were seated at an enormous island in the left of centre of an extremely spacious designer kitchen. Perched on bar stools, Rachel was nursing a steaming cup of coffee whilst Ben, leaning back, was talking to their mum.

As Dan entered the room, Louise looked up before warmly saying good morning to them as she motioned to sit at some seats opposite Ben and Rachel. Dan and Kate complied, sliding onto the bar stools, Dan starting to appreciate his surroundings. The enormous granite worktop that formed the island he was seated at was spectacular. Glistening black, green and brown quartz flecks caught the light. Almost two metres wide and eight metres in length, it was an impressive feature.

At the far end of the kitchen, a commercial-grade set of units, hobs and oven were accommodated alongside a very fancy-looking set of kitchen knives and utensils all hanging neatly on magnetic strips. The kitchen positively oozed class; it could have been one of those kitchens you saw on a TV cookery show Dan mulled.

A member of staff served coffee before scurrying back to the far end of the kitchen, returning a minute later with a tray of warm pastries. The variety of Danish pastries, all freshly baked, smelt amazing. Dan dived in, but not before Ben reached across to grab what appeared to be his second or maybe third. Dan afforded himself a grin at the speed his brother wolfed down the pain aux raisins he'd only just picked up.

"The car is on its way."

Louise choosing to get immediately down to business made good sense, mused Dan. A single night under her roof wasn't going to suddenly get his siblings to a 'happy families' place. He looked across as Rachel who, for the main, had been concentrating on the contents of her half drunk mug of coffee. She had clearly been letting Ben do all the early morning chatter.

"That's great, thanks, Mum," Dan shot back with a degree of gratitude.

He pinged a smile in his mum's direction before reducing it somewhat as he caught his sister's face. Her eyes, trained on Dan, emitted a flash of anger as she clocked his smiling face. No softening in Rachel then, he reflected.

As the four sat there, munching their way through breakfast, Xav appeared in the door frame, initially unnoticed. Silhouetted against the bright lights emanating from the corridor, he stood motionless taking in his surroundings. As Louise looked up, he nodded his head solemnly in her direction before he took several steps into the expansive kitchen.

Dan looked up, to see first Xav and then three men file through the kitchen door. Silhouetted, he couldn't make out their facial characteristics, only their shape, as they entered the room, but the gait and shape of the third man was something he would never forget. Etched into his mind, the third man was blue beanie man.

Dan shot up, leaping off his stool in a flash, adrenaline coursing through his veins. But he only got a couple of metres back from the island worktop before his plight came into an awful and desperate focus.

"SIT DOWN!" screamed Louise, anger almost fire in her voice.

"DON'T FUCKING MOVE," boomed another voice as one of the three men stood a mere eight metres away pointing a silencer-fitted Glock directly at Dan. Henkl's English was perfect, a slightly clipped Germanic accent but perfect, nonetheless.

The atmosphere in the room had changed in a millisecond. An almost pleasant breakfast setting had suddenly become a confused rush of contradicting thoughts. Dan computed a plethora of contrasting facts as he took in what was happening. The man who had been chasing them for seven days across France was now standing in his mum's kitchen alongside two other assassins, three guns trained on them, his mum part of it. *What the fuck?* thought Dan.

Across the island, Ben, also standing, had made a beeline for the man to the left of Henkl. It had been completely reactionary, as had been the response of the killer he bore down on. Zebra squeezed his trigger. The bullet punched a hole into Ben's thigh, causing him to crash to the floor. Both Rachel and Kate screeched, their voices lost in a melee of screams and orders barked out by Henkl, Zebra and Louise.

"NOT IN HERE," boomed Louise, directing her orders at Henkl as she looked across the kitchen towards the prone figure of Ben.

Blood had trickled down his leg, a few small splatters visible on the floor. Rachel had leapt off her seat and was crouching down holding Ben, who remarkably wasn't making too much noise given the bullet wound to his upper leg.

"What the fuck, Mum…" screamed Dan, "…is this you?" he carried on, wild-eyed as he started to take in the situation.

"Sit down and shut up, Daniel," came a firm and patronizing instruction from Xav.

Dan acquiesced, recognizing the dire situation they were now presented with.

"What is this, Mum…?" quizzed Dan. "…What the fuck is this?" He searched into his mum's eyes as he fired across his questions.

Louise no longer looked like the motherly figure from the night before. Gone were her soft facial expressions, replaced by a cold, hard grimace as she stared Dan down.

He listened intently as his own mother told him he wouldn't understand, that he'd never understand.

"You're all freaks," she intimated as she motioned with her head towards Dan, Ben and Rachel.

Clear now to Dan was the fact this entire thing was all about his siblings, Helen's death and Kate's involvement merely collateral damage.

"You're our own mother," part plea, part defiance as he highlighted the obvious.

He was searching for answers, an explanation. Nothing computed and he hated not understanding. The not knowing gnawed at him. His head felt like a woodpecker was perched on it, pecking away furiously at his skull.

Kate, to that point, hadn't done much more than let out some shrieks. Seated the nearest of the quartet to the standing Louise, an almost involuntary action came over her. The death of her best friend, her beautiful, happy-go-lucky 'chica' Helen Waters, had been ordered by this vile human now standing over her. She leapt up. Rapidly closing the gap to Louise, she managed to swipe her across the face, a half slap, half claw, leaving a tramline of blood running diagonally down the older woman's left cheek. Kate's nails had sunk deep into Louise's fleshy cheekbone.

She was like a woman possessed as she ploughed on attempting to strike Louise with her other flailing arm. She didn't, though. Harry lurched forwards and planted a crushing blow to Kate's left shoulder, knocking her off her feet. She crashed to the floor, sliding a little over the smooth, tiled surface. Slightly winded, she didn't move initially as Dan jumped to her defence, to no avail though. As he made to charge at Harry, he almost poked his own eye out as he got an eyeful of gunsight aimed directly at him.

Harry standing with gun arm outstretched, his silencer-fitted Glock pointed directly at his face. Dan didn't twitch a muscle as he stood defiantly staring him down. The killer prodded the gun into Dan's face prompting him to move backwards a touch before sitting back on his stool.

"I'm going to fucking kill you," growled Dan, almost spitting his words out. Harry grinned at him, enjoying the power he finally had over his quarry.

"You fucking wish…" he replied, "…you fucking wish, sunshine…" continued Harry triumphantly.

"Get it done," spat Louise as she composed herself, whilst running a hand across her bleeding cheek.

With that Henkl and his thugs, Zebra and Harry, started to usher the quartet out of Chateau Forestier. The 'get it done' wasn't lost on Dan and could only mean one thing. The four of them were being led to their death.

Uncompliant, Dan got a gun poked violently in the nape of his neck for his troubles. Begrudgingly he obeyed, as the four were frogmarched out of the kitchen in the direction of the two speedboats moored at the lakeside. A watery end maybe, wondered Dan. No, she wouldn't want that. As he weighed up the likely method, the where and when of their demise, he searched his brain for a way out of the situation, interrogating all kinds of thoughts and scenarios.

Looking across at his brother, their situation didn't look at all rosy though. In a degree of discomfort, Dan's biggest concern was Ben's inability to run. Limping heavily, Ben was currently being assisted to the boats with Rachel's help. The armed men had guns trained on all of them as Louise and Xav looked on. Step by step, they neared the jetty, whilst Louise and Xav remained, standing impassively on the stone steps outside the front door of the imposing chateau.

Harry boarded first, moving to the bow of the boat, followed by Zebra who holstered his Glock as he moved to the cockpit. The quartet clambered slowly aboard; a mixture of reluctance combined with Ben's wound helping to slow down the process.

"Fucking move," growled Henkl from their rear as he gave Kate a healthy prod to the dead centre of her shoulder blades. Encouraging Kate to move quickly didn't have the desired impact, so, using the soul of his boot, he kicked her firmly on her arse. She lurched forwards with a jolt, letting out a small yelp as she did. Dan twisted round, intent on closing the gap to Henkl, but thought better of it as he spied the Glock pointing right at him.

With the quartet all aboard, Henkl started unlashing the mooring line, bending down to unhook a loop of rope off the solid-looking, metal, mushroom-shaped post; the shiny chrome post presenting a very nautical feel to the lakeside jetty. Zebra started the engine, patiently waiting for Henkl to free the boat from its moorings as Harry, with his back to the lake, stood watching the quartet very attentively.

It all happened so quickly; initially Dan didn't react. Floating in the middle of the lake, no one had taken any notice of the static boat anchored a couple of hundred metres away. Apparently fishing, the boat had gone entirely unnoticed. Lying prone, Robert Warner had his rifle aimed at Harry, his dead centre mass directly in the cross hairs.

The first bullet penetrated Harry's back, puncturing a lung, as he lurched forwards upon impact. A second bullet punched a hole in his neck. Neither bullet killed him, but he died, nonetheless. Harry keeled overboard to a slower demise as he drowned struggling to cope with his bloody wounds.

Zebra and Henkl didn't react quickly either. The sound of the shots rang out across the water a fraction of a second after the two bullets penetrated Harry, but the sound of the speedboat purring helped to reduce their initial reaction. Harry's movement forwards and overboard was the main catalyst. Dan reacted first, charging forwards in the direction of Zebra, delivering a brutal headbutt as he and Zebra crashed to the floor of the cockpit. A third shot, then a fourth rang out, a couple of thuds heard as two bullets implanted into the wooden post standing proud to Henkl's right. The German took cover as he leapt from the wooden jetty, dashing up a couple of steps before diving over the small, ornate stone wall set five metres back from the water's front. More shots rang out; bits of stone particle bursting off the top of the wall protecting Henkl.

As the shots continued, a speedboat cut across the lake from right to left, piloted by Meek with JT and Nic standing holding the gunwale of the boat, such was the speed she was applying to the craft. A beach landing would have been ideal; Meek would literally have piloted the boat at full speed, grounding her craft on the land to afford her crew to quickly disembark, but that wasn't possible at Chateau Forestier. The chateau had a beautiful water's front, edged neatly with a small, man-made wall that sat proudly half a metre above the waterline. All Meek could do was run the boat parallel to the water's edge whilst ramming the engines into reverse to kill her speed – not the quickest of landings.

Meanwhile, Dan was in a fight to the death with Zebra. Shots rang out above their heads as the two men wrestled each other. Zebra's nose trickled with blood courtesy of the searing headbutt Dan had delivered. Kate had joined the fray, as had Rachel, as they both rushed towards the cockpit. Zebra dished out a ruthless blow to Dan's torso, but the diminished space helped reduce its effect, Dan still grunting in pain from its impact. Kate had picked up the best weapon available, a small, black plastic tackle box. Wielding it wildly at Zebra, she caught him a telling blow to the left side of his forehead, the tackle box body snapping from its handle, leaving her clutching the handle as the box and contents cartwheeled beyond the bow of the boat.

Zebra returned the favour; his blow to Kate's face knocked her backwards as she collapsed into the onrushing Rachel. Zebra, meanwhile, managed to retrieve his Glock whilst Dan fought for control of it too. Both men's hands intertwined around its handle, Zebra attempted to rain a barrage of knee strikes into Dan's torso in his effort to free the Glock from his opponent's grip. Dan hung on as if his life depended on it – it did!

Having managed to stand up, Ben rushed towards his brother as best he could. Grimacing as he closed the gap, doing his level best to ignore the searing pain emanating from his thigh, Ben made to strike Zebra in the face but landed as much of his forceful punch on his own brother as the two men jostled. The gun fell to the cockpit floor, Ben's second punch the most telling. Dan crashed to the ground too under the weight of Zebra and his brother, but the fight wasn't over. Dan breathless, with the wind knocked out of him, was momentarily out of the fight and Zebra sensed this too. Turning his attention to Ben, he jerked his right arm backwards, catching younger Fletcher brother with a crunching elbow to the bridge of his nose. In a bobbing boat, with shots ringing overhead, Zebra felt and heard it; Ben's nose was broken. Ben fell backwards, almost seeing stars as he collapsed to the floor.

Zebra started to get to his feet, realizing his position of superiority as his two main protagonists, both nearly unconscious, lay prone on the floor. He glimpsed his Glock in the footwell of the cockpit, reversing his motion, he went to retrieve it. As he did, Kate, having regained her feet, hurtled across the deck like a screaming banshee, utilizing all 60 kg of her body weight as she squashed Zebra against the boat's wheel. Zebra's 85 kg of honed muscle took the blow easily. In a dual motion, he grabbed Kate by the shoulders and flung her to her left whilst managing to deliver a thudding kick to Dan's midriff as he attempted to get back to his feet.

It was game over, or so Zebra thought. Looking up from the prone Dan, he stood motionless as his eyes focused on Rachel. She was stood holding his Glock, pointing it directly at him, her arm wavering ever so slightly. Nerves maybe? Zebra didn't get more time to figure it out. Rachel squeezed the trigger, hitting him in the chest. He lurched forwards, attempting to disarm her to no avail. She fired again; her second shot killed Zebra as he tumbled unceremoniously to the floor. She shot again at the already dead killer and a fourth shot too before Kate managed to get to her. The two girls momentarily hugged as they took in the desperate sight around them.

Behind them, the action continued unabated. Henkl had managed to scuttle across the lawn, returning fire from behind a large stone statue, one of two that stood sentry either side of the main entrance door. JT was putting suppressing fire down on Henkl, his shots rained down on the statue the German hid behind. As he did so, Nic made ground along the left side of the lawn, gaining some cover from the neat stone wall that created a border for the lawn in front of the jetty.

Louise and Xav had already retreated inside the chateau. As JT reloaded, Henkl took his opportunity, rushing the five-metre gap from statue to the haven the chateau presented. Nic got a couple of shots off, the second of which embedded itself in the door as it slammed shut.

The front door of Chateau Forestier was a sturdy, imposing, thick wooden barrier. Solid wood and oversized, had it been locked with its deadbolt it might have presented JT and his team a significant problem. Fortunately, in Henkl's rush as he beat a retreat, the door was slammed shut on its latch-locking mechanism only. Still, time was of the essence and every second counted. As JT momentarily weighed up his options, Nic made his ground to join him, leaving Meek to tend to the Fletchers.

JT and Nic decided to crash the door rather than enter via one of the windows. Crashing through a glass window always looked easy in the movies, but the reality was a very different thing. Picking up a significant laceration was a quick way to take you out of the game. Nic stood ready to cover JT as he attempted to put his boot through the door. The oversized door meant his boot was much lower than the lock mechanism. The door flexed a little, and he guessed the internal frame may have soaked up some of the impact too. Either way, his attempt failed, the door didn't budge.

A second attempt made no difference as valuable time was lost. Changing tactics, JT charged the door with his shoulder, the impact of his body weight landing much higher up the frame, closer to the latch. It had an effect, the frame made a crunching sound as the lock housing moved an inch inside its wooden frame allowing the door to open a sliver. Nic looked on, a frustrated expression plastered across his face. JT sucked it up, retreated a metre and charged again, this time with enough force to clatter through, as the door finally broke from its frame, splinters of wood trailing from the door casing as he crashed inside. Nic, standing a metre back, trained his gun into the vacant hallway. Breaching the front door had taken over 20 seconds, a very costly 20 seconds. The MI6 team swept through the chateau, room by room, methodically searching for Henkl and his paymasters.

Another 30 seconds ticked by before JT arrived in the kitchen, scene to the moment Dan Fletcher learnt of his biological mum's intent to kill him and his siblings. Off the back of the kitchen stood a very large storeroom cum rear entrance. The back door hung open; a two-metre broad gravel path led directly to the gravel road that almost entirely circled the chateau. The road turning left allowed direct access to the front of the chateau and, more tellingly, turning right led out of the chateau grounds.

There was no sign of Louise, Xav or Henkl; they had managed to flee during the melee. JT and Nic backtracked to the boats, the priority had been to secure the Fletchers, and at least that part of their mission appeared a success. But how were they? In the ensuing gunfight, JT had no idea who was and wasn't OK.

On the jetty, the Fletchers presented a bedraggled sight. Ben and Kate looked the worst. Kate had a huge welt forming on the side of her face and a split cheek revealing an inch of red raw flesh. Ben was worse still, though. His broken nose looked a mess, black eyes would certainly be forming shortly, and his squashed nose and blood-splattered face weren't pretty either. More significantly though was his leg. Immediate medical attention was required to treat this. There was no exit wound, so the bullet would need fishing out. At least that meant Ben only had one hole leaking blood. Nonetheless, he needed a hospital.

JT identified himself as the MI6 team went about managing the situation. Nic was attending to Ben's leg wound, whilst Meek brought their boat adjacent to the jetty. Boarding the quartet as swiftly as they could, she gunned the launch as soon as they were aboard. Slightly ahead, Robert Warner's craft left a white trail in the water for Meek to follow. As the boat speeded along, JT did his utmost to explain himself to the quartet. Relief flooded the faces of the Fletchers and Kate as they exchanged details of their recent ordeal.

More questions than answers rushed through Dan's mind as he processed recent events. An MI6 rescue, following seven days on the run left him perplexed. His own mum had tried to kill them.

"Show me ID." Suddenly becoming suspicious, Dan barked the order at JT. His mind was in overdrive, the exhilaration of the fight was subsiding, allowing him the opportunity to mull things over, paranoia sweeping through his thoughts. Was this an 'out of the fire into the frying pan' moment shot through his brain.

"It doesn't work like that..." JT shot back, "...you need to trust us," he continued as he looked Dan directly in the eyes. JT applied all his experience and training, interpersonal skills at that single moment were critical to contain the understandably jumpy Fletchers, but Dan wasn't having it. Who were they? Yes, they'd saved them, but MI6, really?

"Fucking prove it," barked Dan as he stood up in the boat, grabbing the gunwale for support. He glanced at Ben; his searching look got the message he intended across to his brother. His look wasn't lost on JT either. Dan was prepping Ben to be ready for a fight. JT had remained seated as Dan towered above him, pacifying Dan had now become his number one priority. His training kicked in as he remained calm and meek, allowing Dan to feel he had the upper hand.

"We have Sam..." JT replied. "...He's safe," he continued. "You can speak to him," he offered, thinking on his feet.

Dan's face changed noticeably as he reflected on JT's suggestion.

"Right now," replied Dan, closer to an order than a question.

Nic retrieved a phone from his pocket and hit a dial button. After a short conversation, he ended his call.

He'd heard Nic say the name Sam Fletcher, was it a ruse? Dan's forearm flexed, sinews tightened as he grew more agitated. He looked across at Kate and Rachel before returning his gaze on his wounded brother. A storm was spreading across his face as paranoia took full control. The speedboat lurched across the water, bouncing off the wake, every jar added to the tension on board.

"Bro, you OK?" asked Dan, but he wasn't asking if Ben was OK, he was telling him it was time to act. Ben knew exactly what his brother meant. JT knew too and he was ever grateful his phone suddenly rang. No one heard it, but JT felt the vibrations in his pocket.

"Yes," came JT's single word response as he hit the green call button. "Roger that," he carried on as he looked up at Dan whilst extending his outstretched arm. Phone in hand, he offered it to the standing brother.

"Is that you, Dan?" came the voice of Sam Fletcher through JT's iPhone. Dan relaxed a touch as he started to reply.

"Are you safe, Sam?" quizzed the eldest sibling, before more paranoia kicked in. Coercion suddenly came to the fore. "If you're OK, tell me what you prefer on toast," asked Dan.

"Marmite, buddy," came Sam's response in double quick time.

"Fuck... oh thank fuck..." Dan responded, "thank fuck for Marmite," as he sank back in his seat.

Ben allowed a grin to spread across his face, whilst Kate and Rachel instinctively hugged each other. JT visibly relaxed to as he witnessed a sea change in the quartet's body language. Never had the word Marmite given more happiness than it did it that moment. Clearly Sam loved Marmite, mused JT.

Dan ended the call and passed the phone back. He flashed JT

an apologetic look and breathed a huge sigh of relief. They were safe. Finally, their ordeal was over.

As the boat skipped across the lake, bouncing lightly over the small eddies created by the wake trailing Robert Warner's craft, JT finally had the confidence of the quartet; a more relaxed feel enveloped the group.

"We have a lot to discuss," voiced JT over the sound of the boat as its bow intermittently thumped the water. His chiselled jawline and bright eyes exuded energy. He could have passed for Kate's older brother mused Rachel, as she took in his facial features and lithe, muscular physique.

JT continued to brief the quartet, but it was one short on detail and it was the detail they craved. He hid behind the 'Official Secrets Act', explaining that until he got them safely back to London and ensconced deep inside MI6 HQ at Vauxhall he couldn't tell them much. Signing the Official Secrets Act would be required first and foremost. Dan was of course intrigued; his mind was racing as he pondered over the facts.

JT clammed up when Dan asked the obvious. The obvious being 'was his mum pulling the strings', orchestrating the assassins hunting them down. The craft continued dancing across the water as Meek aimed for the small landing jetty.

The team leader mostly focused on the practicalities, a jet at a local, private airfield was waiting to whisk the quartet straight back to the UK. Having stemmed Ben's blood loss, he was to be included too. Robert Warner moored his boat first, quickly tethering it to the left-hand side of the small wooden jetty. Meek pulled her craft to the right, as Nic jumped across the narrowing gap between gunwale and wooden planks that formed the spine of the jetty.

The speed and efficiency of the MI6 team gave the impression that they were still all under the threat of danger, thought Dan, but he guessed it was probably just their way. Dan and Kate climbed in the back of the first of the two matching black SUVs, whilst Rachel helped Ben climb gingerly into the back of the other one.

Nic jumped in the driver's side, with JT riding shotgun. As Nic gunned the SUV, gravel spewed from under the tyres as he did so. The second SUV, driven by Rob, exited the gravel car park in a similar fashion, Rob working hard to keep his SUV in a compact convoy as the two vehicles hared along. Kate sank back in her seat, visibly depressing the seat's backing as if she were almost pushing her body into its comfortable padding.

Dan looked across at her. For the first moment in almost an hour of bewildering events, things were quiet, almost tranquil. Even with a bloody, open gash to her face, she still looked beautiful. He reached across, putting his left hand on Kate's thigh before giving it a tender, loving squeeze. She reciprocated his affection, taking his hand in hers as she turned in her seat to face Dan. The couple, both aware they were being observed, JT out of the corner of his eye and Nic in his mirror, didn't care.

Dan, ever so gently, cupped the side of Kate's head, carefully avoiding her facial injuries, as he kissed her tenderly, drawing back a little, so he could look her in the eyes.

"We're going to be alright," he whispered reassuringly as he maintained eye contact. Kate pulled him back, locking lips again just as gently.

CHAPTER 27
HENKL ESCAPE
TO SITKA

Thursday 12th January 2017

The dark blue Audi Q5 hurtled out of the driveway, its engine whining under duress as Xav only just made the right-hander on to the main road. Gravel spewed out between tyre and driveway, some of it spraying the grass border as he fought for control of the wheel.

Louise, with a panic-stricken face, turned to check behind them. There didn't appear to be any of the black-clad men following. She caught Henkl doing the same from the back seat. In the rush to escape, it had been Xav who'd got to the Audi first. Henkl, almost missing the ride, had jumped in the back as Xav commenced their escape.

Although not driving, the head of Apfel quickly took an element of control over the situation. Initially allowing Xav to gun the Audi for all it was worth, he instructed Xav to slow down once they'd put a couple of miles distance between them and the chateau. Minimizing attention over pure speed didn't feel right to the inexperienced driver, but he complied, nonetheless.

Ever attentive, Henkl spent the next 15 minutes constantly observing before instructing Xav to pull over. He switched places with the driver, allowing Xav the freedom to do what he did best, plan, Louise too.

First the trio switched cars. Henkl argued the point with Xav who was initially unconvinced the time lost was worth the sacrifice, but that was why they paid Henkl, ran the argument, as the experienced operative explained that the black-clad men were highly likely to be government agents. Which government? Well, Henkl wasn't too sure, but Americans or British would almost certainly be able to access satellite imagery. It was a crystal-clear day, the lack of cloud cover making it very easy to track the Audi as it flew the nest. Xav had to admit it, Henkl's logic was good and that was why he had him. So begrudgingly he allowed Henkl to pull into the large multistorey car park and switch cars.

Meanwhile, Louise had slowly changed from panic to fury as the gravity of their situation sank in, her face turning a deeper shade of purple with every mile Henkl put between them and the chateau. With no one to direct her anger at, her companions took the brunt of her ire.

"WHO WERE THEY?" she growled as she turned to look Xav directly in the eyes.

Henkl glanced in the mirror, keen to gauge his reaction. Disappointingly, Xav's face was an almost picture of calm.

"DO YOU KNOW?" screamed Louise, this time directing her anger at the German.

Henkl shot a second glance at Xav as he stumbled to reply, searching for some support, of which he found none. He used eye contact to respond, looking her directly in the eyes via the central mirror before returning his focus to the road as it swept by. He hadn't uttered a word, but Louise understood. She knew that Henkl was as much in the dark as Xav.

Although unable to give her any insightful intel on the events that morning, Henkl could still prove his worth to Louise. He had never been anything other than proactive; he certainly didn't wait for 'life to happen around him'.

Aged 22, he left university with a first-class degree in engineering. Spurning several generous job offers, he opted for military service. Seeking adventure, he hoped the army would be the answer. It wasn't. In just five years, Henkl excelled and gained several promotions in his short time in the military. The army didn't quite satisfy his enquiring mind and thirst for adventure. Frustrated with pushing paper and playing a dull geopolitical role, he looked for other opportunities. From an early age he had been a 'go-getter'. At 27, he left and took a position on the bottom rung of the ladder in the BND. The German intelligence service satiated Henkl's every need and desire.

Highly intelligent and with five years' experience in the military, the tall, athletic Henkl was an ideal candidate. He had superior language skills too. Fluent in English and Russian, with passable French, he took to life within the BND with ease, quickly making a good impression with his superiors. He loved the work and the lifestyle. Trotting the globe, delving into matters that others couldn't or shouldn't appealed to his psyche. In the course of his work for the BND, Henkl skirted with many issues that only existed in a grey and decidedly murky world, a world where right and wrong didn't matter, just subterfuge, intelligence and silence. He was the master of this unique environment. Within a few years at the BND, he had started working both sides, the other side being his personal fiefdom.

Initially accepting private jobs for large multinationals, Henkl didn't start out with murderous intentions. Becoming an assassin was more accidental, almost like a drug addict starting out life on soft drugs, yet bit by bit moving on to the class A hard drugs. He began by providing information for cash, but one thing, or rather one job, led to another. After a couple of years of earning money on the side for intel, he took a job requiring the use of coercion. Previously his biggest payday had been €30 000 for a single job, but then a shady multinational CEO offered him €300 000 for a job. How could he refuse? The simple conclusion he arrived at was he couldn't.

Henkl knew his own mind, he always had, and this was one of his finest attributes, an ability to weigh up a problem in a moment before being quick and decisive. In this instance, the only thing that surprised him was just how quickly he had decided to accept the offer – no guilt, no second-guessing. Accepting this job was the first time Henkl stepped over the line. No longer was he just providing information for cash, an activity he had always justified as a simple research task where no one got hurt. Now, though, he was going to hurt someone. No amount of self-justification could square the circle in his mind.

But he didn't bat an eyelid.

The job in question was simple enough. Paying a prostitute to seduce a middle-aged executive, all the while capturing the entire bedroom scene, had been a simple matter, blackmail in its simplest form. After expenses, Henkl netted €280 000 of his gross, but earning more than his annual salary in just a couple of weeks hadn't been the motivating factor to repeat this service, he had enjoyed it, pure and simple. A darker side to his psyche had stirred and, at that point, he never looked back. As time passed, he took more work on, fostering more contacts in the grey world as he continued to carve out an alternate life to his work with the BND.

Eventually he took his first contract. Guilt never played a part; killing for money became as easy as any other aspect of his employment. In fact, for him, the reason he considered himself to be so good at it was because of his lack of emotions. The colder, darker side to Henkl gave him the necessary freedom to carry out contract after contract, error-free.

During his university years, he had a relationship with a beautiful, energetic girl called Sabine. His parents loved Sabine, wrongly assuming her to be their future daughter-in-law. As a young man, Henkl was polite, charming and respectful. Outwardly, he seemed the perfect 'boy next door'. After three years, tragedy struck the seemingly perfect relationship. In Sabine's final year at university, her parents died in a horrific car crash, understandably having a seismic effect on Sabine. Struggling to cope, she started attending 'grief counselling' sessions to help her come to terms with the tragic event in her life.

As weeks turned into months, Sabine gradually made headway as she processed the loss of her parents and the effect it had on her psyche. During this process, Henkl took an interest in human psychology as he witnessed the steps Sabine took during her healing process. She took almost a year to come to terms with her loss and, during that time, he learnt a great deal about himself.

Although self-diagnosed, he was certain he was a long way down the psychopath spectrum. Psychopaths are often misunderstood; the mass public wrongly assume a psychopath to be a serial killer, a common misconception.

The defining characteristic of a psychopath is their lack of empathy, and it was this particular trait that Henkl first noticed was something he lacked. Rather than join Sabine in being distraught for her loss, he simply wasn't bothered. Then, when the end of university approached, he simply ended the relationship, without fuss, care or attention. He moved on, not because he needed to or wanted to, in his mind, it was just a functionary action, a logical step for him to take.

He owed Sabine a debt of gratitude though. Aged 21, an initial interest in psychology became one of his passions. He read around the subject thoroughly, he devoured all the available research and experiments, all of which helped him to understand what made people tick, and for that he had Sabine to thank.

Henkl's first contract paid €500 000, a handsome amount given his official salary at the BND was €120 000 before tax. A South African gold-mining company approached him during an aggressive takeover. AnGad, the company in question, owned the mining rights to a significant diamond-rich region of Angola. AnGad was doing its utmost to resist the takeover and, significantly, this was driven by one man, Wouter de Boer. De Boer, half Dutch, half French, owned the controlling interest in AnGad alongside his wife and brother.

Having failed to win De Boer over with an above market offer, a quicker more efficient solution was sought. That solution was Henkl. The logic was simple as was the maths. Henkl's kill contract easily out trumped the above market 50 m Euros offer that was bluntly turned down. And so, it was. He took the contract which for many years remained one of his simplest jobs. A distinct lack of CCTV, the biggest boon and a much more laissez-faire-style of policing made Angola an easy place to carry out the kill. Henkl's trickiest dilemma being his exfil, Angola having only one truly international airport was a problem to solve. He overcame this with a circuitous overland journey to neighbouring Namibia. A few days' hardship seemed a price worth paying for a €500 000 payday.

He continued his double life, working for the BND benefitted him greatly, accessing intelligence and building up a significant little black book of useful individuals really helped kick-start his solo enterprise. After eight years, Henkl had built up a significant list of repeat clients matched only by an even more useful set of who's who contacts, people who sat both sides of the murky intelligence game across the globe, the kind of people that often needed paying in intelligence over hard cash. And eight years into a very successful career in the BND, Henkl met Xav.

He was tasked with investigating a Russian pharmaceutical company committing industrial espionage against a large German pharma. During his investigations, he crossed paths with the calculating, erudite Xav Picamole. The two men quickly formed an amicable, symbiotic relationship, starting as always with cash for intel. Within two years, more than 70% of his private work came via Picamole. He could have joined Xav years before he did, but the ever-patient Henkl bided his time, making full use of his lofty position with German intelligence.

Shrewd, intelligent and extremely logical, Henkl took the most pragmatic approach to his new employment, future-proofing his access to intel after he departed the BND. Using his final three years there very wisely, he hedged his bets by entrapping the two obvious candidates to make the top job within the BND.

He glanced back in the mirror, this time catching Xav's attention with a telling look. A look that said, 'back me'. Xav understood.

"If he knew we'd know, cherie," Xav intervened.

She was venting and it fell upon the Swiss man to adopt the more controlled, calmer approach. Right now, they needed Henkl and his mercurial skill set more than ever. Louise barking at him wasn't helpful, safety was.

"Speak then… sort this shit out," she growled, her demands a little unclear as to who she was directing them at. A pregnant pause ensued as both the men determined who should answer.

Henkl broke the silence first. With clarity of mind, he spelt out a plan, the only logical plan in fact. He couldn't arrange the details, but he knew exactly what needed to be done and who and how it could be actioned. For two minutes, Henkl took leadership of the trio as he navigated out of Geneva. First, he changed direction, moments before he started to dish out instructions to his paymasters. Completing a U-turn, he headed for the Centre Commercial they had just driven past 2 km back.

"Your phones," he demanded with a tone of firm assurance, "remove the SIMS," continued Henkl.

And with that, Louise and Xav immediately understood. One way or another, they had been breached. It was time to take back control. Henkl pulled to a stop in the large car park in front of the Centre Commercial. He jumped from the car returning five minutes later with three new pay-as-you-go phones.

Next Henkl pointed the car in the direction of Berlin or, to be precise, a small airfield 45 km south-west of Berlin. Schönhagen Airstrip fell under the stewardship of a man called Wolfgang Kohl. Kohl owed him, or rather, Kohl was owned by him. Indiscretions over decades, previously uncovered during Henkl's time at the BND, had been carefully and cleverly concealed by Henkl. He had benefitted hugely over the years, the threat of sending Kohl to jail with a release of information had served him well. A discreet flight plan and departure was required and Kohl's airstrip at Schönhagen was perfect.

Sitka. A single word uttered and both Louise and Xav understood immediately. Henkl was right. The only haven, their only option, was Russia and Vitaly Urinov. Knacc was destroyed, and although Sitka was up and running, it was in its infancy. Urinov was also hurting, reeling from the total destruction of Knacc. Henkl drove home the point, surely the Russian would be pleased to offer safe haven; he'd almost certainly leverage his help for improved terms at Sitka. He told Louise to call Urinov and set it up.

First, Louise contacted Urinov and, as Henkl had predicted, he was both eager to help and keen to use his assistance to his advantage. The haven Taly provided came at a price. A shift in the balance of power towards him made her uneasy, but Henkl was right, and Louise knew it. There and then, she had no cards left to play.

Meanwhile, Xav expedited a private jet to be ready and waiting at Schönhagen Airstrip, but not the BioDS private jet. He made a private booking under Wolfgang Kohl's name. With the extraction plan formulated, Henkl fell silent as he concentrated on the long drive north from Switzerland to Berlin, close to 13 hours without stops.

Various items of street furniture flashed by in a blur as Henkl drove. For the first time in over two hours, a silence fell upon the trio. Just after 10 a.m., the day had started triumphantly yet turned into chaos and failure in spectacular fashion. Henkl, lost in his own thoughts, navigating almost autonomously, as he started to analyse what had just happened and who was to blame. Did they have a mole? As he cogitated, he caught Louise studying him in the mirror. She didn't smile, but he detected a warmth in her, an appreciation for what he'd just done for the trio. Without saying a word, he instinctively dropped his forehead a touch, giving her the tiniest of nods by way of response.

Henkl started with the Apfel. Could it be his own men? Bush was dead, so too were Harry and Zebra. His Gruppe Drei, Drey and Mex, had been with him for years. Neither man had any obvious weaknesses. He couldn't see how, or even why, they'd have been got at, but as he knew only too well, almost anyone could be compromised. It was just a matter of finding the right button; learn enough about any human being would always lead to the location of 'where to press'. Then there were the new recruits, but the new team hadn't been brought into the fold yet and, as such, barely knew anything. Henkl couldn't see how it could be them. He dismissed his own team, he'd spend some time later doing the obvious checks on them, but he couldn't see how it was any of them.

So that left either the staff at BioDS, Urinov or an electronic invasion. The BioDS staff would require Xav to explore that further. Urinov presented a much more complicated problem and one that under no circumstances could be brought to the attention of Louise or Xav. He could hardly advise a dash to the House of Urinov and instantly question out loud the possibility of him being culpable of the breach. Henkl would need to investigate this though, after all, the big winner right now was Vitaly Urinov. Maybe this was a truly clever plan masterminded by their Russian principle.

If it wasn't Urinov, that most likely left the Yanks, in which case it meant an electronic breach of some sort, but it didn't add up. Forestier was off the grid, deliberately so, as was BioDS. Henkl had been the main protagonist behind this course of action many years ago. He'd spent a great deal of energy arguing the point to Xav about the difficulties in cyber protection. The only guaranteed way to prevent it was to be entirely off the grid. Xav finally capitulated, creating a home computer system that couldn't talk to the outside world, with a similar set-up at BioDS. It had of course caused enormous issues, but the security it provided made it worth the sacrifice. Something wasn't right! Stumped, Henkl continued to mull over the few facts he had. The long drive north offered him plenty of time to contemplate.

In the back of the car, Louise and Xav sat quietly brooding. Thoughts of a betrayal ruminated through their minds. Sadly, both had many more questions than answers. Xav focused entirely on the who and how. A mole seemed most likely. As he prodded and probed the integrity of their entire staff, he started creating a compelling list of possibles and probables.

Louise, battling thoughts on two fronts, struggled to make any semblance of a plan. An inner rage didn't help her either. Her mind raced; thoughts leapt across the synaptic gaps in her mind as she contended with how to deal with Urinov without losing control whilst solving the breach, their problems now magnified with the loss of the children. Dan and his siblings were safe for now and that was a big blow. Matters could worsen further if the Brits uncovered the motivation for killing the Fletchers. Louise parked those thoughts as she returned her focus on Urinov and Sitka. Things had changed considerably. She was now well and truly in the Russian's pocket.

CHAPTER 28
JT AND DAN
Friday 13ᵗʰ January 2017

Jack 'JT' Thomas sat upright on his seat at the end of the elongated table within the 'Crypt'. Smouldering good looks, athletic physique and a constant twinkle in his eye helped JT navigate through life with ease. He came from Leeds, the youngest of his three siblings to first-generation British Jamaican immigrants. Having spent the last two decades away from Leeds, a once strong Yorkshire accent had faded considerably. When he spoke, a discerning ear would detect a northern England accent with a slight Jamaican hint courtesy of his mother's influence.

He was a fascinating man, nicknamed 'Obe' by his best friends. His nickname emanated from a shortened version of 'odd bod' and went a long way to explain a great deal about Jack Thomas. JT excelled at school; lofty expectations were placed firmly on his shoulders by his pushy, overachieving mother. His parents were both highly successful professionals; his father was a professor of sociology at Leeds University and his mother was a partner in a large law firm.

Finishing school with straight A's, JT spurned a place at Cambridge University to study maths for a career in the armed forces, much to his mother's chagrin. His father took a more laissez-faire approach to JT's decision, whereas his mother was furious. Unable to contain her disappointment, the more she tried to sway him, the more it reinforced the decision he'd already made. His sisters and father did their utmost to placate his mother, all to no avail. Nonetheless, JT left home aged 18 for a career in the British armed forces.

His mother had fretted needlessly, JT excelled. After just three short years, he put himself up for 'selection'. 'Selection' was the one-word description for applying to join the SAS, the best of the best, elite special forces unit. Famous for being the most gruelling selection process going, JT managed to pass selection at the first time of asking. He embraced the SAS, spending nine of the best years of his life training, learning new skills and constantly honing them. He loved every aspect of SAS life, the camaraderie, the challenges and the continual evolvement of his skill set.

He hadn't planned to leave the SAS, life was good, but that was all before he met Jonno. As was often the case, the SAS got tasked to work alongside MI6 and this was how JT came across Jonno. Aged 45, he was the assistant head of MI6, possessing a brilliant mind and an ability to see right through people. Chris 'Jonno' Johnson was a man who had a unique ability to galvanize people, inspire them and importantly, in his line of work, sway them to do his bidding. He had a small job requiring a four-man SAS team headed up by Jack Thomas. Almost from the get-go, JT and Jonno hit it off. An immediate bond was formed, maybe it was chemistry, but either way, they just got on.

As soon as the job was over, the assistant head had approached JT and offered him a job. Under other circumstances JT would have declined. The pay offer alone was three times what he was earning, but it wasn't about the money. He accepted the offer, but his decision was solely due to who he'd be working for – Jonno!

The nine years JT spent in the SAS had flown by in a flash. He astounded himself with how he took to his new life with MI6. His surprise emanated from how much he embraced his new line of work. Having loved the SAS so much, he had always harboured concerns about how anything else would ever be enough. His old school nickname Obe, earnt in part by friends teasing him, wasn't a fair and accurate assessment of him. JT was more a maverick than an odd bod. Where some people are driven by money, he was motivated by a multitude of other, more unusual factors, many of which were immediately satiated by his new job working for Jonno in MI6.

JT's charm and good looks hadn't gone unnoticed. At the opposite end of the table to the team leader, Rachel Fletcher sat motionless sandwiched between Dan and Kate, the fourth member of the quartet, her brother Ben, still in hospital. Upon entering the Crypt, Rachel spent the first couple of minutes taking in her surroundings. A nondescript room, all plain walls, a couple of items of office furniture and a blank VDU didn't occupy her thoughts for long, whereas the faint crease lines running from the corner of JT's sparkling, brown eyes, perfect white teeth and an easy smile all framed by a strong jawline made for a far more interesting vista.

Probably 10 years her senior, Rachel allowed her thoughts to drift a little. Suppressing a wry grin as she pondered 'yes she would' to herself, Kate clocked the timing of her little smile. Giving Rachel the teeniest of nudges with her elbow, Kate shot her a knowing glance. Rachel blushed ever so slightly, silently admonishing herself, as she waited for the meeting to begin. The devil in Kate didn't get the chance to be playful at Rachel's expense though, the silence interrupted by Johnson as he entered the room.

"This is Jonno." JT, breaking the silence, introduced his boss as the man strode confidently to the end of the table, taking the vacant seat to the left of JT. Dan, Rachel and Kate all muttered a soft reply, almost in unison, as Jonno made himself comfortable.

Chris Johnson immediately took command of the room, though not in an overbearing way, projecting a calm, reassuring manner as he kicked proceedings off.

"JT," prompted Jonno, nodding his head at him as he spoke. JT didn't reply, he just slid three identical, slim, brown Manila files across the table to each of the trio. Positioned centrally, in plain, bold font, each read 'Official Secrets Act'.

"Before we begin, you need to sign the OSA," Jonno began, as he looked all three directly in their eyes. The room had fallen stony silent as the gravity of the debrief hit home. JT had given them a little info during their flight home, stopping short of revealing any significant information. Citing the Official Secrets Act or OSA for short, JT had explained they would all be 'read in' as he put it, but only after signing an OSA.

"You can of course refuse…" Jonno offered before continuing, "but then…" He stopped mid sentence, as he saw first Dan, then Kate and Rachel in quick succession sign and date the back page of the document before sliding them back in JT's direction. No fuss, no questions, just an efficient, expedited process borne out by an eagerness to know. Jonno nodded his head approvingly, partly a gesture of thanks but as much an acknowledgement that the trio in front of him had been through an ordeal and now wanted answers.

"Let's crack on then," he commenced.

The last week had been a traumatic, life-changing ordeal. All three had spent copious hours silently deliberating and questioning what had happened and even more time soul-searching concerning 'why'. Now, deep inside MI6 HQ, in a quirky room called the Crypt, an explanation would be revealed – finally.

"In 1997, your biological mother, Louise Walsh, left the UK to continue her research work in biogenetics with the American government." Jonno's use of the phrase 'biological mother' wasn't lost on both siblings. Rachel particularly appreciated this more clinical label of her mother. "Prior to this point, she had been kind of working for us."

"Kind of?" quizzed Dan. JT fidgeted slightly in his seat whereas Jonno didn't flinch.

Facing him directly, Johnson continued to explain. "Your mother worked with our support. We provided funding and a comprehensive research and development facility."

"Developing what?" interrupted Dan, feeling uncomfortable as the briefing took on a dark, ominous change in direction.

"Louise is a world-leading biogeneticist, she had a brilliant mind."

"HAD?" interrupted Dan again assertively.

"We never say 'has' for someone who turns to the dark side," he shot back.

Dan caught Rachel silently nodding her head in approval as Jonno continued.

"Her field concentrated specifically on neonatal gene manipulation."

He paused as soon as he'd delivered his first really telling piece of information. The two junior doctors in the room shot each other a worrying glance, for once leaving Dan Fletcher as the one with the least understanding.

"Manipulating who?" asked Rachel.

Jonno twitched ever so slightly as he took a moment to consider his words. "Louise developed a technique to enhance neonates. She calls them 'MorphEns'."

A cold chill shot down Dan's spine as he suddenly got up to speed with the subject matter. Giving them names, whatever these things were, suddenly lowered the temperature within the Crypt.

"So, is that who was chasing us?" he asked, desperately trying to understand.

Jonno briefly looked away from the trio, catching a glance from JT before he turned back towards them.

"You are her MorphEns…" he didn't sugar-coat it, as he ploughed on with his briefing, "…all four of you," referring to the four Fletcher siblings.

Kate instinctively reached across and held Rachel's hand as the news sank in.

"What… what the fuck!" blurted Dan, whilst an enraged Rachel Fletcher sat glaring at Jonno. "What does this mean… what's wrong with us?" Dan carried on.

As he asked the question, he wasn't entirely sure how much of his emotion centred around a concern for his personal health or the ethical issues of his now very estranged mother.

"It's OK," Jonno jumped in, recognizing Dan's worry over his and his siblings' health. "The procedure she developed enhanced both physical and mental attributes considerably. In layman's terms, you are all extremely high achievers. Put clinically, the lab guys use the term *altae facultates* which translates to 'high capabilities', when it worked." Dan was about to drill him further, but before he could, Jonno intervened. "The process involved didn't always work, many newborn babies died as she carried out the procedure. She lost a child of her own, your sister born in 1992, amongst many other newborns."

Chills continued to tingle through Dan, Rachel and Kate's entire bodies as they took on board the information.

"You're all extremely talented," Jonno explained, nodding at both Dan and Rachel as he continued. "The four of you excel at sport, you can run the 800 m in close to 1 min 50, and your brother Sam is close to the national selection times for the 100 m. You all score extremely highly in every mental aptitude test going," making direct eye contact as he spoke, first with Rachel then Dan. "Your brother Ben too, whilst Sam scores the highest of all of you, in part because Louise had improved her technique by the time Sam came along. However, from what we understand, it's still much more about the material she starts with."

His use of the word 'material' made the process sound extremely clinical.

"Her procedure seems to generate a 'more or less 20% uplift' in the subject, the subject being the neonate child. In other words, the likelihood is that Sam scoring the highest of the four of you is probably because he was already a slightly more gifted candidate."

"So why does she want to kill us?" growled Rachel.

JT looked on empathetically as Jonno responded.

"That's the bit we don't know," he replied, as he motioned to JT to turn on the VDU sitting dormant on the wall behind them. JT moved efficiently towards the VDU, hitting the 'on' button before grabbing a remote-controlled device from the bureau.

The screen displayed a photo of Louise Walsh alongside Xav Picamole. "As you all know, Picamole is Louise's partner."

Rachel's face turned crimson, unable to suppress her hostility as she took in the photo of her biological mother. JT clicked the remote, the photo reduced in size as it swished to the left as a second photo rotated from the right, taking a prominent position in the middle of the screen. It was a photo of BioDS and the company logo, Dan figured it for a screen grab of the company website's home page.

Jonno joined the dots, explaining that Xav Picamole was both

Louise Walsh's unmarried partner as well as her BioDS co-director – complicit in everything.

"Next, JT," prompted Jonno. As the team leader clicked the remote in quick succession, the first of four photos flicked across the screen, the first showing a photo of Henkl, then Zebra, Harry and the fourth a photo of Bush. "These are the four assassins sent to kill you. We don't currently know much about them, but we will," he explained confidently.

"Red beanie man," blurted Dan as he stared intently at the photo of Bush. "That's the FUCKER," he continued uninterrupted.

For the first time, both JT and Jonno remained silent as they listened intently. Dan stopped short of saying that he and Ben had killed Bush in a fight for their lives in France, preferring to leave it unsaid.

"Interpol reported finding him dead in a péage lay-by," said Jonno resuming his briefing.

Dan didn't flinch, nor Rachel or Kate.

"We think he was the one who killed Helen Waters," offered JT, deliberately presenting the information as a subtle way to help justify any guilty thoughts Dan might have had.

He needn't have bothered, a slight smile crept across the eldest Fletcher's face as he bullishly looked across at his sister and Kate, both of whom defiantly returned a half smile of their own.

JT clicked his remote again, reversing the photo carousel, bringing back the photos of Harry and Zebra together on a split screen.

"These two were killed in the firefight at the chateau, and we think this one escaped with Walsh and Picamole." As Jonno spoke, JT clicked away on the remote returning a photo of Henkl.

"Americans," prompted Dan, urging Jonno to carry on with his story.

An ever so slight wry grin crept across his face as he recognized Dan's insightful thought process. JT suppressed a smirk too, getting to know Dan explained a great deal of why it had been so hard for his team and Louise Walsh's assassins to 'track and kill' the Fletcher clan.

"We had reservations about the ethical issues Louise was employing, spiralling costs and ever-increasing demands she put on us. So, in 1997, we cut her programme. We of course kept tabs on her and in 1997 she started working with the Americans." Jonno controlled the narrative, outlining a carefully thought-out explanation, a well-crafted version of events to match the timeline. Dan's mind raced through the facts presented, he reasoned, and he analysed.

"Ethics or money?" he quizzed, never one for wasting words as he got directly to the heart of the matter.

"It was before my time," Jonno explained, "but between these four walls, I'd say it was money." The honesty Johnson displayed won Dan over. "So, we lost Louise to the Americans because we weren't prepared to fund her. The death of the infants involved certainly played a part though. You need to understand that. The UK government grew increasingly uncomfortable with her practices. Eventually the elastic just snapped."

Dan wasn't convinced, but to his left Rachel and Kate seemed to believe this a little more. Maybe their Hippocratic oath persuaded them a little more than it did him.

"With the support of the Americans, Louise created more MorphEns. We don't exactly know why, but they also cut her loose."

Jonno gave a subtle nod of his head in JT's direction, prompting him to point and press on his remote. The VDU sprung to life as a photo of Harry zipped leftwards across the screen followed by Bush, to be replaced by a screen full of headshots with a 'one-line' description below each.

In all 10 headshots were proudly displayed alongside their name, age and, chillingly, the word '*DECEASED*' in bold font. Dan grimaced; Kate suppressed a tear, whilst Rachel fidgeted uneasily in her seat as the trio stared intently at the VDU.

"All 10 were assassinated, we assume by the men we have just shown you. They were all MorphEns," Jonno exclaimed emphatically.

Dan stared intently at the VDU, absorbing the information in its entirety. JT clocked this, impressed with everything Dan presented. He'd make a fabulous agent mulled JT.

"So, Mum has created us and now she's killing us," interrogated Dan, the 'us' referred to his siblings and the dead Americans.

Rachel scowled at Dan's use of the word 'mum'.

"We wouldn't keep you in the dark," assured Jonno, sensing Dan's lack of belief.

"BOLLOCKS," Dan boomed, deliberately raising his voice. "What the fuck aren't you saying?" he continued, unable to suppress his anger.

The room fell quiet as Jonno took a moment, carefully weighing up his response.

A few seconds passed, Dan stared Jonno down, not averting his focus as he awaited a response, a negotiating trick Dan had learnt years ago. Don't be the first to break, holding out for a reply almost always worked. It did.

"There's a Russian connection," highlighted Jonno as he motioned to JT, who obliged, clicking the remote until he reached the desired frame.

The photo of the headshots disappeared, to be replaced by a photograph of the tall, angular Vitaly Urinov, labelled with his name and position, standing next to bull of a man with no name. A third photo showed an athletic, late twenty-something woman, with a name caption 'Natalia Andreeva?' and no position.

"We aren't certain if these are official Russian government assets, but this guy was FSB," Jonno pointed at Urinov as he spoke. "This one, we have nothing on," pointing at the photo of Sergei Asmov, "but we think he's Urinov's enforcer." Turning to the photo of Natalia, "We think this is Urinov's 'right-hand woman' and her name, still unconfirmed, is Natalia Andreeva." As Jonno spoke, JT kept pace, bringing up a single word and definition.

Классовый
Meaning: class (social grouping, based on job, wealth, etc.)
Класс

The word 'Knacc' stood out, splashed across the screen in large, bold font. "We honestly have no idea what this is. Logic dictates that 'Knacc' is the code name / programme name for whatever they are doing with Louise."

Dan was captivated by the Cyrillic words emblazoned across the VDU, Rachel and Kate almost mesmerized too, none of the trio understood the real meaning, and maybe there was nothing to understand. A code word could just be a code word – right?

"Walsh and Picamole have gone to ground. We tracked them initially as they flew the nest from Forestier." Jonno referred to Louise's chateau by its name as he detailed the firefight and escape. "If they're still in Europe, then we'll find them," he stated with an air of assuredness.

"You think they're in Russia," a statement not a question, Dan bounced back.

Searching for a 'tell', he studied both Jonno and JT for a reaction. He didn't need to, neither man bothered to hide their ire.

"We honestly don't know," explained Jonno with a sincerity the entire room picked up on. "But it seems highly likely. Tomorrow, I intend to meet my counterpart at the 'Agency', they should have some useful satellite imagery that might point us in a better direction."

"The Americans," JT intervened, recognizing Dan was about to clarify Jonno's term 'Agency'. Dan nodded his head appreciatively in JT's direction.

"If I get this right, we are genetic mutants created by a woman who switched to the Americans and now for the Russians," Dan summed up.

"Genetically edited super-humans would be a more accurate summary," Jonno shot back.

The term 'super-human' resonated around the room; Kate Harper looked over at the man she had recently fallen in love with. Not quite sure how it made her feel, would this change anything she pondered.

"How many of us are there?" quizzed Dan.

JT fidgeted in his seat as Dan's words rang out; an obvious unease didn't go unnoticed. Rachel picked up on his twitchiness immediately, as did Dan. Jonno frowned, lengthening the creases emanating from the corner of his eyes. The facial lines and folds served to further enhance an already interesting face.

Finally, Dan had hit upon the million-dollar question, the question that would explain everything. Jonno turned towards JT, silently suggesting for him to return to his seat. As JT complied, Jonno leant forwards on his arms, leaning in towards the trio across the table, his body language adding gravitas to what he was about to say. None of which was lost on Dan, Rachel or Kate.

"Can you imagine a world superpower run by super-humans?" Jonno asked rhetorically. Without waiting for an answer he didn't want, he carried on. "You Fletchers, some undisclosed American MorphEns and whatever the Russians have. But you do the maths. She…" referring to Louise as 'she' was very deliberate as Jonno concentrated on amplifying her evil, "…started working with the Russians almost 20 years ago. She created 14 MorphEns that we know about in just two years in America, 10 of which have now been assassinated. What do you think she has done for the Russians," he more stated than questioned.

"Cast your mind back…" instructed Jonno, "…to Russian practices in the days of the USSR." He expanded, "Ethics was a redacted word to them back then.

"We're still learning and unearthing information about some of the schools they ran. We have compelling evidence detailing 'pedigree human' farms akin to how we have produced pure-bred dogs over the centuries. Perfect women and men, hand selected to procreate, to produce Olympic athletes. Children taken from their home aged two and schooled all their lives to create a 'designated outcome'. This was a very rudimentary form of 'gene manipulation'. Now they have Louise. We SHUDDER!" He rapped his knuckles on the table for effect as he said the word 'shudder'.

"The word 'knacc' means class," Jonno spoke softly, going full circle as he reintroduced the subject, "as in a school class."

"You don't think it's a code word," interjected Dan. Tingles ran down his neck as the penny dropped. "It's a school full of them… RIGHT!" he continued, not pausing long enough to allow Jonno to respond.

"We think a factory," Johnson replied grimly, his suggestion visibly affecting the faces opposite him.

Jonno sat back, allowing this final piece of information to sink in. For the last 40 minutes, he had carefully detailed what they knew and skirted softly around what they didn't know. For the most part, he'd employed a scalpel, metaphorically speaking, to brief the trio. Just now though, he had used a sledgehammer and Dan, Rachel and Kate were collectively picking up the pieces.

"Technically, the Russian MorphEns are 'second-generation MorphEns', whilst you and the 14 Americans are 'first-gen', but we don't know the difference other than the coding used to create them was different." Jonno detailed the information retrieved from Chateau Forestier, explaining that the information collected was still being analysed and interpreted.

"Are they better than us?" asked Dan immediately.

"The data doesn't suggest so..." he replied, "but we aren't 100%," he continued, failing to conceal a concerned look as he spoke.

"Before you ask, we are dark on this," Jonno leapt in, responding before Dan could resume his interrogation. "The files discovered describe 'first-gen MorphEns' – that's you and 'second-gen MorphEns', that's the 200 listed creations in her studies." Rachel flinched at the use of the word 'creation', uncomfortable thoughts ricocheted through her mind as she weighed up the label others might put on her very being. "For all we know, these second-gen MorphEns may have a far greater set of attributes than you first-gens. We simply don't know," surmised Jonno.

"Are we safe?" asked Rachel, clutching Kate's arm for comfort as she searched Jonno's face for an answer.

"You are now..." he replied. "We have plans already in motion," he continued in a calm, reassuring manner. "You'll be securely located with 24-hour protection. It's where we have your brother Sam." Jonno methodically spelt out the details. "JT is on overwatch, he'll take you there today, and as soon as your brother Ben is fit to leave the hospital, he will join you too."

"What about our life?" flashed Dan testily, quick to ascertain the offer of protection hadn't come with any kind of a timeline.

"We'll be doing everything humanly possible. You need to appreciate that us sharing this level of intel with the Americans is a huge thing. That alone is a demonstration of how serious we are taking it," Jonno spelt out. "We can't give you a time, for the moment our priority is your safety. After that, well it's complex, it's more fluid, a situation that currently we are unable to provide anything concrete on."

His response didn't adequately satisfy Dan, misgivings etched across his face. For the moment, Dan would have to lump it.

Jonno brought the meeting to a close, leaving JT to escort the trio out of the Crypt. Jonno walked the first couple of lengths of corridor with JT before bidding his farewell, diving through an unmarked door, not before promising to keep the trio updated. JT and the trio filed down the remainder of the corridor, all plain white walls. The bland, sterile interior thoroughfare led to a lift shaft. As they stood waiting, the lift headed towards their floor, B3, a low, whining noise could be heard as the lift slowly stopped, followed by a soft '*bing*' noise indicating its arrival. The display initially showed a small, green arrow pointing upwards that disappeared as the doors of the lift opened.

A handsome, thirty-something man stepped out first, but not before flashing a flirtatious smile at Rachel as he brushed past her. Tony Hunt was a married, low-level analyst with limited professional aspirations. Those aspirations didn't carry over to his personal life, though, in that department he had always enjoyed a colourful approach to a myriad of relationships. His easy smile, although flattering, was quickly ignored by Rachel Fletcher.

The man gave JT a nod of the head as he made his way past the group, down the corridor, in the direction the Crypt. JT chose to ignore him as the four took to the lift. He was now on point; his only priority was the safe passage of the trio in his care.

CHAPTER 29
TOUCHDOWN

Friday 13th January 2017

The sleek Cessna Citation Mustang swept low across the horizon as it made its final descent, lining itself perfectly with the strip of red lights indicating the approach up to the runway. Weather conditions were almost perfect, crystal-clear blue sky with a light breeze cutting left to right across the flight path on landing.

Mid January in Mirny, the temperatures were typically well below zero and, as the private jet touched down, the thermometer proudly standing on a pole outside the main hangar doors showed -8°C. A handful of technicians stood impassively; plumes of freezing breath visible each time they exhaled demonstrating the bitterly cold winter air.

Vitaly Urinov, tall and angular, stood motionless wearing an oversized brown bearskin jacket, looking every part the chief of his tribe, watching on as the Cessna touched down. The pilot allowed the plane to reduce speed gradually as its wheels spun rapidly across the tarmac, bringing the plane to a halt before turning it round and returning in the direction of the large hangar.

Sergei Asmov, known as Бочка, fidgeted, mainly to keep warm, stepping from toe to toe on the spot. He was a barrel of a man, short and stocky; it made for an almost comical sight when stood side by side with his boss, Vitaly Urinov. Бочка despised the cold and the entire relocation of Knacc to Sitka near Mirny had pissed him off more than anyone. Omsk would get cold in winter but nothing like the bitter freezing lows Mirny had to offer. Pissed off didn't go near to summing up Sergei Asmov's ire at the destruction of Knacc.

The Cessna neared the hangar and carefully negotiated the enormous doors, entering the cavernous building. As Vitaly Urinov and Бочка scurried back inside, the gaggle of technicians busied themselves, initially closing the hangar doors before wheeling some large telemetry kit and a refuelling line to the jet. As the pilot shut down the engines the roar of the jet diminished, leaving a subtle hum from the technicians' mobile workstations.

Louise first, quickly followed by Henkl then Xav, descended the small flight of stairs, and were greeted first in Russian and then English by Vitaly Urinov.

"Здравствуйте… welcome," said Vitaly, offering a slight nod of his head as was the formal Russian way to demonstrate 'deference'.

"Спасибо," replied Louise, the word 'thank you' wasn't the only Russian she knew but it was limited, as she quickly reverted to English.

Бочка followed suit with a similarly formal welcome as Vitaly welcomed Xav and Henkl too. Henkl, initially providing a verbose reply to Urinov in fluent Russian, curtailed the warmth as he returned Бочка's nod with an equally formal, frosty reply. Deeply suspicious, Henkl had never liked Бочка and the feeling was mutual. Neither man had ever enjoyed the other's company despite the closeness of their respective bosses. Sharing a home at Sitka was going to prove challenging for both, more so for Henkl given he was the guest.

Бочка took command of proceedings, steering the trio to a couple of black Mercedes SUVs. Standing holding the SUV door open for Louise, the perky-faced Ilya beamed at her. Louise had initially not recognized Ilya, but as she closed the distance to the SUV his bright, alert eyes and shock of blond hair suddenly brought a huge smile to her face. As she sped up to give Ilya a special hug, he nodded his head leftwards. Standing holding the door to the second SUV was the bright-eyed Katerina. No words were uttered as the three of them closed on each other, creating a three-way hug cum huddle, Louise doing her best to suppress a tear. Ilya and Katerina Sokolov were almost like son and daughter. Her first second-gen MorphEns created at Knacc had become Vitaly Urinov's golden couple, not because they were the first couple, but because they were the first couple to have had their second child. Both only aged 18, they had also proven themselves the top of their class, the brightest in the classroom and the strongest in the gym.

Drivers for Vitaly and Louise was further proof of the unique trust Urinov held for them. Бочка interrupted the greetings, all efficiency, as he prompted the group to climb into the cars. There would be plenty of time for catching up later, once they were safely ensconced within the protective walls of Sitka.

Katerina, with Бочка riding shotgun, gunned her SUV, leading the two black Mercedes out of the hangar, Sitka bound. Ilya followed suit, accompanied by the vigilant Henkl upfront as Louise and Xav took the rear.

CHAPTER 30
MOLE

Thursday 19th January 2017

Tony Hunt entered the hotel lobby. To the left of the vast room, soft seating, designed to allow breakout areas for people to read a paper or maybe wait for a taxi, sat on top of a lusciously thick, expensive-looking carpet. An elegant black-and-white-tiled floor separated the plush, comfortable settees from an oversized, elongated reception desk, the counter made from a single piece of brown-green-flecked quartz. The ornate reception desk was the centrepiece of the hotel's entrance room. A couple of members of hotel staff stood between the desk and a back wall adorned with the hotel's name and some artistic, visual photographs of a few historic London buildings. To their left, a doorway led to a back office, a third member of staff, half visible, seated in front of a computer monitor.

Tony strode across the foyer, calm and confidently, as he made his way to the far end beyond the comfortable seating, ignoring the attentiveness of one of the members of reception as he did so. The pretty, young, twenty-something hotel receptionist returned to a more pressing matter, having failed to get his attention.

In the far corner, a doorway led to a reading room, at least that was what the label above the door suggested. The title was a throwback to a time decades earlier. Now the room served as another more secluded breakout area cum quiet place to enjoy a coffee.

The room had a perfect symmetry. A walkway ran down the exact middle of the room, with four matching clusters of furniture to the left and right of the central aisle. Each cluster contained a large two-person chesterfield, accompanied by two single-seater captain's chairs and a stylish, low coffee table placed neatly in the middle of each seated area. The room oozed style and panache. Whoever had designed the interiors had managed to create an elegant yet understated room. The chesterfields were a mixture of different browns, with a few oxblood reds and deep greens thrown in.

An old couple sat quietly nursing coffees at the cluster immediately to the right as Tony entered. Other than that, the room was entirely unoccupied apart from the fifty-something woman sat at the far end of the room. He advanced towards her; out-of-the-bottle blond hair was tightly tied back, almost in an attempt to smooth out the wrinkles on her face.

To Tony the woman was called Catherine, he didn't know her real name was Katya Stepanova, but he figured Catherine wouldn't be her actual name. Catherine had Tony in her pocket. As such, he hated her with every fibre in his body, although it was entirely his stupidity that had landed him in the predicament he now faced, or to put it bluntly, his inability to keep his cock in his pants.

The oldest and simplest of honeytraps had landed Tony Hunt, a very steady away, low-level analyst at MI6, in hot trouble. Catherine had done her homework, studied the MI6 staffers she could find out about and singled out Tony Hunt. Aged 37, he had worked for MI6 for a decade. Although a talented analyst, he lacked the drive and motivation to ascend the ranks within MI6. Outside of work, he'd married well. Having come from a modest background, the highly intelligent Tony had got a first-class degree from Cambridge University, which had the effect of improving the jobs on offer to him and the friendship circles he moved in. Initially working as a financial analyst for a blue-chip London finance house, MI6 came calling. Aged 26, he started working for MI6, almost coinciding with his marriage to a beautiful, fun-loving girl called Harriet. Even better from his viewpoint, Harriet was rich or, to be more accurate, Harriet's parents were rich and one day Tony and Harriet would get half the family estate, to be shared between Harriet and her sister Mia.

But Tony was a self-diagnosed cock. He walked through life talking to himself as he did. His own summary went 'you are a top bloke, but you are a cock' and so it was. He had everything, a great wife and a super job, but somehow he just couldn't stop himself with casual flings or one-night stands. Harriet never knew, as stupid as Tony was, he wasn't that daft. Always careful enough, as the saying went, he didn't 'shit on his own doorstep', but as he sat opposite Catherine, these thoughts leapt through his cerebrum at the speed of light. Caught in a honeytrap didn't fully do it justice.

Well and truly set up, an attractive, young lady had come on to him. He didn't give it a second though and within two hours Tony, having almost run from bar to seedy hotel, proceeded to have sex with the woman. Probably only 25, with a figure to die for and oozing sexuality, how could he not, he justified.

Very graphic, sexual acts got caught on camera, and although half drunk, his recall was 100%, the evening in question had involved some very explicit action indeed. The next day, Catherine casually introduced herself in the queue for a coffee-to-go at his usual café. His world instantly darkened at that first meeting. That had been two years ago, and there was seemingly no end in sight.

Blackmailed for intelligence, Tony didn't even know who he was working for. The analyst in him suspected the Russians or Americans, but he had no idea. All he had to go on was currently sitting opposite him in the reading room, a fifty-something British woman called Catherine, no surname.

"He had a meeting with three young Brits," Tony explained, whilst he studied Catherine, searching for any clues about her, who she was, where she came from, who she worked for.

"How do you know they were British…?" she quizzed. "…Details…" she demanded as she interrogated Tony and his intel.

He explained as best he could. He was certain they were British; he overheard them as he exited the elevator, he felt confident the man had a British accent. With just a 10-second time frame to take in three faces, his description left a lot of blanks. Tony was able to recall a great deal of Rachel Fletcher's features, but other than a white man and a black woman, hair colour and height was as much as he had been able to take in. It had been enough though. Catherine deliberately looked nonplussed, but that had been an act. Outwardly, she expressed her disappointment in his intel, reprimanding him before issuing a threat that better information had to be forthcoming at their next meet, but secretly she was glowing.

Catherine was in possession of some first-grade quality 'intel' and she knew it. Her mole in MI6 had come through and this would be the boost to her career, not to mention her wealth, when it made it back to her superiors.

As much as Tony Hunt was a poor, underwhelming analyst, he never missed a pretty face. A 6 ft tall white man and a 5 ft 8 attractive black lady was pretty good, but his description of Rachel Fletcher was something else entirely. Catherine could have commissioned a police photofit artist off his description of Rachel Fletcher.

Katya Stepanova exited the reading room first, never keener to report back to her superiors.

CHAPTER 31
PAV AND WENDY

Monday 23rd January 2017

Drake was standing so motionless he could have been mistaken for a statue. Dormant as he was, he was still ultra alert as he studied his environment meticulously. His work tonight had to be millimetre perfect; 'zero wiggle room' had been the phrase Wendy, aka the Mega Bitch, had used.

Not that he had needed it spelt out though, the fallout of tonight's mission would be huge and no stone would be left unturned to find him, should he fuck it up. In fact, 'fucking it up' was genuinely not an option. Working alongside Mike Gratton bothered him too, the Mega Bitch's PA clearly had skills, but Drake never enjoyed working with people he didn't know. Gratton was unproven and this fact alone weighed uneasily on his mind.

Gratton silently nodded his head, prompting Drake to take the lead along the darkened alley of the Hilton Arlington. As the pair approached the service door, a crack of light amplified as the door opened wider, presenting the instantly recognizable silhouette of Wendy Angel. No words spoken; the two men followed her as she scurried back inside.

Careful to avoid human contact, the trio made their way to the service elevator, ascending a single floor where Wendy led the way into one of the two main stairwells. Seldom used by guests or staff, the stairs afforded the safest route to room 308 on the third floor of the Hilton, just a few miles to the west of downtown DC.

She reached room eight, conveniently located halfway down the corridor on the left-hand side. Tapping lightly on the door a couple of times, Drake and Gratton fidgeted as the seconds dragged before the door finally opened. Standing inside stood Martin Pawlowski. At first greeting Wendy with civility, his face soured the second he saw Mike Gratton and positively growled as Drake came into focus.

"What part of ALONE did you not get?" boomed Pav, directing his anger at Wendy.

"We hit a problem, and I needed you to hear it from the horse's mouth," she replied meekly, her subservience helping to pacify Pav a little.

Having calmed down, Pav looked Gratton and Drake in the eyes before demanding their news. Pawlowski, assistant director of the CIA, was widely known for his impatience. Intolerant of subordinates, with a dislike of surprises too, it was no wonder Pav came across abruptly. With what was about to happen though, his abruptness was water off a duck's back as far as Drake was concerned.

Wendy nodded to Gratton, Pav looked on, assuming the briefing just mentioned would begin to flow from Mike Gratton's lips. The PA stepped closer to Pav, intentionally conspiratorial, by way of helping relax Pav's guard, then Gratton, with an alarming turn of speed, lurched forwards in Pav's direction. Covering the assistant director's mouth with his right hand, Gratton swung his body across Pav's left-hand side, flinging his left arm around Pav, bear hugging him from behind with a vice-like grip. Pav, taken by surprise, started his struggle far too late. In a flash, Drake pounced forwards. Gripping the smallest of handheld needle guns in the palm of his right hand, he planted his left hand firmly on Pav's forehead whilst cupping his right hand neatly and precisely behind his victim's right ear. The faintest of clicks could be heard above the muffled noises coming from Pav as he struggled to free himself.

Once injected, Drake joined the bear hug, helping Gratton to hold Pav as still as possible as the drug's effect set in. As he did so, Wendy almost casually retrieved a bag of cocaine from her pocket, before blocking one nostril whilst forcing a spatula of cocaine up the other. Pav struggled more as the cocaine first inhaled and then blew back from his nostril in a white dust cloud. She repeated the process with the other nostril and then revisited both nostrils for good measure. Pav fought for his very life, but the battle didn't last long, 40 seconds ticked by before he slumped in the arms of his killers.

The injection killed Pav. The cocaine forced into him might well have done so in its own right, but that wasn't its purpose. The cocaine was merely a decoy, something to point the coroner in the right direction. Not that it would strictly matter, Wendy had a 'belt and braces' scheme planned, the coroner would be guaranteeing the right outcome for her.

As Drake busied himself placing Pav's body on the two-seater settee adjacent to the coffee table in the centre of the room, Wendy got to work setting up the table. Wearing surgical gloves, Gratton retrieved a credit card from Pawlowski's wallet. Carefully dipping Pav's finger and thumb in the open bag of cocaine before shaking it off, Gratton then took Pav's limp right hand and forced his cocaine-smeared finger and thumb to grip the card. The credit card was then left on the table, not before Gratton used it to create two lines of cocaine, ready for the next user. The open bag of cocaine was left too, but not before getting similar fingerprint treatment.

Drake, as per Wendy's instructions, retrieved the bottle of champagne and left it on the table alongside two glasses. Unopened but ready, these items were also given the fingerprint treatment. Setting the room was critical, the scene had to be believable, it had to suggest the events even though Wendy had the coroner in her pocket. Drake had been part surprised, part impressed and even more terrified by the coldness that she displayed that evening. He and Gratton were both heavily trained and experienced combatants, but she hadn't flinched, not a muscle fibre twitched as she not only watched but played her part in forcing cocaine into the wild-eyed Pav's nostril just before he finally exited this world. *Fuck*, thought Drake, *the Mega Bitch truly has ice running through her veins.*

With the room finally set, the murderous trio exited as silently and subtly as they entered. Pav would be found a little later by the expensive call girl he himself had booked earlier in the week. Wendy

Angel had known about Pav's dirty little secret for several years. Biding her time, she had always known this would serve as a useful tool. Originally, she had considered simple blackmail but stopped short of carrying it out having considered that Pav would probably ride his luck with his wife, and she strongly doubted whether the director would be overly bothered about Pav's use of a discreet, high-class call girl service. She figured Pav would probably wave it off, justifying it due to his line of work. So, she had decided to keep this knowledge up her sleeve, ready for when it might better help her cause.

Finally, it had. What better cover for the sad demise of the assistant CIA director than a massive cocaine-induced 'myocardial infarction', commonly known as a heart attack. Cocaine, champagne and a high-end prostitute served to take out Wendy's boss, leaving her the keys to the CIA assistant director throne and another step closer to complete control.

Exiting the street behind the Hilton, the trio returned quickly to their car. Wendy took her seat in the rear behind Gratton, while Drake rode shotgun, as Mike assumed control of the dark blue BMW X5. As the PA put miles between them and the Hilton, the SUV fell silent, Drake allowing his thoughts to wander as he ran through the events of the evening. His first significant assignment under the personal direction of Wendy Angel made him directly culpable for the death of the current assistant director, CIA. Drake had protection, protection in that the soon-to-be new assistant director was complicit in the murder, but that didn't exactly warm his cockles. As he continued to ponder, Wendy broke the silence.

Sitting in the darkened rear of the X5, she had dialled and was now starting to speak to someone. Drake strained to hear the conversation, but all he could hear were her words and an extremely faint, tinny voice. As Drake strained further with no success, he clocked Gratton noticing his eavesdropping efforts.

"We're good," spoke Wendy, her words presumably kept to a minimum on purpose. "When I know you will," she replied having listened to the tinny response down the phone line. "Possibly next week," she responded, the other half of the conversation annoyingly lacking.

Drake reckoned it might be a man that she was speaking to, but in truth that would be quite a big guess too. The other end must have said something to end the call, leaving Wendy to voice one last thing.

"OK, I'll call then," as she rang off.

Drake sat silently contemplating what he had heard. Someone else was in the loop, a fourth person with knowledge of Pav's assassination – Wendy's paymaster? Or maybe someone with a more sinister level of control over her? No, it hadn't sounded antagonistic mulled Drake. She had sounded almost friendly, well as friendly as the Ice Queen was capable of sounding. As Gratton took the X5 out of the city limits, Drake disappeared deeper into his own thoughts, wondering what exactly he had let himself get into.

www.ingramcontent.com/pod-product-compliance
Ingram Content Group UK Ltd.
Pitfield, Milton Keynes, MK11 3LW, UK
UKHW011334131125
8957UKWH00022B/203